CERTAIN JEOPARDY

CERTAIN JEOPARDY

CAPTAIN JEFF STRUECKER
WITH ALTON GANSKY

B&H
PUBLISHING GROUP
NASHVILLE, TENNESSEE

978-0-8054-4853-5

Published by B&H Publishing Group,
Nashville, Tennessee

Dewey Decimal Classification: F
Subject Heading: UNDERCOVER OPERATIONS—
FICTION \ ADVENTURE FICTION \
ESPIONAGE—FICTION

Jeff Struecker is represented by The Nashville Agency,
P. O. Box 110909, Nashville, Tennessee, 37222.
www.nashvilleagency.com

Publisher's Note: This novel is a work of fiction. Names, places, and incidents are either products of the author's imagination or used fictitiously. All characters are fictional, and any similarity to people leaving or dead is purely coincidental.

"DOD Disclaimer"—The views presented are those of the author and do not necessarily represent the views of the Department of Defense or its components.

1 2 3 4 5 6 7 8 9 10 • 13 12 11 10 09

To Aaron:

I hope you will turn to our Savior
when facing Certain Jeopardy.

MILITARY ACRONYMS/ ABBREVIATIONS

AGL—Above Ground Level

AO—Area of Operations

CAS—Close Air Support

COB—Chief of the Boat

DIA—Defense Intelligence Agency

DIM and DISIP—Venezuela's Secret Police

FLIR—Forward-Looking Infrared

HALO—High Altitude Low Opening

ICM—Improved Conventional Munitions

LVRS—Lightweight Video Reconnaissance System

NSA—National Security Agency

SEAL—Sea Air Land

XO—Executive Officer

PROLOGUE

GOATS.

Sgt. Major Eric Moyer hated goats. He had a burning desire to swear at the top of his lungs. Not that it would do any good. He stuffed the urge.

TAT-TAT-TAT-TAT.

The urge returned.

"Junior, get that radio operational. If we don't reach CAS soon, we'll leave this mountain in body bags."

"Working on it, Boss. The snow is giving me grief. I can't find a stable spot for the satellite antenna. Getting shot at from six directions isn't helping."

TAT-TAT-TAT-TAT.

AK-47 bullets whistled over their heads. Moyer pushed himself up from his shallow trench and fired a few quick rounds from his M4 carbine. He pulled the trigger again but nothing happened. Flattening himself in the trench, he barked, "Reloading."

In a practiced move, Moyer ejected the spent magazine and rammed a full one in its place, giving him another thirty rounds.

The weapon could fire seven hundred rounds a minute. Only discipline and training kept him from emptying the magazine in a few seconds.

The sound of enemy gunfire erupted again. Staff Sgt. Pete Rasor grunted and raised his hands to his face.

"Junior. Junior! You hit?"

Slowly, the soldier lowered his hands and stared at them. "I don't think so. Snow and mud splatter. That was too close." He returned his attention to the antenna.

The sputter of automatic weapon fire echoed down the mountain. Colt had unleashed his M249 SAW.

Sgt. First Class J. J. "Colt" Bartley and Master Sgt. Rich "Shaq" Harbison were paired a dozen yards away, almost invisible in their white camouflage and hunkered in a shallow trench. A few yards beyond them were Jose Medina, the team medic, and Martin Caraway. Caraway was the cause of all this—Caraway and the goats.

Moyer wondered at the irony of it all. Years of training, the best intelligence, the finest equipment, a score of missions under their belts, and they get upended by goats. He could see the writing on his tombstone: Trained by the Army. Betrayed by a goat. Killed by the Taliban.

A rumbling split the frozen air. Moyer didn't have to see it to know that Shaq had launched a 40mm grenade. Two of his six-man team carried M4s with grenade launchers. The grenade had an effective range of more than 1,100 feet. The enemy was much closer than that.

"Any day now, Junior. These guys are getting on my nerves."

"I need another minute. I can't get a bounce off the satellite."

Moyer fired off a few more rounds. In the distance a man screamed. Lucky shot.

Three days they had been in Afghanistan, and two of those days had been spent on this mountain in knee-deep snow and temperatures that dropped below zero every night. He had been cold from the moment he and the others had walked out the back of an Air Force C-130 transport at 30,000 feet. They jumped in the dark, landed on the desert floor in the dark, and marched to the mountain in the dark. It took them twenty-four hours to reach their observation point and dig in.

They were there to watch, not engage the enemy—that was the mission. The Taliban had a camp on the mountain, and Moyer and his team were to observe it at a distance. But that was before the goats.

Sgt. First Class Caraway had landed hard, the bottom of his rucksack taking the brunt of the fall. Caraway always carried beef jerky and trail mix on missions—dietary good luck charms. This time one of the bags of trail mix had opened on impact. No one gave it a thought, not until they were on the mountain. Not until half-starved goats had picked up the scent.

As Caraway and Doc took their turns sleeping, the goats helped themselves to the trail mix, chewing through the bottom of the rucksack.

Moyer, who had been on watch, spotted the animals and keyed his radio. "Hey Caraway. Intruder alert."

Moyer saw his surveillance expert sit up, then heard, "What the—" Caraway sprang for the rucksack, but one goat, driven by weeks of hunger, refused to give up easily. The creature began to drag the pack away. Caraway reached for him but missed, as laughter rolled out of the trenches.

"Stow it," Moyer ordered. Noise carried too well over snow and sloping mountainsides. Caraway had removed his Colt .45, ready to shoot the animal, but returned it to his holster; the report of a .45-caliber round would be heard for miles in these conditions. Caraway opted for a more direct approach: He tackled the rucksack, frightening the goat enough to send it bounding through the snow toward a ridge—and toward a man with an AK-47. Caraway froze.

Moyer followed Caraway's gaze. "Not good."

The man turned his head, and Caraway sprinted the short distance to his trench and dove for cover.

A second man joined the first. He too carried an AK-47, but that fact alone didn't make the men Taliban. Almost every adult male in Afghanistan carried such a weapon, especially shepherds who used them to defend their flocks from thieves and predators.

The first man said something to the second and pointed in Caraway's direction. The team's position had been compromised. Even if these guys were just shepherds, they might tell the Taliban camp what they had seen. A muffled whiff, like a loud puff of air, came from Caraway's position and the pointing man fell. The second man turned to run, but Moyer heard another *pfftt*, and the fleeing Afghani grabbed his side with one hand. It wasn't a kill shot. He fell and involuntarily yanked the trigger of his weapon. The sound of five rounds—five very loud rounds—filled the air. Another shot from Caraway's position struck the man's head. He dropped into the snow.

Moyer's radio came to life. "I'm sorry, Boss. I'm really sorry. I had to stop him. My first shot was off."

Moyer ignored Caraway. He keyed his radio. "We have to assume our position is blown. Things are about to go from awful to horrible. Prepare for firefight." He turned to Junior. "Get on the satellite (sat) radio and get us some air support."

That seemed like a month ago, but in fact only minutes had passed. From the previous day's reconnaissance they knew the enemy numbered close to one hundred. Six men against one hundred made for lousy odds.

The Taliban fighters slowly approached their position. Moyer's team held a distinct advantage from a distance of three hundred meters with their advanced scopes and noise-suppressed weapons. Close combat against superior numbers would be a different story. He whispered into the radio, "Let's keep them as far away as possible." No one responded; response wasn't necessary.

Rich Harbison, assistant team leader, took the first shot, and a Taliban soldier folded. "Nice shooting, Shaq," Moyer whispered to himself. Shots were fired from Caraway and Doc's position. Moyer squeezed off round after round, each time dropping an enemy combatant.

Seeing several of their own fall without hearing the sound of gunfire told the Taliban force they were facing a military opponent. They immediately began dividing.

Moyer triggered his radio. "They're trying to flank us. Keep alert."

What Moyer really wanted was a fallback position, a place to regroup, a position easier to defend, but no such place existed—not one he and his men could reach without being cut down.

Gazing over the rim of his trench, he spied a Taliban fighter moving to a rock outcropping and steadying his weapon on a boulder. They're sniper, Moyer reasoned. He quickly fired three rounds at the shooter. As best he could tell, five rounds hit the man. Another of Moyer's team had spotted the sniper as well.

Five minutes passed like an ice age. They had killed a dozen men in that time, but scores more were pressing in. Soon the enemy would have the advantage. Moyer and his team were taking fire from several directions, fire from people who knew this mountain better than he did.

"Give me some good news, Junior. My wife is going to be real angry if I get dead out here."

"We can't have—"

TAT-TAT-TAT-TAT.

Junior ducked and paused. "That is really starting to annoy me. I need a few seconds of uninterrupted work."

Moyer could hear the adrenaline-laced fear in the young man's voice. Fear was a good thing, as long as it didn't displace duty and training. Moyer keyed his mike. "Cover for Junior. Now."

From their trenches, each man sent heavy fire at the enemy. Junior popped up and slammed his palm repeatedly on the snow, making a firm, flat surface. He set the antenna and slipped back into the trench. He checked for a satellite signal. "Bingo! Got a bounce." He took a breath. "Any Storm element overhead, this is Quebec-Nine-Seven. We need immediate suppression. Over."

Moyer strained to hear a response.

"Any Storm element overhead, this is Quebec-Nine-Seven. We need immediate suppression. Over!" The seconds chugged by. "Come on, come on, guys. Throw us a bone here."

Several AK-47 rounds tossed snow and dirt into the air just a foot away from the trench's edge.

"Any Storm element overhead, this is Quebec-Nine-Seven. We need immediate suppression. Over!" Rasor turned to Moyer. "We must have caught them at lunch."

"They're Air Force, it takes them a few moments to realize the voice they're hearing isn't in their heads." Bullets whizzed by. Moyer tried to press himself deeper in the trench.

Junior raised the mike to his lips, but before he could speak an unfamiliar voice filled the small space. "Quebec-Nine-Seven, this is Storm One-Three. What is your location and target description?"

Moyer almost let out a whoop.

Junior wasted no time responding. "Storm One-Three, our location is FC 17584539. We are surrounded by a hundred dismounted enemy fighters. They are moving to fifty meters of my position and advancing. We need immediate suppression on our position. We are dug in. Set all ordinance for airburst. My elevation is 3,147 meters."

"Roger, Quebec Nine-Seven. Understand your location is FC 17584539, elevation 3,147 meters."

"Roger that."

"Stand by Nine-Seven."

Junior looked at Moyer, who nodded. "They're asking for authorization. It should only take a few seconds." The familiar sound of the SAW belching bullets rolled across the mountain. Colt must have found a target.

The satellite radio squawked back to life.

"Quebec Nine-Seven, this is Storm One-Three. We are four minutes out from your location, coming in on a westerly course. We are dropping two times ICM bombs. Repeat, two times ICM. Fuses are set at five meters AGL. We understand we are dropping on your position. Confirm that this is danger close and you are dug in."

Five meters above ground level wasn't very high, not when two improved conventional munitions bombs would be going off and sending scores of smaller bombs over an area the size of two football fields. This was going to hurt.

"Roger that, One-Three, this is danger close and we are dug in. Repeat, we are dug in."

"Stand by, Nine-Seven."

Moyer checked his watch. Four minutes was three minutes longer than eternity. He raised his weapon and pointed it at two Taliban soldiers scampering toward another rock outcropping. Neither made it more than halfway.

The cold air turned acrid with the smell of spent gunpowder.

"Quebec, we are three minutes from your position. Are we cleared hot?"

Moyer caught Rasor's glance. "Give the confirmation, Junior."

"Okay, Boss. Storm One-Three, you are cleared hot. Repeat, you are cleared hot!"

Moyer could see the man's hand shake. He understood; his own guts quivered like Jell-O.

The pilot's words traveled via satellite, but no distance and no amount of electronics could hide the concern. "Quebec Nine-Seven is inbound to your position." Then softly, "God be with you, gentlemen."

Moyer keyed his mike. "Birds are inbound in ninety seconds. Get into your holes! Fall out! FALL OUT!"

He didn't need to look to know what each man did next. When they first set up the recon position, each man had dug a trench and in the side of the shallow wall he had carved out a hole—a cave just large enough to hold one man and his weapon. They did so because they had been trained to plan for any contingency. They made these tiny caves for a reason—a reason no one wanted to experience.

Scrambling with all the speed he could muster, Moyer pressed himself into his hole, leaving just enough room to point the barrel of his weapon out. Fewer than five minutes had passed from first contact with the F-18s, but those minutes had aged him ten years.

A new sound rolled through the icy air—the sound of Air Force jets bearing down with purpose. In moments bombs would explode fifteen feet above their heads.

"The antenna!" Rasor shouted and rolled out of his protective lair.

"Junior!"

Rasor seized the antenna from the snow pad he had worked so hard to establish and dove back into his hole. Several shots landed near where he had been a moment before. Junior pressed back into the small cave, clutching the radio and satellite antenna close to his body.

"Please God," Junior mumbled, "let them get the fuses right."

Moyer heard several of the Taliban shout something, but their words were drowned in the wash of jet noise. Moyer guessed there were two aircraft. A second later Moyer heard the F-18s pass overhead and scream into the night.

"Here it comes," he said.

They had trained for this. In the worst of situations, a team leader might have to call for bombs to be dropped on his location. His team's only advantage was in knowing when it would happen and taking cover.

He waited. One second. Two seconds.

An ice pick jammed his eardrums, and a flash of light pushed through his closed eyelids. The ground seemed to depress as if a giant foot had stomped on his position, intent on crushing him like a bug under a boot.

The world shook.

Heat poured down like ejecta from a blast furnace.

Moyer clenched his jaw. Dirt and stones rained down like hail. The concussive force of the bombs pummeled the ground, while two dozen fists pounded Moyer's body at once.

Then darkness sucked Moyer's consciousness into a void.

"... DO ... READ?"

Moyer came to with a start. Where was he? What happened? Two seconds later it all came back to him. He coughed up a lungful of dust and rolled out into his trench. His head hurt like his

brain was trying to break free of his skull. A consistent, annoying tone played in his ears. Something wet hung just beneath
his nose. He raised a hand and ran a finger along his upper
lip—blood.

"Quebec . . . come in."

Moyer blinked a few times. The radio? Junior? He crawled to
the sat radio. Junior lay still in his hole.

"Quebec-Nine-Seven, this is Storm One-Three, do you copy?"

Moyer snatched the mike. "Storm One-Three, this is Quebec-
Nine-Seven, stand by one."

"Roger, Nine-Seven. Good to hear a voice."

"Junior?" Moyer laid a hand on the young man's shoulder.
"Junior. You okay?"

Rasor opened his eyes, looked around, but didn't move. "We
dead, Boss?"

"Not yet, but the night's not over."

Junior slipped from his cave, careful to stay low.

Moyer triggered his radio. "Who's still with me?"

"I'm here, Boss," Shaq said softly.

"Oorah, Boss." No matter how bad things got, Colt remained
Army.

"I don't recall reading about this in the recruitment brochure,
Boss."

"It's in the fine print, Caraway. You with us, Doc?"

"Shaken and stirred but still in one piece."

Relief flooded Moyer. "Injuries?"

"I could use a nurse, Boss."

"You're hurt, Caraway?"

"No, I just like nurses."

Before Moyer could respond, Shaq spoke up. "I don't see any
movement. I think that did the trick."

Overhead the F-18s scorched the sky. Junior's satellite radio crackled. "Quebec-Nine-Seven, we see no movement around your position. Repeat, we see no movement."

"Understood, One-Three . . . and thanks," Junior said.

"Don't mention it. Extraction copter is ten minutes out. Do you have wounded?"

"Negative, One-Three, but I don't think anyone wants to do that again."

"Roger that, Nine-Seven. Glad we could help."

Moyer glanced at the sky. "I don't know who that guy is, but I think we owe him dinner." He activated his radio. "Let's secure the area. Slow and easy." He turned to Junior. "You stay by the sat. I wanna know when the helo is two minutes out."

"Will do."

The scene looked as if it had been snatched from the pages of a Stephen King novel. Bodies lay akimbo across a field of snow and in the crevasses of rocks. Some bled from the ears and eyes; others were riddled with shrapnel, pincushions for superheated metal fragments. Much of the snow had been melted by the six blasts and pooled around lifeless forms.

Smoke settled to the ground, soiling what snow remained. The site of what had been a fierce firefight moments ago was now shrouded in funerary silence.

A faint *thumpa-thumpa* of large rotors grew in volume. Through his earpiece Moyer heard Junior. "Chopper is two minutes out, Boss."

"Grab your gear. I want everyone ready to evac in two. Is that clear?"

"OORAH." The response came in unison.

Moyer started to return to his trench when he noticed one of his men standing a short distance away. "Colt, get a move on."

J. J. didn't budge. Moyer jogged to his position. Colt stood over the body of the first man shot in the fray, the one who had pointed in their direction.

"I don't think he was Taliban, Boss." Colt's voice was soft. "I think he and his buddy were just shepherds."

Moyer could see the man was troubled. He had fought bravely and in past missions always showed courage and dedication. He had never heard Colt question an order. "Noncombatants die in war. You know that. We did what we had to do."

"I know."

"Got your Christian conscience upset, does it?" Colt was the only committed churchgoer on the team. Until now Moyer had never considered that a weakness.

"I guess so."

"You gonna be all right? You still with us?"

"Yeah, Boss."

"Then get your gear."

"Will do." Colt jogged to his trench.

A CH-47 Chinook helicopter appeared overhead, its back ramp opening as it descended. The vehicle was loud, gangly, and the most beautiful thing Moyer had ever seen.

CHAPTER 1

THEY SAT IN THE "special" room reserved for large parties or VIP patrons. Ricardo Estevez's father served the three men personally, but the busy restaurant kept him dashing from table to kitchen to table. Ricardo's job was to keep the water glasses filled, the beer flowing, and warm tortillas on the table. His father had been clear—Ricardo was never to be out of earshot of the three customers. Until they left, they were to be his only concern.

"You are not to bother these men," his father said. "Understood? The two foreigners are guests of a very important man."

"You mean, Minister Santi?"

"Yes, and keep your voice low. Minister Santi comes here because he knows that we will provide for his privacy."

"And because you have the best kitchen staff in Caracas."

Reuben Estevez slapped his son on the back and laughed. "Are you trying to get a raise out of your old man with flattery?"

Ricardo laughed and the sound of it lit up his father's face.

The evening passed smoothly. The men ate their meals and Ricardo brought whatever they desired. After the dinner the three began to talk in hushed tones. With little to do, Ricardo cleared the table, brought more drinks, and then retired behind a curtain that separated the large room from the passageway to the kitchen. The small space contained a sink and a set of wood shelves that held plates, silverware, napkins, and glasses. Behind the curtain was also a small stack of Spanish and English comic books that Richard read on his breaks. At sixteen he had yet to outgrow the need for superheroes. His life consisted of school and work. Nothing exciting ever happened. Comic books provided a vicarious means to a life of adventure.

Ten minutes later he set the magazine down, peeked through the curtain at the men, and his stomach dropped: He had left a plate on the table. His father would consider this a lapse of restaurant etiquette. The men were bent over the table, heads huddled close, lost in the conversation. What appeared to be a map lay before them.

Ricardo slipped through the curtain and walked softly to the table. No one seemed to notice him. He recognized Foreign Minister Santi from the newspaper his father made him read every day. His father believed in self-education and insisted Ricardo stay current.

The two foreigners were strangers to him. Their skin was slightly darker than his, except below the beard line. He assumed the men once sported facial hair but had recently shaved it off.

Ricardo moved slowly so as not to startle the men. As he reached the table he picked up snippets of the conversation. "Hector Cenobio . . . nuclear . . . fast capture . . . airport . . . nuclear . . . Iran." The words meant little to him at first.

He reached for the offending plate, and the conversation abruptly ended. The harsh gaze of the three men froze Ricardo mid-motion.

"I forgot this plate," he stammered. "May I bring you anything else?"

"How long have you been in the room?" Santi snapped.

"Only a moment. I came to clear the last plate and to see if I can be of service to you."

"What do you mean? Service?" Ricardo thought he heard the foreign minister growl.

"I only meant to ask if you wanted more water or beer or perhaps dessert."

"No. Take the plate and leave."

"Yes, sir. I am sorry I disturbed you. I will wait behind the curtain should you need me."

"Curtain?" Santi looked over to the small room where Ricardo had been moments before. One of the foreigners sprung from his seat and yanked back the curtain. The small room was empty.

"Is something wrong?" Ricardo felt his heart skip.

"Leave us," Santi ordered.

Ricardo retreated quickly and pulled the curtain closed.

Moments later the three men left.

The rest of the night, Ricardo waited for the scathing words of his father. His father was fair and loving but strict, and to offend such an important customer as Foreign Minister Andriano Santi would be inexcusable. But the tongue-lashing never came. Could it be that Santi had not complained?

Ricardo spent the remaining hours helping to clean the kitchen and close up the restaurant. Just before midnight, he dragged a large can of trash out the back door and into the alley. He struggled to lift the heavy plastic container filled with unfinished meals, empty containers, and a broken dish or two. The contents raised a clatter as they were poured into the large dumpster. Then Ricardo turned back toward the rear door of his father's business.

"Boy."

Ricardo looked up. A dim light at the end of the alley struggled to push back the darkness but gave just enough light for him to see a man silhouetted there.

The man raised his arm and pointed.

"May I help you?"

Ricardo's head snapped back. A half second later something hot punched him in the chest and he took two steps back. Something thin and white came into view. The moon. A sliver of the moon. But the moon was in the sky, how could he . . . ? It took a moment for Ricardo to realize he was no longer standing.

The moon dissolved into the blackness.

CHAPTER 2

"... BLOOD ... UNCOMMON ... TESTS ..."

Eric Moyer didn't respond. The voice was little more than background music. Images that flashed like a strobe on his brain occupied all his gray cells.

"... your age ... health ... worry ..."

The mental pictures flashed one after another like images cast from an old slide projector. He could almost hear the *click-clack, click-clack* of slides moving up and down in the carousel.

"... Mr. Moyer ..."

He saw his wife, strawberry blonde hair tickling the tops of her shoulders when she wore that yellow sundress he liked so much. Her image faded, replaced by Gina, his twelve-year-old daughter. He had no free will with her. She could ask for the moon to be painted pink, and Moyer would grab a ladder and have a go at it. Rob was a different matter. Sixteen years old and pushing every border and pressing every button Moyer had. They had argued just the night before, and Moyer lowered the boom. Odd, he was having trouble remembering what the argument had been about.

5

"Sir? Mr. Moyer?"

Another flash, another image. One from yesterday. From his bathroom.

"Are you all right, Mr. Moyer?"

Moyer looked up. The question came from a bulky man seated behind a mahogany desk. A half halo of hair reached from ear to ear, his smooth, clean dome reflecting the overhead lights. He shifted in his chair and straightened his white lab coat. Stitched over the left breast were the words *Miles Lawton, M.D.*

"Yes. I'm fine. Sorry. Didn't sleep well last night, so I'm a little drifty."

Lawton nodded. "Understandable. This kind of thing can cause a great deal of stress."

"Normally, I'm pretty good with stress."

"No one is immune, Mr. Moyer." The doctor directed his gaze to the chart on the desk. "I notice that both of your parents are dead. It says here that your mother died of . . . a heart attack at the age of sixty-eight. Is that correct?"

If it weren't, I wouldn't have written it down. "Yes. A massive coronary."

"Was she under a doctor's care?"

"Not for heart trouble. She had always been in good health, and I know she had frequent checkups. She was a bit of a health fanatic."

"I see. And your father? You checked off 'deceased' but don't give a cause. May I ask how he died?"

"Colon cancer."

The doctor looked up. "I imagine that has ratcheted up your anxiety some. Understandable." He made a notation in the chart. "This is your first time in our office, Mr. Moyer—"

"Call me Eric."

"Very well, Eric. As I was saying, this is your first time with us. Do you have another doctor? I may need to consult with him."

"No," Moyer lied. He was good at lying. It came with the job. "I've been healthy all my life, and I have a thing about doctors."

"Well, many men do. When was your last checkup?"

"Maybe ten years ago. I don't remember. I switched my life insurance and they insisted that I get a checkup." Another lie. He'd had a routine physical six months ago.

"That's a long time between checkups."

"Like I said, I have a thing about doctors."

Lawton smiled, but Moyer didn't see any humor in it. "Well, as I was saying, blood in the stool is not unusual. The blood can originate from anywhere in the digestive tract. Overall, your health seems excellent, but the guaiac smear test did show the presence of blood. Of course, it can't determine cause, but there's no reason to assume the worst. True, blood appearing as it has in your case may indicate colon cancer, but there are many other things—less challenging things—that can cause such a symptom: bleeding esophageal varices, a polyp, an ulcer, or angiodysplasia of the colon. Although the latter usually occurs in older people."

"I don't understand."

"Angiodysplasia of the colon simply means that fragile and stressed blood vessels in the colon release blood into the GI tract."

"Oh." Moyer twisted in his chair. He didn't feel comforted. "What next, Doc?"

"Several things. We need to take a blood sample and look for cancer markers, check for anemia and a few other things. Of course, we need to schedule a colonoscopy; that's the best diagnostic tool. We just go inside the colon and take a look. That can be a little uncomfortable, so they'll put you under for a short time."

"How soon?"

"I'll have the nurse set up for the blood draw, and we'll get that to the lab. She'll also set up an appointment for the colonoscopy. If they find anything suspicious, they'll take a biopsy." He paused. "Look, I know this is scary, but you're in good hands. We'll find out what the problem is and deal with it."

"And if it is cancer?"

"There's no need to worry about that now."

"Answer the question, Doc."

Lawton frowned. "If it's cancer, then many factors come into play. Size, location, spread, and a dozen other things. If a tumor is found, you'll be scheduled for surgery."

"Surgery didn't save my dad."

"Medicine has advanced since then. Most likely surgery will take care of everything. There may be some chemo involved. There's no use in speculating until we know what we're dealing with." He rose. "I'll get the nurse started. You can wait here if you like."

He moved to the closed door and opened it, but before crossing the threshold he turned. "Try not to worry, Mr. Moyer . . . Eric."

"Sure, Doc. No worries."

Lawton closed the door behind him, and Moyer brought his hands to his face and rubbed his eyes. Everything was going to change. *Everything.* He shouldn't even be in this office. There were doctors he should report to, but if they knew they would immediately—

No, he wouldn't tell them yet. If the tests come back positive, then he'd have to let them know. But maybe it was one of the things the doc had said. Maybe it wasn't so bad. Maybe after the surgery he could return to work. After all, he was only thirty-eight and in far better shape than most men half his age.

He chastised himself for the thought. He knew several people who had that kind of surgery, and it had taken months, maybe a year, for them to get up to speed. He doubted he could ever return to the thing he loved.

And then there was his family. They'd sacrificed so much because of him. How would he tell his wife? *When* would he tell his wife?

Moyer had gotten where he was in part by believing himself invincible, invulnerable. Superman in a different costume. Now . . .

His cell phone chimed. He pulled it from his pocket and checked the caller ID. There was no name, just a phone number: *8035559115*. Only three of those numbers mattered to him: 911. Moyer's heart began to pound like a piston in a NASCAR engine.

He rose, pocketed the phone, and marched from the doctor's office and through the lobby. Sixty seconds later, he pulled his car from the parking lot.

His only thought: *Why did I have to pick a doctor so far from base?*

CHAPTER 3

J. J. BARTLEY FORCED HIS breathing to slow, choosing deep inhalations over panting. The key rested in controlling one's body and not letting it control the mind.

J. J. forced the right pedal down with slightly more strength then the left, slowly increasing the number of revolutions and thereby driving his Ellsworth Evolve 29 mountain bike faster up the long dirt grade. Ten yards in front of him and riding an identical $2,200 bike was Paul, his twin brother.

"Is that heavy breathing I hear, Pauley?" J. J. had to shout to be heard over the distance separating them. "You fading on me so soon?"

"I'm ahead of you."

"Yeah, but for how long? I got plenty of time before we reach the top of the grade."

Although twins, they looked nothing alike. Paul was three inches taller than J. J. and bore thirty pounds more muscle. No one confused the two. Yet despite their physical differences they had much in common. Both excelled at sports, loved the outdoors, attended the same church. They even enlisted in the Army the same day. Being assigned to Fort Jackson together was a plus. They spent their off hours together, double dating, watching sports, or as today, riding the trails of the South Carolina hills.

It was time to turn up the heat. J. J. drove the pedals with piston-like efficiency, his eyes fixed on the small of his brother's back. The bike, which weighed just a hair over six pounds, responded like a race car. Pressing uphill kept his speed down but not his technique. This race was all about endurance, and it was endurance that had separated their Army careers.

Early on the brothers had decided to join the Rangers, the elite of the elite. Together they worked on their strength, speed, knowledge, and endurance. You don't just join the Rangers, they had been told; you earn the name. Nine weeks of training, twenty-hour days, and few meals took a heavy toll. The physical and mental stress forced many to drop out. Only about half made it to graduation. J. J. was one of those. Paul wasn't.

J. J. knew Paul regretted not earning his Ranger tab, and he walked softly around the issue. Although Paul was stronger and just as determined, he lacked endurance—the ability to shut out the pain and press forward. He possessed enormous courage, but courage wasn't enough to be a Ranger.

"Look out now," J. J. said. "You're about to be passed."

"Ain't gonna . . . happen."

The distance between them had closed to three yards. J. J.'s heart threatened to pop out of his chest, but he kept up the assault. "Do you prefer that I pass on the left or the right?"

"I prefer quiet."

"Sorry, I didn't realize you were meditating."

Paul's legs began to move faster as he rose from the seat, using his weight to drive the pedals down. The fight was against the grade and gravity. The path started as a shallow slope but grew more intense with each mile. Five miles in, J. J. felt as if he were riding up Mount McKinley. He had two advantages: First, he was smaller, so simple physics said he had to do less work to reach the top. Second, he had the mental ability to block out pain—which was good since every joint in his body complained and every muscle was ablaze.

Fifty yards from the crest of the trail, J. J. poured what little energy he had left into the race and shot past Paul. He tried to offer a smart-aleck remark as he passed, but that required wasting a precious breath. Paul reached the peak thirty seconds later, sucking air by the barrelful. J. J. tried to appear nonchalant about the climb, but he couldn't maintain the act. He too was drawing air in noisy wheezes.

"I . . . thought I had . . . you this time." Paul leaned over the handlebars as if studying his front tire. "At least it was close."

"Well, I stopped for lunch back there."

"Yeah, right. Lunch. I'm going to beat you someday. You know that. It's as certain as the sunrise."

"Never going to happen. I have a reputation to protect." J. J. hoped the trembling in his legs wasn't obvious.

"It's not a fair race. I'm older than you."

J. J. faced his brother. "No you're not, we're the same age. That's why they call us twins."

"I'm twenty-two minutes older. Besides, it's not the years; it's the mileage."

"Oh, is that what it is? You got twenty-two minutes more of hard life than me?"

"Okay, smart guy, I'm going to come over there and pummel you."

J. J. laughed. "It's a good five feet between us. Think you can make the distance?"

Paul shook his head. "No, but give me a couple of minutes . . . days . . . weeks . . . then I'll show you who the real man is. In the meantime, I'll just add it to my list."

"What's that bring me to?"

Paul straightened and stretched his back. "I think you're up to thirty-five pummelings, fourteen poundings, and three kicks in the seat of the pants."

"A man could get hurt enduring that kind of beating. Good thing you're in no hurry."

"I'm a patient man and—"

The chirping of a cell phone interrupted. J. J. pulled the device from the pocket of his jersey and glanced at its face. *8035559115.*

"Creditor track you down?" Paul asked.

"We gotta go."

"There's no rush. I need a few more minutes to rest."

"Sorry, bro. No can do. We have to leave now." He turned his bike around. "Why does it have to be today?" He caught Paul staring at him. "What?"

"You're being called up?"

"I'm wanted at the base. I've got an hour to get there. You're going to have to drop me off." He watched his brother open his mouth to speak, then close it. He'd been in the Army long enough to know what the call meant. J. J. also knew his brother was too much of a professional to ask.

"At least it's all downhill from here."

J. J. started down the slope, moving as fast as was wise. A serious spill now could mean an injury. And this wasn't the time for injuries.

CHAPTER 4

PETE RASOR STRUGGLED TO seem interested. It had been an hour-long effort, a marathon torture session he knew wouldn't end before dinner.

"I'm thinking of rose-colored gowns for the bridesmaids. What do you think, honey?" The question came from Samantha Whitmire, soon to be Samantha Rasor, who sat to his left at the dining room table. Her mother, Ruby, sat to his right. He was surrounded.

"Rose or pink?" Pete asked. "They're pretty much the same, aren't they?"

"Not at all, Petey. Rose is darker, prettier."

He hated being called Petey, and Samantha knew it. "Rose is fine with me." His eyes drifted to the television that had been left on. Every time he visited Samantha's mother's home, the television was on, and if it was daytime, then he could bet heavy money that it had been tuned to a soap opera.

"Look, I know this is hard for you, sweetheart, but we do have to make decisions about the wedding. Please try to pay attention."

"Yes, ma'am."

"Don't 'yes, ma'am' me. I'm your fiancée, not your commanding officer."

"Yes, ma'am . . . I mean, you're right."

His future mother-in-law joined in. "What I want to know is what kind of tux you're going to wear. I think tails are nice."

Pete glanced at the woman. Was she kidding? Or maybe she'd gone senile since the last time they had this discussion. "I'll be wearing my dress uniform, Mrs. Whitmire."

"I had so hoped you would change your mind. And I've told you to call me Mom."

"We've already decided that the base chaplain will perform the wedding. My uniform is the appropriate thing to wear."

"But it's so ugly—olive green with all those colored pins."

Pete tried not to bite through his lip. "The dress uniform is blue, not green. It looks sharp. The best uniform in the military."

"But don't you think a tux would be—"

"Leave it alone, mother," Samantha snapped. "We can talk about it later."

"What's to talk about? Military wedding means military dress uniform."

Ruby's brow creased. "That's why I think a civil ceremony would be better. Besides, Samantha tells me—"

"Mother!"

Pete studied them. "What?"

"Nothing." Samantha's dismissal came too fast.

"It doesn't sound like nothing. What were you going to say . . . Mom?"

"Sam just mentioned that she felt you'd be leaving the Army soon."

"Is that so?" He turned to Samantha. "When did I say I was leaving the Army? This is my career. You *know* that."

She redirected her gaze to the pad of paper on which she had been documenting wedding plans. "Honey, it's just that I don't like to be separated from you. And at some point we'll be starting a family, and with children involved it would be better if you were a civilian."

"*I* grew up in an Army family, and I turned out all right. Good enough for you to accept my proposal."

"I know, but I don't want our children to have to go through all that."

"What did I go through? My father was strict but fair. I had a great childhood."

Samantha frowned. "You know what I mean."

"No, I don't. Why don't you tell me?"

"It's just . . . the Army interferes with our life. Who knows where they're likely to send you? And I'm left home to worry. I can't even plan my own wedding without consulting the Army."

"Your wedding? I thought it was *our* wedding."

"Of course it is. I didn't mean it like that."

Ruby spoke up. "A girl dreams of the perfect wedding. It's *her* day. Surely you understand that."

"And what about the groom? He's just decoration?"

"Now you're being ridiculous." Samantha began to tear up.

Pete stiffened. Crying was unfair; it changed all the rules. No matter what he said now it would be wrong, and in the end he would be responsible for putting a damper on her "special day."

"Maybe we should talk about the flowers," Ruby suggested.

"I don't feel like talking anymore." Samantha rose and moved from the dinning room table to the living room, plopping down on a well-worn sofa.

The one thing the Army didn't teach me was how to deal with women. Pete slipped from his chair and joined her. At least Ruby had the good manners to go to the kitchen and wash some clean dishes.

"Samantha, don't be this way. This is supposed to be the greatest day of our lives. I know there's a lot of planning to do and a bunch of expectations, but we'll get through it."

"I know." She lowered her voice. "Mom is putting a lot of pressure on me. Not to mention my sister and my aunt. Everyone seems to know what I want better than I do."

"I know what *I* want: you." He kissed her on the forehead.

She smiled. "I love you more than anything, but I do want you to think about what I said about the Army."

"I could ask the same of you."

A tinny rendition of a Rolling Stones tune erupted from his pocket. He retrieved the cell phone and saw the string of numbers.

"Uh-oh. You're not going to like this."

CHAPTER 5

ADRIANO SANTI WAVED ONE more time as he watched the helicopter rise into the cerulean sky, point its nose toward Caracas, and thunder off. The rotor blast mussed Santi's hair, something he couldn't abide. The moment the craft began to move away, he removed a comb from his suit coat and ran it through his black and gray hair until every strand rested in its proper place. Returning the comb, he brushed the dust from his handmade suit. Despite the aircraft's assault on his fastidiousness, he remained in place until the helicopter reached altitude, carrying his president back to the palace.

Santi had his own palace, this ten-thousand-square-foot hacienda in the Cordillera de la Costa Mountains. It had been in the family for two generations before passing to him. His wealth, drawn from oil interests, allowed him to renovate it to his tastes. And he had expensive tastes.

With the president of Venezuela on his way, Santi strode across the manicured lawn and into the white courtyard fronting the mansion. A fountain with a marble representation of the Roman goddess Fortuna greeted him with calming, quiet bubbles. He stopped and studied the statue for a moment. He had seen it count-less times, but given the gambit he was currently undertaking, the thinly garbed statue took on a new meaning. Fortuna, goddess of fortune and fate. He had the previous quality in abundance and hoped the latter would not turn against him.

He moved to his spacious office and took a seat behind his handcrafted Honduran mahogany desk. He had barely settled in when a servant in a white coat appeared and set a cup of thick, rich coffee before him then silently slipped from the room. No words were exchanged.

Four days were all that remained. Ninety-six hours and the operation would begin. He sipped the Ethiopian coffee then looked at his phone, a wasted gesture. His team would not call on the phone, even though it was a secure line. Word would come by per-sonal messenger.

Setting the cup aside, Santi pulled close a file that rested on his desk and opened it: a security report on the movements of the president of the United States. A routine document. His trip to Australia held nothing of concern for the foreign minister. On the other hand, the American president's planned trip to Brazil next month provided greater interest. He opened another file. The document inside revealed a rising discontent in Cuba and with Fidel's successor, Raul Castro. This was to be expected. Latinos were a hot-blooded people, and protesting against their leaders was a heritage. Santi knew that as well as anyone, having served Hugo Chavez for many years. He had seen and heard his share of angry citizens.

He rose and moved to a window overlooking the dense forest that surrounded his compound. There was work to be done— letters to be dictated and reports to review. But his mind was anchored four days in the future.

REUBEN ESTEVEZ STOOD BY the grave, his arm around his wife, Estella. He crossed himself with his right hand as the priest, robed in white with a purple stole, finished his prayer. The priest, a young man of thirty, continued to speak, with an older priest standing by his side. Reuben didn't hear the words. His ears were filled with the sharp report of a gunshot, a sound he heard every hour of every day since it first assaulted his ears three days before.

Three days. Such a short time had passed with excruciating slowness. Minutes stumbled by like hours, especially at night. The dark of evenings served as an amplifier that magnified each piercing stab, heating every emotion to a molten mass of pain—fury, regret, guilt, and despair. Three days and nights, and he had slept less than a dozen hours the entire time.

Sleep doesn't come to a man who finds his sixteen-year-old son dead in an alley, holes in his forehead, chest, and abdomen. Such a sight branded the brain, infecting the memory until every neuron became tainted with the image.

Estella raised a handkerchief to her nose. He pulled her tight. Without his support she would have crumbled to the moist ground the moment the service began. She barely spoke these days. Her voice would return, he told himself, but his heart held doubts. Tears flowed from a bottomless reservoir. Reuben could not comfort her; he could not comfort himself. He spent hours holding her, communication riding on waves of silence and through empty eyes.

Reuben was a quiet man, a sensitive man, a man content to serve others and share a laugh with the customers who patronized his small restaurant in the eastern part of the city. Many of those stood behind him now, silently offering prayers to God and willing their strength to the man they called friend.

The priest's words continued to hum in his ears but failed to become packets of meaningful communication. To Reuben it was little more than the buzzing of a bee.

Someone touched Reuben on the shoulder. He turned and saw the gray eyes of the old priest who had stood by his young charge. The man's eyes held the images of a thousand tragedies. "The Lord bless you and keep you, my son."

Reuben nodded but couldn't form words. Others stepped forward and spoke soft sentences of grief and support. Estella offered the families their gratitude, proving again that she was the sturdier of the two. Reuben struggled to stay strong enough to support his wife. Anything else would tax him beyond his power.

A few moments later only Reuben and Estella stood at the edge of the grave. A short movement to his right caught his attention. A glance showed three men waiting to lower the casket and fill the hole.

"We must go. The men are waiting."

Estella raised the handkerchief again. "I know. Just a moment or two longer."

He tightened his arm around her. "Another moment then."

"Why our boy?"

"I don't know. Why anyone's boy?"

"They killed me when they killed him."

Reuben nodded. They had only the one son—only Ricardo, and no parent ever had a better child. "It should be me in the grave. Had I known, I would have taken out the garbage." He lowered his head. "To be killed doing something so simple, so insignificant." He wanted nothing more than to straddle the casket, to be lowered into the grave with his son and let the men cover him over. His own death seemed so inviting.

"It was his job, husband. You did nothing wrong."

"Still I wish to God it were me in that box."

Estella didn't respond. She didn't need to. He knew she wished for the same thing, not because she hated him that much, but because she loved Ricardo that much more. He would be hurt if she felt any other way.

Five minutes later Reuben Estevez led his wife from the grave and into a dark gray future. Their reason for living would be in the ground soon.

CHAPTER 6

LUCY MEDINA LAUGHED AS she watched her husband tuck the Nerf football under his arm, struggling toward an imaginary goal line and besieged by three tiny players who grabbed his legs and held on to his trousers. Weighed down by five-year-old Maria, six-year-old Matteo, and eight-year-old Jose Jr., Jose Medina staggered a few steps then crashed to the ground like a fallen redwood, careful not to squish any of his children. The kids cried, "Tackle!"

Maria jumped to her feet and shouted to Lucy, "Did you see, Mother? Did you see?"

Lucy rose from the picnic table and applauded. "Good job, children. Your father had it coming."

Maria clapped her hands and jumped. "We tackled you, Daddy. We tackled you."

Jose said something that made the kids squeal. A moment later the four were wrestling in the grass.

It's going to take me a week to get out the grass stains. Lucy chuckled. "Get him, kids. Make him take us out for ice cream."

"Ice cream! Ice cream!" The three children chanted in unison and attacked again.

A smooth breeze wafted through her black hair, carrying the sweetness of mowed grass mixed with the aroma of hot dogs roasting on one of the park's barbecues. The day was perfect, with a high sun shimmering through a clear sky—a great day for a family picnic. There had been too few of these.

She rubbed a hand over her belly and felt her unborn child kick. Lucy was thirty-two, married, with three children and one on the way. Her sister called her "the baby factory." She once told Lucy, "You should have married a Navy man. They ship out for six months at a time." But having babies fit nicely with Lucy's ideal for life, and the man who made her life perfect lay on his back in the grass getting the stuffing beat out of him by his own children.

Lucy watched the hubbub, the earlier smile still etched on her face. But the grin dissolved as the football-turned-wrestling match came to a sudden stop. Jose stood and removed his cell phone. The kids were still chanting, "Ice cream." She saw him look at the caller ID. He didn't open the clamshell device; he just stared for long moments. His shoulders slumped and he raised his eyes to meet hers.

Lucy buried her face in her hands.

They had just been evicted from Eden.

ORLA CARAWAY DIDN'T WANT to take the call. The caller ID told her all she wanted to know. He had received the letter. He must have. She lifted the office phone and said hello.

"You know I can't do this, Orla. I can't believe you would even ask."

"Hi, Martin. It's good to talk to you too."

"Don't be snide with me, Orla. You send me this letter then expect me to be chatty?"

"I didn't send the letter, Martin. My attorney did." She moved several contracts to the side and rested her elbows on the desk. Her "office" was an eight-foot-by-eight-foot cubicle. A dozen other Dilbert spaces filled the open area of the Los Angeles real estate office. She'd have to keep her voice down.

"Same thing. You wouldn't need more money if you weren't forking over big bucks to shysters."

"They're not shysters. They've taken very good care of me."

"Yeah, by running me into the ground. What about your new fiancé? You two are shacking up. Isn't he supposed to support you and Sean?"

"After we're married, but that's not for six months. And, for the record, we're not shacking up. I have my own apartment."

"That doesn't make a difference."

"You should know."

Her comment brought silence from her former husband. He had left her for another woman. Two months after they divorced, his new gal pal left him for another man. The karmic payback brought her no joy. She didn't want to see him hurt, but she did intend to hold him responsible for his obligations.

"I don't understand why you need extra money, Orla. You have a good job. Real estate is big business."

"For one, I live in Los Angeles now and it's expensive. Auto insurance alone is twice what we paid in South Carolina. Second, I'm just an agent working in a lousy economy. I'm barely getting by. And don't forget, I have a six-year-old child to take care of, and he's not getting any smaller. There's clothes, child care, school expenses, medical—"

"Then hit up your boyfriend. Aren't you Christians supposed to help the poor or something?"

"He's not Sean's father; you are. You can divorce me, but you can't divorce your responsibility."

"Orla, I'm just a lowly sergeant. I don't make that much money. How am I going to come up with an extra thousand a month? I mean, I have to hire an attorney to properly answer this letter. That'll cost an arm and a leg."

"I don't know. But you haven't been overly concerned about how I manage to support myself and our son." She heard him sigh, then heard paper crumpling. She could imagine him squeezing the letter into a tight little ball.

"Well, bottom line is I can't do it. So don't expect it."

"You should think that through, Martin. Talk to your attorney. Becoming a deadbeat dad could affect your standing with the Army."

Hot swearing poured over the line. Orla wished she had recorded the conversation. She might need it if they ever had to go back to court.

"Look. Maybe we can work . . . something out . . . Hang on."

A soft ringing poured through the receiver. She waited, searching her mind for a way to end the call.

"Um, I gotta go."

"What shall I tell my attorneys?"

His voice tightened. "Tell them whatever you want."

"When can I expect the child support?"

"Not anytime soon." There was a clear element of glee in his voice. "I'm being called up."

The line went dead.

She had been a Spec Ops wife long enough to know what that meant. Her anger cooled, and a few moments later Orla began to pray.

CHAPTER 7

DR. HECTOR CENOBIO SETTLED into the first class section of the Alitalia Boeing 757 and leaned back against the headrest, letting his eyelids close. He felt weary, worn to the bone. The conference of physicists held in Milan had been intellectually thrilling but tiring, and there had been little time to recoup during his guest lectureship in London. As the jet engines came to life, he allowed himself to believe that the craft would soon be winging him home, but such was not the case. This aircraft was flying to Rome where he would attend yet another symposium, this time with engineers who built nuclear power plants. He would share his latest work on "Plutonium and Uranium Reclamation and New Elemental Processing." His new techniques for reprocessing nuclear waste had made him a star in the science and engineering communities. Outside those ingrown groups he remained unknown—and that was the way he liked it.

He looked at his watch. His family would be in the air by now, flying from Toronto over the United States to Caracas. Venezuela was still home, though he had not visited the country of his birth in nearly fifteen years. He wondered how much had changed. It didn't matter. Four more days and he would be landing in his home country and he could show Nestor and Lina the old neighborhood. It would be the first time out of the country for the ten-year-old twins.

Twins. The word made him smile. No two children could be more different. The fraternal twins were miles apart emotionally and in their interests. Lina, whom he assumed would be a studious girl, was rambunctious, loud, and seldom read. She lived to play soccer and send countless text messages to her friends. Nestor, on the other hand, cared nothing for sports and spent as much time with his nose in a book as possible.

Hector kept his eyes closed and imagined himself with his family. Every time he traveled he vowed that never again would he be gone more than a couple of days at a time. This was his second week away.

One dark cloud shadowed his thoughts about the trip to Venezuela: He had been invited to attend a formal dinner with President Hugo Chavez, something he didn't want to do. Chavez's bluster and arrogance toward the United States annoyed him and reflected badly on the country. Of course, these days everyone criticized the Americans. It had become an international sport.

What he dreaded most were the questions he knew would come. "Why does an imminent scientist such as yourself not live in his own country? Why live in Canada?"

"You see, Mr. President, it is where I teach. I have tenure and research facilities at the university there."

"We could provide such things," the president would say.

"I'm afraid I have been gone too long for my family to feel comfortable with a move."

No doubt Chavez would make some comment about how a family goes where the man goes, and things would descend from there. Still, as much as he hated the idea of attending, one did not snub the president of the country—especially when that president is Hugo Chavez. Perhaps Hector could simply lie and say he would consider moving back, but Hector was uncomfortable lying.

A brown-haired beauty took her position at the front of the first class cabin. She opened the metal door of a small compartment and pushed a button. A moment later a video played reminding the passengers how to buckle their seat belts. Hector snapped his belt in place and pretended to watch the instructional movie. What he was really doing was praying for his family.

☢ ☢ ☢

ERIC MOYER PULLED HIS red '64 Ford Mustang, a gift from his grandfather, through the gate of Fort Jackson and worked his way along its paved streets. Fort Jackson was more city than military base, with more than a thousand buildings dotting its fifty-two thousand acres, and harbored everything from weapon ranges and field training sites to a family water park. Thirty-nine hundred active-duty soldiers and their fourteen thousand family members called the place—and nearby Columbia, South Carolina—home.

Moyer had started his military career here by surviving basic and advance individual training. Every year forty-five thousand men and women civilians became warriors on these grounds. Drill sergeants trained here; chaplains trained here; recruiters trained here; even polygraph technicians trained here.

Of the nearly twelve hundred buildings on the compound, only one interested Moyer at the moment: a plain-looking, windowless, three-story cement building dubbed the Concrete Palace. Several buildings made up the Palace, but one held special interest for him.

The architects had done a masterful job of making it look as non-descript as possible.

He parked in an open stall and stepped from his car onto the hot macadam of the parking lot. South Carolina knew how to put on the heat.

"Isn't it about time you gave that car to a real man?"

Moyer locked the car door then turned his attention to the large African-American man who'd spoken. "Hey, Shaq. I might, if I knew a real man."

"What? You're looking at a prime specimen. 'C'est moi! C'est moi! I'm forced to admit 'tis I, I humbly reply.'" Master Sergeant Rich Harbison's dark face split with a wide grin.

"Shaq, I can't tell you how badly it creeps me out when you quote show tunes. It just ain't right, man."

"Hey, even big guys like me have a sensitive side."

Big was right. Rich stood six foot six with a shiny bald head and the build of a giant redwood. People who didn't know him assumed him to be a dumb jock. He was neither. He liked sports enough, but culture interested him more. Over the last three years, Moyer had come to admire and respect his second in command, even if there was an actor in there dying to come out. Because of his size few risked poking fun at the man.

Moyer shook his head.

"What? It's Lerner and Loewe. You know, *Camelot*? Lancelot—"

"If they don't show it on HBO, I don't know it."

They started toward the building. Moyer dropped his keys in his pocket. "What'd they catch you doing?"

"Yard work. I hate yard work. Robyn had me on my knees pulling weeds. The call came just in time."

"Why? Were you going to tell her to pull the weeds herself?"

"You kidding? A man could get hurt saying such things."

"Robyn's been nothing but nice to me."

"It's all an act."

"At least you had time to say good-bye."

The men walked to a manned gate in the chain-link fence surrounding the compound. Each pulled a military ID from his wallet and presented it to the guards. One of the guards compared the names to those on a list, then held the ID up and moved his eyes from photo to face and back to photo. Moyer waited patiently. The photo didn't match his present appearance. His longish hair and goatee made him look anything but military. That was part of the illusion. In their line of work, it was important that he not look Army sharp. Not even his neighbors knew what he did for a living.

The guard waved them through, and the two entered one of the most restricted areas on any military base.

"I take it you didn't have time to go by the house." Shaq's tone grew more somber.

"You know the drill. Call comes in, we got one hour to get here. I was on the other side of town. Must have broken every speed law in Columbia. I'm lucky not to be cooling my heels in jail."

"How did she take it?"

The question lacked specifics but Moyer knew where Rich was headed. "Like the trooper she is. I could hear the concern in her voice, but she didn't say anything. Except 'Come home to me.'"

"You know, I don't think we do our marriages any favors by going out to run an errand and not coming back for a few weeks." Rich shook his head. "Sometimes I think Robyn is the more courageous of the two of us. Did you get to talk to the kids?"

"No. They're at school."

He already missed Gina, his twelve-year-old daughter. The image of her blue eyes and blonde, streaked hair flashed to the forefront of his mind. She laughed more than any child he had ever met. Rob was a different matter. At sixteen he had reached the age where he knew everything and cared for nothing. Unlike many his age, he didn't want to be a rock star or an athlete or anything. He didn't fit in at school, and he didn't fit in at home. Last night Moyer and he came close to blows. This morning he refused to talk at breakfast. Instead, the boy grabbed his backpack and two pieces of toast and bolted through the front door without so much as a good-bye.

The Concrete Palace had no street-facing doors, forcing Moyer and Rich to walk halfway around the building where they stopped at a gray steel door. Moyer punched a six-digit code into the keypad above the door handle. A second later he heard the sound of the automatic lock disengaging. He pulled the door open and followed Rich into the room that only a handful of soldiers entered. The room was small and Spartan. No artwork hung on the walls, nothing to indicate what lay deeper in the building. A gunmetal-gray desk sat in the middle with a uniformed Sgt. First Class, who looked too young for the rank, seated behind it. He also looked too young to wear the handgun on his hip.

"Gentlemen." He pushed a small chrome box with a red plastic plate forward but said nothing. They either knew what to do with it or they didn't. The fact that Moyer had been in this building many times and even met this sergeant before meant nothing. He still had to go through the motions.

Moyer stepped to the desk and placed his thumb on the small plastic plate. The sergeant's eyes never left his computer monitor. "Thank you, Sergeant Major." He pushed the biometric device toward Rich. A second later the computer cleared him as well. "You are cleared to go back. The colonel is waiting for you."

They started away from the desk. "Just a moment." The guard held out a small wicker basket holding several cell phones. Moyer and Rich surrendered their phones.

At the back of the small room was another steel door with another encrypted keypad. Again Moyer entered a six-digit code and pushed through the door to a wide corridor. Unlike the room they'd just left, the walls of the hall wore general military posters, though nothing unit specific. Moyer looked down the hall—every door was closed. Doors were always to be closed and locked. No exceptions. Moyer and his team had access to every door in the building except three. He had no idea what lay in those rooms.

He never asked.

Four doors down they entered a large open space populated by desks and military personnel of varying rank, each involved in some task on their computers. These walls bore more than vague military posters. They portrayed Special Ops soldiers on mission around the world, in China, Vietnam, Afghanistan, and Iraq.

A few steps more and another door later, Moyer and Rich entered the team room and closed the door behind them. Ten desks filled the room. On six of the desks rested laptop computers. At the back of the room were two workstations used to analyze satellite photos and recent intelligence information. Moyer had used them before. On the walls hung art depicting Special Ops forces jumping from an airplane in Afghanistan, ready to capture an airfield in Panama.

Of the ten desks, four were occupied. Pete Rasor sat with his eyes glued to the laptop's screen. Even from the door, Moyer could tell his communications man was involved in a gripping game of Solitaire. Next to him J. J. Bartley, weapons and demolitions specialist, used a pen knife to clean his fingernails. Medic Jose Medina sat behind J. J. and studied photos of his family. Martin Caraway, two rows over, slumped down with his chin resting on his chest, eyes closed.

"I take it I'm not late." Moyer spoke a few decibels louder than necessary to make sure everyone heard him. The Solitaire game disappeared, the pen knife was folded and dropped into a pocket, and Caraway's eyes snapped open as he repositioned himself in the seat. Only Medina continued his previous activity for a moment before looking up from the photos to gaze at Moyer and Rich.

J. J. looked at his watch. "Two minutes early, Boss. If I know Colonel MacGregor, he'll be here in . . . eighty-four seconds."

"That should be enough time for you girls to look like you're interested in the mission."

Caraway leaned back. "We don't know what it is yet, Boss. How do we know if we're interested?"

"You're paid the big bucks to be interested."

Several of the men chuckled.

"Big bucks. That's a good one, Boss." Rich slipped behind one of the desks, checking, as he always did, that his computer was on and that he had easy access to pen and paper.

Moyer moved to the front of the room and faced his team. J. J. was right; Mac was well known for punctuality. He could almost imagine the Special Ops leader standing at the door with his hand on the knob, ready to plunge into the room the moment the second hand of his watch swept past the twelve.

"Let me have your attention. Is there anything I need to know before the briefing begins?"

No one spoke for a moment, then Caraway nodded. "Yeah, the Yankees stink this year."

"We all know that, Billy. I'm asking if we're ready to go. Any problems I should know about?" He thought about what the doctor had told him less than an hour ago, but that was his secret to keep. It made him wonder what secrets his men kept.

"I want a new nickname, Boss. 'Billy' just doesn't fit a man of my skill and training."

Shaq grunted. "You let a goat steal your rucksack. You're stuck with the name."

"That wasn't my fault. How could I know the local wildlife would go after my chow?"

"Don't feel bad, Billy," Pete said, "I'm sure the other goats call *him* 'Caraway.'" The others laughed.

Enough. "Stow it." Moyer snapped the words. "Do we or do we not have anything I need to know about?" No one answered. "Then I take it we're good to go."

"OORAH."

"Good."

Before Moyer could speak again the door opened and Col. MacGregor stepped in, followed by his master sergeant, Alan Kinkaid. Kinkaid carried several folders. Before the colonel took a second step, the men were on their feet, at attention.

"As you were, gentlemen." He took Moyer's spot at the front of the room. Moyer took a seat behind a desk. "We got some business that needs attending. In less than eight hours from now you will be on recon. We have intelligence with high confidence that al-Qaeda has set up, or is in the process of setting up, a new training facility. We have reasonable confidence that the training camp will be used to raise up terrorists for action in North America. In a nutshell, your mission is a low-vis recon to confirm or deny."

Moyer said nothing. Training camps were nothing new, neither were missions to observe them. What Moyer wanted to hear was the *where*. Although he would go without complaint, he fervently hoped Afghanistan was not in his immediate future. The last time he had been there, he'd ordered bombs to be dropped on his location. That left a bad taste in his mouth.

"You will ship out in pairs, fly on different airlines, depart at separate times, and meet up for the mission once on scene." Colonel Mac paused. "I hear Venezuela is warmer than the mountains of Afghanistan."

CHAPTER 8

THE BODY CAME DOWN the jungle river floating face up. Didn't bodies normally float face down? She always thought they did. That's what they showed on television. The body that had captured her attention was one of six. The other five had already passed her position on the shoreline, each headed for the lip of a massive waterfall fifty yards to her right.

Stacy closed her eyes, but it didn't help. The scene pressed through her closed lids and exploded like a bomb on her brain. She had recognized each and every body. She had recently attended a barbecue with these men just a few weeks before to celebrate a safe homecoming from a distant land none of them would discuss. She had watched them down seasoned T-bone steaks, corn on the cob, and mountains of potato salad.

J. J. had been the first body down the river, his youthful, always-smiling face twisted into the anguish he had felt moments before he breathed his last. Rich and Pete, the one they called Junior, came next. Both bled from holes in their chests. Jose came next, his lifeless eyes gazing at a cloudless sky. His throat had been cut. Martin followed a few moments later, his head twisted awkwardly to one side. Stacy knew little of such things, but she recognized a broken neck when she saw one.

She tried to step back from the river's edge, to ease back into the jungle behind her. Danger might wait there, but it couldn't be worse than what she knew was coming down the river. Her feet wouldn't move.

She lifted her eyes and saw others standing on the shore around her. There was the statuesque ebony-skinned woman watching her husband, Rich, approach the waterfall's edge. A few yards from her stood a pregnant woman with three children at her side, each wailing at the loss they were forced to witness. The sight of people tortured by indescribable grief forced Stacy to avert her eyes upriver, and her knees buckled beneath her.

Her husband's body moved along the surface of the water like a tree limb—a battered, bloodied tree limb.

"Eric!"

Tears flooded her eyes. She stepped into the water, first to her ankles, then to her knees. She fought the powerful tug of the river, felt the muddy bottom pull at her feet. "ERIC!"

He was dead. He must be dead. All the others were, but he twitched then turned his head. One eye was missing, as was much of his scalp on the right side. The sight froze her heart and set her soul ablaze.

"I'm . . . sorry." His words were weak, and she heard his lungs rattle with each shallow breath. Love conquered her repulsion and she reached for him, taking hold of his arm. The effort moved her deeper into the river until it was several inches above her waist.

Stacy pulled with all her strength, but her husband's body would not move. The current turned her in place as she fought to maintain her grip.

"I'm sorry, baby." Eric's voice sounded distant and tinny, as if coming from an old radio.

"Don't talk, sweetheart. I'll get you to shore—"

"No. You must let go of me."

"Never! I won't do it."

"Tell Rob I'm sorry I yelled at him. Tell him I love him. Tell Gina she's my heart and soul—"

"Don't talk. Save your strength." She pulled again and again. Water splashed in her face and hair. Her feet dug into the mud as the water rose.

"Let go, baby. You must let me go."

"No."

The current increased its hold on Eric's body, unwilling to let go of its prize.

"I shouldn't have put you through all this. It wasn't fair to you. Not fair to the kids."

"I won't let go of you. I'll never let go. I promise. Not now; not ever."

"Please . . . sweetheart. It's all right. It's—" A death rattle drowned out the last word. Eric's remaining eye went blank.

"No . . . no . . . I won't let go."

The river ripped her husband from her hands, and she watched his corpse float toward the waterfall's edge.

"ERIC!"

His body disappeared.

Stacy couldn't cry, couldn't think, couldn't move. She had no sense of time. Her only awareness was that some invisible scorching tool had just hollowed all the life out of her.

She lowered her head.

She raised her feet.

The view of the river gave way to the cobalt sky. At the edge of her vision she could see the jungle scrolling by as she let the river carry her downstream.

A distant roar grew louder with each moment that lumbered past. The waterfall was near. She had no idea how far the drop would be, but it didn't matter.

Mist filled the air. The roar grew in a steep crescendo.

A minute later, the river disappeared and Stacy began to fall.

STACY JERKED, GASPING FOR air. She sat on the sofa, pressed into the corner where arm met back and seat cushion. On the television a CNN reporter spoke of the damage caused by a freak tornado in Alabama.

Scooting to the edge of the sofa, Stacy raised a tremulous hand and drew it across her eyes. Tear-moistened mascara left dark marks on her skin. Her heart stuttered and her stomach roiled. She forced herself to inhale deeply and slowly.

"A dream." She whispered the words. "Just a stupid dream. A nightmare." She knew the cause of it.

At the bottom right of the CNN broadcast, in the news crawl, was the time: 2:12 p.m. Four hours after Eric called to say that he wouldn't be home for supper. That was his code word. In their home the evening meal was called *dinner*. She received the news the way a Spec Ops wife should, calmly and with understanding. She expressed her love and said, "Come home soon." He promised he would. She hung up the phone and, grateful that the kids were at school, went to the bedroom and cried for a half hour.

She wept for shorter periods of time every hour after.

Weeping was hard work. Draining. So were fear and worry. She'd settled on the sofa to watch the news, hoping to hear something that would reveal the possible destination of her husband. Sometime after, she fell asleep.

This wasn't the first no-notice call she'd received from Eric, nor was it the first time she'd dissolved into tears after hearing the news, but it was the first time she'd experienced a daytime nightmare. Why?

Perhaps the answer lay in the fact that he always had time to stop by the house for a few minutes before leaving for the base. It wasn't much time but enough for a physical touch and a proper parting. This time he was too far from the base. He never said where he'd been.

Stacy rose from the sofa, retrieved a dust rag, and began expunging dust from the furniture. She always dusted when Eric left suddenly.

CHAPTER 9

ALL JOKING AND VERBAL jabbing ended the moment Col. Mac stepped through the door and announced their mission. Moyer's team was comprised of competitive, opinionated, confident men. They trusted each other implicitly but could, and often did, annoy one another to a point just shy of a fist fight. Once on task, that all changed. The occasional quips and jokes remained, but the business at hand took priority. The nature of their work required a level of trust few men experienced. No matter how irritating the guy next to you might be, he could be trusted to lay down his life in exchange for yours. They never talked about it; they all knew it.

"Do we know how large our AO is?" Moyer asked.

"Ground intel has identified two primary areas of al-Qaeda operations." Mac pointed at a map digitally projected on a screen. "Here in the industrial area of Caracas are several concrete tilt-up complexes, two that are of special interest to us. Intel has identified these buildings and observed unusual activity associated with them."

"Did they recon the buildings?" Shaq asked.

Mac shook his head. "The spooks have their hands full with other matters in Venezuela. As you know, Chavez hasn't been playing nice of late. The intel has limited eyes in the area. They do have one resource who says he has seen Middle Easterners going in and out of the buildings. That's why you're going in. We want a deeper understanding of what they're doing."

"Can we trust the spy guys?" Caraway was looking at Moyer when he asked the question. "Their reputation has been pretty spotty of late—nonexistent WMDs and all that."

"The colonel said the intel came with high confidence." Moyer didn't take his eyes from the map. He was memorizing everything.

Mac added, "We have corroborating intel from DIA and NSA sources."

"You said there were two locations of concern," Moyer said. "What's the other, Colonel?"

He grinned. "You gotta love this, gentlemen." He motioned to Kinkaid and the digital image changed from a satellite photo of industrial Caracas to a mansion in the jungle. The satellite photo was detailed enough for Moyer to make out individual tiles on the roof and several cars on the ground.

"Is that Chavez's crib?" J. J. spoke for the first time.

"He should be so lucky. This little ten-thousand-square-foot shack belongs to Andriano Santi, Chavez's foreign minister and attack dog."

"Must be the best-paid civil servant in the world," Shaq said.

"The mansion and grounds have been in the family for generations, built with and maintained by oil money and, we believe, drug money. It's located in the Cordillera de la Costa Mountains."

Moyer studied the photo. "The man has his own jungle retreat. I assume it has heavy security."

The image on the screen cycled to a close-up of one quadrant of the property. Mac said, "Satellite surveillance shows a fence perimeter. Our image techs think the fence is a fairly recent addition, replacing an older chain-link one. We have photos from one and two years ago, and they differ from this one taken four days ago."

"So the foreign minister has become more security conscious." Shaq ran a hand over his bald pate.

"Maybe he has a new art collection," Caraway ventured.

"We can only hope. Native sources tell our people that helo traffic to the compound has increased over the last few weeks. We also have a witness who can put him in the area of the industrial buildings. Another thing: The Caracas papers carried a story about a boy killed outside his father's restaurant. Intel had a man and woman tail Santi to the restaurant, where they saw him in the company of several men with Middle Eastern features. To preserve their cover, they left before the meeting broke up. The kid, just a teenager, bought it that night. Three shots: head, torso, gut."

"An assassination." Moyer looked at the file folder he had been given and found a copy of the article. His limited Spanish was insufficient to read the document, but it contained a photo of a dark-haired youth that made him think of his own son. Regret over last night's argument percolated once more to the top.

Mac's voice cut through his thoughts. "It has all the hallmarks of a hit. Santi has the kind of influence to make that happen."

"Nice guy," J. J. said.

"It's common knowledge that there's no love lost between Chavez and the U.S. Compared to Santi's hatred of Americans, our strained relationship with Chavez is a love fest. We don't know why, but the guy has a real big ax to grind against anything with *USA* stamped on it. Chavez doesn't need help keeping his hatred simmering, but Santi certainly stirs his pot."

Moyer decided it was time to get to the bottom line. "What are our orders, sir?"

"You and your team are to recon and gather on-the-ground intel on the industrial park where we suspect al-Qaeda activity and training. Second, you are to conduct surveillance on Santi's compound and the industrial buildings in question. If the field agents and desk jockeys are right, then Santi has been snuggling up to al-Qaeda, and that isn't good. An AQ recruitment-and-training facility in Venezuela is not something we want. You will fly to Caracas from Atlanta, arriving on different flights. You will travel under new U.S. passports, which will be given to you following the meeting. You will be traveling as businessmen: two as oil execs, two as real estate investors, and two as World Health Organization scientists."

"Scientists?"

"Yes, but don't worry, Caraway. You're a real estate developer. Tickets and flight times are in your folders. You will also receive business cards, laptops, and other material to support the cover."

"Weapons and equipment, sir?"

"Once you select the equipment for your mission, it will be flown to a private airfield in a neighboring country and trucked in by operatives and cached for later retrieval. You will set up in different hotels." Mac looked at his men. "Do us proud, gentlemen. Kinkaid will bring you up to speed on the essentials."

Over the next hour, Kinkaid gave Moyer and his men a crash course on Venezuela and its capital city, Caracas. Every detail was accompanied by a PowerPoint slide. Moyer made a mental laundry list:

- Venezuela was officially called the Bolivarian Republic of Venezuela.
- The country had a 1,700-mile coastline and laid claim to seventy-two coastal islands, of which Margarita was the largest.

- A Spanish colony for more than three hundred years, Venezuela declared its independence in the early nineteenth century.

- Seventy percent of the twenty-five million inhabitants were *mestizo*, people of mixed European and native bloodlines. Only about 5 percent of the people were of indigenous descent.

- Ninety-four percent of the people were Roman Catholic, and most lived in urban areas.

- Spanish was the country's official language, and literacy rate for adults was 94 percent.

- Life expectancy for the region was seventy-five years, better than most countries and nearly as good as the U.S.

- Venezuela was a founding member of OPEC. Oil made the country rich, but much of the population lived in poverty.

- The monetary unit was the bolivar.

- This time of year they could expect mild temperatures in the city, warmer temperatures inland.

- Venezuela was ostensibly a democracy, but President Hugo Rafael Chavez, a one-time military officer who attempted coups twice in 1992, had moved to consolidate his power in recent years. The National Assembly had twice voted to grant Chavez broadly defined powers to rule by decree.

"It's not news," Kinkaid said, "that relations between our country and Venezuela are strained. A military coup in April 2002 briefly ousted Chavez from office. He blamed the coup attempt on the Bush administration. Visit the Venezuelan embassy's Web page and you will see a list of accusations made against the U.S. It's easy to dismiss the country; after all, it doesn't look like much on the map, and Chavez's public persona is almost comical. However, he and his country sit on what some claim is the second largest oil reserve in the world. The Orinoco Belt has an estimated 236 billion barrels of extra-heavy crude. Only Saudi Arabia has more. Bottom line, when your government sits on that kind of reserve, well, other countries take notice. And so do terrorist groups."

Kinkaid placed his hands behind his back and paced the front of the room like a university professor. "The Venezuelan leadership is convinced that our government has been trying to destabilize the region. They don't trust us much, especially our military."

Moyer didn't ask whether Chavez's paranoia had some basis in fact.

Kinkaid stopped his pacing. "Chavez is convinced that the U.S. plans to invade Venezuela. He learned of a military simulation called Operation Balboa. The simulation does involve Venezuela, but it was nothing more than a simulation carried out by Spain. All that to say that you're heading into unfriendly territory. Your presence and activity will be denied if push comes to shove. Is that clear?"

The team acknowledged the fact.

"You will be issued credit cards in keeping with your passports and IDs. Use the credit cards. Don't carry a lot of cash. Thieves work the airport. A number of tourists have been abducted and forced to withdraw cash at ATMs. Several have been murdered. Even taxi drivers with what looks like proper paperwork can't be trusted, so watch your backs, gentlemen."

Kinkaid looked around the room. "Questions?"

When there were none, Mac nodded. "That's it for now, men. You go with my prayers." He paused. "I wish I were going with you."

"We'll bring you a pretty senorita, Colonel."

He chuckled. "Don't bother, my wife has cut down on the amount of dating I do."

CHAPTER 10

"HURRY, CHILDREN. GATHER AROUND." Julia Cenobio motioned for her twins to come to the laptop computer sitting on the desk in their hotel room. "Papa wants to see you."

"Papa!" Ten-year-old Lina raced from the bedroom to the living quarters of the suite. Her brother Nestor followed behind at a slower pace, a book in his hand. Both children had hair just a shade paler than coal, just like their mother.

Julia pushed her chair back so the children could stand in front of her. She pulled them close and gazed at the image of her husband on the computer monitor. Sitting atop her computer was a small Webcam similar to the one being used by Hector.

"Hello from Rome, children!" Hector's grin widened.

"Hi, Papa." The children spoke in unison.

"How was your first airplane flight?"

"Scary—"

"Fun—"

"I had peanuts and they brought us soda to—"

"They gave us cookies too. I liked them—"

"Slow down, children." Julia placed her hands on their shoulders. "Papa won't understand you if you both talk at once. Lina, you go first."

Five minutes passed as the children poured out details about their adventure. Her husband smiled, nodded, said, "Ah" and "Wonderful" and "You don't say" whenever he could squeeze a word in. They slowed, more because they needed to breathe than the lack of things to say. Hector took advantage of it.

"I will see you soon. I have two more days here in Rome then I'll fly straight to meet you."

"Will you bring us something, Papa?"

"Perhaps, Lina. What are your plans for today and tomorrow?"

Nestor shrugged. "Mamá can say it better."

Julia looked into the camera. "Today we rest. We will watch television and maybe a movie then have dinner in the hotel. Tomorrow they've arranged for a tour around the city and a boat ride."

"I've never been on a boat before." Lina jumped in place, unable to suppress her excitement.

"I wish I could go with you. Maybe if you like the boat trip we can do it again when I get there. I also want to show you where I grew up."

"Okay," Lina said.

"I want to go into the jungle." Nestor remained more reserved than his sister.

"I'll see what I can do. Now let me talk to your mother."

The children disappeared into the adjoining room.

"They're so excited, Hector. This has been a big adventure for them."

"I'm glad. And what about you? Is it such a big adventure?"

"Yes . . . most of the time. I worry some. We're so far from home."

"You grew up in Caracas just as I did."

"I know, but we've been gone so long. I feel out of place. My family . . ." There was no need for her to finish. Hector and she were dating when her parents died in an auto accident. An only child, she was all that remained.

"I feared this might stir up old pains." Even thousands of miles of Internet connections couldn't hide the concern in his face. "It is why I suggested we turn down the invitation."

"Nonsense. I'm a woman. I have the right to feel down from time to time. I want to be here when they honor you. It is one of the joys of being married to a great man."

"I'm not a great man, Julia. I'm just a man who loves his work."

"You're a nuclear scientist. How many women can say, 'I married a nuclear scientist'?"

That made him laugh. "If you were with me at this conference, you would be surrounded by such women. And men too."

"So you are well?"

He nodded. "I feel fine. A little weary from the travel and the difference in time zones. It is already late here. I am six hours ahead of Caracas time."

"You must be exhausted."

"I'm fine. Did you have any trouble at the airport? Did they ask you questions?"

"Someone from the government met us. He showed his identification to the customs agents and security. No one stopped us or asked questions. He even carried our bags."

"It sounds like they're treating you well."

"The hotel room is beautiful. I didn't expect such luxury. It's a suite with two bedrooms and a large common room. It has a kitchen with a refrigerator filled with food and drinks. I'm having trouble keeping the children from eating it all."

"Let them have some fun. This is all new to them."

"Spoken like a father who will not have to get up in the middle of the night and tend their upset stomachs."

"Just make sure they're well when I arrive. I plan to spoil them unmercifully."

"You always do."

"I'll be praying for you."

Her voice softened. "And we'll be praying for you."

They said good night and Julia ended the video call. As she did, it seemed as if the distance between them had grown. It was good seeing his face and hearing his voice, but it came nowhere close to having him near enough to touch, to hug, to kiss.

"Mamá, Nestor hit me with his book!"

"No, I didn't. Liar!"

Julia sighed, rose, and walked from the computer.

☢ ☢ ☢

THE MAN IN THE adjoining room winced when the child shrieked. He pulled his headphones away from his ears just before the boy replied with equal volume.

"Brats."

He replaced the headphones and continued listening to the activity on the other side of the wall.

CHAPTER 11

J. J. BARTLEY LEANED BACK in his chair in the Atlanta airport waiting area and watched his team leader scowl. Moyer wore a light-blue shirt, a dark-blue tie, charcoal-colored suit pants, and dress shoes and looked more uncomfortable than J. J. had ever seen him. J. J. wore a similar set of clothes, except his shirt was white and his tie yellow. The shoes needed walking in to loosen the leather at the heel and to scuff the slick sole. He only owned one suit, which he wore to weddings and funerals. There had been no time to return home and retrieve it. The off-the-rack garment he wore would have to do.

"You okay, Boss . . . Eric?"

"I'm fine, why?"

"You look pretty uncomfortable. Suit getting to you?"

"Nah, it's not the suit."

"Ah."

Moyer furrowed his brow. "What's that mean?"

"What?"

"That all-knowing, smart-alecky 'Ah.'"

"Not a thing. It's just that I have a friend who hates to fly. Any time he has to get on a plane he squirms, sweats, and spends a lot of time in the head. Flying upsets his, um, digestion."

"J. J., how did we get here?"

"We flew in on a commuter."

"Did I look afraid on that flight?"

"No, but—"

"We've done several . . ." Moyer looked around the waiting area, and J. J. did the same. The place was empty. Their flight didn't leave for two hours, so they had settled on a less crowded waiting area fifty yards down the terminal. "We've done several missions together. You've seen me fly on helos and military transport craft. You've seen me do HALO jumps. What makes you think a ride in a Boeing 737 is going to put any sweat on my brow?"

"I don't know. Maybe you don't like commercial craft. I'm not saying you're afraid to fly, just that you remind me of my friend. Still, you look uncomfortable."

"It's not the suit, and it's not the flight."

"You sick? I mean, you've hit the latrine several times since we landed."

"That was two hours ago, J. J. A man's got the right to use the bathroom when he wants."

"You'll get no argument from me."

"Good. What say we drop the subject?"

"Will do."

"Good. Watch our luggage."

"Where you going . . . never mind. See you when you get back."

☢ ☢ ☢

MOYER FELT BAD ABOUT giving J. J. such a hard time. The man had just been asking about his welfare. J. J. was observant; he had been trained to be that way. Still, being pressed by a junior member grated his nerves.

J. J. had been right about one thing: Moyer had been using the restroom more than usual. His stomach twisted as if he had eaten a three-week-old sandwich. As much as that bothered him, it wasn't nearly as disturbing as seeing blood in the toilet.

CHAPTER 12

"WHEN IS HE COMING home?" Gina sat at the dinner table with her mother. Stacy had set the table for three, but only two of the family sat around the oak dining set.

"I don't know, sweetie." Stacy set a bowl of mashed potatoes on the table. "You know that Daddy takes these trips from time to time and we never know how long he'll be gone. Maybe this will be only for a few days."

"I hope so. I miss him when he's gone."

"He misses you, too." Stacy looked at her daughter: straight brown hair with blonde highlights hanging past the shoulder, blue eyes that at times seemed brighter than possible, thin frame, and an infectious smile. At twelve years she was still at that wonderful age where parent and child enjoyed each other's company. Her father often claimed that he lost his free will the day Gina was born. Stacy believed it—and so did Gina. She could play her father like Beethoven played the piano.

Gina was the light in the family, but Stacy wondered how she would change as twelve became thirteen, fourteen, fifteen, and—

heaven help her—sixteen. Already she was showing signs of shedding childhood and embracing the world of young adults. Soon the hormones would increase from a trickle to a flood, parents would suddenly seem stupid and stifling, and being popular would become as important as breathing. Then again, maybe Gina would be one of those who flew through the teenage years with grace and purpose. Or she might go through it as Stacy had. Stacy's mother had promised that one day her children would pay her back for the way she treated her mother. So far, one had.

"You made gravy." Gina pushed the ladle through the thick fluid. "I love gravy."

"So does your father. I planned the meal before he called."

"Where's Rob? He's late for dinner."

Stacy wondered when the question would come. "I don't know. Did he say anything to you?"

"No. He never tells me anything. Did you call his phone?"

"I've tried his cell phone several times, but no answer."

"Did you leave a message?"

"Leave a message? You can leave messages on them fancy no-wire phones?"

Gina put the ladle down. "I'll take that as a yes."

"I left several messages."

She moved back to the kitchen, removed the fried chicken from the paper towels she used to sop up the excess grease, and placed it on the platter. There was enough food for six people. Rob ate like he had two stomachs, and Eric packed down more food than he should. He remained trim through daily exercise, but someday that would end. His metabolism would change as he approached his late forties, and she feared he would balloon. Considering he was headed to an unknown part of the world to do some kind of military work to complete some kind of mission, a little weight gain seemed like a small thing. He never spoke of the places he went and the work he did. Maybe someday, but not today or tomorrow or the next few years. Maybe never. She often told herself she didn't want to know.

"Fried chicken, mashed potatoes, gravy." Gina arched a brow. "My health teacher would have a cow if she saw all this."

"Invite her over, we can barbecue the cow."

"Mom, you know what I mean."

"You know, we don't eat like this every night. Your father seemed distracted the last few days, and I thought he might like an old-fashioned, heart-clogging meal. You don't have to eat it."

"Bet me." Gina spooned out a mound of potatoes.

Stacy sat in her usual seat and let her eyes drift to the two empty chairs around the table.

"YOU LOOK A TAD pale, Eric. You sure you're okay?" J. J. knew he was pressing his luck. Moyer was fair but often impatient.

"I told you, I'm fine. Good to go. Ready to rock. You don't believe me?"

J. J. forced a smile. "Just wondering if you're contagious."

"Thanks for your concern, but you're safe. Like I said, I ate something that hasn't settled well. I'm feeling better, so let it go."

"Will do. You da boss. I'm just a lowly middle executive for an oil company."

"And don't you forget it." Moyer sat and stretched his legs. "I hate airports. As a kid, I loved them: so many people, noises, and things to see. Now it's just something to endure to get from one place to another."

"At least you don't have to wear a parachute."

"I'd feel better if I did." He sighed. "I'm making quite a sacrifice to be here, you know. Stacy thought I needed a pick-me-up and promised fried chicken with all the fixings. Man, she makes a mean fried chicken."

J. J. closed his eyes. "My mother used to fix country meals. Now I feel guilty if I eat food like that."

"Well, danger is our business, and if it means going toe-to-toe with potatoes and gravy, then I'm willing to risk it."

"Except your upset stomach would ruin it all."

"I'd risk it."

"You miss her already."

Moyer nodded. "Goes with the territory. I know it. She knows it."

"That's the advantage of being single."

Moyer shook his head. "That's the *dis*advantage of being single. When you have a family, you're fighting for more than patriotic ideals. You fight to make sure your family remains safe." He paused. "How come you don't have a girl? A good-looking guy like you should have women dogging his steps. This isn't one of those don't-ask-don't-tell things, is it?"

J. J. laughed. "If it were, then you just asked. No, nothing like that. I do my fair share of dating but haven't found the right fit. Made lots of friends but haven't made the connection I'm looking for."

"This is one of those church things, isn't it?"

"I suppose. I want to marry, but I need a spiritual woman who understands what I do. I've met a number of women who have been impressed that I'm Army, but no matter how fascinated they seem I can tell they don't like the idea of being married to a military man. They ask, 'Have you ever been stationed overseas?' and when I mention being stationed in Germany for a couple of years, the sparkle goes out of their eyes."

Moyer nodded. "Takes a special woman to hang with men like us. I don't know how Stacy does it."

"That's the thing. In my case, I need someone who understands my travel needs, my work, my love for—" he grinned—"hardware and things that go boom. *And* she has to be a person of faith. A lot of people fall in love with love, but then it isn't long before the relationship starts taking a beating. I believe in marrying for life. The one thing I don't want to do is have to choose between career and marriage. It's not fair to the woman, but it comes with the package."

"I don't know how you do it. I couldn't do this work and be a Christian. I'd have to give up one."

The words soured J. J. "I couldn't do this *without* being a Christian. It's how I keep my sanity. It keeps me human." He studied Moyer's expression. "I'm talking about me and no one else, you understand."

"Yeah, I got it." After a moment, Moyer said, "You had me worried. I thought the team was going to lose you."

"Lose me? Why would you think . . . oh. Afghanistan."

"You looked pretty shook—no, not shook—troubled. You looked deeply troubled at the end."

J. J. looked down the aisle: a man and woman, each towing a rolling suitcase, walked by. He waited for them to pass before speaking again. "I won't lie to you, Boss. It bothered me. Still does. I helped kill a couple of men who did nothing more than follow their sheep into the wrong place at the wrong time. Still, we made the world a slightly better place by defeating a terrorist cell. No worries. I'm not going anyplace the Army doesn't send me."

"That's good. The Army spent a ton of money training you. I'd hate to think my hard-earned tax dollars went for nothing."

"Hey, I pay taxes too."

Moyer laughed, and it seemed to J. J. that he was looking better. Moyer laughed again. "I gotta tell ya, I've never met a man who loves Jesus *and* guns so much. I don't claim to understand it."

J. J. took his fair share of ribbing for being a Holy Roller, but he never let it bother him. Jesus had hung on a cross; the least J. J. could do is take a few jokes and jabs.

He looked down at the luggage near his feet. "Neither do I."

CHAPTER 13

THE DARKNESS OF THE alley threatened to swallow the dim light from distant streetlamps and a late-rising moon. It also threatened to swallow the man who sat on the concrete stoop behind his restaurant. To his left were two dumpsters. In front of the dumpsters, shrouded by the dark, was the blood-stained pavement where his son had died.

The restaurant appeared more tomb than business. A single light burned inside and dribbled through the open back door. The concrete stoop was hard and dirty, but Reuben didn't care. The pain in his heart and mind was so fierce he could feel nothing else. Estella was inside writing thank-you notes for those who had sent cards and well wishes. She had paused to weep and that was when Reuben moved outside.

He needed air.

He needed to be alone.

He needed courage.

The latter was slow in coming. He knew what he wanted to do, what he longed to do. For the last ten minutes he had stared down the alley toward the street that ran in front of his eatery. The killer had come from that direction. He didn't need to be a policeman to figure that out. He had walked down the alley, raised a pistol, and pulled the trigger three times. And a good boy, a smart boy, a loving boy, *his* boy had breathed his last.

Reuben prayed. He prayed God would send the man back down the alley. Perhaps to revisit the crime, maybe to gloat. Maybe to mock Reuben. He didn't care, just as long as his son's killer appeared.

The gun in Reuben's hand felt heavy and cold. It wasn't a fancy weapon, just a cheap .38 he bought at a sporting goods store. He kept it near the register in case someone thought he had a right to Reuben's money. But the money didn't matter now. The restaurant no longer mattered.

He looked at the weapon in his hand and wondered if it would hurt once he placed the barrel in his mouth and squeezed the trigger. He was close to doing it. The courage had at last arrived, but one thing kept his hands resting in his lap: Estella. She would hear the sound. She'd know what it meant. She would run to the back door and find her husband with half his head missing and lying in a pool of blood.

The thought of her losing a son and a husband in one week made the gun too heavy to lift, the barrel too difficult to point.

"Reuben?"

He didn't look up. He knew every nuance, every unspoken message that rode on the notes of his wife's voice.

Estella lowered herself to the stoop. Without looking he knew she saw the gun in his hand. At first she said nothing. Minutes passed like days.

"First, a favor." Estella's voice was soft, not much more than a whisper.

"What favor?"

"Put the gun to my head first."

He snapped his head around. "What?"

"Before you kill yourself, kill me. I have no life without you and Ricardo."

"I can't. I won't!"

"I know you, Reuben Estevez. I have lived with you too many years to not know what you are thinking. There are days when I know your thoughts before you do."

He believed that. "This time you are wrong."

"Am I? Before you put that gun to your head, you must first put it to mine. I deserve that much from you."

"I could never do that. I am no murderer."

"If you kill my husband, the last human being I love, then you will be a murderer. You will kill more than just yourself; you will destroy my soul. I will be dead one way or the other."

The pistol in Reuben's hand began to shake. Tears fell from his eyes onto the smooth metal.

He raised the handgun.

He put his finger on the trigger and felt its metallic curve beneath his rough finger. He withdrew his finger and pressed the safety to the on position. He then opened the cylinder and emptied the rounds into his hand. A short distance away rested a paper sack. He had seen the likes of it many times before. A few of the local homeless like to drink in the alley from time to time. Reuben rose, retrieved the bag and empty whisky bottle, dropped the gun in the bag, stepped to one of the dumpsters and deposited the bag.

Estella joined him. He handed the bullets to her, and she took them in her hand. Then they embraced and wept—wept together on the spot where their son had died.

☢ ☢ ☢

SEVERAL DAYS HAD PASSED since Reuben had found his son in the dark alley. The restaurant had remained closed in the days that followed. Reuben employed two managers he could trust to run the business, but none of that was important now. In a way, the restaurant he built over twenty-five years seemed more tomblike than the grave his son lay in.

After the police had left, Reuben sent his employees home, closed and locked the doors. Unwashed dishes lay in the large stainless-steel sinks, surrounded by dark, dirty water. Tables waited for an employee to clear their surfaces of dishes, coffee cups, glasses of beer, and silverware spotted with dried clumps of cheese.

Estella turned the knob of the faucet and hot water began to flow.

Reuben picked up a few cooking utensils and set them near the sink. "I promised Ricardo that I'd add a commercial dishwasher this year. He said it would clean the dishes better and make them more sanitary. I wish I had acted earlier."

"He was right." It was all Estella could say.

"Will things return to normal, Estella?"

She reached into the sink, unplugged the drain, let the water escape then replaced the specialized stopper. Hot water began to fill the basin. "Normal?" She shook her head. "No. Not normal. Not ever again. Everything will be different, but life goes on. The pain will become manageable but never go away. We go on."

"I don't think I can."

"You can, husband, and you will. It would disappoint Ricardo if we didn't."

"How can you be so strong?"

"Strong? I'm not strong. I'm broken. Time may patch the broken parts, but it will never heal them. We go on."

"Everything here reminds me of him. Every memory is a knife to the heart."

"I know. But I would rather have the pain than not have the memories."

Reuben marveled at his wife. She had just saved his life. Like a fallen figurine she was shattered in myriad pieces, yet there she stood, washing dishes and reminding him that life goes on.

"I'll clear the tables and bring in the dishes."

Estella opened her mouth to speak, but no words crossed her lips. She nodded instead.

Reuben was a systematic man. As such, he chose to start at the most distant corner of the building and work back toward the kitchen. When he reached the private dining area, he stopped at the small bussing station where Ricardo had last worked. He pushed back the curtain and imagined his son there.

The station was cramped with just enough room for one person to fill water glasses, pour coffee, and do the other little things patrons seldom noticed. Colored paper on a shelf above the sink caught his attention. He reached for it: American comic books. Reuben smiled. He had felt the comic books were a waste of money, but they did help his son with his English. More than once Ricardo had said he wanted to visit the U.S. He didn't say it in the restaurant and never to anyone but family. Reuben had insisted on that. These were not good days to speak of such things.

He started to put the comics back when he noticed some writing on the backside of one issue: *Hector Cenobio, nuclear, fast capture, airport, Iran.*

He had no idea who Hector Cenobio was, but the words *nuclear* and *Iran* caught his attention. Why would his son make such notes? He lifted his eyes from the comic book cover to the private dining room. He looked at the table and thought of who sat there the night his son died—and found a reason to live.

CHAPTER 14

J. J. LOOKED AT MOYER, who leaned against the small window of the Boeing 757, eyes closed, head back, mouth agape. Every so often a soft snore would rumble out of the man's mouth. J. J. smiled. If his team leader got any noisier, J. J. would gently put an elbow in the man's ribs. Not that it mattered much. Half the passengers on the aircraft were in some form of twisted, painful-looking sleeping position, something that made J. J. envious. He never could sleep while flying, no matter how late the hour.

On small screens mounted the length of the aircraft, George Clooney was wooing some actress, J. J. didn't bother to find out whom. They were three hours into a slightly-longer-than-five-hour flight. Five hours didn't seem right to him. Flying across the U.S. took as long if not longer. He reminded himself he should be thankful. A 757 was a good deal more comfortable than a military transport or doing a HALO—high altitude, low open—jump in the dark. Missing a little sleep wasn't so bad.

Boarding the plane had proved an eye-opener for J. J. He knew of and had been briefed about the ongoing tensions between

Venezuela and the U.S. What he hadn't expected was the number of people flying to Caracas. Although the State Department had not blacklisted the country for Americans traveling abroad, its Web site info was far from complimentary of Caracas as a tourist destination, spotlighting robberies, kidnappings, and other forms of violent crime. Yet this aircraft was filled with Americans—men and women who could be his neighbors, sleeping, watching the movie, knitting, reading, or working on laptop computers.

J. J. leaned his head back and closed his eyes. He was having stomach trouble of his own. Not like Moyer, who just looked ill and worried. No, a different illness troubled him: a disease he caught on a mountain in Afghanistan. He never spoke of it, never let on that regret traveled with him wherever he went.

This was his first mission since the recon-turned-firefight on the snowy slope. He had told Moyer he was good to go, but there were moments—usually when he was alone, lying in bed, staring at the ceiling—that the ache of doubt burned. A thousand times he had returned to the mountain, saw himself pressed down in his hand-dug ditch, leveling his weapon at the chest of one of the men with AK47s. The Afghani pointed their direction. Someone on the team fired, indelibly tattooing the *fsst* sound of a suppressed round on his mind. A half second later instinct and training took over. The trigger of his weapon moved beneath his finger, recoil slapped his shoulder, and the man spun.

Had he delivered the kill shot? Everyone else on the team seemed to think Caraway had tapped both men. J. J. tried to convince himself that there was no way to know, but he did know his round punctured the Afghani's sternum. If that wasn't a kill shot, he didn't know what was. J. J. had earned his nickname, Colt, for his love of and proficiency with weapons. He had many talents, but marksmanship was his signature skill.

When he relived that night, his heart broke over the shepherd he killed, although he gave no thought to the al-Qaeda fighters who tried to swarm their position. This dichotomy didn't bother him. The AQ had chosen to attack, and they did so with deadly force; J. J. had done what he had to do for his team and for himself. When he joined the Army, when he determined to earn his Ranger tab, when he allowed the government to spend $100,000 to train him, he knew he would one day be called on to lower the hammer on the enemy.

But the shepherd had not been the enemy. He had been a simple working man in the wrong place at the wrong time. If the guy had been a carpenter instead of a sheepherder, he'd still be alive. Moyer had reminded J. J. that innocent men died in war. It was the way of the world. J. J. knew that—he just couldn't feel it. What he could feel was that somewhere halfway around the world a shepherd and his friend lay in graves. And a young wife sat alone, a child wept, and another young man grew angry at the world.

"Are you okay?"

J. J. opened his eyes and looked across the aisle at a woman in her mid-fifties: brown hair with gray at the roots, thin, and wearing a lime-green pantsuit that made J. J. wish he were wearing his sunglasses. "Excuse me?"

She had a Ken Follett book on her lap. "I asked if you were feeling all right. You look a little pained."

"I'm fine. Just resting my eyes."

"If you say so. But if you were my grandson, I'd say you were having gas pains."

"Wha—? How old is your grandson?"

"Six months. He's a chunk, like his father. The kid is born for the NFL."

J. J. chuckled. "Lots of fathers say that."

"He didn't say it. I did. He's why I'm on this flight. My grandson, I mean. I've only seen pictures, and that won't do. A grandmother can't spoil a photo."

"I suppose not."

"My son works in Caracas. He's been down there for two years now. I only see him at Christmas."

"That's rough. Being separated from family for long periods is no fun."

"No, it's not. What about you? You have family?"

"Just a brother. My parents are gone now."

"Judging by your age, I'd say they died much too early."

J. J. nodded. "It's always too early to lose the ones you love."

"From your mouth to God's ear."

More often than you think.

"So why are you making the trip to Venezuela? Business?"

"Yes, ma'am. A few days of business and maybe a little recreation."

"What business are you in?"

J. J. didn't want to go down this path. He had his cover down pat, but there was always the chance of a mess-up. "I work for an oil company."

"Really? What company?"

"Oklaco. They're a firm in—"

"In Oklahoma. My son works for them. Maybe you've met."

J. J. pushed out a smile, struggling to make it seem real. "I doubt it. It's a big company, and I'm not a regular employee."

"What's that mean?"

"I do consulting work. Oil companies hire me for extended periods of time. After my contract is up, I move on."

"That doesn't sound right to me. It seems you could take company secrets to the competition." She narrowed her eyes.

"Not a chance. That's what nondisclosure agreements are for. First, I'm an honorable man. Trust matters a great deal to me. Second, the last thing I want is to find myself in a legal battle with a company like Oklaco. I know where my bread is buttered."

"I suppose. So what do you consult the company about?" The woman wouldn't give up.

"I review geological surveys and offer an outside opinion. That's all I can say. Being something of an insider, you'll understand."

"I suppose I do. Maybe I could have your card."

"I wish I could, but I wasn't planning on talking business on the trip. My card holder is in my luggage, and I don't think the pilot will pull the plane over for me to retrieve it." He winked at her. She seemed to like it. "You know, I've never read Follett. Is he any good?"

"Oh, he's great . . ."

She talked for the next half hour about the books she'd read.

CHAPTER 15

JAY LENO HAD JUST started his monologue when Stacy Moyer heard the rattle of keys at the front door. She didn't bother to turn on the light. She'd been sitting in the glow of the large flat-screen television for hours. She pressed the MUTE button on the remote.

The door opened slowly and a familiar, rail-thin figure slipped between the jamb and the partially opened door. The figure quickly closed the door as if the night might follow him in.

"Thanks for stopping by."

The figure jumped a foot and spun. "Mom. What are you doing up? It's late."

"Ya think?" She rose from the sofa. "Last I checked, school let out at three-fifteen. Did that change without the parents being informed?"

"No." At sixteen, Rob had already reached six-foot-one, which made him a hit on the intramural basketball team, but he lacked the skill and desire to make the varsity team. He wore a black T-shirt emblazoned with the image of a human skull wearing sunglasses and smoking a cigarette. His jeans were worn and one of the pockets torn, not from hard work but by an elusive fashion sense.

She waited. "'No'? That's it?"

"What do you want?"

"Well, let's see, what could a mother want at eleven-forty in the evening, seven hours after her son should have been home? Hey, I know: How about an explanation?"

"I went over to Freddy's after school. He's starting a band and asked me to join."

"You don't play an instrument, unless you've taken up the tuba behind my back."

"I can sing."

"Yeah, but can you answer a cell phone?" Anger warmed her face.

"You didn't call." He started to move from the door.

"Yes, I did. I called at least six times and left a message every time."

"I don't know. Maybe I had it turned off."

"Give it to me." She stepped to him and held out a hand.

He stepped back. "What?"

"Your cell phone."

"Why?"

"Have you ever seen me this angry?"

"No . . . no."

"Then don't trifle with me, son. Give me the phone."

He pulled a small Motorola from his pocket and placed it in Stacy's hand. Before she flipped open the clamshell device, it beeped.

"Odd, it seems to be on now. And look, it says you have several messages."

"I guess I wasn't paying attention."

Stacy worked another button on the phone. "Hmm, the call history says you received several calls tonight, some of them near the times I called. It looks like you answered those."

"You can't tell that."

"You're right. I'll just call one now and ask the caller if he or she spoke to you." Stacy moved her thumb over the green-lit button marked SEND.

"All right, I saw your calls, but I didn't answer because I knew you'd go ballistic on me, just like now."

"How often have I done that . . . not counting tonight?"

He didn't answer.

"I asked you a question."

Rob shrugged. "Not often. But Dad does. You saw how out of control he was last night. Who wants to come home to that?"

"As I recall, you started it."

"As I recall, *Dad* started it. He always starts it. He hates me because I haven't grown into a gun-totting jock." Before Stacy could respond, he added, "Where is Dad? I thought he'd be here to beat me down."

"Your father has never hit you and you know it."

"There are other kinds of beatings, Mom. Where is he?"

She lowered her voice. "He was called up this morning."

"So he's taken off again to who-knows-where for who-knows-how-long."

"That's part of his job. I knew it when I married him."

"Too bad I didn't know it before I was born. Can I have my phone back?"

Stacy didn't reply. Fighting back tears took all the willpower she could muster. Finally she held the device out and Rob took it.

"What now?" Some of the defiance drained from Rob's voice.

"Go to bed, and please don't ever do this to me again."

"I wasn't trying to do anything to you. I'm not a kid anymore, Mom. I don't need you checking up on me all the time."

"You haven't proved that to me yet. Adults make the effort to keep contact with their families."

"Really? You expecting a call from Dad tonight? Because, if this 'business trip' is like his others, we won't hear from him for days, maybe weeks." He started toward his bedroom.

"Rob."

"What now?"

She turned and when she spoke the anger was gone from her voice. "I fell asleep this afternoon. I had a bad dream—a nightmare about your father and his team."

He shrugged. "Everybody has nightmares."

"Rob, what I'm trying to say is that there may come a day when I need you to be more than a rebellious sixteen-year-old boy."

Stacy watched her son stare at her for a moment. He nodded slightly and disappeared down the hall to his bedroom.

☢ ☢ ☢

STILL CLOTHED, ROB MOYER lay on his bed bathed in a light from a nightstand lamp. He thumbed through a skateboard magazine not seeing the photos, not reading the words. His emotions churned, alternating between anger, hurt, frustration, and guilt. Guilt was losing.

A soft sound pressed through the door. He closed his eyes.

His mother was down the hall. Weeping.

Rob fought back his own tears, then—did nothing.

☢ ☢ ☢

THE BLACKNESS OF THE ocean beneath them gave way to the lights of Maiquetia as the 757 banked over the shore and descended into Simon Bolivar International Airport. J. J. peered past Moyer out the window, watching the flashing running lights bounce off the runway. A second later they were wheels down and taxiing to one of the airport's two terminals. They had made better time than expected.

The moment the aircraft came to a stop, the *clack* and *click* of seat belts releasing filled the passenger compartment. Scores of people stood as if doing so would get the exit doors open sooner. J. J. stayed in place. He saw no sense in standing in the narrow aisle pressed between strangers like salami on rye.

Ten minutes later they stood in a line, computer bags hung over their shoulders, waiting for their turn in immigration. J. J. reminded himself that nothing could go wrong here, though neither he nor Moyer carried anything suspicious. Even the bags they had checked in the U.S. contained what anyone would expect to find in the luggage of two men traveling on international business. A decade ago they might have tried to smuggle personal weaponry, broken down into its most basic parts for later reassembly, in special luggage, but not now. In August 2006 Venezuelan authorities searched and seized diplomatic cargo intended for the U.S. Embassy. The authorities claimed they found parts for a military aircraft ejector seat and 176 pounds of chicken. The U.S. lodged complaints about the improper search of diplomatic packages. J. J. wondered what the embassy needed with an ejector seat and chicken.

If diplomatic material could be searched, then certainly the luggage of two Americans could fall under close scrutiny. They had other ways of getting the equipment they needed.

"Passports, please." The words belonged to a short, dark man with a thin mustache that hung to his lip below a heavily veined nose. He oozed contempt and boredom. "Anything to declare?"

"No." Moyer handed over his passport.

"Nature of your visit, please?" The man studied Moyer's documents.

"Business."

The immigration officer squinted as he looked at Moyer's picture and ran a thumb over the image. "Your passport looks new." He studied the small book's spine and fingered the other pages.

"It is."

"Do you travel on business often?" The officer's English was good.

"Several times a year." J. J. saw Moyer's shoulders tense.

"Yet your passport seems only days old."

Moyer chuckled. "It's my wife's fault. She washed my other one. Let me tell you, it's a real pain in the fanny to get a new one on short notice. If you know what I mean."

"Do you have another form of identification, Señor?"

"Sure. Would a driver's license do?"

J. J. could do nothing but act bored, even as his mind raced like an Indy car. His passport looked much like Moyer's. Everything else about the documents was perfect, but no one had guessed that some civil servant would care about how new or old a passport appeared.

Moyer removed his driver's license with the false name and address and handed it to the man.

"I can't believe some of these people." The voice came from behind J. J. He turned and saw the grandmother that tried to talk his ear off on the plane. "What's the hang-up?" Her voice rose above the ambient noise of the airport.

J. J. started to warn her against irritating the immigration officer, then decided against it. Odds were that the man wouldn't be too hard on a woman, and she might just cause enough disruption to distract the man.

The officer compared Moyer's driver's license photo to the one on the passport. He fingered the license. J. J. had never seen such a tactile man. "Your driver's license also looks new. Did your wife wash that as well?"

"Are you married?" Moyer asked.

The man nodded.

"Have you ever made your wife mad? Yes, she washed my driver's license and everything else in my wallet—my passport, my license, my credit cards. My cell phone too. I'd had a few too many the night before. She claimed it was an accident. I think it was revenge."

The man nodded.

"Come on, mister," the woman said. "My family is waiting for me."

The immigration man lifted his head and frowned.

"Look," J. J. said to the woman. "I don't have anyone waiting on me. Why don't you take my place?"

"Thank you." She pushed past him, jostling J. J. with her shoulder bag. She was now one behind Moyer and much closer to the officer.

The official looked at the woman and tightened his jaw. He handed the passport and driver's license back to Moyer, pulled a small booklet from a pile to his left, made a couple of notes and slammed a rubber stamp on one of the pages. "This is your three-week visa. Welcome to Venezuela. Enjoy your stay." The words were delivered in robotic fashion. He waved Moyer through.

The woman was cleared in what had to be record time. J. J.'s heart picked up a few beats as he handed the man his passport. To J. J.'s surprise he cleared immigration with no trouble. The man glanced at the passport, then at J. J.'s face. "This is your three-week visa. Welcome to Venezuela. Enjoy your stay." The immigration officer was still working, but part of him had already checked out for the day.

J. J. made eye contact with Moyer. They had just dodged a bullet.

Customs went smoothly and minutes later they entered the main terminal. For some reason J. J. had expected a trashy building with technology just this side of the Stone Age. Instead he saw a newly remodeled structure, with colorful walls, large windows, and highly polished floors. He should have remembered: never make assumptions.

"Think you can get us a rental car?"

J. J. turned to Moyer. "I think I can manage."

"Good. There's the rental car counter."

He looked at the signs over the counter. *Aco Alquiler, Amigo, Auto 727, Avis, Budget, Hertz, Margarita Rental,* and *Rojas.* "I think I'll go with Hertz."

"Got a reason?"

"Yeah, I recognize the name."

"Works for me. While you do that, I'll take care of some other business."

Before J. J. could ask, Moyer moved at a brisk pace to the men's restroom.

CHAPTER 16

MORNING LIGHT PUSHED THROUGH a gap in the heavy draperies, falling across Moyer's face as he lay in bed. The radio alarm-clock read 6:15. He had been awake for over an hour. For him, this was sleeping in. Still, being awake didn't necessitate crawling from bed. Clean white sheets and a thick comforter conspired to keep him in place, and he felt content to let them do so.

After leaving the Caracas airport, he and J. J. had checked into the Palacio de Sol, an upscale business-class hotel near the center of the city. When Moyer pushed his credit card across the marble-topped check-in desk and signed the room agreement, he saw his tax dollars were paying over $300 a night for a two-week stay. They were warmly welcomed and their baggage carried to their rooms by a bellhop in a red uniform that looked as if it had been salvaged from a 1950s movie set. A twenty-dollar tip put a smile on the man's face.

Both rooms were on the eleventh floor of the twenty-five-story hotel. At the briefing that morning, Kinkaid had described the hotel as a step above most of the other facilities in the area, complete with luxury suites. Neither Moyer nor J. J. got a suite. They had to settle for a "standard room," but standard proved better than he hoped. White plaster walls supported a coffered ceiling. Thick blue drapes hung over sheer inner drapes, the former being pulled back to let in the lights of downtown Caracas. A king-size bed dominated the space. A workstation of cherry-veneered wood occupied one corner. Two heavily padded chairs anchored the other corner. Photo artwork of the Venezuelan countryside hung on the walls.

Moyer had wanted nothing more than to unpack and crawl into bed. The day had been long and taxing. In less than fifteen hours he had gone from sitting in a doctor's office, hearing how he might have colon cancer but not to worry, to being shipped to a foreign country.

Despite the lure of the bed, Moyer had more work to do, though it wouldn't appear like work to most people. He and J. J. were to meet in half an hour and make their way to the hotel bar. Sometimes the best way to maintain low visibility was to keep a high profile. They had to assume that someone might be watching them. They had done nothing thus far to draw attention to themselves, and they wanted to keep it that way. They were traveling as businessmen, so they had to do what traveling businessmen often did—knock back a drink or two. It was all part of hiding in plain sight.

The bar looked like most bars Moyer had been in but with better furniture. Flat-screen televisions hung from the ceiling, each strategically placed to allow anyone in the bar an unencumbered view. Each television had been tuned to a sports channel. Clips of soccer and baseball games beamed from the screens.

An hour later Moyer crawled into bed, turned on the television, found ESPN Deportes, and tried to make sense of the Spanish sports news. Not that it mattered. Five minutes later he was asleep.

Now that the sun had crawled over the eastern horizon, Moyer was ready to get to work. He shaved, showered, and dressed in a pair of loose-fitting jeans and a pale yellow shirt with the words OKLACO OIL stitched over the right breast. He replaced yesterday's black dress shoes with a scuffed pair of leather work boots.

As he retrieved his wallet and hotel key, his Nokia E61i chirped. A text message had arrived: *Lunch meeting is confirmed.* The innocuous sentence would mean nothing to anyone reading over his shoulder. To Moyer it meant Shaq and Caraway had arrived and checked into their hotel. He studied the PDA display and noticed that another text message had arrived while he was in the shower: *Hi Sweetheart. I miss you already. Junior misses his daddy. Call when you can.*

Jose and Pete were on scene. Moyer smiled. Cell phones were normally devices so open that a high school student with a little knowledge and the right equipment could intercept a call or text message. The cell phone Moyer held was different. The modified Nokia phone carried the latest encryption software. A dual-layered RSA 1024-bit/AES 256-bit military-grade encryption had been loaded into the phone. To carry on a conversation free of prying ears all he had to do was key in a single digit. Even a text message was safe once the encryption was turned on. The phones were not new; many government leaders carried them.

"So far, so good."

Someone knocked on the door. Moyer, with phone still in hand, peered through the peephole and saw a spread of white teeth. When Moyer opened the door, he found J. J. leaning close to where the door had been a moment before, still grinning like the Cheshire cat.

"What's with the cheesy grin? You win the lottery or something?" Moyer stepped back, letting J. J. enter. He wore a gray shirt similar to Moyer's, as well as jeans and work boots.

"Every day a man can climb out of bed is a good day." J. J. closed the door behind him.

"That's how you got it figured?"

"Absolutely. Optimism is my middle name." He looked at the phone in Moyer's hand. "Receive any interesting calls?"

"Usual stuff." Moyer's cryptic response carried enough meaning for J. J. to understand. "You ready to rock?"

"And roll—just as soon as I use the latrine."

"What? They didn't give you a bathroom?"

"Coffee. It's all about the coffee."

☢ ☢ ☢

AFTER A BREAKFAST OF eggs and chorizo in the hotel restaurant, Moyer and J. J. pulled their rental car from the parking stall and started across the surface streets. Moyer drove, leaving J. J. free to take in the sights. Were it not for all the signs in Spanish, he might have confused his surroundings with any U.S. city of two million people. Like most cities, Caracas had an industrial area, a downtown business section, and numerous suburban neighborhoods. It was to one of these neighborhoods the onboard GPS led them.

The neighborhood comprised row upon row of small homes. Judging by the size of the trees near the street, J. J. figured the community to be more than thirty years old. The houses sported pale paint on hand-applied stucco. This was a working-class neighborhood, chosen because very few people would be home. Children would be at school, parents at work. The few people who might see them would be mothers of small children or the elderly.

They moved down the street slowly, though not so slow as to attract attention, and parked behind a dark green panel truck. The vehicle was ten years old if it was a day but looked well kept. Moyer pulled the sedan behind the truck and switched off the car.

He glanced at J. J. "Open the hood and fiddle around for a couple of minutes."

"I'm not much of a mechanic."

"You don't have to be. Just look and touch a few things, then we'll be on our way."

J. J. didn't need the explanation, but talking helped quiet his nerves. Moyer had been more somber than usual on the ride over.

They moved to the panel truck. Moyer unlocked the door and pulled the hood release. J. J. peered into the engine compartment. It was surprisingly clean for a vehicle of its age. He wiggled the radiator hose, studied the fan belts, and made certain the spark plug wires were in place. They were, of course. He expected to find nothing wrong. All of his activities were for the benefit of anyone watching. Two minutes later he stepped back and nodded to Moyer. The engine fired to life, and J. J. closed the hood.

Moyer drove off down the street, with J. J. following in the sedan.

CHAPTER 17

THE PHONE RANG AT 9:12. Stacy dusted grainy laundry soap from her hands and picked up the handset. Already she had run and emptied the dishwasher, dusted the living room, and vacuumed the house. It was what she did when Eric went on mission.

"Hello."

"Um . . . good morning. Is this the Moyer residence?" A male voice.

"It is. Who's calling please?" Stacy leaned against the wall. She wasn't in the mood for a telemarketer. "We're on the 'Do Not Call' list, so if you're a salesperson . . ." She heard the man chuckle.

"I'm not selling anything. Is this Mrs. Moyer?"

"Yes. Who is this?"

"My name is Dr. Miles Lawton. I'm a physician. Is Mr. Moyer in?"

The voice sounded calm and pleasant, nonetheless the word *physician* made Stacy's heart jitter. "Are you sure you have the right number? There are a lot of Moyers in the world."

"I'm looking for Eric Moyer."

"My husband is Eric Moyer, but he's not in at the moment. May I ask what this is about?"

"Mr. Moyer came to my office yesterday for an examination and consultation. I stepped from the office for a few minutes, and he was gone when I returned. I thought I'd give him the day to call, but when he didn't I decided to call."

"He gave you this number?"

"Yes—well, sort of. The number he left is similar, but the last two numbers are transposed. It happens all the time."

That sounded like something Eric would do if he were being secretive. "I'm sorry about all the questions, Doctor. I'm one of those privacy nuts. Sometimes my husband forgets to update my calendar as well as his, so I'm often a day or two behind."

"I understand. I've done it too. Must be a guy thing. You say he's out for a while?"

"Yes, he's been called away on business. That happens sometimes. Everything is an emergency with his firm."

Another forced chuckle. "Is there a way I can reach him? Phone? E-mail?"

Stacy's mind began to spin. This could get complicated. "I'm afraid not. Why don't you just give me the information and I'll see what I can do to run him down." Seeing a doctor without telling her gave "run him down" new meaning. What was Eric doing seeing a civilian doctor?

"Just a moment."

Stacy heard paper shuffle.

"Yes, here it is. He gave your name as a contact and signed the release."

"Release?"

"HIPAA Privacy Rule. Basically it means I can't talk to anyone about a patient's health without permission of the patient. But I see here that he signed the release."

Of course he did. He also gave the wrong phone number. Why was he being secretive about his health? And how to make the doctor think she knew what was going on? "I know he's sensitive about the problem. He had a difficult time talking to me about it."

The line was silent for a moment. "So he's spoken to you? That's good. Such matters should be discussed between spouses."

"When he calls, what shall I tell him?"

"I'd like him to come back in for the blood test and to arrange for the colonoscopy. We don't want too much time to pass before getting the tests done. As I told him, colon cancer is only one possibility. Most likely he has a far-easier-to-treat ailment, but we don't want to take any chances. Sometimes it's hard for men to follow through on these tests. I'm hoping that you can encourage him to do so. We men like to act brave, but we're often more fearful than we let on." He paused. "I'm not saying your husband lacks courage, you understand. I'm sure he's very brave in other ways."

"You have no idea, Doctor."

Stacy set the phone back in the cradle after three tries. She staggered to the sofa on legs that felt made of overcooked noodles rather than bone and muscles.

"Colon cancer." They were the only two words she could muster.

J. J. WAS IN HIS element. Standing in the back of the panel truck, he made a quick survey of the equipment and weaponry smuggled across the border from Colombia. Entering the country by commercial airliner made bringing weapons and recon gear impossible.

J. J. didn't know who brought the truckload of equipment, but it must have been a long drive across Venezuela.

"Everything there?" Moyer directed the truck along one of the city's highways.

"They forgot the kitchen sink."

"Figures. What about the incidentals?"

"Side arms, field knives, M4s, and enough surveillance equipment to make Caraway slobber all over himself. There's even some stuff to make things go boom."

"You know what they say: 'There is no situation in the human condition that cannot be solved through a properly sized, shaped, packed, placed, timed, and detonated charge of high explosive.' It's a motto we can all live by. Electronics?"

"Yup. Digital Soldiers-R-Us. Looks like we're set for anything. This truck is a rolling weapons locker."

Moyer nodded. "All we need is the small stuff. Can't walk around with M4s slung over our shoulders."

J. J. lifted a 9mm pistol. "I can see how that might get noticed."

"Let the others know the rendezvous is on. Time to earn our pay."

LUCY MEDINA SETTLED INTO her husband's easy chair. She did so for two reasons. First, the chair reminded her of him; it carried his smell, and sitting in it made him seem close even when he was far away— wherever far away might be. She wore one of his T-shirts that she slept in for the same reason. The second reason was physical. She had been busy getting three children ready for school and driving them to the campus. Fortunately all three went to the same school. Matteo and Jose Jr. would be in school until nearly three, but Maria would need to be picked up at noon when her half-day kindergarten class ended. Still, that left her a couple of hours to rest her body and mind. Taking care of three children under the age of nine was difficult with help; alone was an impossible task. She wondered how she would manage once the baby was born. She could handle days all right as long as Jose was there to help in the evening—which he wasn't today and might not be for weeks.

She closed her eyes and tried to nap.

The baby moved, then kicked. Lucy rubbed her belly.

Another kick, then a sharp pain. She winced.

Lucy took a deep breath and released it slowly. The pain eased. "What are you doing in there, little Niña?" Again, Lucy tried to relax in the chair. Being pregnant was hard work. She could grow tired just sitting around. This was her time to rest. With the children at school these quiet hours were her sanctuary.

She moved her hands over her basketball-size belly. In another three months "baby within," as Jose called his daughter, would become "baby out and about." Lucy took rest when she could get it—there would be precious little of it soon.

Another kick, this one to Lucy's bladder.

Another pain . . . and another. Something within her tightened. A small moan escaped her lips. Her skin oozed perspiration.

"Oh, God," Lucy prayed.

CHAPTER 18

THE U.S. EMBASSY IN Venezuela would have been a perfect place to meet if it weren't under constant surveillance. The 100,000-square-foot building sat on the side of one of the Andean foothills. The five-story brown building contained a room encased in steel walls that could be used for meeting and planning, but Moyer didn't have that luxury. His mission was as covert as they come. If captured, the State Department would deny any connection with his team.

Instead, he and the others found a rundown bar near the center of the city. The place was large, dingy, and had colored film pasted to the windows like a poor man's stained glass. The pub catered to unsuspecting foreigners. The price of beer was a third higher than what he and J. J. paid in the upscale hotel bar the previous night.

"Nice tourist trap." Shaq took a seat at a long table near the back.

"More like a roach trap." Caraway wrinkled his nose.

"I didn't know you were such a sensitive spirit." Moyer sat at the middle of his team, allowing him to keep his voice down and still be heard.

"Sensitive? Me?" Caraway laughed. "I just like my beer and food to be free of insects."

"Protein is protein," J. J. said.

"Put a sock in it, guys." Moyer paused long enough to make eye contact with each man. "We're here for a reason and we're going to drink beer and eat chicken wings and act like we're enjoying every moment of it. Clear?"

The others nodded.

"Good." Moyer looked at Caraway. "You comfortable?"

Caraway pulled a small, black electronic device from his shirt pocket and gave it a glance. The small device looked very much like an MP3 player but could detect hidden microphones in the 1 MHz to 6.5 GHz range. "Can't do a full sweep, of course. That'd be a tad obvious. But the mini-sweeper says we're good." He dropped the device back into his pocket.

Moyer gave an approving nod. The device wasn't foolproof but provided enough reassurance for Moyer to continue. "We begin tonight. We stay low-vis on this, so we'll be keeping hardware to a minimum." His team nodded. The quickest way to attract attention was to shoulder an M4 automatic rifle. "Martin, bring what you need for the job. We're going to need eyes and ears. I surveyed the equipment and it's all nonmilitary issue."

"Nothing to tie us to our origins," Caraway said.

"Exactly." Moyer stopped as a waitress cleared empty mugs of cerveza from the table and replaced them. J. J.'s mug was still full. When the waitress left, Moyer continued. "We go in full team tonight. Once we have the lay of the land, we'll split into teams for round-the-clock recon. We stay in the same teams we arrived in country with. I know I don't need to say this, but I will: This is an urban recon, so the odds of someone spotting us are much higher than parachuting into some desolate backwater and hiking in."

"That's been bugging me," J. J. said. "These camps—places—are usually away from population centers unless they're in a friendly country. There's miles of jungle around here; why set up in the industrial area of a major city?"

Moyer pursed his lips. He didn't have an answer for that one. "It doesn't matter. Intel said that's where they are and so that's where we go. My best guess is they're getting co-op from the government."

"Still seems odd."

Moyer ended the discussion by ignoring the comment. "Be ready at 2200. Mess up your beds before leaving. I don't want the maids wondering why someone pays big bucks to stay in a hotel then sleeps elsewhere."

They stayed another hour, drinking and eating like business-men off the home leash. The group broke up over the next thirty minutes until only Moyer and J. J. were left. Moyer planned to fin-ish his beer then make his way back to the panel truck. J. J. would drive the rental car back to the hotel.

"What's the matter, J. J.? You look bothered."

"Something doesn't feel right, and I can't put my finger on it."

"We don't operate on feelings, J. J. We operate on intel and gut instinct."

"It's my gut that's bothering me. The M.O. just doesn't seem right." J. J. lowered his voice. "How can a terrorist group train in a downtown industrial park?"

"Not all training has to do with guns and explosives. Maybe they're teaching them something else. Maybe they have other sites in the country. That's what we're here to find out."

"Maybe I shouldn't listen to my gut so much."

"Well, my gut has plenty to say, and I prefer it says it back at the hotel. I'm less likely to catch a disease there."

☢ ☢ ☢

JULIA CENOBIO WAS ON her knees, her elbows resting on the edge of the
bed, her head bowed and eyes closed. She held her hands out to
each side. In each hand rested a smaller hand.

"Thank you, Jesus, for the fun day we had today." Nestor had
been praying for several minutes, and Julia wished he'd find his way
to the end. He was this way every night. At bedtime Julia would
kneel with the children, hold their hands, and lead them in prayer,
allowing each child to pray as they saw fit. Nestor and Lina were
competitive even for twins. At times one would try to eat faster
than the other or read more books or do more cartwheels—they
even tried to out-pray one another.

"And thank you for breakfast and lunch and dinner and the
snakes. And thank you for the man who drove us around the city.
And thank you for this room and this bed . . ."

If only Hector were with them. He had a way of controlling
the children's *enthusiasm*, or at least directing it. "Never squash a
child's enthusiasm," he often said. "The word *enthusiasm* means
'God within.' It is a holy thing."

She tried not to smile. Right now it was an endurance thing.

"And bless Mamá and Papa and the people we saw at the
museum and the waiter who brought our food and—" Julia
squeezed Nestor's hand. He got the hint. "In Jesus' name, amen."

"Amen," Julia and Lina said in unison.

Lina was first on her feet. "God won't answer your prayers,
Nestor."

"Yes, he will. Why not?"

Lina's grinned morphed into a smirk. "Because your prayers are
so long they put him to sleep."

"Do not. Shut up!"

"That's enough, children. I'm sure God heard every word. He listens very closely to everyone who calls on him. Now it's time for you to crawl into bed."

IN THE ADJOINING ROOM the man who served as their chauffeur listened to every word carried through the headphones he wore. No one was more thankful to hear the children were going to bed than he. He had tolerated their unending chatter and bickering all day and then through the early evening. Now his ears would have a rest.

He made a note in a computer: *Children said their prayers then started arguing.* It wasn't much of a note, but at least his report would be accurate. Now all he had to do was wait for his replacement, who was due in two hours.

He knew what came next. The children would chatter in bed. The woman would tell them to be quiet at least four times before they surrendered to slumber. Julia Cenobio would watch television for two or three more hours then go to bed. This part of the job was tedious, not that he would ever complain.

To pass the time, the man removed a pistol and a handkerchief and began wiping down the weapon. He handled the gun tenderly as if it would respond better to a caress than rough handling.

The gun felt good in his hand. He pointed the barrel at the wall that separated his room from where the children slept and closed an eye, taking aim.

"Boom," he whispered.

CHAPTER 19

THE 2:00 A.M. MOON hung high in a cloudless obsidian sky. Moyer lay on his belly peering over the short parapet of a two-story truck supply a half block from the suspected row of concrete tilt-up structures. He held a monocular NVG unit to his right eye. Similar to the Army-issue PVS-14 night vision scope, the device allowed him a near daylight view of the north and west sides of the target buildings.

"One guard smoking a cigarette near the north street-side corner. Looks bored." Moyer studied the man for a moment.

"Standing alone during the wee hours can do that," J. J. said.

"He's the only signature I have on the FLIR." Caraway kept a low profile while moving the handheld forward-looking infrared device. "He seems to be the only one on duty. Maybe the others are sleeping in the building, but there's no way I'm gonna get a reading through concrete walls."

"Here," Moyer said, handing the NVG to Caraway. "See what you can tell me about the fence."

Caraway raised the monocular to his eye. "Full-perimeter chain link, six feet high, no razor wire. Of course, you already know that." Moyer gave the man time to study the situation. "I don't see anything to indicate the fence is electrified. Checking for motion sensors." Caraway could be a pain, but he was thorough. "I don't see ground sensors or anything to indicate a passive detection system. Of course, I wouldn't expect one. Having a guard walking the grounds would set off motion sensors and any other intruder alert system. I think we have one guy and a fence."

J. J. eyed Moyer. "Those buildings could house several hundred hostiles."

"No doubt, but I don't think they do," Moyer said. "If you had that many men, then why only one guard? I doubt there's more than a handful of people inside." Moyer retrieved the night vision device from Caraway and studied the situation again. "It's not right. They're too casual about their security. Why?"

"No idea, Boss."

Moyer rolled over on his back, removed his encrypted cell phone, and made a call. A second later he said, "Whatcha got?" Rich, Medina, and Pete had taken position on the roof of a furniture manufacturer.

"We have a good view of the south and east quadrants. Nothing happening."

"Okay, set up the LVRS. We'll do the same. We'll monitor at distance."

"Understood." The line went dead.

Moyer faced Caraway. "Set her up."

J. J. helped Caraway erect a small aluminum tripod supporting a video camera and transmitter. The lightweight video reconnaissance system allowed surveillance at a distance of six miles. The panel truck would serve as a base station. Live surveillance from the rooftops would be impossible during the day when the streets came to life. This way, at worst, someone might discover the equipment on the roof and the government would be out some pricey toys. Better than having a team member observed or even arrested and tipping off the targets.

Thirty minutes later Moyer and J. J. sat in the panel truck. The others returned to their hotels. There was nothing to do now but watch nothing happen on two LCD monitors.

LUCY MEDINA COULDN'T SLEEP. What had been a sharp pain in her uterus this morning had evolved into a dull, persistent throbbing. Not enough to make her double over but enough to keep her from sleeping more than a few minutes at a time. She rose from bed, made her way to the living room of their small home, and tried to find a comfortable position on the couch. She turned on the television but kept the sound low. The children didn't need to be awake at 4:00 a.m. Neither did she. Finding nothing of interest, she stopped on a program that promised to make her rich through real estate.

Lucy closed her eyes. Why did everything inside her seem to burn?

STACY BOLTED UPRIGHT IN bed. The cool air touched her damp skin, chilling her. She took a breath, then another. Her heart ricocheted against her ribs. She raised a hand and touched her sternum. The dream had been so real, so startling, so horrible. As the nightmare drained from her mind, it left a residue of pain, like boiling water over tender flesh. She moved from the bed, bent over the toilet, and emptied her stomach.

When the retching ended, Stacy tossed cool water on her face. Compared to the heat of the night terror, the cold water was refreshing. Pushing back the drapes that covered the bathroom window, Stacy gazed at the moon and wondered if Eric could see it from wherever he was.

CHAPTER 20

HECTOR CENOBIO PREFERRED THE privacy of his office and lab. He was comfortable lecturing to the few upperclassmen and graduate students that attended his classes, but standing before fifty scientists and journalists made him uneasy. Of course, only a handful of these were journalists. The rest were researchers from the various disciplines that orbited the world of nuclear physics.

Hector had become something of a celebrity in the science community. Yet outside of those whose research touched on nuclear power generation, he was largely unknown, and he liked it that way. What he didn't like was answering questions from the media. Most reporters didn't know enough about the subject to make insightful queries. A few science writers had a fair grasp of the concepts at hand, but he still felt the need to dumb things down.

He had already made his opening remarks, methodically laying out the principles of reprocessing spent nuclear fuel. His reasoned explanation fell on deaf ears. Apparently reporters could only ingest information preceded by a question.

A squat man in a rumpled coat stood. He held an MP3 recorder in his hand. "Dr. Cenobio, isn't it true that the recycling process is more expensive than you've let on, and that the end result is fuel that costs more to make than the fuel is worth?"

Hector had just covered this but managed to hold back a frown. "As I mentioned a few moments ago, the world is changing at unexpected speeds. The costs of oil and natural gas have reached new levels and will continue to climb. While most people worry about the increase of fuel at the pumps, there is a greater concern: power generation. The population is not decreasing. Third-world nations are not walking into the high-tech world; they're skipping in, leaping over the stepping stones first-world countries had to traverse. There are countries whose citizens have never used a phone attached to a phone line. They have graduated straight to cellular. The up-and-coming countries are going to need more and more power. Nuclear is the only way to provide consistent power that isn't dependent upon oil from other countries."

"But the process is still expensive, right?"

"Every power source is expensive. Yet my new techniques have brought the price of reprocessing down and will continue to do so in the decades ahead. Besides, expense is not the only concern. There are other matters in play."

"Such as?"

Whatever happened to one question per reporter? "Storage. Fuel used in reactors is not eternal. It has a limited lifespan. Spent fuel must be replaced. Unfortunately spent fuel is still radioactive and requires special care. This spent fuel is stored in cooling pools, but we have reached the limits of what such pools can hold. Many companies have begun storing spent fuel in dry casks, concrete and steel canisters, but this is an expensive proposition. Each cask holds about ten tons of waste. A one-thousand-megawatt reactor generates enough spent fuel to fill two casks a year, and each cask costs approximately one million dollars."

The reporter started to ask another question, but Hector stopped him with an upraised hand. "It was generally thought that spent fuel would be sequestered in underground facilities like Yucca Mountain, Nevada, in the United States. Yucca Mountain was to begin taking deposits in 1998. We are over two decades past that date. The best estimates state the facility will open in 2017. In the meantime, more and more spent fuel is accumulating in what remains of cooling pools and dry casks.

"There are four hundred and thirty-nine nuclear power plants in the world, with another thirty under construction and two hundred more on the drawing board. Those numbers will increase, as they should. My technique will allow the world to make use of the spent fuel from these and future plants."

Another man stood. He was tall, wore a tweed jacket, sported a thin mustache, and looked a few years beyond sixty. He spoke with a heavy Italian accent. "Dr. Cenobio, as I understand it, your process is similar to those used by the United Kingdom and France in which you—and forgive me for being so basic—extract and enrich the plutonium in used fuel."

"The end result is the same, but my process is different, more efficient and cost effective."

The man grinned. "Of course it is, Doctor. Your reputation precedes you. My question centers on the unintended use of such plutonium. Isn't it true that plutonium is relatively easy to handle and is thus a target for terrorists?"

Hector had been expecting this. "It is true that the current state of spent fuel is too dangerous for terrorists to transport. Too many harmful gamma rays. It is also true that plutonium is less dangerous, but that doesn't mean that it can be easily stolen or—"

"Forgive me, Doctor, but over the last decade plutonium—enough to make several nuclear bombs—has been reported missing from Los Alamos in the United States and Sellafield in the UK—"

"It is my understanding the Sellafield was an error in auditing."

"So we are asked to believe. My question is this: Why should a process such as yours be allowed when it leads to the creation of a material that can be stolen, illicitly sold, or otherwise find its way into the hands of terrorists?"

Hector stepped back from the lectern for a moment. He had been answering questions like this for the last five years. He stepped to the microphone again. "Such a thing is highly unlikely. We can control who has access to such technology. I cannot imagine any sane country making this new technique available to a government that supports or harbors terrorists. Security measures will be in place."

"India, 1974."

"What about India?" Someone in the group called out.

Hector fielded the question. "I believe he's referring to India's efforts to separate plutonium from fuel used in a nuclear power plant."

"A nuclear plant with technology provided by the United States. India made a bomb and joined the world's superpowers with a nuclear arsenal."

"We've learned a lot since 1974," Hector said.

"Have we?"

CHAPTER 21

MOYER WAS GLAD TO see the sunrise. Another couple hours and Jose Medina and Martin Caraway would spell them. Medina would be bored stiff, but Caraway would enjoy it. Anything that involved electronics was candy to him.

J. J. sat on a metal folding chair reading a pocket Bible by penlight.

"Found anything interesting?" Moyer asked in low tones.

"Excuse me?"

"You've been reading that Bible for a couple of hours now. Have you found anything interesting?"

"It's all interesting. Cover-to-cover interesting."

"Can't say I've spent much time in the book. Don't see much relevance for the twenty-first-century warrior."

J. J. tilted his head to the side. "The Bible is the most relevant book ever."

"Yeah, well, maybe. It doesn't seem to have done you any harm."

"Any shortcomings in me came from someplace other than the Bible."

"Caraway doesn't seem to care much for your Bible reading." Moyer turned his eyes back to the two monitors. The most exciting thing they'd seen so far had been a stray dog sniffing the gutters for food.

J. J. lowered the Bible. "You've noticed that, have you?"

"I notice everything that goes on in my team. It's my job. So what's his beef with you?" Moyer didn't look away from the monitors. The remote video setup was working as planned. They were parked five miles from the site but still received a strong signal from both LVRSs.

"It might be better if you ask him."

"I'm asking you, J. J."

J. J. shrugged. "He blames me for his wife's desertion."

That got Moyer's attention. He turned in his chair. "You're responsible for Caraway's wife leaving him? Do I want to know why that is?"

J. J. shook his head. "It's nothing like that. The only time I met her was at the barbecue you threw for us when we returned from Afghanistan. Even then I didn't spend more than fifteen or twenty minutes talking to her. Martin was there the whole time. Nothing happened—I want to be clear about that."

"That's good to hear, but I still don't understand the problem."

"He doesn't like my faith."

Moyer raised an eyebrow. "How do you figure?"

"He told me so. Not long after Afghanistan. That night back at the airfield the guys were blowing off some energy talking about the men we killed. I didn't feel like joining in, and Caraway noticed. I guess he also saw me looking at the shepherds we killed and put two and two together."

"You mean your regret about killing the civilians."

"Yeah. Anyway, he began razzing me pretty bad. He told me his wife won't come back to him because she's a Christian. I still haven't figured that out."

Moyer hesitated. How much should he say? "Caraway is a man who likes women—likes them a lot. Apparently marriage didn't quench his thirst. His wife decided not to stay after she learned of his most recent affair. He was fine with that until his new girlfriend left him. No wife, no mistress. The guy's alone. He doesn't do alone well."

"Should you be telling me this?"

"I'm telling you enough so I can also tell you to give the man a little space. You don't have to like him, and he doesn't have to like you. But on this team we work as a unit. I don't care what my men do in their off time as long as they don't disgrace the Army."

"Can I ask how you know all this?"

"My wife bumped into his just before she left. Word got back to me. I'd appreciate it if you didn't mention it to Caraway. I'll talk to him at the right time. Understood?"

"Understood." A moment later J. J. said, "Can I ask a question and not lose my head?"

"Depends."

J. J. took a deep breath. "How bad is it?"

Moyer stiffened. "How bad is what?"

"I'm sure you're going to tell me to mind my own business, but I think you're sick."

Moyer studied the video monitors, but their images didn't register. "I'm fine. Feel great. Never better."

J. J. chuckled. "You know my brother is a chaplain, right? He once told me that if someone makes three statements when one would do, they're concealing something."

"You think I'm lying?"

J. J. took several moments to answer. He closed his Bible and set it on the equipment console. He licked his lips. "Yes." The word was soft and carried no animosity.

"That's either an incredibly gutsy thing to say to your Master Sergeant, or incredibly foolish."

"I know." J. J. looked at his hands. "There's something wrong, isn't there?"

"I told you I'm fine."

J. J. leaned back in the metal chair and let slip a near silent sigh. "You know what my dad taught me to do? When we traveled and stayed in a hotel, he would always bring the luggage in, set it on the bed, then go to the restroom and toss a little toilet paper into the commode, then flush it. He used to tell us that one thing both cheap and ritzy hotels had in common was plumbing problems. He's an executive with an envelope-manufacturing firm. He travels a lot and has stayed in more hotels than any ten men combined."

"And your point is . . ."

"When I came to your room today, I slipped into the head. The toilet didn't flush well when you last used it."

Moyer licked his lips. His stomach dropped like an untethered elevator.

J. J. leaned forward again and rested his elbows on his knees. "My father had colon cancer. He used to pass blood."

There it was. He had been found out by a faulty valve-flush toilet. "So now you think I'm unfit to lead."

J. J. shook his head. "If you say you're good to go, then I believe you."

"Then why bring it up?"

"Because a man shouldn't go through such things alone. The diagnosis scared my father to death. It was the only time I saw him weep. The thing is, he went through the surgery and treatment and is alive today."

"I don't know that I have cancer. The doc says it could be other things."

"So you've seen the doctors."

Moyer tore his eyes away from the monitor. "I was in the office when I got the call."

J. J. straightened. "You were at the infirmary when the call came down?"

Moyer didn't answer. "We were setting up tests."

"I'm surprised the Army docs let you respond."

"Look . . ." He took a breath. "I went to a civilian doctor."

"Why would you . . . oh. You were afraid they'd take you off mission status. Makes sense. I would be too."

"Wasn't much time to think about alternatives. I did what I had to do. Now let me be clear about this: You will say nothing to the team. Once this mission is completed, I'll get the doctors to do what they need to do, but right now my focus—and that means *your* focus—is on this mission. We're done talking about it, and you are not to bring it up again. Got that?"

"Loud and clear."

CHAPTER 22

HECTOR CENOBIO PREFERRED TO travel light. If his wife were with him, he would be carting several large rolling bags. Traveling alone, while not his preference, was easier on his back. One green, medium-sized wheeled suitcase and his computer bag were all he needed. He checked the suitcase at the airport in Rome, leaving him only the computer bag to carry. The computer was loaded with everything he needed: work files, speeches, downloaded magazine and journal articles, and several audio books. The flight to Caracas was long. He hoped to sleep as much as possible, but snoozing in the air wasn't something he did well. Most likely he would spend his time reading or daydreaming about how soon he would be holding his wife in his arms and teasing his children.

Traveling first class was a treat for him. His professor's salary didn't afford him such luxuries. Usually he had to wedge his generous frame into the narrow seats of economy class. This trip, however, was courtesy of the conference coordinators in Caracas. They had made all the arrangements, and he was happy to let them do so.

After clearing security, Hector strolled down the long corridor, avoiding the surging waves of people moving in different directions. Hundreds of people with scores of different gates and destinations in mind—a classic case study for chaos theorists. *If a passenger from Rome bumps into a passenger from London outside the duty free shop, will it set in motion a series of events that will ultimately cause a downpour in Toronto?* He had never accepted chaos theory, seeing instead more plan in the universe than randomness.

He had arrived at the airport early and found the first-class lounge nearly empty. A dark-skinned man sat in the far corner flipping through a magazine. Hector caught his eye and nodded. The man returned the gesture. Taking a seat in one of the padded leather chairs, Hector pulled his computer from the bag and turned it on. As the device booted, he glanced at the man with the magazine. Something about him seemed familiar. Another scientist? If so, he had not attended any of the colloquia or seminars. The press conference? He shifted his gaze to his computer screen then back to the man. He didn't want to appear to be staring. There were close to a hundred and fifty reporters at the conference; the man certainly could have been among their number. Hector decided it didn't matter. Clearly the stranger wasn't interested in him, and truth be told, Hector wasn't interested in the stranger either.

The computer finished its warm-up exercises, and Hector called up a downloaded article from *Physics and Power Engineering*, an obscure but respected journal. Hector had decided in graduate school that the hardest work of science was not experimentation or even scrambling for grants; it was keeping up with the literature. Reading journals was practically a part-time job.

An hour passed and more first-class passengers entered the exclusive lounge. A uniformed man in his twenties appeared and offered snacks and drinks to the waiting passengers. At the

appropriate time the steward reminded the passengers it was time
to board the plane. Hector shut down the computer and slipped it
into the bag. He glanced at the dark-skinned man, who folded his
magazine and replaced it on the coffee table, rose, and walked past
Hector.

Passengers boarded the aircraft in a long, slow-moving line that
started and stopped with each passenger who struggled to lift a
bag into the overhead compartments. A stewardess who looked too
young to hold the job brought Hector orange juice. Across the aisle
sat Magazine Man, sipping a mixed drink.

Thirty minutes later, the stewardess closed the door and the
Alitalia Boeing 757 pushed back from the gate. *On to London, then
to Caracas, then home.* He longed most for the final destination.

Just before the hatch had been closed and latched, Hector saw
the familiar man place a short phone call. The moment he ended
the call, he looked at Hector and smiled.

Hector found this unsettling.

PETE RASOR AND RICH Harbison sat at a small table near the side wall of
the restaurant. Pete set his chopsticks down and leaned back.

"That was the best lo mein I've ever had."

"I assumed that, since you've done everything but lick the
plate."

"That may happen yet."

Rich chortled. "Where did you learn to wield chopsticks like
that? If I had to use those things, I'd starve."

"I've seen you eat—you'd manage."

"You sayin' I'm fat?"

Pete wasted no time answering. "I'd never do that. You're a perfect specimen of manhood. Every girl's dream, every man's idol, every—"

"You can stop right there. I'm not paying for your lunch."

Pete shrugged. "Can't blame a man for trying." He decided to change subjects. "It seems odd to be an American in Venezuela eating Chinese food."

"Not really. I was in a mall in Southern California and had lunch in the food court. I ordered Japanese food from a Chinese woman who gave the order to a Hispanic cook who passed my plate to an Anglo worker while an African-American girl poured my soda. Not all that weird."

"It was weird enough for you to take notice."

"Let's get back to the hotel. I want to snag a few hours of shut-eye before starting the swing shift."

"Sounds good to me."

Pete paid for the meal and followed Rich from the small restaurant. "We should come back here tomorrow. I want to try their kung pao shrimp."

"Don't hold your breath. I think we have a tour of the jungle coming up."

Part of the mission was reconnoitering the Santi mansion. Moyer's plan would split the team into two three-man teams. Now that remote surveillance was up and operating, the secondary recon could be done—assuming some handyman didn't find one of the two LVRSs and take it home to show the kids.

They moved down the sidewalk and stopped at the corner. The hotel was only three blocks away, a pleasant walk on a lovely day. Still, they had driven in case Moyer needed them in a hurry. "Mind if I drive?"

"It's only a couple of blocks," Rich said. "Not enough to satisfy your wanderlust."

"I can turn a three-block drive into a three-hour tour."

"I believe that. You never were very good at navigation."

Pete feigned shock. "You wound me. I was at the top of my class."

"Was it a class of one?"

"C'mon, let's take the long way back. We need to check other routes." By "other routes" he meant paths of evasion should escape become necessary.

"All right." Rich tossed him the keys.

They walked another half block to their car, which was parked next to the downtown curb. Pete pushed the unlock button on the key bob and stepped between their car and the one parked in front of it. Rich slipped into the passenger seat. Pete reached for the handle on the driver's side door.

He heard it first. Then he saw it.

The roar of a car engine. The screech of tires on pavement. The flash of blue to his right. Reflex made him jump, but no ordinary man could have gained the height necessary to clear the sedan, which struck him mid-thigh. Pete landed on the metal surface, rolled over the windshield, and tumbled down the back of the vehicle. It took a full five seconds for him to realize that he was lying on asphalt. It took another five seconds for Rich's voice to penetrate the shock and confusion.

"Pete! Don't move, buddy. Just stay there."

"What? Where . . ." He looked up to Shaq's face. He had seen the big man angry, happy, drunk, even bewildered. This was the first time he had seen him afraid.

"Take it easy, buddy."

Pete could hear the roar of a car racing away. He wondered who was in such a hurry. Something was wrong—he knew that much. His hearing was good, but off. A single sharp tone ran in one ear and out the other.

Then the pain arrived. Pete tried to rise.

"No you don't, buddy. You're staying down."

"Okay. My leg hurts." The dull ache soon became white-hot needles jabbing his legs, back, and neck. As the shock faded, the pain grew. "What happened?"

"A car hit you. Stay still." Rich turned to the gathering crowd. "I need an ambulance. *Ambulancia*!" He returned his attention to Pete and whispered, "Tell me you're not packin'." He leaned over Pete and gently patted the area around his belt, looking for what wasn't there—a 9mm handgun.

"Of course not. I wouldn't . . ." The pain began to dim, as did the sun.

☢☢ ☢☢ ☢☢

JULIA CENOBIO HEARD A knock on the door of her hotel suite and was surprised to see Miguel Costa standing there with a small brown bag.

"Miguel. You're not due to pick us up for another hour." She and the kids had planned to visit the artificial lagoon and small zoo at Parque del Este.

"Yes, senora, I know. I had to pick up a few things from the store. I brought the children some treats." He held up the bag but didn't offer it to her.

"Treats?"

"Yes, but I do not wish to give them to the children without your first approving. I will take away what is not suitable. May I come in?"

"Yes, yes. Of course."

Miguel entered the room and locked the door behind him.

CHAPTER 23

JOSE MEDINA STROLLED INTO the Clinica Caracas as though he had done so countless times. He wore a loose-fitting long-sleeved shirt untucked, blue jeans, and sneakers. He looked like half the other men moving through the corridors of the five-story structure. The emergency room was at the back of the hospital, and Jose took his time making his way through the hallways. He could have parked in the back lot but chose the front entrance hoping that he would be able to blend in with the dozens of people who moved in and out of the building every minute.

A sign on the wall pointed the way to EMERGENCIA. It had taken him nearly thirty minutes to travel from the remote surveillance site to the hospital. It took all the willpower he had not to run red lights and scream past the ALTO signs.

A pair of double-hinged swinging doors with porthole-like windows separated the emergency room from the rest of the facility. Jose pushed through the doors.

Banks of fluorescent bulbs illuminated a highly polished vinyl floor and pale-green walls. The air was thick with odors of

123

antiseptic cleaners and recycled air. Rows of standard hospital lobby chairs were filled with mothers holding crying children, a man with a bloody cloth wrapped around his left hand, a woman who stared at the floor and rocked back and forth in pain. Others looked drugged with discomfort. A tall, ebony-skinned man leaned against a wall, his arms crossed over his chest.

"We have to stop meeting like this." Jose whispered the words.

"You got that right. I'm glad you're here. You come by yourself?"

Jose nodded. "Moyer thought it best if I came alone. Too many of us hanging about in one place isn't good. He sent me because he thought my Spanish might be better than yours."

"Ya think? My ten words of Spanish don't go very far."

Jose looked around the room. To his relief, no one was staring at them. "How is he?"

Rich shrugged. "Can't say for sure. He went out about a minute or two after he was hit. I did a quick field survey. Best I can tell, there were no broken bones."

"That's good. Do you know if he hit his head?"

"No. I was in the passenger seat. I heard the driver hit the brakes and snapped my head around in time to see Pete roll over the top of the car. I think he jumped at the last moment. If he hadn't, he might have gone under the sedan." Rich looked away. "The guy didn't even stop."

"Was fluid coming out of his ears or nose?"

"His nose was bleeding."

"Anything else? Any clear fluid."

Rich shook his head. "Not that I saw. Is that important?"

"Sometimes in head trauma cerebrospinal fluid can leak out. It doesn't mean he's in good shape if you don't see it, but it sure means trouble if you do."

"You're the doc. I'll take your word for it."

"You okay?"

"A little shook. Who wouldn't be?"

"Let me see what I can find out." Jose moved to the triage nurse's station, nodded, and said in Spanish, "My name is Jose Isea, and I understand that one of my foreign consultants has been hit by a car. Do you have any word on his condition?" Jose felt relief that he had remembered to use his in-country name.

"Name?"

It took a second for Jose to recall Pete's pseudonym. "Pete Tanner."

She studied her computer monitor for a moment then said, "One moment please." She rose and entered the treatment area of the ER. Jose glanced back at Rich but made no comment. The nurse, a stout, dour woman, emerged from the bowels of the ER, her expression no different than when she went in.

"They're bringing him up from X-ray now. It will be another thirty minutes before you can see him."

"Thank you. My friend and I will wait."

She said nothing, and Jose walked back to Rich. "It'll be another half hour before we know anything. Let's grab a cup."

The cafeteria was a wide-open, well-lit expanse of tables and chairs. Jose bought two cups of coffee. As a Master Sergeant, Rich outranked Jose, but the nature of the team allowed a freedom of communication not often experienced in other units. Because of this, Jose had no problem pressing Rich for more information.

"I told you all I know. We had just finished lunch at a Chinese joint a few blocks from the hotel. You know how Pete likes his Chinese food. Our car was a block away. He wanted to drive around a little, so I gave him the keys to the rental. Traffic was light. He stepped into the street, rounded the car. By that time I had already plopped down on the passenger seat. I heard tires squeal and looked up in time to see Pete go flying over the vehicle. Next thing I know, I'm kneeling in the street next to him."

"Was he conscious the whole time?"

"Just some of it. He was conscious but confused. He didn't seem to know what happened."

"So you don't know if he hit his head?" Jose took a sip of the strong coffee.

"I can't be sure one way or the other. I didn't see anything that looked like a head wound."

"What about his eyes?"

Rich cupped his hands around the cup as if warming them. "Pupils were equal and looked normal."

"Speech?"

"Good, but as I said, he was confused about what happened."

"Not unusual. I've heard of accident victims who were unable to recall anything about the event."

"Sounds like a blessing to me."

"I suppose so. Did the ambulance crew seem to know what they were doing?"

"They impressed me." Rich looked up from his coffee. "You're the medic—what happens next?"

"It all depends on how badly hurt he is. The first concern is his brain. The fact that his pupils were equal is good, but that could change. If he hit his head hard enough, he may have more than a concussion. There might be bleeding in the brain. Another concern is internal bleeding. How fast was the car going when it struck Pete?"

"Fast enough to make his tires squeal, but I can't say how fast he was going when he hit Pete."

Jose frowned. "This isn't good. Not good at all. Even if he's just a tad banged up, we got problems to deal with. The police will want some answers."

"I've been thinking about that. The cops showed up about the same time as the ambulance. I told them what I knew. Of course, they checked my ID and stuff. They let me follow the ambulance to the hospital, but not before telling me they're going to want to interview Pete."

"We can do without that. I'm also concerned what he might say under anesthesia."

Rich narrowed his eyes. "What do you mean?"

"Let's say they have to operate. It's possible that Pete could say something he shouldn't while going under or coming out. Or depending on the kind of surgery and his condition, they may not even use a general anesthesia. I had a hernia surgery a few years back and all they used was a spinal block and a med to make me not care about what was going on."

"We may have another problem." Rich rubbed his eyes.

"I don't want to hear this do I?"

"No, and I'm pretty sure Moyer won't want to hear it either." Rich straightened as if doing so would make the telling of it easier. "Pete came out of the shower this morning. I was still kicking it in bed. Maybe he thought I was asleep. He still has the tattoo."

Jose closed his eyes and wished he could close his ears. Before joining Special Ops Pete had been regular Army. Proud of his service, he did what many soldiers had through the decades: got a tattoo. That was not unusual in of itself. It was Pete's choice of tattoo that created the problem. On his upper shoulder the tattooist drew a pair of dog tags in indelible ink. One had the name of his father, a Vietnam vet; the other bore his own name. Moyer told Pete to get rid of it.

He didn't.

"Moyer's gonna choke him with his bare hands."

Rich shook his head. "I'm assistant team leader; I should have followed up with Pete. It just never occurred to me."

Jose stared at Rich for a moment.

"What?"

"I'm hoping you won't order me to tell Moyer."

"Nah, I'll do it." He rose. "If I'm not back in ten minutes then know that Moyer found a way to kill me over the phone."

"NOT THROUGH THE LOBBY. Take the hall to your right."

Julia Cenobio didn't argue. She couldn't. Not with her two children by her side. Not with the gun Costa flashed. He walked behind her. She kept the children in front in a useless but brave effort to provide a shield between them and their abductor.

At the end of the hall stood a man with thin features and a beak-like nose. He wore casual dress. He stepped into the middle of the hall and removed a shiny rectangular object from his coat pocket and raised it to his face.

"Smile." The small digital camera flashed.

"Through the doors and into the van."

Julia placed a hand on each of the children's shoulders and tried not to cry.

CHAPTER 24

PETE RASOR LAY IN one of two hospital beds in room 201. The other bed was empty. Rich walked in with Jose and felt an immediate sense of relief that his partner was sitting up and had no tubes protruding from his nose or anyplace else. That relief melted at the sight of the dog tags tattoo poking out from beneath the sleeve of the hospital gown.

"How are you feeling, Junior?" Rich kept his voice low.

"I'm fine. Good to go."

"What about pain?" Jose asked.

"The only place I hurt is my head, neck, back, hips, legs, and arms. My eyelids however are pain free."

"That's good to hear, buddy." Rich stepped close to the bed and watched Jose move to the other side so he could keep an eye on the door. "Any idea what the docs say?"

"Yeah, the ER doctor speaks great English—told me he studied in San Francisco. He said I'm a lucky man. No broken bones, no internal bleeding, nothing but some bruises the size of Delaware."

"Did he say when you would be released?" Rich asked.

Pete shook his head then winced at the motion. "He said he wants to keep me a few hours for observation. He's worried about my head, which is strange. I'm sure I didn't hit my head."

Rich exchanged glances with Jose. "Did he or anyone comment on your tattoo?"

"My tattoo . . . oh, no." The color drained from Pete's face. "I know I was told to get rid of it. I even had a doctor's appointment set up for next month. You know how the military medical complex works. Like everything else, it's hurry up and wait."

Jose ran a hand through his dark hair. "They may be keeping him for more than observation."

"That's what I'm thinking."

"Oh, man. It's not bad enough that I let myself get hit by a car, but I may have blown our cover."

"When did you come to?" Jose asked.

"In the ambulance. I remember Rich kneeling beside me. Then things went dark, but I woke up before they put me on the gurney."

"That's good. At any time did they give you anesthesia?"

"No, I've been conscious the whole time."

Rich looked around the room. "We can't stay here. The doctor may have reported that an American with a dog tags tattoo just came through his ER."

"Lots of people have tattoos." Pete spoke in a tone that said he didn't believe himself.

"That's not our only problem," Rich said. "The cops said they had more questions. They could arrive any minute."

"Can you walk?" Jose asked.

"I said I'm good to go, Doc. Walk? I'm ready to dance." He scooted up in the bed and moaned. "Okay, maybe I'm a little stiff."

"I'll get a wheelchair," Rich said. "See if there's a robe in the closet."

Rich found a wheelchair at the end of the hall. He also noted that the second floor nurse's station had only one nurse behind the counter and assumed the others must be about their duties with patients. A pegboard mounted to the wall held several white lab coats. The phone at the nurse's station rang and the nurse snapped up the handset. Rich snatched one of the doctors' coats.

Back in the room he tossed the lab coat to Jose. "Put this on. I'm pretty sure it won't fit me." Pete was on his feet like a man standing on marbles. Rich pushed the wheelchair close, and Pete lowered himself onto the seat. He made no complaints, but Rich could see the pain on the man's face.

"We should avoid the ER where we might be recognized."

"My rental is in the front lot. Let's get him to the car. I'll drive around back and drop you off. You can follow us to the hotel."

"Let's do this," Rich said.

"That brown bag on the seat is my clothes. Get it. I don't want to walk into the hotel wearing a robe."

Rich grabbed the bag and set it in on Pete's lap.

"You push him," Jose said. "I'll walk alongside."

"One problem," Rich said. "The elevator is the other side of the nurse's station. Someone might want to know what we're doing with the new guy."

"That could be a problem," Jose said, "but what are our options?"

Rich stepped to the open door and moved it so he could study the emergency plaque on the back. "There's a stairwell at each end of the corridor. Nothing but rooms along the way."

"I could change clothes in the stairwell," Pete said. "That way I'll be less conspicuous."

Rich thought for a moment. "Let's go."

☢ ☢ ☢

"ANYTHING?" MOYER ENTERED THE panel truck; Martin Caraway followed behind and quickly shut the back door. Getting in and out of the truck without raising suspicions was tricky, but they chose their spot carefully, parking in the lot next to an abandoned industrial business.

"Not a thing." J. J. yawned. He had been up most of the night and only grabbed a couple hours of sleep before being dragged from his bed and put back on surveillance duty while Moyer retrieved Caraway from the hotel. Jose's mission to the hospital had left Caraway twiddling his thumbs in the hotel room. "The guard changed again, but there is still just one."

"Okay, you and Caraway keep up the surveillance. Got word from Shaq that they sprung Pete from the hospital and that he's going to be fine. Judging by Shaq's tone, he didn't check Pete out through normal channels."

"Sounds like him," Caraway said.

"Keep me posted."

Moyer exited the vehicle, and a moment later J. J. heard him drive off.

Caraway took the empty metal folding chair and sat. "So, do you think Boss will kill Junior with his bare hands or use a weapon?"

"You mean because of the tattoo thing?" J. J. shook his head. "I can tell you he was not a happy camper."

"Rasor could have killed the whole mission." Caraway tilted back in the chair.

"Thank God the car didn't kill him."

"You thank him if you want, just leave me out of it."

J. J. sighed. "That didn't take long."

"What?"

"Whenever we're alone you start ragging on my beliefs."

Caraway raised his hands. "Sorry, pal. Didn't know you were so sensitive."

"You can't bait me into an argument. We have a job to do."

"Most people who avoid arguments do so because they know they're going to lose."

"What's your real problem, Caraway? I don't get in your face. I give you all the room you need."

"My problem? You really want to know? You're weak, and that makes you a danger to the team."

"I went through the same training as you. I've been on just as many missions, so how am I weak?"

Caraway leaned forward and lowered his voice as if someone were trying to listen in. "It's all this Jesus nonsense. If you believe it too much, it makes you slow to act, to pull the trigger when necessary. That may get me killed."

"Nonsense."

"I saw the way you looked at those dead shepherds in Afghanistan. Some of us know that ancillary casualties are part of what we do. Can't be helped."

"You don't need to worry about me."

"Someone does. Somehow you've got the boss's ear. He's taken a shine to you."

"He doesn't treat me any different than he treats you." J. J. refused to look Caraway in the eyes.

"Yeah, whatever. Keep lying to yourself, but you know I'm right."

J. J. turned to face his accuser. "You've been aching to say this for a long time."

"You got that right. You gonna run to Moyer and tell him I talked mean to you?"

"This is how it lays out, Caraway. My faith is part of me. You're not going to change that. Not even death can change that. I'm not responsible for your wife leaving you. The fact that she's a person of faith now is what eats at you, not me."

"You're all alike. And leave my wife out of this!"

J. J. pointed a finger. "Oh no, you don't. You don't get to waltz in here and chew my fanny and expect me to sit and take it. If you think that's how Christians respond, then you know even less about what we believe than I thought."

"You little—"

Caraway seized J. J.'s upper arm. Before he finished locking down his grip, J. J. had a hand around the man's throat. "Think, Caraway. Think. Is this how you want to end your career? Right here, right now, in the back of a truck in Caracas? Do you really want to do this?"

Long seconds clicked by, then Caraway furrowed his brow and cut his eyes to the monitor. "What's that?"

J. J. didn't look at first, expecting Caraway to try something sneaky. Finally he cut his eyes to the image. He let go of Caraway's throat and focused on the video feed.

"Let me in," Caraway ordered. J. J. relinquished his seat. Surveillance was Caraway's specialty.

"It's a van."

"Well done. You recognized a van with no help."

Caraway worked the controls that tighten the shot.

The dark vehicle pulled to the double-wide chain-link gate and waited. The lone guard jogged to the gate, removed the lock and chain that secured it, and pulled it open, stepping to the side to allow the vehicle in. The moment the back bumper crossed the threshold, the guard closed the gates and locked them again. He then jogged to the van, which had pulled to the large metal roll-up door on the south side.

J. J.'s eyes switched to the second monitor, which played the feed from the other remote video unit. The van blocked much of the view, but he could see the dark open space just beyond the open door.

"Uh-oh," Caraway said.

J. J. swiveled his head back to screen one.

Three men exited the side door of the vehicle. Between them were a woman and two children.

"They don't look happy to be there," J. J. said.

"Agreed. If body language means anything, I'd say the family is there against their will."

As he spoke, Caraway tightened the shot from both video locations, swinging the camera in an effort to capture faces. J. J. didn't know when he did it, but Caraway had activated the recorder.

Fewer than two minutes after the van arrived, the roll-up door closed and the building and lot returned to the very picture of inactivity. But Caraway wasn't done. He zoomed in on the van, first focusing on the license plate then surveying as much of the exterior as the cameras would allow.

J. J. activated his cell phone. "We got activity, Boss."

CHAPTER 25

MOYER PULLED INTO THE parking lot of Hotel Azteca, parked, and walked into the building. His gait indicated a man of leisure, untroubled by the pressures of the day. It was a lie. The man inside, while calm and thoughtful, fought a battle to keep his anger in check.

He made eye contact with no one. Instead he stared at his cell phone as if looking up a phone number. The lobby design and décor told Moyer that this place was a notch or two lower on amenities than the hotel he and J. J. were set up in.

He stepped into the elevator, joining a mother with a young girl whom she held by the hand. He guessed she was four or five. She waved at him. Moyer smiled and waved back but said nothing. The mother tensed, so Moyer returned his gaze to the phone he had no intention of using.

The mother and daughter stepped from the elevator cab on the fourth floor; Moyer continued to the twelfth. Green letters on yellow signs with arrows pointed him to room 1222. He knocked lightly on the white door. It looked like wood but felt like metal. A fire door, he assumed.

A moment later the door opened. Rich stood just over the threshold and seemed to fill the doorway from jamb to jamb. At times Moyer forgot how big his assistant team leader and friend was.

Rich stepped aside and Moyer entered. Jose sat in the chair by the work desk.

"Hey, Boss."

The greeting came from a man reclined on the bed. He started to rise.

"As you were, Pete."

"It's okay, Boss. I'm fine. Just a little stiff."

"I said, 'As you were.'" There was heat in the words.

Pete lowered himself back to the bed. To Moyer's surprise, he saw no bruises or contusions on Pete's face. Both hands sported a road rash but nothing that couldn't be concealed by placing his hands in his pockets.

Moyer looked at Jose. "How is he?" The heat in Moyer's delivery cooled. He was as mad at Pete as he had been at any man, but Pete had proved himself a good soldier time and time again. Staring at a man that had just missed the express train to death tempered Moyer's fury.

"I'm fine, Boss. A little banged up, but—"

"I'm asking Doc."

Pete blanched. "Understood, Boss."

Jose looked at Pete then back to Moyer. "He is the luckiest dog I've ever seen. His injuries include a deeply bruised right thigh, bruised upper arm, separated—but not broken—ribs, and some abrasions."

"He jumped just before he was hit," Rich said. "Rolled over the top of the car. If he'd hesitated a split second, we'd be sending him home in a body bag."

"It was just reflex," Pete said.

"Reflex or not, it saved your life." Jose leaned back in the chair. "They gave him something for the pain at the hospital. That should be wearing off pretty soon. After we got him here, I slipped out to a pharmacy and bought some ibuprofen and acetaminophen. He can take those in tandem for pain and inflammation. It should keep the edge off."

Moyer nodded. It was all good news, especially considering how bad it could have been.

"Boss, I'm sorry about the tattoo thing. I really did mean to get it removed, but you know how it is. I just couldn't—check that— I *didn't* make the time. I couldn't decide between having it surgically removed, which might take me off duty for a few days, or go the laser or abrasion method."

"Well, you're going to have time to think about it the next few days. I want you to take it easy." Moyer looked to Rich. "When do the maids come by?"

"They came by about 1100 hours yesterday and were just down the hall today when we went to lunch."

He faced Pete again. "When the maid comes by, take a walk, but get back in here when she's done. Clear?"

"But, Boss, I'm still good to go. The pain relievers will handle the aches. I want to do my job."

"This is not a discussion, Junior. Doc will check up on you from time to time. When he gives me the go-ahead, I'll put you back in the rotation. For now, I want you to lie low. Got it?"

"Got it, Boss. But why are we worried about the maids?"

"Anyone want to answer that?"

"We sprung you from the hospital without telling anyone," Doc said. "The medical staff got a good gander at that tattoo and may put two and two together. If they do, they'll call the local police. If you were a Caracas cop looking for an American with a military tattoo on his arm, what would you do?"

"Search the hotels," Pete said and raised a hand to his eyes. "Of course."

"There's also a good chance that they'll notify the military." Moyer leaned against the wall. "It's time to be a little paranoid, gentlemen. We carry on as if nothing happened, but vigilance is the order of the day."

Moyer's cell phone rang. He answered and listened. "Stay put. I'm on my way."

THE CHILDREN WERE FRIGHTENED, and although Julia tried to hide it, so was she. During the drive from the hotel, they had not said a word.

"Where are you taking us?"

No answer from the driver, the man in the passenger seat, or from Miguel Costa—if that was his real name—who sat behind her with a handgun.

"Let the children go. You don't need them. You have me."

No response.

"My husband is due to meet with President Chavez. If I'm not at the airport to meet him, he'll appeal to the president for help. He's an important man—"

That was when it hit her. This wasn't about her or the children; it was about Hector. *Dear Jesus, protect Hector. Protect us.* She needed to keep the children cool, and the best way to do that was for her to remain calm.

Her mind raced to make sense of things, to find something she could do to protect Nestor and Lina. For a moment she had thought of jumping from the van as it slowed to turn a corner, pushing the children ahead of her, but she quickly abandoned the idea as foolhardy. She could have pounded on the window and screamed for help, but that would last only a moment before Miguel struck her or shot her or hurt one of the children. She even considered jumping forward and grabbing the steering wheel. She wore no seat belt. She could do it. If she could crash the van, or just cause the driver to swerve, then perhaps the erratic driving would draw the attention of the police or another driver. If she sideswiped a car, then the driver would certainly call the police. But she was not a strong woman and it would be just her against three men. She dismissed that idea but did not give up trying to formulate a plan.

Julia forced herself to think. Many times she heard Hector tell the children, "Nine out of ten times your brain will help you more than your brawn. Think first. Always think first. Use the brain God has given you."

The more Julia thought, the more disturbed she became. Some things didn't add up. Miguel was clearly Venezuelan, or at very least, South American. His Spanish flowed naturally, and he used local colloquialisms. The other two men didn't fit. The hue of their skin was different. The only communication between them had been one way, with Miguel doing all the talking, which he did in English.

Clearly this was about her husband, but why kidnap her and the children? They were not wealthy. They lived well on a professor's salary, and Hector said that they would be rich once the commercialization of his new project was sold. But until then, they were strictly middle class. They must want something other than money, and the only thing that could be was her husband's knowledge.

One other thought bothered her: Her captors had not blindfolded her or the children. That meant they didn't care if she memorized the way to their destination—wherever that might be. If they didn't care what she knew, then they might not intend to let them go. She started to pray again.

The inside of the building they had come to was dark and smelled of oil and dust. The building had housed some kind of industry, maybe a machine shop. Now it was a shell, an open expanse with a few small rooms she assumed had once been offices.

Miguel motioned to the distant wall. Another small room with white exterior walls was tucked in the corner. The structure had two doors. Placards identified the doors as leading to the restrooms.

"Get in." Miguel pointed to one of the doors. Julia saw no choice but to obey.

The bathroom was small, with one filthy toilet, a sink, several plastic bottles of water, and a chipped plate with a pile of energy bars on the floor. Like a hen guiding her chicks, Julia kept the children in front of her and stepped into the dark room.

"Against the wall."

"Why? What do you want?"

"Back against the wall. Children in front of you."

He's going to shoot us. Right here. Right now. In this filthy bathroom.

"No."

Miguel didn't blink. He pointed his gun at Lina's head.

"Mamá!"

Julia stepped in the line of fire. "Leave her alone. What do you want?"

"I want you to stand with your back against the wall, with the children in front of you."

Julia did as she was told.

Miguel motioned to one of the other men, who appeared with a digital camera.

"Say cheese," the man said.

Julia recognized a Middle Eastern accent, possibly Arab, maybe Persian.

The flash made her eyes water. A second later the door closed.

CHAPTER 26

HEATHROW AIRPORT IN LONDON bustled with activity. After the flight from Rome, Hector had a two-hour layover before boarding the plane to Caracas. He used the time to walk the stiffness out of his legs, to drink coffee in one of the sports bars, and watch the last fifteen minutes of a soccer game. Shortly before boarding the aircraft, he tried to call Julia. It was still midday there and a ten-minute chat would make the next long leg of the journey more tolerable. Julia never answered. He tried again once seated in first class. Still no answer. Perhaps her cell phone battery had died. He looked up the number of the hotel in Caracas that he stored in his phone and dialed. The front desk rang the room, but again no answer. He shook his head. He would have to talk to her about keeping her cell phone charged and in working order.

He leaned back in the seat and toyed with the idea of taking a pill in hopes that he could sleep more than ten minutes at a time. He hated taking medication, but there were times when it made sense to use pharmaceutical magic. He reached for the pill he kept in a plastic baggie in his front pocket then stopped. The man who had traveled in first class with him from Rome to London stepped through the doorway. They looked at each other for a moment, exchanging glances. He didn't seem as surprised as Hector to be sharing yet another flight. What were the odds that the same man would fly from Rome to London to Caracas? Not impossible, certainly, but it struck him as odd, and for some reason made him uncomfortable. To make matters worse, the man sat down next to him. This time he spoke.

"We travel together again, I see." The man's accent sounded odd, as if it were an affectation—like a Brit trying to sound American, or a Frenchman trying to speak like an Irishman.

"So it seems. I was just wondering about the odds."

"A little odd but not out of the bounds of possibility. At least as far as I can tell. Math is not my strength."

"It's one of mine."

The man slipped a computer bag beneath the seat in front of him and fastened his safety belt. "Really? What do you do?"

Hector chose to be cautious. "I'm a teacher."

"You teach math?"

"Science." He wanted to end this conversation, so he opened his cell phone again and dialed Julia. It had only been a few minutes since his last try, but he hoped the act would erect a barrier between them. Something about the passenger made Hector uneasy. He let the phone ring. No answer. Nothing to worry about, he told himself. He worried anyway.

"I was in Rome on business. I import Italian furniture. How about you?"

Hector said, "Never owned Italian furniture."

The man laughed. "You are a clever man. I meant to ask, 'What brought you to Rome from Venezuela?'"

"I live in Canada. I'm just visiting Venezuela."

"Oh, I shouldn't have assumed . . . Forgive me, but you don't sound Canadian."

"I grew up in Venezuela but moved away to study in the United States then Canada. This is my first trip back."

"I see. A homecoming."

"Of sorts."

"Were you in Rome to teach?"

Hector stifled a sigh. "No. A conference."

The man nodded. "Oh, I see. Were you at the symposium on nuclear power?"

The question chilled Hector. "Why do you ask?"

"I don't mean to pry. I've been traveling alone for weeks now and have grown hungry for conversation. I read about the symposium in the papers and saw a news report on the television. You said you teach science, so naturally I thought there might be a connection."

"Naturally." If the man had followed the news about the gathering then he might already know that Hector was there. "I attended."

"May I ask your name?"

"I'm a little tired. I don't travel well. I'm not much in the mood for conversation now."

"I understand," the man said. "Flying makes me weary, too. I will let you rest."

A tall, thin steward closed the door. Fifteen minutes later they were in the air and flying over the Atlantic.

☢ ☢ ☢

THE BATHROOM FAN IN the ceiling rattled as it spun on aged and overworked bearings. The rattle concealed the sounds of activity outside the door. It also masked her conversation with the children from anyone standing by the door. And someone *did* stand at the door— she could see the shadow of his feet at the gap between the bottom of the door and the floor.

"Why are they doing this, Mamá?" Lina was shaking.

Julia put an arm around her. "I don't know." She wanted to tell her that everything would be all right, but she had never lied to the children.

"It's Papa. They want Papa." Nestor sounded angry, but Julia could hear the fear in his voice. He was doing his best to be brave.

"I think you're right, Nestor. I don't know what they want him for or want him to do."

"It's because he's smart about nuclear stuff," Nestor said.

The thought had occurred to her as well.

"What are we going to do?" Lina asked.

"I don't know. Let Mamá think."

Julia took stock of the situation. She first looked for a surveillance camera and couldn't detect one. She wondered about a listening device, but if their captors wanted to listen in on the conversation between a frightened mother and two terrified children, they would have fixed the noisy exhaust fan.

Next she looked for something that could be used as a weapon. She wasn't a fighter and had never been in a physical altercation, not even in grade school. But this involved her children and her maternal instincts prepared her to fight anyone who would harm her own.

"What are you looking for, Mamá?" Nestor stood by her side.

"Something we can use for a weapon."

"Like what?"

She shook her head. "I don't know. Something. Anything." Her eyes took stock of everything. Could the chipped plate be broken to make sharp shards that she could use? The bottles of water could be

wielded like a truncheon. She remembered enough of her basic science classes in college to know that water could not be compressed,
meaning a plastic bottle could be made to strike as hard as a rock.
The problem was striking the person correctly. Hitting one of her
captors with the side of the bottle would probably split the bottle,
thereby releasing the water and diminishing the effect. She would
have to strike with the butt end of the bottle. But how many times
could she do that? If she were lucky, she'd get in one blow before
one or more of her abductors were upon her.

She studied the sink. Plastic pipes ran below it. The connection was made with hand-tightened rings, but hollow plastic pipes
would be useless. Even if she could weight them with water or
something else, she wouldn't be able to wield it effectively enough
to down one man, let alone three.

The toilet was all that remained. Julia lifted the tank lid and
looked in: stopper, overflow tube, a small chain that linked the
stopper to a metal arm connected to handle. The metal arm was
a rod about three millimeters thick, with a flat end with holes to
which the stopper chain was attached.

An idea formed.

ANDRIANO SANTI WALKED THROUGH the hallway of the capitol building
when his cell phone rang.

"Yes."

"Package one has arrived. Package two is airborne."

"Thank you."

Santi hung up.

☢ ☢ ☢

ONE HOUR AND TEN minutes into the flight, after the passengers had
settled into their seats, reading newspapers and paperback books or
watching the in-flight movie, the stranger next to Hector removed
the computer bag from beneath the seat, turned in on, then nudged
Hector.

"Dr. Cenobio, I have something to show you." He whispered
the words.

Hector turned his head slowly and looked the man in the eyes.
"You know my name."

"Yes. I'm afraid I was playing a little game with you."

"Why—"

"Please keep your voice down. The others do not need to hear
our conversation."

"Your accent has changed."

"I have never been a good actor. I have something to show you.
Please keep control of yourself."

The man clicked on an icon and the computer displayed a
photo—a photo of people whom Hector recognized before the
man had finished turning the screen toward him. There were his
wife and children standing against a wall and wearing expressions
of terror.

Hector tried to speak but only managed a croak.

The man turned off the computer and closed it. He leaned
toward Hector and whispered, "They are fine. No harm has come
to them, and none will if you cooperate. Do you understand?"

Hector nodded.

"I received that photo shortly before we left London. It is my
job to show it to you and to insist that you follow my directions
without question. If you try to be a hero, if you alert anyone,

then I will not be able to make my scheduled reports. And if that happens—well, I will no longer be able to vouch for the safety of your family. Is that clear?"

"Yes. What do you want?"

"For the moment, just your cooperation. The rest you will learn in time."

CHAPTER 27

STACY MOYER MOVED THROUGH her day in a daze. She had spent part of yesterday searching the Internet for information on colon cancer. The doctor's words had been calm and reassuring. He had told her not to worry, that cancer was only one possibility, that a number of other conditions could explain her husband's passing of blood. She knew that to be true, but knowing something with the mind was not the same as knowing it in the heart.

So far she had said nothing to the kids. Eric would be upset if she spoke to them without first consulting him. After all, he had gone to great lengths to keep the news from the Army and from her. At least last night had been uneventful as far as Rob had been concerned. He came home after school and even went so far as to tell her when he was leaving to go practice with his new rock band. As he started for the door, she stopped him to say thanks. Anything more and he would have considered it an overreaction—too much of a "mom thing."

Last night she had caught Gina staring at her. A girl insightful beyond her years, she often sensed the emotions of others. She said nothing, asked nothing, perhaps intuiting that her mother wouldn't or couldn't talk about the new burden.

Alone again, Stacy fought off the inclination to sink into fear and despair. The nightmares continued, though none were as frightening as the first. Those she kept secret too.

Special Forces soldiers, her husband had told her, know when it's time to step back. Sometimes the body just couldn't keep up anymore. Sometimes the nature of the work became so burdensome that they couldn't take on any new assignments. Sometimes they would say, "I'm getting too old for this." It was different with every man. She doubted Eric would ever step away. He'd give up his position when they dragged him from the base and changed the locks.

What Stacy wondered was what happened when the wife "got too old to do this." She felt she had aged over the last forty-eight hours.

The phone rang.

"Stacy? This is Lucy Medina."

Odd. Lucy had never called the house before. "Hello, Lucy. How are you?"

"Not good. I think there's something wrong."

"Wrong?" The word made Stacy's heart beat faster.

"With me. With the baby. I can't reach my sister. I don't know who else to call. I think I'm going to lose my baby."

A WET SENSATION BENEATH her had awakened Lucy Medina. Her afternoon nap had become a ritual with her. Each school day she would lay five-year-old Maria down for her nap then take one herself. Matteo and Jose Jr. were still at school. It was one of the few times the house was quiet enough to hear the birds outside in the oak tree sing.

She pushed herself up and looked down at the sheets and her legs. Water and blood. Her uterus contracted sharply, and Lucy released a squeal of pain. Something was very wrong. She reached for the phone by her bed and called her sister. No answer. She tried her sister's cell phone. Nothing. Another contraction. The baby wasn't due for two months.

Panic set in. She moved to the bathroom and wiped her legs with a towel. She wanted to change clothes but feared she wouldn't be able to. She needed help. It took more effort than she thought it should, but she walked into the living room, one hand holding her stomach. She and Jose kept a personal phone directory on the coffee table. She retrieved it. The first listing she saw was that of Eric and Stacy Moyer. She had met Stacy at a barbecue held at the Moyers' house. She seemed smart and caring.

Lucy made the call.

STACY PUNCHED LUCY'S ADDRESS into the GPS unit in her Chevy Trailblazer and rolled out of the driveway. She didn't know why Lucy had chosen to call her, but it didn't matter. The woman needed help, and Stacy wasn't going to turn her down.

Her stomach churned at each stoplight. She did her best not to speed, but she did press the word *limit* in "speed limit." Before leaving she had taken just enough time to text-message the children that she would be gone when they got home. She'd call them later.

It took fifteen interminable minutes to cross town on the surface streets. She parked in the driveway and raced to the front door and knocked. A little girl answered. "Hi," Stacy said. "I'm here to see your mommy."

"My mommy is sick. She's lying down."

"Your mommy asked me to come over. Will you tell her I'm here?"

"I can't."

"Why not."

"She's sleeping."

"I'm sure she wants to see . . . me . . ." Through the open door Stacy saw Lucy lying on the floor. She pushed past the child.

Lucy was unresponsive. Stacy tried to rouse her but failed. "Where is your phone, sweetheart?"

The little girl started to speak when the phone rang as if on cue.

"I got it!"

Stacy watched her retrieve a handheld phone from its cradle on the kitchen counter.

"Hi, Aunt Charlene. Mommy's sick."

"Let me speak to your aunt." Stacy took the phone. "My name is Stacy Moyer. Who is this, please?"

"Charlene Pena. I got a message from Lucy saying she was in trouble."

"She is. She called me too. I just found her on the floor. She's hemorrhaging. I was just getting ready to call the ambulance. Where are you?"

"I'm in my car, five minutes away. I was in a meeting and turned my phone off."

"Get here as soon as you can. I'm calling the ambulance."

Stacy didn't wait for a good-bye. She hung up and dialed 911.

☢ ☢ ☢

MOYER WATCHED THE VIDEO several times before speaking. "And there's been no further action since they closed the door?"

"Nothing," Caraway said.

"Their expressions and body language say they were brought here against their will," J. J. said. He stood out of the way, giving Moyer and Caraway all the space they needed—at least as much as the back of the panel truck would allow.

"I've downloaded the video to the laptop, converted some of it to stills, and tried to get the best face shots I can." He worked the keyboard. "First, the woman." A headshot of a woman filled the screen. Her face was turned in profile. "It's not much, but it's the best I can do here."

"Doesn't look familiar," Moyer said.

"Now the bad guys." Another profile shot filled the screen. "I make him out to be in his mid-thirties, Hispanic. The others stood to the side when he exited, probably to cut off any attempt by the woman and children to run, but it also looks like they're show-ing deference to him. They allow him to follow the woman in."

Another keystroke and the image of another man appeared. His head was turned more to the camera, revealing more of his face. Moyer leaned a couple inches closer. "I have serious doubts about this guy being Hispanic."

"That's my take, Boss. It's just a guess, but he strikes me as Middle Eastern. So does his buddy." A new picture flashed on the screen.

"I agree with Caraway," J. J. said. "I know we're making a judg-ment at a distance, but it fits with previous intel about the building."

Moyer nodded. "The question is, Who is the woman and what do they want with her?" He straightened. They had come to recon a possible al-Qaeda training site and had stumbled upon a kidnapping. Possibilities chugged in his mind. Drug-related kidnapping? Then why the Middle Easterners? Why intel about an al-Qaeda presence? If it was an AQ operation, then why abduct a family? Business execs and journalists had been abducted for terrorist purposes, but Venezuela was a long way from Iraq, Afghanistan, or other AQ playgrounds. To abduct and hold someone in another country was risky. It would be easier to have killed the woman and kids and achieved a greater shock value. No, something else was afoot.

"Let's assume this is an abduction. Kidnappers do what they do because they want something. The question is, What do they want?"

"Don't have a clue, Boss, but I'm worried about those kids." J. J. ran a hand through his hair.

Moyer was worried two. Of the three men present, he was the only one with children. The look on the little girl's face broke his heart. His first impulse was to assign weapons to J. J. and Caraway, sneak onto the site, make entry, and put a bullet or two in the brains of each man in that building. But such an impetuous act would not only destroy the mission but could lead to the deaths of the very people he wanted to save.

"What now, Boss?" Caraway asked.

"Send what you have to Ops Command. Maybe they can identify the players."

"And after that?"

"We wait for now."

"But, Boss—"

"I said, we wait for now. If they wanted them dead, they'd be dead by now."

J. J. wasn't satisfied. "There are other bad things besides death."

"I know that, but we have our orders for now." He turned to Caraway. "Get that info to Ops."

"Will do."

CHAPTER 28

STACY COULDN'T SIT STILL. She had done all that anyone could expect of her. She had called an ambulance and stayed with Lucy and her five-year-old until Lucy's sister arrived. Stacy followed the ambulance to the hospital while Lucy's sister stayed with the children. Stacy promised to keep her informed of every development. The paramedics followed protocol and took Lucy to the nearest ER. Now she waited. No one would blame her if she went home. It wasn't like Lucy was a family member, not as most defined family. She was, however, family in a different sense—they were both Army wives. More than that, they were married to Special Ops soldiers, both of whom were in some foreign land doing things neither wanted to know anything about.

So she stayed. The ER was like the others she had been in. Being the mother of two children had meant several trips to the emergency room over the years. This one offered the same highly polished floor, pale walls, a television five years beyond its life expectancy, and well-worn chairs occupied by people in various states of pain and illness. Waiting rooms had to be among the most depressing places people ever visit, and this one depressed Stacy.

Every time a nurse poked his or her head out the door leading to the ER, Stacy's spine stiffened. She had been waiting for over two hours but refused to feel sorry for herself; Lucy was the one with the problem. At most, Stacy had been inconvenienced.

As the time passed, she tried to replace the vicarious fear and empathy she felt with planning. Most likely she would be home before dinner. Gina and Rob could get along without her until then. Rob would likely shut himself away in his room with his iPod ear buds jammed deep in his auditory canals, while Gina would sit at the dining room table doing her homework. If Stacy couldn't leave on time to make dinner, she would order pizza and have it delivered. The kids would like that.

The next hour crawled by and Stacy passed the time looking at an entertainment magazine just a few months old. The television blared a courtroom reality show. Stacy did her best to put as much distance between her and the TV. She had very little tolerance for daytime television.

She had just started an article about the misbehavior of another under-twenty-five star who didn't have the maturity to handle success when a thirty-something male nurse called her name.

"Here." She tossed the magazine on one of the few empty chairs.

"Come with me, please," the man said.

The ER bustled with activity. Doctors and nurses ministered to patients or sat in the nurses' station filling out paperwork.

"Ms. Medina is in bed three." He pointed to one corner of the room. The ER held twelve beds, all but three of which were occupied. Lucy's was in the corner with the drapes that separated the stations drawn nearly shut. "The doctor stepped away for a moment, but he'll be back in a minute."

Before Stacy could thank him, the nurse was gone, off to attend some other patient. She took a deep breath and pulled back the thin drape enough to enter. She found Lucy lying on her back, staring at the ceiling. Tracks of tears marked each side of her face. Without words being spoken, Stacy knew she gazed upon a broken woman.

Stacy started to speak, but the words wouldn't line up in any way that would be meaningful. Instead, she moved to the edge of the bed, took Lucy by the hand, and gave it a squeeze. More tears ran from Lucy's eyes. Matching tears started down Stacy's cheeks.

"They say . . . they want to take . . ." Lucy couldn't finish the words.

"Take? No. You don't mean they want to take the baby?" Stacy had worked hard to keep her thoughts orderly and her emotions in check. Lucy's words struck her, scattering her thoughts like books flying from the shelves of a library in an earthquake.

Lucy nodded and wiped at her eyes with her free hand. "They say the baby is a danger to my life. I don't remember what they called it, but it's bad."

"The ER doctor told you this?"

"Yes. They had an obstetrician examine me. He said my life was in danger and that I shouldn't continue the pregnancy. I don't want to lose this baby." Lucy dissolved into sobs. She managed to utter one more thing: "I need my husband."

"I need to make a phone call." Stacy released Lucy's hand. "I'll be right back. I promise."

Stacy walked from the ER.

☢ ☢ ☢

STACY'S PALMS WERE WET and she wiped them on the jeans she wore. She hadn't bothered to change from her sitting-around-the-house clothing. She had barely taken time to grab her purse. Matters of appearance seemed insignificant at the moment.

She stood by the waiting room window, watching each car pull into the parking lot and gazing at each driver. It had been thirty minutes since she placed the call. Half that time she spent at Lucy's bedside, watching the woman cry and trying not to join in the weeping. Wanting to appear strong for the woman, she had tried to sound confident, offering words of hope and failing miserably. Several times she caught a female nurse glancing her way, her face a poster of despair.

Eventually a pair of nurses came to move Lucy to a hospital room. Stacy used it as an excuse to step away and took up her post by the window. Her focus centered on a particular parking space across the lot, one with a white sign: CLERGY. She had called the office of the base chaplain. She made the call not because she was religious by nature. Truth was, she'd be hard-pressed to say how long it had been since she and the family had been in church. She called because of a different kind of connection: one of Eric's team had a brother on base, a chaplain. Certainly calling for a chaplain made sense, but it was even a better idea in this situation.

A dark-green sedan pulled into the designated space. Stacy didn't wait for the man to find her. She exited through the sliding glass doors and approached the car. A tall, well-built man dressed in an Army combat uniform emerged, turned, and gave her a brief smile. The smile was a courtesy; his eyes showed a deep concern. He wore a silver cross on his chest.

"Mrs. Moyer?"

"Yes. Call me Stacy. You must be Captain Paul Bartley."

"I am. I got here as quickly as I could. The name Moyer got my attention. My brother J. J. serves with your husband."

"That's why I called you. I don't suppose you know where they are."

Bartley smiled. "I don't, and as you know, I couldn't tell you if I did."

"Sorry, I'm not at my best right now."

"Fill me in."

"Lucy Medina's pregnancy is in serious trouble. I haven't spoken to the doctors, but I know bad when I see it. She called me for help. When I got to her home, I found her unconscious on the floor. She tells me that the doctors want to perform an emergency abortion to save her life."

"It's that serious?"

"As near as I can tell. Like I said, I haven't spoken to the doctors, and since I'm not family, the nurse won't tell me anything." She took a deep breath. "She wants her husband. That's natural. What woman wouldn't? She needs her husband, but as you know, the team is on a mission."

"He's with your husband and my brother?"

"Yes. Jose is the team medic. Can you help?"

"I will do everything I can. Is she still in the ER?"

Stacy shook her head. "They moved her to a regular room about twenty minutes ago."

"Let's go see her. I also want to talk to the doctor."

"Will he be up-front with you?"

"Clergy don't have special rights in hospitals, but we chaplains can be pretty persuasive. He'll tell us what we need to know."

Chaplain Bartley took her by the arm and started for the ER doors. It felt good not to be the only one on the scene.

☢ ☢ ☢

"THAT WAS QUICK," **CARAWAY** said. The satellite radio system came alive. "Ops Command must have learned something."

Moyer slipped on a headset and listened. His heart sped up then tumbled to a stop. "Understood. Will advise." He removed the headset.

"Forgive me for saying so, Boss, but you look like death warmed over. Did they get a hit on the people in the video?"

"No. They're still working on that."

"Then what."

Moyer lifted his cell phone and dialed. "Shaq, I need you at the truck ASAP—and make sure Doc stays put."

Moyer hung up, leaned forward in his folding chair and raised his hands to his face.

"What is it, Boss? What did they say?"

Moyer tried to find the best way to share the news. He gave up and blurted the message: "Doc's wife and baby are dying."

Caraway's next three words couldn't be repeated on television.

CHAPTER 29

"CAN WE DRINK THE water, Mamá?" Nina's small voice sounded all the more pitiful in the small confines of the restroom. Julia almost didn't hear her over the rattling of the exhaust fan and the slight scraping of metal against the concrete floor. Nothing could be done about the overhead fan, but the latter ceased when Julia stopped scraping the metal lift arm she'd retrieved from the toilet tank.

"Maybe. Hand me a bottle." Nina, who like her mother sat on the concrete floor, retrieved one of the many water bottles.

Julia took it and studied the cap. Its seal looked intact. She squeezed the bottle, but no liquid escaped through holes in the bottle, holes that might have been made by a hypodermic needle. Next, she shook the bottle. The fluid gave no sign of being anything other than pure water. She knew she was being paranoid, but being abducted at gunpoint had that effect on some people. Twisting the lid, she listened for and heard the familiar sound of the safety seal breaking. Still, she sipped the water before handing the bottle to her daughter.

"Do you want water too?" she asked Nestor.

Nestor sat on the toilet seat. "No. I'm not thirsty."

"I think its safe, sweetheart."

"I don't care. It's *their* water."

Julia understood. She returned to the slow act of scraping the flat end of the flush lever against the floor, occasionally stopping to run her finger along the edge to test its sharpness. It would do. It wasn't much of a knife, but it was all she had.

Please, God, don't make me use this.

"LET'S WALK," MOYER SAID. "You okay to be alone, Junior?"

"I'm fine, Boss. Don't worry about me."

Moyer led Jose from the room and to an emergency stairway at the end of the corridor. Once Shaq had relieved him, Moyer had headed from their observation point to Jose's hotel. He spent the time forming his words and planning where and how to break the news.

"This isn't fancy, but it will give us some privacy." Moyer opened the door that led to the enclosed stairway.

"I'm not going to like this, am I?"

"Have a seat." Moyer motioned to one of the concrete steps.

Jose did. "The first thing they teach us in medic school is that it hurts less to rip off a Band-Aid fast than slow."

"Got a message from Ops Command. Your wife is in the hospital."

Jose blinked several times but said nothing.

"They say it's bad, Doc." Moyer sat down next to his medic. "The baby's in danger. The doctors feel that continuing the pregnancy might endanger Lucy's life."

"They want to abort the baby."

"They didn't say that in the message, but I think that's right."

Moyer saw Jose's vision shift to something only he could see. "Did they tell you the medical condition that caused this? Did they give it a name?"

"No. They did say my wife took her to the hospital and that a chaplain had been by."

"There are a number of possible causes for such a prognosis," Jose said. "None of them good. Perhaps it is—"

"Jose. Don't analyze. It won't do any good."

"It's how I cope, Boss."

Moyer understood. Every man had a different way of coping with bad news or overwhelming situations. Jose's approach was to deny the problem and keep working. "Understood. I want you to pack your things. I'm shipping you out on the next available flight."

"What about the mission?"

"We'll get by. Ops may send a replacement, but that'll be their call. All you need to worry about is getting home. Also, I don't need to tell you that you can't call her from here. While you try to get a flight, I'll see if I can't get someone in Ops Command to get an encrypted phone to your wife."

"Thanks, Boss."

"Is there anything else I can do?"

Jose shook his head. Moyer saw the man's eyes moisten as the seriousness of the situation bored in on him. Moyer put his arm around Jose and extended to him the courtesy of silent support.

A tear escaped but Jose made no attempt to hide it. There were those who thought brave men didn't weep. Brave men knew better.

☢ ☢ ☢

HECTOR STARED OUT THE aircraft window at the ocean below. It would still be several hours before his plane touched down in Caracas—a time span that seemed as wide as the sea below. The stranger next to him sat unperturbed by the situation. He thanked the steward each time he brought a drink or a snack. He read the paper, two news magazines, and a business journal provided by the airline.

Nothing in his speech, appearance, or behavior betrayed his present occupation: kidnapper.

CHAPTER 30

ANTONIO SANTI HAD HEADED home for the day. Although the day's activities would have tired most men, Santi felt energized. Juggling his duties as foreign minister with business dealings even President Chavez didn't know about provided him the intellectual thrill he longed for. Younger men might bungee jump, ride a kayak over churning rapids, hunt big game in the jungle, or cheat with other men's wives. Santi got his adrenaline rush from working behind the scenes. The danger he faced was discovery, pure and simple. Chavez was not a man of scrupulous honesty, but he was a priest compared to his own foreign minister.

The plans had been in place for five years. Santi had operatives working in various parts of the world, as well as in country, carrying out the details of an often complicated scheme. Unlikely alliances had been formed. Money from drugs as well as legitimate business interests lubricated his way through many tight passages. Twenty-first-century men were still driven by greed. Greed led to money and money to power. Santi had plenty of each but craved more.

He slipped into his study. A servant brought a small cup of strong coffee. Santi activated his computer and entered a fifteen-digit alphanumeric password to retrieve his e-mail, several of which had to be run through encryption software.

One particular message—or more accurately, the sender's address—caught his attention. The suffix of the digital address was *.ir*. The message was from someone in Iran.

☢ ☢ ☢

"**NEXT FLIGHT OUT IS** in the morning, Boss." Jose hung up the hotel room phone. "It's the earliest I can get away. It leaves shortly before lunch."

It didn't seem right to Moyer that Jose had to wait overnight to catch a five-hour flight, but nothing could be done about it. "I had Caraway ask Ops Command for updates. I don't think there will be any, but if . . . I mean . . ."

"Thanks. Any info will be helpful."

Moyer pursed his lips then looked Jose in the eyes. The man remained calm, professional, feigning detachment, but he couldn't hide the weight on his shoulders. The hours between now and when he arrived home would be the longest of his life. Moyer couldn't imagine it being any other way.

"If it's okay with you, Boss, I'd like to take my shift on the surveillance. It'll help pass the time."

Moyer shook his head and saw Jose's head dip in disappointment.

"I have another job for you."

☢ ☢ ☢

J. J. TRIED THE BED again but couldn't rest. He had been up most of the night and needed sleep, but it evaded him. Every time he closed his eyes, he saw the frightened faces of the two children and their mother. It ate at him that he sat in a nice hotel room while they were held in the bowels of that industrial building.

He reminded himself that they didn't know for sure that the three were abductees. For all he knew, the woman was the wife of one of the men in the van. Yet he did know. He knew in his heart they were in trouble. He also knew Moyer was right to hold back. They could rush in and snatch the family; such rescues were part of their training. It would be a small matter to make a forced entry, pop the bad guys, and lead the family to safety. Most likely none of the hostages would be killed. Most likely.

But then what? Their mission would be blown and leaving the country would become difficult if not impossible.

J. J. rose from the bed and began to pace the room. That's the way the world was—full of evil. Bad people harmed good people for impossible-to-understand reasons. Life was tough all over the globe. In church one Sunday the pastor had preached a mind-melting sermon on global responsibility. J. J. learned that thirty thousand people, mostly children, died of starvation every day. Every day! Five thousand peopled perished daily for lack of water or from consuming contaminated water. Thousands of others died from diseases that could be treated by what most Americans kept in their medicine cabinets. The sermon stuck with him.

A strong sense of justice was one of the reasons J. J. had joined the military, why he had chosen the most grueling, demanding work. Someone had to do something, and this was his way of doing his part. He recited that truth daily, and he believed it. At the moment, however, it failed to satisfy his impatience.

His cell phone rang. Caraway was on the other end.

"Sorry to mess up your beauty sleep, but Shaq wants us on premises ASAP."

"On my way."

Sleep would have to wait.

"IT'S TIME TO GET up close and personal," Rich said. "Boss wants a closer look. The sun will be down in thirty minutes. You go at 0300 hours."

J. J. started to say, "Finally," but caught himself. Instead, he just nodded.

"Ops Command gave us the go-ahead. You and Billy—"

Caraway groaned at the nickname.

"You and Caraway will make entrance at the northwest corner of the perimeter fence. It's the darkest corner on the lot. There are no video surveillance cameras that we can detect on that side of the building. There are two just above the front door and the roll-up. You are to gain access to the roof, where Caraway will set up additional surveillance."

Caraway called up a still image of the north side of the building. "There is a roof-access ladder centered on the back wall. As you can see, it has a safety rig on it."

J. J. knew of the ladder. During his hours of surveillance he had studied every inch of the building the video system allowed. The safety rig Caraway mentioned was little more than a panel of plywood attached to the rungs of the metal ladder. He had seen them on many commercial buildings. The plywood made it difficult for kids to climb, thereby removing the "attractive nuisance" element.

Caraway zoomed in on the wood panel. It was painted dark green, as was the ladder. Caraway pointed at a round, shiny disk to one side. "The panel is hinged on one side and held in place on the other by a three-dollar cabinet lock."

"Gather your gear, gentleman. I want this done fast, I want it done right, and I want it done without incident. Clear?"

"Clear." J. J. and Caraway answered in unison.

CHAPTER 31

HECTOR CENOBIO'S PLANE TOUCHED down in Caracas and began to taxi to the terminal. The man next to Hector, the man with the pictures of his family, continued to read his magazine. Hector ran through the possible actions he could take to free himself of the situation. He contrived several that might get the man arrested or at least detained for questioning. Hector could scream, "Bomb! This man has a bomb!" Or he could run the moment he entered the terminal until he found a policeman to help him. But that did nothing for his family. Any such action might get them killed—if they hadn't been killed already.

He refused to believe they had. He had to have faith that God protected them. A part of his mind, the part that harbored doubts and fears, reminded him that horrible things happened to people of faith every day. Faith was not an exception card that spared the holder of life's difficulty; it was the glue that held the believer together in difficult times.

"I don't have to explain the price of foolish behavior, do I?" The mystery man set down his magazine.

"No. I understand."

"Just stay by my side. We'll pick up our luggage together. A car is waiting for us. Do you understand?"

"I already said I understand."

"No need to get testy, Dr. Cenobio. I'm just trying to save you from making any costly mistakes."

"Let's be clear." Hector turned to the man. "Despite your tone and words, I know you are not here to do favors for me."

"Please do not test my patience, Dr. Cenobio. You would not like to see me angry."

Hector started to tell the man that his threats meant nothing to him but thought better of it. All that mattered was the safety of his family. He would endure the threats. He would jump through hoops if it meant the safety of his wife and children.

The aircraft came to a stop, and the passengers readied themselves to disembark. Hector gathered his things and his wits. He had no idea what lay ahead, but he determined to meet it head-on.

☢ ☢ ☢

"THE VAN IS LEAVING," Rich said. Caraway and J. J. had been going through their personal rituals before the mission.

For some reason known only to him, Caraway carried a small package of trail mix. He never explained why and when questioned about it always gave a different answer.

J. J. sat in a quiet corner with his eyes closed. The moment Rich spoke, he opened his eyes. "Leaving? How many people in it?"

"I saw only one person. Judging by the way he tore out of the lot, he must be late. I'll bet his superiors don't like to be kept waiting."

"That means there are only two black hats in the building." J. J. moved to the monitors.

"Only two we know about. Remember, we don't know who or what is inside the building."

"I know how to find out," J. J. said.

"We follow the plan, Colt. You two do your job right and we might have a better idea of what we're facing."

Rich fired up the truck, drove to an area a half mile from the target site, and parked in an alley that ran between the industrial buildings.

"Do it quick, gentlemen. For all we know the van went to pick up a pizza. He could be back any minute. I don't want him to see you guys shinnying up the ladder." He turned to the two soldiers. "Do me proud."

J. J. and Caraway slipped from the truck.

☢ ☢ ☢

MOYER FOLLOWED THE DIRECTIONS on the dashboard GPS navigator.

"You okay?"

Jose glanced at Moyer. "Yeah, I'm fine. Glad to be out of the hotel room."

"Why is it that every time I ask one of my team members if they're fine they say, 'Yeah, sure, you bet, good to go!' even when I know they're not?"

Jose kept his eyes straight ahead. "Before you had your own team, and your commanding officer asked you that question, what did you say?"

"That's different."

"Is it?"

Moyer made a wide left turn on a commercial street. "Okay, it's not different."

"We're not paid to be depressed; we're paid to do our jobs."

Moyer grinned. "Yeah, I know. Maybe I'm just getting old."

Jose didn't say anything.

"This is where you jump in and tell me I'm still a young man."

"Oh." It was all Jose offered.

"Everyone's a comedian." Moyer let a few moments pass. "We need to take it easy with this guy. He doesn't know us from Adam, and while he might take you for a local, he's going to spot me as a foreigner the moment I open my mouth. We can't be sure he'll tell us anything. He may not have connected Santi to his son's death."

"Have we made the connection?"

"Intel tells us Santi was at the restaurant with some Middle Eastern men. That night, the kid is shot and killed. The pattern of shots indicates a hit. It's worth a try. Maybe the kid heard something he shouldn't."

"A lousy way to lose a loved one. Not that there is a good way."

Moyer found the restaurant with no trouble, and soon they sat at one of the tables. A man bustled between the kitchen and the dining room. He was older than the other waiters and his eyes seemed empty. Moyer guessed this was their man.

A busboy brought tortilla chips, a bowl of deep-red salsa, and two menus to the table. Ten minutes later one of the waiters approached. Moyer's first impulse was to ask for the owner—get right to work—but he and Jose had discussed it on the drive in. First they would eat and study their surroundings, search for any indication that they were being watched. They wanted to know how the restaurant "felt" and who sat at the tables. Moyer felt whiter than normal. Many Caucasians visited and lived in Venezuela. Like

Los Angeles, New York, Dallas, Atlanta, and other major American cities, Caracas had its share of immigrants. He had seen scores of non-Hispanics at the hotels and on the streets. Here, however, he felt like the lone oak tree in a wide, green pasture. Clearly the eatery was a favorite spot for locals rather than tourists.

"*Petróleo?*"

"Excuse me?" Moyer said in English and immediately wondered if he had just blown it.

The waiter, who was all of eighteen, pointed at Moyer's shirt and the emblem, OKLACO.

"Oil company?"

Moyer studied the kid. "You speak English."

"Yes, sir."

"That's good. I'm afraid my Spanish is not very good. Yes, I work for Oklaco."

"American company. My uncle works the oil fields. A different company."

Jose smiled. "Yes, my friend is a consultant. I'm his translator. We heard this is the best food in Caracas."

The waiter smiled. "No one complains. What can I get for you?"

Moyer glanced at the menu then decided on something safe. "Enchiladas, *por favor.*"

Jose ordered something Moyer didn't recognize.

As they gave their order, Moyer noticed the man he assumed to be the owner staring at them. Moyer gave a slight nod. The man frowned and disappeared into the kitchen.

For appearance Moyer and Jose made small talk while studying the dining room. Neither found anything to cause them concern. The food arrived fifteen minutes after they placed their order. Moyer had to admit the food was good. No wonder the place was packed.

The older man worked the tables, stopping by each one and chatting with customers as if they were family. Many of the customers wore expressions of sadness, patted his hand, and spoke softly.

Moyer and Jose drank beer with the meal and ordered another bottle each as the waiter cleared the table. "So how do we chat with the owner?" Jose asked. "I suppose we could just ask to see him."

"Direct but maybe a tad bold. Unfortunately I don't have a better—"

Jose turned to follow Moyer's gaze. "What?"

"Looks like our problem just solved itself."

The owner moved from the bar to their table. He carried two bottles of beer.

"*Gracias*," Jose smiled at the man as he set the bottles on the table. "*Está usted el dueño?*"

The man answered in English. "I am the owner, yes. I have not seen you here before." He clipped his words as if biting off the last syllable.

"We're in Caracas on business," Jose said. "The front desk at our hotel recommended your restaurant. The food was wonderful. I especially liked—"

"You are here to see me?"

Jose glanced at Moyer, who took a moment before answering. "Why would you say that?"

The man closed his eyes then slowly opened them as if his eyelids held back a fury ready to erupt. "You are here to see me?"

"Yes." This time Moyer didn't hesitate. "We would like to talk to you."

"We close at ten. The employees leave at eleven. Be here at eleven thirty. Come to the back door off the alley." He didn't wait for an answer. Turning, he marched to the kitchen.

"That was weird," Jose said.

"Yeah. Why is my gut uneasy?"

"Maybe it's the salsa."

"I hope that's all it is."

CHAPTER 32

CARAWAY LED THE WAY and J. J. was happy to let him do so; he had never been comfortable with Caraway at his back. Before leaving the truck, both men had changed into dark shirts and pants. Each man carried only a 9mm handgun strapped to his thigh and a backpack over his shoulder. Radios hung at their belts and lightweight headsets clung to their scalps. The alley they moved through was nearly as dark as a tomb, lit only by a setting moon and one dim bulb near the rear door of one of the buildings.

They walked the half mile in silence, listening for the sounds of a truck, the conversation of late-night workers, or the snores of a wino sleeping off a bottle of red wine. They heard none of those things. To J. J. it seemed he and Caraway were the last two men on Earth. The thought chilled him.

Something crunched under J. J.'s boot. He stopped and directed the thin beam of light from his small flashlight to the ground. "Charming." The single word carried his disgust.

Caraway directed his light to the same spot. "Cockroaches. Man, they grow them big down here."

"I've seen smaller dogs."

"You can apologize to the bug's family later. Let's get a move on."

They crossed a street, making sure no one was about to see them do so. The target building was one block down. They continued through the alley until they reached the chain-link fence.

J. J. studied the building, the grounds, and the fence. "I don't see anything to indicate the fence is electrified."

"We'll know soon enough. I see no surveillance cameras. These guys are either stupid or overconfident."

"Or they don't plan to be here very long."

Caraway placed his hand near the fence then touched it. "We're good to go." He keyed his mike and radioed Rich. "Making entry."

"Roger that."

"I'll go first."

J. J. nodded to Caraway and unholstered his weapon.

They had considered cutting the chain link to gain access to the property, but that would leave evidence of their presence. The fence stood only eight feet high, with no razor wire at the top. Caraway raised his gloved hands and slipped his fingers through the wire mesh. A few seconds later he pulled himself over the top and dropped to the ground.

The second his boots hit the pavement Caraway drew his handgun.

J. J. holstered his weapon and followed Caraway over the top, doing his best not to jiggle the fence enough to create noise.

In a crouch the men sprinted across the open macadam lot until they reached the windowless wall of concrete. Again they paused and listened for the sounds of human activity. Nothing. Conversation between the men was over; all communication from here on out would be done with hand signals. Caraway pointed at

J. J., then to his own eyes. J. J. nodded and took two steps away from the wall, his 9mm at the ready.

Caraway studied the lock that held the hinged plywood barricade that covered the bottom third of the ladder. He shook his head and stepped back. The initial plan had been to force what looked like, on the surveillance camera, a cheap cabinet lock. Apparently Caraway saw something he didn't like. A second later he turned, pressed his back to the plywood and interlaced his fingers. J. J. needed no explanation.

He returned his weapon to the holster, took a step toward Caraway, and placed his foot in the makeshift stirrup. He pressed down on Caraway's hands and let the other soldier lift him up until J. J. could take hold of the second free rung above the plywood panel. He pulled himself up and slipped a foot onto a rung. Moving to the side of the ladder, J. J. slipped his left arm around one of the vertical supports and reached his right arm down to Caraway. Caraway jumped, catching J. J. by the wrist. J. J. pulled himself up, dragging Caraway with him. It was like lifting several bags of concrete with one arm.

He didn't have to hold the man for long. Caraway seized a rung with his free hand and released his grip on J. J. He now had two hands on a rung but his feet still hung loose, the toe of his boots touching the plywood.

Without a word, J. J. squatted again and reached for Caraway's belt. One heave later, Caraway stood on the ladder. J. J. held his place to the side and let Caraway scale the rest of the distance to the roof before following.

The decomposed granite over the hot-mopped roof presented a problem. The gravel crunched beneath their boots, forcing them to take measured steps, each stride considered before a boot was moved. Caraway went first, and J. J. waited until his partner had made it to the front of the building before following the same path.

Once he reached Caraway's location, J. J. removed his backpack and set it next to Caraway's then studied the roof.

J. J. had worked a few of his high school summers in construction. While he didn't learn enough to pass the contractor's license exam, he had picked up a few things. He easily identified the HVAC fan unit that helped with the heating and cooling of the building. He also saw a couple of plastic pipes he knew to be vents for restroom plumbing. Before leaving the van they had decided to set up the surveillance first in what they assumed to be the work area of the building, the dark area they had seen when the van brought the woman and children to the concrete tilt-up.

Caraway pulled a palm-sized handheld drill from the backpack and a six-inch-long bit. He moved to the estimated center of the building, knelt on the gravel and brushed clean as many of the small stones as possible. Caraway removed a hand towel from the backpack and wrapped it around the power tool to muffle the noise of the battery-powered device. The drill came to life and chewed through the tarred paper and into the material beneath. A white, flaky substance traveled up the bit and fell to the roof. Caraway stopped. "Doesn't look like wood," he whispered.

J. J. picked up some of the material and rubbed it between his gloved fingers. "Rigid insulation."

"You mean like fiberglass?"

J. J. shook his head. "It's a different material—similar to Styrofoam but more rigid. Some commercial buildings put rigid insulation over the plywood sheeting to save energy. It's more effective and easier to install."

"How thick is this stuff?"

"Maybe six inches."

"That's longer than the drill." Caraway stared at the 3/8-inch hole.

J. J. pulled a Benchmade knife from his pocket and began carefully cutting a three-inch wide hole in the material. "The stuff is strong enough to stand on, but it still cuts easily." He dug until the knife touched the plywood sheeting that made up the structural membrane of the roof. "Unless you drill right into a beam, you should punch through after about three-quarters of an inch."

Of course, "punch through" was the last thing they wanted. A drill suddenly appearing in the ceiling would be a certain giveaway, as would bits of debris falling to the floor. Caraway activated the drill again and J. J. watched as the man stopped after boring only half an inch. Caraway removed the drill and bit, ejected the battery, then placed the bit back into the hole. For the next few minutes, Caraway twisted the cylindrical power drill by hand. From time to time, he would remove the bit and blow in the hole to dislodge any buildup of sawdust. J. J. had to remind him to move the voice-activated mike away from his mouth.

"Don't like the sound of my breath, Colt?" Caraway whispered.

"I know I don't." The voice belonged to Shaq. "Ease up on the sound effects, Billy."

Caraway slipped the bit back into the hole and slowly turned it, J. J. watching each twist of the wrist. It seemed as if they had been at this for an hour, but patience remained the order of the day.

Caraway's wrist jerked to the right and he stopped. "I'm through. Clear the debris."

J. J. moved his mike up, put his face close to the opening and blew a stream of air over the opening and around the bit. A thin beam of light pressed through the narrow opening. Both men remained still, listening for the opening of a door or the shout of warning. They heard nothing.

J. J. took the drill and bit from Caraway, broke it down, and returned it to the backpack.

"Light."

J. J. switched on his small flashlight and aimed the beam at Caraway's hand. Caraway held what appeared to be a thin, black snake but was in fact an ingenious fiber-optic device comprising a ¼-inch CCD high-resolution color camera at the end of a thirty-four-inch metal-reinforced neck. The camera offered an eighty-five-degree field of view and delivered video at 380 lines. It could focus on something as close as one inch or be set to infinity.

Caraway bent the neck of the device and slipped it into the hole. "Wire."

J. J. bent a stiff wire around the neck of the device to keep it from slipping farther through the hole. Caraway plugged the device's RCA jack into a handheld monitor and turned it on. The color display came to life. Caraway set the monitor on the roof so J. J. could see. They now had a view of the entire main room.

J. J. studied the image then keyed his mike. "We have eyes. I see three hostiles, all asleep."

"The woman and kids?" Rich asked.

"Negative. No sign of them." He paused. "Hold on." Two men lay on bed rolls near the west wall. Next to each lay an AK-47. One man, however, slept off by himself. He sat in a chair positioned in front of a narrow door, an automatic weapon across his lap. Light oozed from beneath the door. "One unfriendly is perched in front of a door. I can see a light beneath it. Best guess is the family is locked in there."

"Understood," Rich said.

J. J. looked around the roof. His spotted a galvanized metal vent with a small matching metal hood over its opening. "I see the bathroom vent, Shaq. I think we can create another peephole and see what's in the bathroom."

"Do it."

Twenty minutes later they had dug another hole through insulation and bored through the plywood. Caraway worked his magic with the electronics and again turned on the monitor. A second later J. J. and Caraway were staring at a woman sitting on the floor, a child beneath each arm. The children seemed to be asleep. The woman, however, remained wide awake. She laid her head back against the dirty tile and looked at the ceiling. For a moment he thought she had spotted the business end of the camera. If she had, she gave no indication. Her lips were moving.

"Who's she talking to?" Caraway asked.

J. J. knew. "God."

CHAPTER 33

MOYER PARKED ON THE street near the alley that ran behind the Estevez restaurant. His watch showed 2330 hours on the dot. He and Jose walked the alley without speaking. From their briefing they knew the owner's son had been gunned down on this very lane. Moyer thought of his own son and family then forced their faces from his mind. He needed to remain focused.

The light that poured from the window seemed paler than when they had dined there a short time before. Nothing unusual in that, Moyer decided. Business hours were over. He and Jose stepped up the stairs that led to the exterior stoop and knocked on the door.

The door opened and Moyer caught a glimpse of Reuben Estevez. He had his back turned to them. The hair on the back of Moyer's neck stood, though he didn't know why. Cautiously he stepped into the kitchen area. Only half of the overhead fluorescent lights were on, casting a dim light on metal tables, an old commercial stove, pots, pans, and a dozen resident objects in the kitchen.

"Señor Estevez." When the man didn't turn, Moyer whispered to Jose. "Heads up. Something doesn't feel right."

Estevez moved through the kitchen and into the dining room. Moyer and Jose followed.

The restaurant, which had been a cacophony of conversation a short time ago, held no noises other than the footfalls of three men and the gentle roar of a water heater firing up. Estevez moved slowly and like a man with purpose. He hung his head and barely moved his arms as he walked, which struck Moyer as odd.

The restaurant owner stepped to a table in the middle of the dining area. Moyer studied it. It looked like every other table in the place: red tablecloth, two bottles of hot sauce, a tall napkin dispenser, and a thin vase with two long-stem flowers. Nothing struck him as dangerous.

Estevez rounded the table and stood behind a chair. Moyer eyed him then closed the distance between them. When Moyer and Jose were five feet from the table, Estevez reached for something behind the napkin dispenser. Moyer tensed. Estevez stood with a gun in his hand, its barrel pointed at Moyer's sternum. Moyer stopped midstep. Jose did the same.

Moyer kept his tone calm. "What's this about?"

"You work for Santi." Estevez's hand shook, which made Moyer all the more nervous. "Do not deny it."

"I'm sorry, Mr. Estevez, but that isn't true."

"He and his foreign friends come to my restaurant then kill my son. I will avenge my boy."

"By killing two innocent men?"

He raised the gun toward Jose. "There are no innocent men." He extended his arm as if he were on a practice range.

"Even if we did work for Santi, killing me wouldn't bring your son back."

Pain-filled eyes fixed on Moyer. "No, it will not, but it will keep you and your kind from killing again."

"How can we convince you that we are here to help?" Moyer moved his eyes to the man's trigger finger. The gun was old and not well kept, not that it mattered. An old, ugly pistol could kill as well as a shiny new one.

"You can't."

Instinct said run; training said attack. Moyer chose the latter. Running only made a man a bigger target. When Moyer saw Estevez's finger twitch, he ducked and moved to the side as the gun went off. He ignored the loud report, ignored the acrid smell of spent gunpowder. It might have been his imagination, but he felt something caress his hair.

Before Estevez could reacquire his target, Moyer took a step forward and launched himself over the table, hitting the man square in the chest with his shoulder. Both went down. Before Moyer could take hold of Estevez's arm, something landed on top of him—Jose, landing on Moyer hard. With two men on top of him, Estevez was going nowhere. Moyer reached for the man's gun hand and found Jose had beaten him to it.

Jose clambered off Moyer. He had pinned the gun hand to the floor. "Release the weapon." Estevez refused. Jose repeated the command then said something in Spanish. Still Estevez refused to comply.

Moyer pushed himself up and took hold of the attacker's throat. Options ran through Moyer's mind—most of them not good for Estevez. But he had not come to this place to kill the man. With his free hand, Moyer put a thumb to Estevez's left eye and pressed. The man squealed. Moyer pressed harder. Estevez released his grip on the handgun.

Jose pulled it away. "Got it."

Moyer removed his thumb from the man's eye. Estevez wept, but not from the pain Moyer had inflicted. Moyer had seen men weep in pain. This was different.

These tears came from unmitigated sorrow.

Moyer stood, freeing Estevez, who rolled over on his side and covered his face with his hands. Moyer let him have a few moments. Jose had already removed the rounds from the handgun and dropped them in his pocket.

"Let's get him up." Moyer took the man by the arm. "Come on, Estevez. On your feet."

A few moments later the three sat at one of the tables. Estevez's tears dried over the next few minutes. Moyer saw no need to rush the man. It would do no good.

Estevez broke the silence. "What will you do to me?"

Moyer smiled. "Let you go home, of course. I told you, we don't work for Santi."

"How can I believe you?"

"If we worked for him, you wouldn't be alive now." Jose pushed the empty gun toward the man.

"Then what do you want?"

Moyer leaned forward. "Santi and some foreigners were in your restaurant. Your son was killed that same day."

"How do you know about Santi and the strangers?"

"I can't tell you that," Moyer said.

Estevez frowned. "You may ask questions but I cannot, is that it?"

Moyer nodded. "I'm afraid so. I know it's unfair, but it is better for you this way."

"If she knows, my wife will be ashamed of me. I am glad she is at home and not here to see what I have done."

"Grief is a powerful thing," Moyer said. "Do you know why Santi and the foreigners were here that night?"

"You are CIA?"

"No."

"American military?"

"We work for an oil company."

Estevez surprised Moyer by laughing. "Of course you do. An oil company." He rubbed his sore eye. "I don't know why they chose my restaurant. I have a private dining room. Someone from the foreign minister's office reserved the room the week before." He looked down at the empty weapon. "I treated them with the greatest respect. I satisfied their every need, and they killed my son." He rose. "Come with me."

Moyer and Jose followed him to a back room. "They ate at that table. My son waited on them. He is—was—a good boy. Never caused us trouble." He moved to a small room just off the reserved dining area. Moyer saw coffee makers, napkins, and other items a waiter might need. He also saw a stack of comic books. Estevez reached for one of the comics. "Ricardo had a . . . how do you say it . . . hungry mind?" He looked at Jose.

"Inquiring."

"Yes, an inquiring mind. Restaurant work bored him. He used to listen to the customers and sometimes jotted down what he heard." He handed the comic to Moyer.

Moyer took in the words. "Hector Cenobio . . . nuclear . . . fast capture . . . airport . . . nuclear . . . Iran."

Moyer began to swear.

"WE CAN DO THIS," J. J. whispered into the mike. "There are only three of them and they're asleep."

"Negative."

"Shaq, we can make entry through a side door. We'd have the element of surprise."

"I said negative, Colt. You are underarmed and undermanned. You don't have the equipment to make entry through a locked door."

"But . . ." J. J. couldn't finish the sentence. Rich was right. If they could just walk through an open door, then he and Caraway could kill off the three guards before they opened their eyes. They wouldn't need more than the 9mm they were packing, but they didn't have an opening. If they made too much noise, the guards would come to and make short work of J. J. and Caraway. A pair of handguns were no match for three AK-47s. In the end J. J.'s bravado might lead to the death of the very family he wanted to save.

"Understood."

"Good," Rich said. "Billy, reposition the spycam and set up the transmitter. I want you two back ASAP."

"Roger that." Caraway withdrew the camera and quietly made his way back to the original hole. Ten minutes later the system was set up. "You should have a signal now."

"Affirm. Signal strength good. Now you two get out of there."

The trip back through the alley was the darkest J. J. had ever made.

CHAPTER 34

STACY PUSHED THE COVERS back on the bed and sat up. There were still three hours before daylight, but sleep had quit and gone home early. At the hospital she had lost count of the number of cups of coffee she'd consumed to keep her sharp while she sat with Lucy. Watching a woman weep proved to be hard work, especially when you're trying not to mingle in your own tears. At eleven, Lucy ordered Stacy to go home.

The house was quiet when she arrived. An empty pizza box sat on the kitchen counter, as did several empty soda cans. Stacy checked in on Gina, who slept soundly in her bed. A light from Rob's room slipped beneath the door. She knocked. "I'm home."

"Okay." Rob offered nothing more.

"Anything I need to know?"

"We're almost out of milk."

"Ah. Well, it's been good talking to you. Maybe next time we can do it without a door between us."

"Don't start, Mom. I'm getting ready for bed."

"Okay. Sorry. I'm a little tired. I'll see you in the morning."

"Whatever."

Stacy shook her head and crossed the house to her bedroom. Sleep had come quickly and left just as fast. She first awoke at one when she thought she heard something, then again at two then three. The last time she awoke she knew sleep had fled for the night and gave up the fight. Perhaps a magazine, a soft throw blanket, and a comfy chair might lure slumber back.

She crossed the threshold of her bedroom door and moved slowly through the dark living room and pulled the chain on a small reading light next to the sofa. Rifling through the magazines she found the latest *Entertainment Weekly*. As she was about to settle down on the sofa, something caught her attention. Rob's room was at the end of the hall. Despite the dim light she could tell the door stood open. A few moments later her fears were confirmed.

Rob was gone.

☢ ☢ ☢

LUCY GAZED AT THE muted television in her room. Hospitals, she decided, are the worst places to sleep. When she did doze, she was awakened by a nurse taking her temperature or blood pressure or changing her IV bag. A small red light on the IV monitor flashed with each drop of medical elixir that dripped through the plastic tube. She had no idea what the clear substance was, and while it did ease her pain, it did nothing to quiet her mind.

She worried about her children. Were they afraid because Mommy didn't come home? How long could her sister care for them? That alone was enough to set ablaze the acid in her stomach, but other thoughts added explosive fuel to the fire. Would she lose the baby? Would she have to sacrifice her life for her unborn? If so, how would Jose Jr., Matteo, and Maria get along without her?

Tears flowed once more from her eyes. She had cried so much since this morning—no, it was yesterday morning—she had doubted any more tears were in her. Apparently the well of sorrow never ran dry.

Lucy wondered one more thing: How long before Jose came home?

☢ ☢ ☢

"NO WAY, MAN. YOU'RE going to the airport and getting on that plane." Moyer sat in the passenger seat, Ricardo's comic book on his lap. Jose drove along the thoroughfare, keeping pace with the early morning traffic.

"Listen, Boss. In almost any other situation I'd agree. I'd swim home if I had too, but this is too important. You read the words."

"We don't know what they mean."

"We've got a good idea, Boss. You know that. 'Hector Cenobio—nuclear—fast capture—airport—nuclear—Iran.' Any sentence with *nuclear* in it makes me nervous. Add the word *Iran* and I get the shakes."

Moyer looked at the man next to him. Could he really be saying what Moyer was hearing? "It's just a bunch of words scratched down by a teenager."

"Boss, you know I got nothing but the greatest respect for you, but that is more baloney than a man can eat. I was there when you read the words for the first time, and unless things have changed, that's not the kind of language you use around civilized people."

"It caught me off guard."

"Yeah, I could see that. Didn't do much for me either."

Moyer took a deep breath and let it out slowly. "Look, there is no way I'm going to let you stay here while your wife is in the hospital. Your replacement will be here soon enough."

"You hope. You know that it might be several days, and I'm thinking we don't have that long." Jose steered off the highway to downtown streets. "Look at what we have: foreign nationals, most likely from an al-Qaeda country, setting up shop in Caracas; a kidnapped woman and two children; the involvement of the foreign minister of Venezuela; a cryptic note that indicates another kidnapping of someone named Hector Cenobio; mention of something nuclear; and the word *Iran*. I'm not much for making up stories, but the way I see it, there's a plan to kidnap and export a nuclear expert to Iran."

"We don't know that Hector Cenobio is a scientist or engineer."

"Come on, Boss, you wouldn't put money on that and you know it. I bet a call to Ops Command will start a little research that will tell us that Cenobio is some big shot in the world of nuclear weapons or some other discipline."

"Doesn't matter. We'll take care of it. You're going home."

"Let me stay until my replacement arrives. You need a Spanish speaker."

Moyer would not be moved. "Forget it, Doc. If something happens to your wife or unborn child while you're here when I could have sent you home . . . well, I'd never forgive myself. I could never look you in the eye again."

"Boss." He stopped. "Eric . . . don't get me wrong. It isn't that I don't want to be by my wife's side. I'd cut out my own heart and give it to her. I'd dig my own grave and crawl in it if I could give her and the baby the rest of the years I have left, but I can't do that. I didn't choose the Army for the money. I didn't choose it for the excitement. I enlisted because I'm an idealist. I believe I can make a difference in the world. I hate to see the little guy get kicked around, especially when I can do something about it. I can't change the world, and I can't save everyone; but I can save a few along the way. It's why I wear a uniform. It's why I'm here."

"I can't let you do this."

"I'm not asking you to say yes, Boss." Jose pulled into the parking lot of Rich and Pete's hotel. "I'm just asking that you don't say no. Especially considering what you're considering."

"You a mind reader now? What am I thinking?"

"Certain jeopardy."

Moyer looked at Jose. Maybe he *was* a mind reader.

CHAPTER 35

THE SOFT BED, THE well-appointed bedroom, the quality food prepared by a chef, the offer of wine or beer—all were nothing more than attempts to curry Hector Cenobio's favor, and he recognized them as such. He didn't need to be a professional spy to know this. Since his arrival at the airport, Hector had been treated like a foreign dignitary. A limo met him and the passenger who had shown him photos of his abducted family and ferried them to a distant part of the airport where a business helicopter waited, its engine already warming.

The limo stopped a short distance away from the aircraft and a powerfully built Venezuelan opened the door. He motioned for Hector to exit. Hector hesitated. "Please, Dr. Cenobio."

The man who had flown with Hector gave him a shove. "Out. Now."

Hector climbed from the vehicle and faced the stranger. "Who are you?"

"You may call me Miguel Costa. I am a . . ." He stopped to smile. "An acquaintance of your wife's."

"If you have hurt them—"

"They are fine for the moment and will remain so as long as you cooperate. You understand this, no?"

"I understand."

Costa nodded at his cohort, took Hector by the arm, and walked him to the helicopter. The craft lifted off the moment the last safety belt had been snapped in place. Hector turned in time to see his unwanted flight companion drive off in the limo.

Even in the dark Hector could see the sprawling mansion in the jungles just outside of Caracas. A butler greeted them, bowing as he opened the door. A meal had been set at a massive table. He and Costa were the only two in the expansive room. Foods far too elaborate and expensive for Hector's tastes were served. Duck, wine imported from France, and more. Hector touched none of it.

"You must be hungry, Dr. Cenobio," Costa has said. "It does no good to go without. It changes nothing."

"I will eat when I know my family is safe."

Costa nodded. "That is too bad."

"I will not eat my captor's food." Hector crossed his arms.

"The choice is yours, Doctor, but I think you are being foolish. When was the last time you had such fine cuisine spread before you. Maybe your stomach cannot tolerate such quality."

"It isn't the food that my stomach can't tolerate; it's the company."

Costa's face hardened then relaxed into a smile. "Very good, Dr. Cenobio. You talk a brave game. Unfortunately talk will not change matters for you. At least drink the wine. I can call for beer if you prefer."

"I prefer to be taken to my family."

"Soon, but not tonight."

Hector took in his surroundings. Whoever owned the mansion must be wealthy beyond what Hector could imagine. He guessed the furniture and art were imported from Europe, but the furnishings did not interest him as much as the shadowy figures that moved past the windows every few moments. The place was heavily guarded. Usually guards were hired to keep people out; he had no doubt these had been hired to keep him in.

After Costa finished his meal, he led Hector to an upstairs bedroom. The room was better appointed than hotel suites he had seen. He noticed one exception: This room had wrought-iron bars on the window and a dead-bolt lock that locked from the outside. Hector had been treated as a guest but knew he was prisoner.

The night passed slowly and the sun rose lazily in the east. Hector had not slept, had not touched the bed. He passed the hours in prayer or staring out the window at the black jungle. He would not sleep in luxury when his family was who-knows-where.

The butler retrieved Hector for breakfast at 7:00 a.m. The elderly man led him down the wide stairway to the dining room where he had sat the night before. This time another man joined Costa—a thin, stately man with dark eyes as hard as marble despite the gracious smile he wore. He rose when Hector entered. A moment later Costa stood, although he seemed puzzled by the need to do so.

The stately man spoke first. "Dr. Cenobio, I've been looking forward to this moment for many months. It is a pleasure to finally meet you."

"I wish I could say the same."

"Please, Doctor. Come sit to my left. The chef is putting the finishing touches on a marvelous breakfast—"

"I won't eat it." He walked to the chair his host indicated.

"Are you certain, Doctor? I am told that you refused to eat last night."

"I did, and I refuse to eat now or at any time in the future until my family is free."

The man nodded. "Does your bravery keep you from sitting?"

Hector sat, as did the others. A second later a server dressed in white appeared with a tray of three plates. The aroma made Hector's stomach come to life. Poached eggs over a white meat covered in a thick hollandaise, small cranberry muffins, and thick, rich coffee. Hector folded his hands on the table.

"Please try the food. The eggs rest on a bed of lobster meat. The hollandaise is the best in the country. My cook makes it fresh, of course."

"No, thank you."

"Oh, Dr. Cenobio, this saddens me. I wish only to show you the best of my hospitality."

"A good host never kidnaps members of the guest's family."

The man chuckled. "No, I suppose not." He took a bite of egg and lobster, then closed his eyes and chewed slowly. After he swallowed, he wiped his mouth with a cloth napkin. "Do you know who I am, Dr. Cenobio?"

"A criminal is all I know."

"Perhaps. My perspective is different, of course. I am Andriano Santi, foreign minister for Venezuela."

"I knew things had deteriorated since Chavez came to power. I just didn't realize he'd hired thugs to run the government."

"Please don't antagonize me, Doctor. I'm trying to be a gracious host, but there is a limit to my patience."

"You don't frighten me."

"I frighten your wife and children."

The words hit him like bullets. "I understand."

"Good. After breakfast, you will be taken to your family. I must insist that you behave yourself, Doctor. The people in my employ are far less patient than I, and the other people—well, patience is not a virtue to them."

"What other people?"

"All in good time, Doctor. I trust you didn't unpack."

"My suitcase was left in the helicopter."

For the first time that morning, Costa spoke. "It's in one of the storage closets."

"Good, that means we do not need to waste time. I know you have spent a great deal of time in airplanes lately, but I'm afraid you must take another long trip."

"Where?"

"I suppose it doesn't hurt for you to know. You and your family are relocating to Iran."

"And if I refuse to go?"

Santi laughed. "You speak as if you have a choice."

"I'm not afraid to die."

Santi set down his fork and dabbed at his mouth with a napkin. "You're testing me, Dr. Cenobio, and that is not a wise thing to do. Why do you suppose we've enlisted the help of your wife and children?" He leaned back in the chair. "A man will die for his principles, but very few men will sacrifice their children. You will go and you will cooperate every step of the way. I have no doubt of that."

"You didn't enlist my family; you abducted them." Hector's courage eroded with each comment Santi made. "People will look for me."

"As if that matters. Once you are in Iran, no one will find you unless our friends wish it to be so."

"They're your friends, not mine."

Santi returned to his meal. "That distinction doesn't matter, now does it?"

"It matters to me."

"If you say so. Now I suggest you eat. It might be sometime before you sit again before a meal of such quality."

"I prefer to be hungry."

"As you wish."

Wishing wouldn't help. Hector preferred prayer, but at the moment not even that seemed to help.

☢ ☢ ☢

MOYER'S MIND MOVED LIKE a brakeless freight train on a steep downhill grade. Ops Command had taken several hours to reply to his report about what was written on the comic book in Estevez's restaurant.

Command's research brought some answers. Hector Cenobio was an expert in the recycling of spent nuclear fuel, a noble goal at its heart but one with serious consequences in the wrong hands.

Rich grimaced. "I didn't get very high marks in science. What makes Cenobio such hot stuff."

They sat in the outdoor area of a nearby coffee shop, sipping thick espresso and lattes. Pete and Caraway were missing, as they manned the surveillance truck. The whole team needed rest, but circumstances kept getting in the way. Only Pete, whom Moyer had ordered to spend the day resting from his injuries, had more than a couple hours of sleep. This morning he had convinced Moyer he was fit for duty, at least for sitting and watching computer monitors.

"As I understand it," Moyer said. "Spent nuclear fuel from power plants can be reprocessed and used again in a different kind of power plant. The problem is the recycled fuel is rich in pluto-nium, which can be used to make bombs."

"And Cenobio has created a new way of doing this," Jose added.

"So the woman and kids are Cenobio's family?" J. J. asked.

"That's our best guess. Command thinks—and I agree with them—that we're not looking at an al-Qaeda training facility; we're seeing the abduction of someone who can help . . . others . . . obtain high-grade plutonium." Moyer didn't want to use the word *Iran* in public.

"Man," Rich said, "I didn't see that coming."

Moyer sipped his espresso. "I've told Command that I'm moving us to Certain-Jeopardy status." He gave his men time to process this. They all knew too well that the Certain-Jeopardy designation was used only in the case of a serious threat to national security. And it changed the formal rules of engagement. They were now on more than a covert intelligence-gathering mission; they were cleared to take direct and forceful action to minimize—or eliminate—the threat to the U.S.

Moyer continued. "Command is sending a shooter team, but I don't think they'll arrive in time. From the look of things, the bad guys will move Cenobio as soon as possible. From what you tell me, J. J., it doesn't look like they plan to stay in the building very long."

"We didn't see much in the way of supplies. They don't even have cots to sleep on. If they were in for the long haul, I'd expect to see more evidence of it."

Moyer noticed J. J.'s speech came unevenly. He and everyone on the team knew why Command would send a shooter team: Their job would be to make sure Cenobio never made it to Iran. By lethal force, if necessary. "Okay. We need to be ready to go on a moment's notice. This changes our exit strategy. I need everyone at his best. I don't need to tell you this can go bad in a heartbeat. Got it?"

The team members nodded.

"Okay, let's get to work. Jose, you sit for a minute. I want to talk to you." After J. J. and Rich left, Moyer leaned over the table and stared hard into Jose's eyes. "Your flight leaves in two hours. Are you ready?"

"No."

"Are you going to make me order you to get on that plane?"

Jose nodded. "I'm afraid so, but I'm hoping you won't."

"Your wife needs you."

"Don't you think I know that, Boss? Every second that passes makes my insides melt some more. I want to be there for her, but I need to be here. Now that we know what's at stake, it's even more important that you have a full team."

"Jose—"

"I know I may lose my wife or the baby or both, and if that happens, I'll never forgive myself. But if something goes south on this mission, if that woman and two children are killed because I'm not here to do my job, that will be something else I can't forgive myself for. Let me stay until my replacement arrives. Not that it matters. I don't think we have that much time."

Moyer agreed, but he wouldn't give Jose the satisfaction of saying so. The problem was this: Jose was right. Moyer did need every man, especially now that the mission objective had been changed to a kill-or-capture effort.

Jose took another stab at convincing Moyer. "I know it's your call, but let me ask this: Haven't you ever bent the rules to work a mission? I don't mean you've defied orders or anything, just that you would go as far as you can to make the mission a success no matter what it cost?"

Moyer didn't want to answer this. Knowing that he might have a serious medical condition should have prompted him to step down as team leader until a full diagnosis could be made. He didn't. He had gone on this mission as if nothing were wrong. "This goes against my better judgment, but I'll allow it."

"Great."

"No, it's not great. It's wrong on so many levels, but you're right about us not having much time. So here's the deal: If your wife blames me for your not being there, I will hit you in the throat. If my wife divorces me over this, I will find you and hit you in the throat. If I get in trouble with the brass, then—"

"Let me guess. You'll hit me in the throat?"

"Twice." Moyer lowered his eyes. "It's your call, Doc."

CHAPTER 36

MOYER FELT LIKE A man juggling chain saws—one mistake and you were toast. He and Rich sat on a patio on the south side of the hotel. The sun continued its climb up the sky as if it couldn't be bothered with the little things of human beings including abductions, nuclear terrorism, colon cancer, and the dying wife of one of his team members. The fact that he sat in comfort while two children and a woman were locked in the bathroom of an industrial building added several tons of guilt to his shoulders.

The hours between breakfast and lunch had left the patio empty, granting them freedom of speech. Nonetheless they kept their voices low. Moyer took a sip of coffee. He had had more coffee since sunrise than ever before and was sick of it. Rich glanced at a newspaper, although he couldn't understand most of the words. The paper was for affect. To an outsider they looked like two travelers enjoying a morning of leisure.

"How do you see it?" Moyer asked.

Rich didn't look up from the paper. "The situation is fragmented. We have players in different locations without a clear idea of their next move. We could rescue the woman without much trouble, but doing so could jeopardize the new mission. We take the bad guys out, which keeps them from reporting in, and we never see Cenobio."

"And if we wait, the hostages could die. I assume they're being kept alive for a reason. Maybe Cenobio refuses to cooperate without first seeing his family."

Rich nodded. "We're also split up. We've got Pete and Caraway in the van and due to be relieved soon. J. J. and Doc are resting because you ordered them to hit the rack and, truth be told, Boss, you should be sacked out too. When did you sleep last?"

Moyer shrugged. "I don't know. It's been a while." He thought for a moment. "We don't have a handle on this. Not by a long shot. We have to get more proactive. If they made their move right now, all we'd have is Pete and Caraway trying to keep track of things."

"Agreed."

"You know the hardest mission in the world, Rich?"

"Knowing you have to do something and having to wait to do it?"

"Bingo," Moyer said. His intestines hurt. He was experiencing more discomfort every day. He had no idea what was going on inside him, but he could tell it wasn't good.

"We know who the family is. Ops Command got back to us pretty quick on that."

"I imagine they've been reading everything they can find on Cenobio. No doubt one of the spook agencies came up with a family photo." Moyer pushed the coffee cup aside.

"So what are the possibilities?" Rich asked. "They bring Cenobio to the building, then move the family to some other location where they hook up with Cenobio and his captors. Or they—"

"Kill the family. I'm not sure I can live with that."

"Not much you can do, Boss. Ops Command said to sit tight and wait for the shooter team."

"Doc doesn't think we have that kind of time, and I agree."

"No disrespect, Boss, but you should have forced him to leave. He needs to be with his wife. If it were me, I'd be gone."

Moyer studied his friend and assistant team leader. "Is that right, Rich?"

"Absolutely. If my Robyn were in Lucy's situation, I'd leave a vacuum in my wake. Wouldn't you do the same if it were Stacy or one of the kids?"

Moyer didn't answer at first. Finally, he said, "I don't know. I don't think a man knows what he'll do until he has to do it. Let's face it, we injure our families every time we make a phone call and say, 'Sorry, Hon, I won't be home for dinner tonight, or any night for the next few weeks.'"

"Can't argue with that. So what's our next step?"

"Like I said earlier, it's time we got proactive."

SANTI STOOD ON THE second-floor balcony of his home and watched the small black dot in the distant sky grow larger as it approached. A sound below him drew his attention away from the approaching helicopter. Hector Cenobio, wearing handcuffs, walked from the door and onto the large carpet of grass that covered the front acre and half of the property. Next to him walked Miguel Costa, his hand clamped on Cenobio's right elbow. So far, his captive had been physically cooperative although stubborn. He didn't expect a struggle. The man had probably never been in a fight, not even as a child. Not that it mattered. Costa was a killer, a man who enjoyed taking the life of another. Fortunately for Santi and his Iranian friends, Cenobio loved his family too much to risk their lives even to save his own. That was the problem with relationships—they punched holes in a man's armor, leaving him weak. Santi had no need for love or family.

The cell phone on his belt chimed. He checked the caller ID: Teodoro Grijalva. The call puzzled him. The Secretary of the Interior and he didn't often talk, and when they did it was at the office. He answered.

"To what do I owe this honor?" Santi said.

"El Presidente asked me to call you. I have information he said you'd find important."

"I'm listening." He heard the man take a deep breath.

"This news has come about in an odd fashion, but I will give you the gist of it. Two days ago an American businessman was hit by a car and taken to Clinica Caracas. Doctors treated him. I am told his injuries were minor."

Teodoro's Department of Interior oversaw the four intelligence agencies that replaced the DISIP secret police and the DIM military intelligence agency in 2008. "And how does this concern me? If an American businessman is stupid enough to step in front of a car, he deserves a trip to the hospital."

"There's more. The attending physician noticed a tattoo on the man's upper arm. It was a picture of military tags."

"Tell me more about these tags."

"The physician remembered enough to draw them for police. The man left the hospital without checking out, and I don't need an intelligence agency to tell me that is suspicious. I have a photocopy of the doctor's drawing. There are two tags—one bears the name 'Mark Rasor' and has the dates '1972–1974'; the other reads, 'Pete Rasor' and the date '2006' but no second date."

"This happened two days ago? Why have you taken so long to speak to me?"

"Layers of incompetence. The doctor didn't realize the patient was gone until the police came to fill out a report. The police launched a search, which came up empty. Since the tattoo was military in nature, they reported it to our military. From there it worked its way up to me. I mentioned it to our president during this morning's briefing. He seemed concerned and insisted that I call you." He paused. "Is there something going on I should know about?"

"No. What is being done now?"

"The search continues. We have some photos taken from security cameras. There are three people: a large black man, a Hispanic, and the injured American. They don't look military, but we both know what that means."

"You still have eyes on the embassy?"

"Always."

"Hotels."

"The police are searching the hotels."

Santi thought for a moment. "They won't stay in the same hotel. Too obvious. Send me everything you have so far. I want these men found." He hung up and called out from the balcony rail, "Miguel! Take him back to the house. We're not leaving just yet."

CHAPTER 37

STACY HUNG UP THE phone and sighed with relief. The school atten-dance administrator confirmed that Rob's homeroom instructor had checked his name off the attendance list. At least she knew Rob was safe. When he got home that might change. A fury grew in her like a funnel cloud itching to touch Earth. The relief she felt a moment before melted like wax. Stacy didn't need this right now. It was bad enough that her husband was off doing something that could get him killed, but he was doing it with what may be a deadly illness—an illness she was not supposed to know about.

She toyed with the idea of going to the school and pulling Rob from class by his constantly mussed hair. It would embarrass him in front of his friends and that made the thought all the sweeter. The thought faded. She would never do that. What would it achieve? Most likely it would make things worse and that was the last thing she needed now.

The more she thought about the situation, the more confused she became. One thing she did know: for the first time in her life, she was glad Eric wasn't around. Eric and Rob's relationship was strained on the best days. This little fiasco would set Eric off, and Rob, ever his father's son, would react in kind.

But something had to be done. Stacy picked up the phone and dialed a number. "Chaplain Bartley, please."

THE DOOR TO THE bathroom opened and the tall, dark-skinned man stepped to the threshold. He held several plastic-wrapped items in his hand. He eyed her for long moments, and Julia didn't need to be a mind reader to know what he was thinking. She remained seated on the floor, partly to deny him any measure of respect, but mostly to keep hidden the sharpened metal lever she had taken from the toilet tank last night.

The man tossed the objects to the floor. She eyed them. Frozen breakfast burritos. She didn't speak, didn't move. The man frowned and stepped from the room, closing and locking the door again.

"Can we, Mamá?" Lina asked. "I'm hungry."

Julia picked up the food items. They were warm. Apparently there was a microwave nearby. She examined the wrappers, scrutinizing every inch. They didn't appear to have been tampered with. She opened one and sniffed. It smelled exactly as she thought it should. Breaking the burrito in half, she stuck a finger in the scrambled eggs, cheese, and salsa then licked it. Nothing offensive.

"I think it's safe." She gave the burrito to Lina.

"I don't want one," Nestor said. "I don't want their food."

Julia opened another burrito and offered it to him anyway. "It is important that we keep up our strength. We don't know what lies ahead."

"They want to kill us, Mamá. That's what lies ahead."

"There will be no more talk like that, Nestor." There was no anger in Julia's words.

"Papa says a man always faces the truth. I'm facing the truth like he would want me to do."

"I am proud of you, son. You have shown great courage. You too, Lina. But facing the truth doesn't mean giving up. We must be prepared. Eat something, son."

Nestor took the burrito and ate, but he made a point of scowling with every bite.

Julia stared at the door. She had a feeling the next time it opened bad things would happen. She reached behind her and felt the metal rod she had fashioned into a knife and wondered if she would have the courage to use it when the time came.

☢ ☢ ☢

THERE WERE TWO OTHER people in the hospital room with Lucy—her mother and her sister—yet still she was alone. The words of the doctor played on her mind in an endless loop. "I'm afraid the tests have confirmed our earlier suspicion . . . baby is a danger to your life . . . must act quickly . . . I know this is difficult to hear . . ."

She couldn't remember much of what he'd said. She did, however, remember her part of the conversation.

"No."

"You understand that your life is in danger. The odds are slim that you can successfully carry the baby to viability." His words were firm but had no edge to them. His face revealed the difficulty he had in delivering the news.

"No."

"Ms. Medina, taking the baby now is the only way I can save your life."

She shook her head. "I will not kill my baby, not even to save my life."

"Ms. Medina, the uterus has already partially detached from the abdominal wall and is causing internal bleeding. If the condition worsens, it will die anyway—"

"My baby is not an 'it'—he is my boy. His name is Tito, named after my grandfather."

"I apologize. It's just that it sometimes makes it easier if we don't think of the fetus as—"

"As what, Doctor? A human? I'm his mother. I feel him moving within me. I feel his soul touching mine."

"Have you spoken to your husband?"

"No. He's in the military. The chaplain is trying to reach him."

The doctor pursed his lips. "Do you have other family to help you make a decision?"

"Doctor, listen to me. I've made my decision. Talking to family won't change that."

The conversation ended there but not before the physician took Lucy's hand and squeezed it gently. "I'll check with you later. We'll continue to monitor your blood volume and other indicators. Rest as much as you can."

"Thank you, Doctor."

"I hope you understand that my only motivation is to save a life."

"I have the same motivation."

When Lucy's mother and sister arrived, she relayed the whole of the conversation. Lucy's mother almost collapsed. Once she regained the composure to speak, the argument began. Lucy could see the devastation on her mother's face; she no more wanted to lose her "baby" than Lucy wanted to lose hers.

When the hot words were replaced by loving words, when the flow of tears had mingled all they could, when conversation gave way to hand-holding and caresses, Lucy let her mind hold a thought she never thought it could: She thanked God that Jose was gone. She knew what he'd say. He'd do anything to save her life, and if he could convince her to follow the doctor's recommendations, then he would slowly poison himself year after year with guilt and regret. In a way, she was trying to save his life as well.

HECTOR CONTINUED TO GAZE out his window and wonder what had happened to alter Santi's plans so abruptly. He tried to comfort himself with the idea that someone—someone on the side of justice—had learned of Santi's plans and interrupted them, maybe even rescued his family. He was content to remain a prisoner for now, as long as his wife and children were safe.

From his window he watched the helicopter land and Miguel Costa board. Although some distance separated Hector from Miguel, he was close enough to see the expression on the man's face—an amalgam of anger and concern.

Hector could do nothing but wait and pray and remind himself that as long as there was life, there was hope.

CHAPTER 38

IT HAD ONLY BEEN four hours—more of a nap than a night's sleep. Or a day's sleep, in this case. J. J. rose, slipped into the shower and emerged twenty minutes later cleaner, a little more alert, and just as edgy as when he crawled into the sack.

His body felt better but his mind remained fixed on the hostage family. An old enemy was gaining a beachhead in his mind—impatience. He had excelled in all phases of his training, from classroom to gun range, but taking orders—especially orders he thought were off the mark—strained his discipline. He had made it this far by keeping his mouth shut. He was determined to maintain that policy, but every few minutes the image of the trapped woman flashed on his brain. He could see her looking up, her lips working in prayer, and there he was, just a few feet from her position, unable to save her and her children.

It wasn't that he doubted Moyer's reasons. He knew that certain aspects of a mission took precedence over others. At any moment a soldier might be called upon to undertake an action that would lead to his death. J. J. had accepted that truth before he enlisted, and his years of experience and training had only deepened his willingness to sacrifice himself for the life of another. Not so acceptable was the idea of sitting on his hands while others faced danger.

He padded across the carpeted room and picked up his cell phone. A text message had arrived while he was in the shower. Jose was awake and restless.

JOSE LOOKED LIKE A man at the end of a fifty-mile uphill hike—stooped, red-eyed, and a shade paler than a Hispanic should be. He slipped into the passenger seat of the rental car and J. J. pulled from the parking lot. Normally J. J. would make a crack about Jose's appearance: *Didn't anyone tell you the zombie look is dead?* But he held his tongue. Jose had a right to look bad.

"Where to?" J. J. asked. "Let's grab a couple of sodas. We only have an hour before we spell Caraway and Pete." He paused. "Do you think Pete can finish the course?"

"What? You mean because of his injuries? Yeah, I do. He's stiff as a board, but I think he can move plenty fast enough if he has to. The pain meds I'm giving him won't affect his alertness or judgment."

"What about you?"

Jose turned toward him. "I'm fine. Besides, my flight already left. I'm here for another day or two at least. You're not going to lecture me too, are you?"

"Moyer give you an earful?"

"He threatened to hit me in the throat—several times."

"Ouch. That might hurt some."

Jose pressed his lips together. "Can't hurt more than what I'm feeling right now."

J. J. could hear the pain in his friend's voice. "You know what, let's forget the sodas. Let's just drive. How about it?"

"Fine with me. I just couldn't stand looking at four walls or watching any more television."

J. J. smiled. "At least you can understand the programs. It all sounds like Spanish to me." He maneuvered the auto through the afternoon traffic. He had no destination in mind. Like Jose, he was happy to just be someplace other than a hotel room. "You know the problem with guys like us?"

"We're too good-looking for our own good?"

That made J. J. chuckle. "That goes without saying, but I had something else in mind. Guys have a problem opening up to each other."

"My wife says we don't open up because we don't have anything inside."

"An astute woman. We don't like to open up, and to be honest, that's the way I like it most of the time."

"Most of the time?"

"I'm not trying to be your counselor, Jose. The Lord knows I don't have any skills in that area, but I gotta believe that you're walking on some pretty hot coals. Who wouldn't be? I'm going nuts thinking about the captive woman and I don't know her from Eve. I can't imagine going through what you're going through with your wife."

"You're not going to ask me to share my feelings, are you?"

"No. I wouldn't know what to do with them if you did. I just want you to know that I'm praying for you and your wife."

"I appreciate that, J. J. I really do. I've been saying a few prayers myself."

"Just so you know, if you ever feel like talking, I'm here. Like I said, I have no counseling skills, but I can be a friend." J. J. saw Jose's eyes moisten. "Have you asked Moyer about calling your wife? With the encrypted phone and all, he might allow it."

"No," Jose said. "She'd need an encrypted phone to hear me. And even if she could hear me, her end of the conversation would be open for anyone to overhear. Can't risk her saying something that might give us away."

"Yeah, that occurred to me as soon as I asked the question. Maybe I should have slept another hour. My brain is still a little fried."

J. J.'s phone chimed. The caller ID showed Moyer's pseudonym. "Yes, Boss."

"Sorry to wake you, but we may have a situation."

"Already awake, Boss. Jose's with me. We're taking a little drive before heading over to relieve Billy and Junior."

"How long ago did you leave the hotel?"

"I left about thirty minutes ago and picked up Jose at his place ten minutes later. What situation?"

"I just walked into the lobby and caught sight of a man and two local cops showing pictures at the front desk. I got a look at one of the photos as I walked by. It was Jose. It looked like a snapshot from a security camera. I have to assume the other two photos are of Shaq and Junior, from the hospital."

"The tattoo," J. J. said. The word made Jose's head snap around. "Hang on." J. J. pressed the button that put the phone into speaker mode. J. J. repeated what Moyer said to bring Jose up to speed.

"Shaq is with me. Actually, he's hiding in the bathroom at the moment. Junior and Billy are on surveillance, so we're clear for now. But you know what this means."

"We've been compromised. Do you know if the person at the front desk recognized the photos?"

"I doubt it. Neither you or I were at the hospital, but if they've checked here, they'll check everywhere."

"Not good," J. J. said. "What do we do now?"

"Our new mission is still a go, but we've lost hotel privileges. We have to assume they'll check with the car rental places and will have a make and model and license number for at least one of the cars. We need to lower our profile."

"Understood," J. J. said. "The others know?"

"No, I called you first. I thought you might still be in the room. Hang one sec . . . They're leaving. Sooner or later, however, they're going to find the other two hotels."

"Sounds like time has turned against us," Jose said.

"It always does, Doc. It always does."

Moyer hung up.

"Now I'm really glad I didn't go to the airport," Jose said.

CHAPTER 39

CHAPLAIN PAUL BARTLEY NEVER felt more like a minister than when helping someone through a crisis. Preaching at chapel services was fun, leading Bible studies was intellectually invigorating, but nothing touched his soul more than standing alongside someone in true despair. Most of his job involved proclaiming truth and offering encouragement. Even when on foreign fields like Afghanistan and his two tours in Iraq, where he worked with soldiers who entered harm's way daily, he felt most valuable when he could stand by those who had been emotionally crushed.

Although he loved this aspect of his ministry, he also hated it. Over the years he had faced countless tragedies that left him speechless. Words were some of the most powerful things on Earth. Wars started and ended with words. Still, there were times when words were utterly impotent. The best he could do was to hold a hand, put an arm around a shoulder, and silently pray. In seminary he'd had a professor who taught, "A minister is never more eloquent than when he keeps his mouth shut and his heart open."

Walking through the corridor that led to Lucy Medina's hospital room, his emotions did battle with his soul. An Army chaplain faced many of the same problems civilian ministers did, but he also faced situations his counterparts couldn't imagine. This was one of those times.

He stopped two steps from Lucy's door. Soft voices came from the room. Lucy was not alone, and he felt thankful for that. Bartley inhaled deeply, closed his eyes, and prayed, "Lord, give me the right words," then stepped over the threshold.

Lucy lay in bed, looking at her three guests. Most hospitals allowed only two visitors at a time, but since the other bed remained empty, he assumed the nursing staff would be flexible.

"Chaplain Bartley." Lucy smiled. A magnificent act of courage, Bartley decided. Army wives often showed strength matching that of their husbands.

"Hello, Lucy. I see you've decided to have a party and not invite me."

"Your invitation must be lost in the mail." Her smile wavered. "Chaplain, this is my mother, Amanda, and my sister, Charlene."

"Everyone calls me Char," the younger woman said.

Bartley shook hands with them and with Stacy Moyer, who stood next to the side of the bed closest to the door.

"How are you feeling, Lucy?"

Tears immediately came to her eyes. "They're controlling the pain, but I worry about what the meds are doing to the baby." Bartley saw Amanda and Char exchange glances. "They decided not to move me to the base hospital. They say I'm too unstable."

"This is a nicer place to be," Bartley said. "I assume nothing has changed since yesterday."

She shook her head and drew a hand across her eyes. "No. They still want to . . . They sent in a couple more doctors. Specialists."

"They all agree, Chaplain," Lucy's mother said, "but she refuses to listen." Her words carried no conviction. It didn't take years of counseling experience to see how conflicted the woman was. Bartley couldn't blame her. She stood to lose her daughter or her grandson or both.

He nodded and waited for words to come, but they hovered in his brain like a cloud of gnats. The very act of reaching made them impossible to catch. He caught Stacy's eye.

"You know what, ladies?" she said. "We should give the chaplain some time with Lucy. Let's take a little walk."

Again, Amanda and Char exchanged glances. Stacy took a step toward them then turned toward the door. They got the hint. Moments later Bartley stood alone by Lucy's bed.

"You have news about Jose?"

"Yes, Lucy, I do. I spoke to his commander on the base, who spoke with Sgt. Major Moyer. Jose was to fly home today, but the situation changed and he's still out of country."

"He's all right, isn't he? Please tell me he's all right."

Bartley took her hand. "As far as I know. If he had been hurt, I'm sure I would have been told."

"But he's not coming?"

"Not right away, Lucy. I don't know why. There are some things I can't be told. I believe he is fine but for some reason can't leave right away. I'm sure he'd rather be here with you."

"Good." Lucy looked to the window that overlooked the roof of an adjoining wing.

"Good?"

"They want to take my baby to save my life, Chaplain. Jose would agree with them. He loves his children more than life, but he also loves me. I know this, and I know that if he had to choose between me and our unborn, he'd feel compelled to save me."

"I suppose that's understandable."

"It is wonderful to be loved so much, but I know we would both pay for the decision the rest of our lives."

"What do you mean, 'pay'?"

"Every time we looked at each other we would remember the decision we made, and the child we sacrificed so I could live."

Bartley felt as if some creature were eating its way out of his gut. "Lucy . . ." He had to start over. "I don't know how to advise you. I used to think ministers had all the answers, but we don't. We never have. I believe all life is sacred, yet I'm in the Army and we are called upon to engage in war. People die—die by our hands. We do this because we also believe in justice. But I don't know what is just here, Lucy. You are willing to die so that your child might live, but there is a good chance that baby may perish with you and we lose both of you."

"As long as there is a chance that I can carry the baby long enough for him to live, then I will try."

"What can I do for you, Lucy?"

"Pray."

"I understand you're Roman Catholic. Do you want me to arrange to have a priest stop by?"

She nodded. "Will you tell my mother and sister about Jose?"

"Yes. May I pray for you?"

"Yes."

Bartley gave her arm a squeeze, closed his eyes, and prayed, trying to sound professional. Fifteen seconds into the prayer, he gave that up and uttered his words with an honesty that came from the deepest part of the soul.

☢ ☢ ☢

STACY WATCHED CHAPLAIN BARTLEY emerge from the hospital room looking thinner and more fragile than when he entered. He stopped to talk with the three women.

"Thank you for allowing me some time alone with Lucy." He paused and looked down the hall. "Let's step over here for a moment." The suggestion made Stacy nervous.

"What's wrong?" Char asked.

"I had some news to share with Lucy. She asked me to let you know."

Stacy saw the two women stiffen.

Bartley continued. "As you know, the Army is trying to get Jose back as soon as possible. He made arrangements to fly home but chose to stay—"

"Why would he do that?" Amanda snapped. "He needs to be with his wife and child."

Raising a hand, Bartley said, "Hang on. Of course, you are right, and I'm certain this is where he wants to be. Apparently something came up."

"What could be more important than this?" Amanda asked.

"I don't have an answer for you. I don't know where the team is or what they are doing. That's not the kind of information they give a chaplain. I can only assume the situation must be serious for Jose to make this decision."

"Serious? This is serious! My daughter may die."

Stacy couldn't remain silent. "The chaplain knows that. He's just doing his job."

Amanda's face darkened. "Lucy said your husband leads Jose's team. Why doesn't your husband let him come home?"

Bartley stepped in. "It's my understanding that Jose chose to stay."

"Mother, settle down." Char placed a hand on the older woman's shoulder.

"Her husband could have ordered Jose to leave."

"We don't know that," Stacy said. "We don't know what the situation is." She knew enough about soldier-thinking to know that something serious was up, and that made her worry about Eric.

Amanda pushed past Bartley, and Char followed.

"That could have gone better," Bartley said. "I don't think I'll be welcome back anytime soon."

"Their emotions are getting the best of them. Not that I can blame them."

"You all right?"

"Just worried about Eric."

Bartley nodded. "Having a rebellious teenage son doesn't help. Let's go to the cafeteria and have a soda or coffee. We can finish our conversation about Rob."

"Are you sure you feel up to that?"

"Of course. It's what we chaplains do."

CHAPTER 40

MIGUEL COSTA STEPPED FROM the helicopter the moment it touched the helo pad and jogged to the mansion. Santi stood on the balcony watching. Costa could feel the man's eyes boring into him. His boss would be pleased with the good news, not so pleased with the bad.

Costa plunged through the front door and up the grand staircase that led to the second floor and the expansive balcony. He found Santi still staring into the surrounding jungle, binoculars held to his eyes. He didn't turn when Costa opened the French doors and stepped onto the deck. He took several deep breaths to replace what he had expelled sprinting up the slope to the house.

"What have you found?" Santi didn't turn.

"We believe the surrounding area to be secure. I did an aerial survey and saw no indication of intrusion."

"The jungle canopy is too thick for a proper aerial survey."

"Yes, Minister, it is. I also sent men to scout the area. All have reported in, and as yet there is no indication of intruders."

"Did they search beyond the motion detectors' perimeter?" He lowered the binoculars and finally turned to Costa.

"Yes, sir."

"Still, a well-trained commando team might escape detection."

"Perhaps, but they wouldn't get past the motion detectors without disabling them. To be sure, I had the men check each detector, and they report that all is as it should be. No one has touched them."

"Video?"

"I've added a guard to the video surveillance post. We have one man watching the monitors and another reviewing footage from the last few days. So far, no sign of intruders."

Santi nodded, but his face remained grim. "We have to assume that something is afoot. If the injured American with the tattoo had stayed in the hospital and cooperated with the police, I'd be less suspicious. His fleeing the hospital tells us that we must keep up our guard."

"I have an operative working with the police. They're searching hotels. I expect to hear from them soon—" Costa's cell phone sounded. He answered, listened, then ended the call. "A rental car employee at the airport recognized two of the men from the hospital surveillance photos."

Santi set the binoculars on the balcony rail and put his hands behind his back. Costa had seen this before. His employer was a methodical man prone to logic over emotion—most of the time. When the emotions kicked in, Santi became as volatile as unstable dynamite.

"Nothing unusual in that," Santi said. "We have an open airport. We know the U.S. sends spies to our land. The question is, what do they want? The fact that they are here during this . . .

operation . . . raises my suspicions. It may be only a coincidence, but we must assume they know about our plans. If they do not, we lose nothing."

"Understood, sir."

"I've made arrangements for additional support. We will have two dozen soldiers here to set up another perimeter and search the jungle."

"What do we do with Cenobio?"

"Our friends are expecting to receive their package. The longer we wait, the greater opportunity we give our enemies to interfere. Have you heard from our people in the city?"

"Yes, sir. I checked with them just before landing. They say they have seen nothing unusual."

"And the woman?

"She and the children are confined to a small room."

"I wonder . . ."

"Sir?"

Santi didn't answer at first. Instead he paced, turning every six steps. "I wonder if the enemy knows about the other location."

"I don't see how that is possible, sir. It is well hidden and known only to a handful of people."

"If these Americans are part of a military operation, then there would have been an advance intelligence team, maybe spies that are already in country." He stopped, tilted his head back, and gazed at the blue sky. "We have three men on scene now, correct?"

"Yes, sir. Well, actually, the Iranians have three men guarding the woman and children."

"Time is running out. We need to act quickly."

"What do you want to do?"

"Get Dr. Cenobio."

☢ ☢ ☢

ON NUMEROUS OCCASIONS MOYER had spent days, hidden from sight, watching some object of concern to his government. In such situations, time moved at tortoise speeds, and that was fine with him. A good soldier not only knew how to spring into action at a moment's notice; he also knew how to hunker down and wait.

This last quality now eluded Moyer.

J. J. had been eager to charge in and rescue the woman and kids. Moyer understood that. J. J. was young, impetuous, full of vinegar and gung-ho attitude. Impatience had killed too many men. Moyer determined that none of his team would die needlessly. He would be patient.

Such decisions are easy to speak even in the vault of one's own mind, but to exercise patience is an entirely different matter. Moyer had struck the calm, reserved, cautious pose of a leader, but inside he was dying to do something, anything.

It was the cancer thing. Every hour his intestines grumbled, cramped, churned, twisted, ached, and occasionally bled. Every abnormal sensation reminded him that cells in his body had turned traitor, ending his career and possibly his life.

Moyer tried to put such thoughts out of his mind. Everyone died. Death held no fear for him. The demise of his career proved a different matter. Assuming the disease didn't kill him, what would he do for a living? He'd have some retirement from the Army but not enough to support a family of four, two of which would probably want to go to college. He thought of Rob. Well, at least one would want to go to college.

Normally thinking of his son made Moyer angry. The kid had so much potential yet chose to waste his opportunities. While Moyer had to admit that his own teenage years had added gray to the heads of his parents, he had never been disrespectful and never flushed his future before it had a chance to become a reality.

For some reason the image of Rob flashing on his mind made Moyer miss his son.

"You okay, Boss?" J. J. looked up from the monitors in the panel truck.

"Yeah. Why?"

"You seemed a long way away."

"Just thinking things through." Moyer directed his attention to the monitors. The images hadn't changed. "Caraway tells me we'll have to replace the batteries in the fiber-optic cam if we want to keep it running."

"The batteries on the LVRS units too. Maybe tomorrow."

Moyer frowned. Every excursion to the rooftop could lead to discovery.

"Do you think they're waiting because of Pete's tattoo?" J. J. asked without moving his eyes from the monitors.

"Yeah, I do. It's what I'd do. If I were running their operation and someone told me about a dog-tag tattoo on an American's arm, and then that American sneaks out of the hospital, I'd be real suspicious."

"How long do you think they'll wait? Everything we've seen makes me think that this was supposed to be a short turnaround. Maybe I should ask, how long *can* they wait?"

"They hold all the aces for the moment."

"I don't know how much longer that poor woman can hold out. She's got to be going out of her mind."

"She'll hang in there," Moyer said. "She's a mother. She'll keep herself together for the kids."

"I've been thinking about how we can make entry. There are windows for the office and a couple that open to the work area.

We split the team. Alpha team breaks the work-area window and tosses a couple of flash-bang grenades. I'm sure they can pop one or two of the bad guys through the window. Bravo team makes entry through the window on the other side of the building, the one that leads to the offices. They can neutralize any targets that remain. Since the woman and children are locked in the room, the grenades won't stun them. We snatch and go."

"And what about Cenobio? How do we find and deal with him? Saving his family won't keep him out of the hands of the Iranians. He's got to be our primary focus."

"But, Boss—"

"Drop it, Colt. I want to save that woman as much as you. Maybe more so; I got a wife and children. We stick to the plan."

"Understood, Boss."

What Moyer didn't tell J. J. was that the plan was about to change. If this was going to be his last mission, then it would be one to remember.

CHAPTER 41

CHAPLAIN BARTLEY, DECKED OUT in his combat uniform, stood in the office of the high school and stared at the somber son of Eric and Stacy Moyer. The kid oozed bad attitude. This wasn't going to be easy.

"Who are you?" the boy asked.

Bartley corrected himself: Rob Moyer was no boy. Although only sixteen, he stood tall and lanky. Yet he wasn't a man either and that was the problem. Rob traveled that twilight area between adult and kid. Most people his age found a way to enjoy these awkward years, while others seemed to twist every bit of pain and angst possible out of this time, choosing to play the role of misunderstood outcast. Such kids seemed to breed misery, as if making others unhappy was their calling in life.

Bartley had seen it more times than he could count. Enduring normal teenage years taxed most people Rob's age; being tied to the Army by no choice of your own made it worse. While some kids relished the idea that their mothers or fathers were soldiers, the rebellious ones despised what their parents did. Rob was clearly a charter member of the latter group.

"My name is Paul Bartley."

"So what do you want with me?"

Bartley handed him a note. He read it. "So my mother put you up to this."

"She did."

"The note says I should go with you. Is she all right?"

"Yes."

"And my sister?"

"She's okay too."

Rob shrugged. "Then I don't see any reason to go with you."

"Interesting."

"What's interesting?"

"You didn't ask about your father." Bartley watched the color drain from the boy's face and his eyes skip to the office staff in earshot. "As far as I know, he's fine." He thought he saw the boy relax slightly.

"Let's take a ride, Rob. I've cleared it with the school."

"I don't want to go with you." He took a step back.

"Listen, Rob. Just relax. I'm not a cop. I'm not going to lecture you. I just want to talk."

Two beefy boys wearing letterman jackets stepped into the office. "I don't want to talk."

Bartley gazed at the athletes for a moment. "It's your call, Rob. If you're afraid, well, I understand."

"I didn't say I was afraid."

"Frightened people seldom do." Bartley started for the door.

"I'm not afraid."

"Good. I was thinking of a burger. I skipped lunch. Let's go." Bartley didn't wait for Rob to respond. He stepped to the office door and held it open. "Coming?"

"Yeah, I guess."

Bartley wasn't sure what Rob expected but judging by his expression he didn't expect a classic black '68 Camaro SS convertible. "You like cars?"

"Yeah, they're okay, I guess."

"You guess, huh? Got your driver's license yet?"

Rob's eyes widened. "Sure. Got it two months ago."

Bartley jiggled the keys. "Think you can handle it? It's an automatic so you don't have to worry about shifting—"

"I can handle it."

"In that case, mount up, cowboy." He tossed him the keys and slipped into the front passenger seat. Rob was in the car a second later.

"Pristine, man. You must have dumped some serious coin to get this restored."

"It keeps me poor. My father bought it. He gave it to me when I enlisted. Gave my brother a '64½ Mustang. Dad was into cars."

"I guess so. Where to?"

"Jimmie's makes a decent burger. Do you know where that is?"

Rob inserted the key and started the engine. The throaty rumble vibrated through the car. "Yeah, I know where it is."

"Then what are you waiting for?"

"I'm trying to figure out the longest path there."

Bartley laughed. "I think I'm gonna like you. Just remember this is a school zone—"

In a single motion, Rob dropped the car into gear. The tires squealed as he pulled from the curb.

☢☢ ☢☢ ☢☢

"YOU SEEM DISTRACTED, ORLA."

Orla Caraway looked up from her chicken salad and stared at the man on the other side of the restaurant table. "Sorry. Lost in thought."

"Lost in thought, is it? I know that expression." Albert Crenshaw wore a gray suit that covered his broad shoulders—shoulders made broad by genetics not exercise. Although trim and fit, the only exercise he committed to was fifteen minutes on a slow-moving treadmill three times a week and eighteen holes of golf as often as possible.

"And what expression is that?"

He set his fork down on the half-eaten broiled salmon on wild rice. His eyes sparkled. "It's sort of a cross between indigestion and pity. It happens every time you think of your ex."

"You know me that well?"

"We've been dating for nine months and been engaged for three. During that time I've made a point of memorizing every detail about you."

Although she could think of no reason to do so, Orla blushed. "It must be the keen legal mind of yours. You attorneys are always looking for ways to gain advantage over other people."

"Wait a minute now. I'm a real estate attorney—only partly slimy."

They met at a continuing education seminar for real estate agents. Real estate law grew more complex every year. A week later, after admitting to some behind-the-scenes research, he asked her out. She was pleasantly surprised when he suggested dinner after a Saturday-night service at his church. Orla accepted. Three weeks later he came to her apartment and met Sean, her six–year-old son. They hit it off. Albert became so fond of Sean that he often insisted on including him on their dates. Orla had had to put her foot down.

"There's nothing slimy about you." She reached across the table and took his hand. Albert was five years older and showing just the right amount of gray at the temples, just the right spread of wrinkles around the eyes.

"So what's on your mind?"

Orla pulled back and looked out the window. A stream of slow-moving traffic clogged the nearby freeway. "You're right. I was thinking about Martin."

"You said he called to give you a bad time about child support."

"He did. I feel awful. I know he doesn't make executive-level money. He's a soldier. Supporting himself and paying alimony and child support can't leave him with much."

"Look, Orla, I've never met the guy. But from what you've told me, you're better off without him."

"I know. He's a good man in many ways but very confused."

"Was he a good father?"

Orla frowned. "No. But he wasn't cruel—just never engaged."

"Look, sweetheart, if it's money that worries you, let me help. We'll be married in two months, and you and Sean will be moving into my condo. What difference does it make if I start taking some responsibility right now?"

Pressing her lips together she struggled with how to explain what he surely wouldn't understand. "I guess it's the principle of the thing. Sean is his son. Martin should step up to that responsibility."

"I agree, but that doesn't mean he will. You are certainly within your rights to pursue payment of back child support. Those are serious, court-mandated obligations. He can get himself into trouble by avoiding those duties."

"If I wanted to get him in trouble, Albert, I'd call his commanding officer. That'd cost him in more ways than cash." She leaned forward again and kept her voice low. "I have no desire to do that. The Army is the one thing he truly loves. Everything else in life is pure infatuation, and that included me and Sean."

"That's just wrong on so many levels."

"I suppose." She looked Albert in the eyes. "You were never in the military, were you?"

"You know I wasn't. I went straight to college then law school."

"I know, I know. Nonmilitary people have trouble understanding the mind-set of men and women who make a career of the service. It's a sacrificial commitment. Low pay, moving every few years, and in times like ours, being shipped overseas where there's a good possibility they may not come back whole if they come back at all. It takes a certain kind of person to do that. Oh, there are those who enlist for a short period of time and are glad to be out once their commitment is up. There's nothing wrong with that, but the career soldier is a different breed."

"I can't imagine every career soldier is like Martin."

"They're not. Most are as honest as a person can be. My point is that a career man like Martin breathes a different kind of air from the rest of us."

"I think you're worried about him."

"Worried? Maybe."

"You never told me much about the phone conversation other than it ended abruptly."

She stabbed at the salad. "I heard his cell phone ring."

"Um, Orla, that's what cell phones do."

"Soldiers in Martin's line of work sometimes receive coded calls. He never explained it to me, but when the call comes they have a limited amount of time to get things together, say good-bye, and leave for wherever their mission takes them. Martin got that kind of call."

"Ah. And you're worried about him." He raised an eyebrow. "You're a remarkable woman, Orla Caraway. Your former husband runs off with another woman; then when he's dumped he tries to come back to you. You divorce, but he refuses to pay alimony and child support. But when he gets called up, you start worrying about him."

"Are you saying I shouldn't be concerned?"

Albert rubbed his chin. "No. It's the Christlike thing to do. The irony of it all is just a bit much for me."

Orla sighed. "I've been praying for him. He hates Christians. He thinks my faith is what ultimately doomed our marriage."

Albert laughed. "I'm sorry. You've told me that before, but I can't wrap my mind around it. He's an adulterer who abandons his family then feels slighted when you won't run back into his arms."

"I came to Christ during the months he was gone. It's what got me through everything. I suppose I would have survived without faith, but not nearly with the sanity and dignity." She gave up on the salad. "In some ways, Martin is a miserable pain in my life, but he is also a man of some honor. Maybe I should pray that he grows up."

"If he did, would it change our relationship? Are you regretting the divorce?"

"No. My pastor believes the divorce is biblical. Martin did commit adultery and abandon his family. I just hate the idea of his being halfway around the world without someone at home caring what happens to him."

"If you didn't care, you wouldn't be praying for him."

"I think I'll drop the alimony and child support case. Sean and I will find a way to get along."

"You've found a way, Orla. I've told you, I'll take care of you. Money means very little to me. Soon we'll be sharing a bank account. You need to understand: I love you and Sean. Nothing brings me greater joy than seeing you two happy."

"You're a good person, Albert."

"My mother always said so."

CHAPTER 42

HECTOR CENOBIO HAD NEVER been in a helicopter before, although he had wanted to do so since he was a child. Not under such circumstances, however. He lowered his head and kept his face turned to the ground to keep the rotor blast from his eyes. Costa moved him forward with a tight hand on Hector's elbow. Surrendering to an urge of defiance, Hector yanked his arm free but continued toward the open door of the helicopter. The fenced perimeter and the thick jungle beyond meant there was nowhere for Hector to run. Besides, he could do his family no good by escaping—at least not by escaping here.

A nylon zip cord held his wrists together, making the climb into the helicopter more difficult than if his hands were free. Still, he managed it without help. The interior of the business craft sported two rows of three leather seats each. The seats faced each other.

"Move over," Costa ordered and slipped in behind Hector. "All the way to the other side."

He did as told, plopping down next to the window on the starboard side. Costa reached across Hector and snapped the safety belt.

"I didn't know you cared."

"Don't press my patience, Dr. Cenobio. I have very little of it left." Although there were five other seats available in the helicopter, Costa sat in the seat to Hector's left. Two minutes later he knew why: Antonio Santi slipped into the cabin. A man with him closed the door once the foreign minister sat. The noise of the large motors and the spinning rotors were nearly shut out by the well-insulated hull. Seconds later the craft lifted into the air, and Hector's stomach dropped like an elevator in freefall, partly from their rapid rise and partly because he feared what the next hour would bring.

"What happens now?" he asked.

"You do as you're told," Costa said.

Hector turned to the window. Below him the variegated greens of the jungle scrolled by. In the jungle lived jaguars, anacondas, and boa constrictors, any of which would make better and safer company than Santi and Costa.

Santi sat at the far end of the opposing row of three seats. Hector surmised that Costa pushed him to the starboard side of the craft to put as much distance between him and his boss. Perhaps he feared Hector would attack the foreign minister.

"When do I see my family?" Hector spoke louder than necessary.

"If you behave, then soon. If you cause trouble, then never."

"Have I caused you any trouble yet?"

Costa looked at him. "Desperate men are prone to stupidity, even intelligent men like you."

Hector turned to Santi. "Does President Chavez know you are doing this?"

Pulling his eyes from the window, Santi stared at Hector for several long moments. "Tell me, Dr. Cenobio, why did you abandon your country?"

"Abandon my country? Is that what I did?"

Santi turned in his seat. "Were you not born here? Did you not receive an early education as good as anywhere in the world?"

"I'm not an expert on grammar school education—"

"Answer me!"

The man's tone startled Hector. He had been aggravating Santi on purpose—a childish effort, perhaps, to show courage where none was present.

"My early education was sufficient."

"Did your country not provide you with safety, health care, a home?"

Hector gave a short nod.

"Yet you leave it behind."

"I was accepted to a college in the United States. After graduate school I was offered a teaching and research position at a university in Canada. Of course, that meant I had to live there."

"Did it mean you had to surrender your Venezuelan citizenship?"

"It seemed the right thing to do if I was going to live in the country for the rest of my career."

"We have fine universities here, Dr. Cenobio. You could have helped your country raise better scientists, but you chose to reject the country of your birth."

"I don't expect you to understand," Hector said. "The science community is rather cliquish. Where one is educated matters as much as the degrees earned. In some cases, having a PhD in a subject isn't enough; the graduate school itself is considered, and in some circles even the major professor who oversaw the research and dissertation work. I had to choose my institutions carefully."

Santi leaned forward and Hector leaned back as if the man's gaze could bore through his skull. "I've spent my life in politics and in power; I know a liar when I see one. All those things may be true, but you left Venezuela for other reasons, didn't you?"

"Yes."

"Tell me."

"Does it matter?"

Santi unsnapped his safety belt and backhanded him. Then, as if he had just swatted a fly, Santi returned to his seat and buckled again. The pain from the blow fired through Hector's head and down his neck. Perhaps Costa sat Hector where he did to protect him from his boss. If so, it hadn't worked.

Hector worked his jaw. "I left because thugs like you were taking over the country." He prepared himself for another assault, but it never came. Instead, Santi nodded.

"This is a difficult world, Dr. Cenobio. Difficult indeed. Unrest in our own country is bad enough, but when it is fomented by foreign interference, it is even dangerous. Every week I must read reports about interference by the United States and its allies attempting to undermine our government and our president. Their spies move across our borders, infiltrate our political enemies, and publish lies about us. We are a noble country with noble goals."

"Lies?" Hector couldn't stifle his laughter. "I've been taken against my will, my family has been abducted, and you plan to turn us over to the Iranians. And you consider yourself noble? You, sir, are a criminal and nothing more."

Costa put a hand on Hector's shoulder.

"No, let him speak," Santi said. "His words don't frighten me."

"Why should they frighten you? You're going to hand me off to an unstable nation, or some faction of that nation. Why?"

"There are certain . . . returns."

"For you or for Venezuela?"

Santi's face darkened. "All I do, I do for my country."

"What you do, you do for yourself."

"I don't expect you to understand."

"I don't expect you to understand this, but God is not mocked. What a man sows, he shall reap."

This time Santi laughed. "I thought scientists were all atheists."

"Not all of us."

"Well, feel free to pray all you want, Dr. Cenobio, because only a miracle will save you."

"I'm in God's hands no matter what happens."

This made Santi smile. "It appears, Doctor, you are in *my* hands. As is the fate of your family."

"You will not kill my family. It is the only hold you have over me. I've given this some thought: The Iranians will need them to keep me working. If my family is killed, then I will have no motivation to do the work they want. And don't think you can torture me into submission. Without my family, torture would just be another outlet for my grief."

"Your words are brave, but surprisingly your logic is weak." Again Santi leaned forward. "You are right. We would not kill your family—not all of them at least. Tell me, Dr. Cenobio, which of your family would you least regret losing? Your wife? Maybe your little girl."

Hector felt sick enough to vomit.

CHAPTER 43

ROB HAD CHANGED THEIR destination since Chaplain Bartley let him choose the burger joint he wanted. To Bartley's relief and surprise, Rob had stayed beneath the speed limit, didn't roll through STOP signs, blow through red lights, or sideswipe any cars. So far, so good. Rob had deftly pulled the car into a space at the Sonic drive-in. Bartley noticed that the young man had surveyed the area and seemed happy that several short-day students from the high school were parked in other slots. He had been seen behind the wheel of a classic Camaro convertible.

A few minutes later they had ordered, and Bartley knew he was dealing with a teenager: Rob ordered enough food for two men.

Rob ran a hand over the dashboard. "This is sure a sweet ride. Wow, is that an eight-track player?" He fingered the controls of the stereo.

"Yup. It still works. Maybe on the way back, I let you listen to some real music."

"Real music, huh? What do you call real music?"

"Okay, it was real music for my dad. Blood, Sweat, and Tears. Tommy James & the Shondells. Otis Redding. The Rascals. Oh, and Donovan. Man, my dad loved Donovan. The eight-track had already given way to cassette players before I was born, but every time I rode in this car with my dad, he played the music of the late sixties and the seventies. Got to where I liked it."

"What's a Donovan?"

Bartley chuckled. "Donavan is a who, not a what. Folk-style ballads, velvety-smooth voice. A child of the Love Generation."

"Never heard of him."

"Pity."

Silence filled the space between them. Bartley started to say something when he saw a Sonic employee exit the front door of the restaurant and walk in their direction. He carried a plastic tray with what looked like their order. A minute later the aroma of freshly fried burgers and onion rings settled in the open cabin of the car. Bartley told the truth when he said he hadn't eaten lunch. The food tasted better than he thought possible.

Rob downed the first burger like a man at the end of a week-long fast. He unwrapped the second and took a bite. With a full mouth he muttered, "So, my mom put you up to this."

Bartley wiped his mouth with a napkin. "Yup. She sure did." Rob stared at him. "What?"

"I didn't expect a straight answer. I figured you'd have some excuse ready."

"I don't need an excuse. The truth works great for me."

"You should tell my dad about it."

"What's that mean?" Bartley grabbed an onion ring. "Your dad not good with the truth?"

"He wouldn't recognize it if he stepped in a puddle of it."

"Ouch. Harsh."

"Maybe, but you're the one who said truth works."

"You think he's been lying to you?"

Rob returned to his second burger but stopped before taking a bite. "He doesn't so much tell lies as he lives them."

"You'll have to explain that to me."

"You wouldn't understand. You're probably no different."

Bartley heard some heat in the words. "Best I can tell, we've only known each other twenty minutes. Can't learn much about a man in twenty minutes. Well, not usually. Twenty minutes in battle reveals a lot about a person's character."

"You see, that's it. That's it right there. Everything is about fighting with you guys. My dad sees everything through Army eyes. He's probably going to force me to enlist the day after I graduate."

"No one can force you to enlist in the Army, Rob."

"Yeah? Well you don't know my dad."

"My brother does and he speaks highly of him. They serve on the same team."

"So your brother is off saving the world, too."

Bartley ignored the sarcasm. "As we speak. Wherever he is."

"He didn't tell you where the Army was sending him? I mean you're an officer and everything. And you're his brother."

"I was with him when he got the call. We were mountain biking. To answer your question, no he didn't tell me and I didn't ask. I'm not part of his unit, therefore I don't have a need to know where he is and what he's doing. My being an officer has nothing to do with it."

"But don't you want to know?"

"Yeah, I do. I pray for him daily. I think of him hourly."

Rob shook his head. "It's not right. My dad didn't even come home to say good-bye. He just left."

"That's a shame. Maybe he couldn't get home in time. You know, guys in your dad's position have to report within a certain amount of time. You were at school anyway, weren't you?"

"What difference does that make? He's done this before. Get a call and leave right after. It's killing my mom."

"She looked pretty strong when I talked to her, but I can tell something is bothering her."

"Ya think? She never knows when he's leaving or if he'll ever come back."

"They also serve who only stand and wait."

"What?" Rob gave a quizzical look.

"It's the last line of a poem written by John Milton. 'On His Blindness.' He was writing about Christian service, but I've often thought those words applied to family members of the military who stand and wait for a loved one to return. In many ways it is as noble a service as that provided by the soldier. Your job is not easy, pal, and knowing that you're not alone in it doesn't help much."

"It doesn't matter. Things are better at home when he's gone."

"If it's so much better, then why didn't you go home last night?"

"So that's what all this is about." Rob delayed his answer, choosing to finish the last bit of his burger. Bartley didn't press him. "Well, I wasn't doing anything illegal, if that's what she's worried about."

"I think she's more worried about you than about what you did or didn't do."

"I can't help that. All I did was go to a friend's for band practice. We practiced late then played some video games. I fell asleep on the sofa."

"And it didn't occur to call your mother this morning?"

Rob turned away. "It's no big deal."

"It is to your mother." Bartley shifted in his seat. "Look, let's do a little man-to-man talking here. You just told me that your father lives a lie, that his work forces him to leave on short notice. I don't have to have a degree in psychology to see that bugs you. Well, it should. No one likes it. I guarantee your dad doesn't like it any more than you."

"I wouldn't bet on it."

"Well, Rob, I would. Here's my point: Last night when you didn't go home and didn't bother to warn your mother, you did the same thing you accuse your father of doing, except he's fulfilling a responsibility. You were just irresponsible."

"I don't need this." Rob reached for the door, but Bartley had a hand on his shoulder before he could move.

"Sit still for a moment. Did you think because I was a chaplain I would pat your hand and tell you to be a good boy? I'm not here to make your life miserable; I'm here to add a little wisdom."

"Fine. Talk. Just do it fast."

"Do you really care about what your father's Army career is doing to your mom and the family?"

"Yes. Of course. Who wouldn't be?"

"You know what I think you're really worried about? I think you're worried about being a man."

"What's that supposed to mean?"

"I think you're worried that one day your father will not come home. I think you're afraid that if he's killed, his death will reveal how much you really love him."

"You're crazy."

"I also think you're afraid of becoming the man of the house."

"That's stupid." Again, Rob turned away.

"Is it? Look at me, Rob. I said look at me." Rob turned. "Being sixteen is tough work. Being the father of a sixteen-year-old is just as hard. Everyday you take a step closer to manhood. It's natural for you and your father to clash from time to time. Being the son of an Army team leader is even worse. Frankly I'm impressed that you're not more goofy than you are."

"Hey!"

Bartley laughed. "Okay, the last line was a joke, but I mean it when I say I'm impressed with you. Most other guys your age have no idea what it's like to be the son of a Spec Ops soldier. Let me tell you something, Rob. I ship out with these guys. I talk to them every day—here and overseas when I'm deployed. They think about two things and two things only: their jobs and getting home to their families. I take it your dad is hard on you."

"You can say that again. He's always pushing me to be more, do more. He just wants to make me into a soldier like him. Well, I don't want to be a soldier."

"So don't become one. Become what you want to be."

"My dad won't let me."

"Has he ever told you he wants you to go into the Army?"

Rob hesitated. "Not in so many words."

Bartley frowned. "Let me tell you what your dad is doing. I've seen this a hundred times, so I recognize it. Your dad is tough on you because he wants you to be tough—not so you can be a soldier but so you can protect the family if the worst happens."

The teenager's mouth opened but no words came out.

"That's right, Rob. The thing that frightens a soldier like your father most isn't AK-47 fire, improvised bombs, or mortar attacks; it's leaving his family in the lurch, leaving his kids fatherless and his wife without a husband. Rob, I've seen big, bold men weep over that one fear. They can look a heavily armed Taliban soldier in the eye without flinching, but the thought of leaving their family alone melts them like butter in a frying pan."

Bartley took his hand from Rob's shoulder. "You and your father are going to knock heads from time to time, but you're too smart not to know that's normal. You're also too smart not to know that I'm right. Whatever happens, son, I'm convinced your mother and sister can count on you."

"Done?"

Bartley nodded. Rob was doing his best to act like the words had just bounced off his steel exterior, but Chaplain Bartley could see the boy got the message.

"Rob, your mother needs you right now. Her plate is full with your dad gone and with the help she's trying to provide to Lucy."

"That the pregnant woman? How's she doing?"

"Not good. Her husband is on your father's team. There's a good chance she may lose the baby. She may even lose her life."

Rob furrowed his brow. "Not good."

"No it's not. I'll tell you something else. I think there's another problem your mother is dealing with, but I don't know what it is. She hasn't said anything, but I get a sense that something is weighing her down. Do you know what it is?"

He shook his head. "No. We haven't talked much the last few days."

"Look Rob, I'm not your conscience. I'm not your father or your uncle. I'm a stranger to you, so there's no reason for you to listen to me, but I think you should talk to your mother. She needs you. She needs you to stop being a pain, but she also needs you to man up. I don't know what else she's carrying on her shoulders, but my guess is that it's pretty heavy."

Rob stared into the distance. Bartley gave him time, gathering wrappers and soda cups, exiting the car and depositing them in a waste container. He slipped back into the car. "You know the way home?"

"Of course."

"Then tallyho."

Bartley couldn't help noticing that Rob drove more slowly than before.

CHAPTER 44

AS FAR AS MOYER was concerned, night came too slowly. On this kind of mission, darkness was a friend, daylight the enemy. The building they had under surveillance sat at the end of an industrial section of town. When they scouted the area days before, they noticed that several of the large structures were empty, perhaps due to a downturn in the economy. Whatever the cause, Moyer was grateful. As it was, there were still too many people moving through the streets.

Jose stood nearby. Moyer knew Jose always stood when he was nervous. It paid for a leader to know the little things about his men.

He turned his attention to the monitors. Two were blank and one displayed a fuzzy image. They had pushed their luck too far. The batteries had died on the gooseneck spy camera, and one of the LVRS units had suffered the same fate. Replacing the batteries was an easy task; getting to the units wasn't. Since J. J. and Caraway had already made access to the building once, they were the logical choice to do it again. Except this time they had to make roof access on three buildings. The lightweight video reconnaissance systems had worked flawlessly, but batteries could only last so long without being recharged.

"Position one clear." It was Caraway's voice over the radio.

"Position one clear, roger that." The blank screen to his right came to life. "Functional."

"So far, so good," Jose said.

"Ever hear about the man who fell off the roof of the Empire State Building? Every floor he passed, he yelled, 'So far, so good!'"

"Feeling pessimistic, Boss?"

"Pessimism gets a bad rap."

The next transmission wouldn't be made until J. J. and Caraway reached the roof with the other video system. Now with one system working he could see part of the target building and its lot. Using the small joystick on the control panel, he aimed the lens across the street and at the other LVRS and waited. Five minutes later, the dark image of two men dressed in black appeared. They slowly moved to the other observation unit, the one transmitting the weak signal.

The screen went black then glowed as the new battery was installed.

"Position two clear." Caraway again.

"Roger, two clear. Functional."

Moyer watched as J. J. and Caraway made their way across the rooftop and down an access ladder. Only one camera remained: the fiber-optic spy cam the two men had set the night before. Caraway believed the battery would last two days. It didn't. Moyer learned long ago that no mission goes according to plan.

This was the tricky part of the operation. The other two buildings were unoccupied, making access easy. The third building, the one that held at least three armed men and three captives, was different. His team had watched the building for many hours and spotted no guard on the ground. Perhaps they were being lax;

perhaps they feared a guard outside the building might draw attention. Whatever the reason, Moyer counted it a blessing. He directed one camera to the front of the building and one to the back fence where J. J. and Caraway had previously made entry to the property. There they were repeating their actions of the night before.

The most difficult task of leadership, Moyer decided years ago, was sending someone else to do a job. Moyer wished it were he sneaking down alleys and climbing the side of buildings, but J. J. and Caraway were younger, faster, and better suited to the task. Such knowledge didn't make him feel better, but it calmed his frustration some.

For thirty seconds the building blocked his view of the two men climbing the ladder, then he saw the head of one appear over the parapet and do what soldiers called a "snoop and poop." Caraway made his way onto the roof. Shortly after that, J. J. appeared. Again they moved slowly, careful not to make noise that could be heard by the armed men below them. Moyer watched as they crouched. They were at the camera—

Thunder was Moyer's first thought but immediately dismissed it. The sound was more familiar than thunder and more frightening. On the monitor he saw his two men freeze and look up.

Moyer's cell phone chimed. He snapped it up and punched the button for speakerphone. Rich spoke before Moyer could finish saying, "Yeah?"

"Incoming, Boss. Three vans just passed our location and are headed your way . . . wait one . . . we hear rotor sounds."

"I hear it too," Jose said.

"Start moving this direction." He hung up.

"Boss." The voice was a whisper but clear enough for Moyer to recognize J. J. "We hear a chopper. Sounds inbound."

"Roger that. We have incoming vehicles. Repeat, incoming vehicles. Bug out, bug out."

Then Moyer saw something that turned his spine to ice: A bright light shone from above, illuminating the area just in front of the target building. Half a breath later the helicopter searchlight began scanning the rooftops.

Jose swore.

Moyer snapped up his cell phone. "We got trouble, Shaq."

☢ ☢ ☢

J. J. HEARD IT FIRST, the distant thumping of a helicopter's rotors beating the air. He tipped his head and tried to locate the direction of the sound. It was coming from the north. Although he hadn't seen it yet, he could tell it wasn't a heavy military craft—more like a business or news chopper. It was coming closer. He looked at Caraway, who kept his head down while changing the batteries on the gooseneck camera. He held a small flashlight in his mouth. J. J. touched his shoulder.

Caraway removed the light from between his teeth, switched it off then looked up. He said nothing, letting his expression ask the question. J. J. tapped his ear and pointed skyward. Caraway tilted his head and listened.

J. J. keyed his radio. "Boss. We hear a chopper. Sounds like it's inbound."

"Roger that," came the response. "We have incoming vehicles. Repeat incoming vehicles. Bug out, bug out."

Caraway whispered a curse and handed the small flashlight to J. J. "Take this. I need sixty seconds."

"We have orders to bug, man."

"Hold the light. Talking will only take more time." Caraway's gloved fingers snapped the battery in place. It took another fifteen seconds to place the gooseneck down the hole they had created the night before.

"Let's move, Caraway." J. J. started for the ladder, still moving as softly as he could. The helicopter might simply fly over them. For all he knew it was an air ambulance on routine duty. Of course, it could be a police helicopter or, worse, a military scout. Moyer's announcement about incoming vehicles made J. J. dismiss the air ambulance idea.

"Hold it," Caraway whispered. J. J. turned in time to see Caraway soft-shoe back across the roof to the camera. He squatted by the device, touched something, then rose again. "I forgot to turn the thing back on."

J. J.'s earpiece crackled to life. "I said, bug out."

Caraway heard the same thing in his ear. "Boss doesn't sound happy."

"You got that right."

The pounding of the rotors sounded closer—much too close.

J. J. reached for the curved top of the access ladder and raised a foot over the parapet when he saw something that made his heart tumble. A bright beam of light slashed through the night, falling on the street in front of the building.

"Uh-oh," was all he could say. He stepped over the parapet and worked his way down the side of the ladder as he had the night before. He hadn't traveled more than two rungs before he saw the bottom of Caraway's boots come over the edge of the roof. Halfway down the ladder, J. J. let go and dropped to the ground. Caraway did the same two seconds later. They kept their backs to the wall and waited. The helicopter circled overhead, its blinding beam of light sweeping the road.

Turning to Caraway, J. J. pointed two fingers at his own eyes then at the corner of the building closest to the street. He moved quickly along the wall, stopping at the corner. He saw what he feared he would see. The light moved from the street to the tops of the building directly across the road. The beam swept left, right, then stopped. It had found the LVRS camera system.

Not good. Not good at all.

J. J. scooted back to Caraway and motioned for him to stay. "Boss, this is Colt. The helo has spotted one of the LVRS—"

J. J. felt himself jerked to the side. Caraway had grabbed his sleeve and was dragging him along the wall toward the other corner. J. J. didn't resist. Caraway was a pain in the fanny, but he was a good soldier. If he felt they needed to move, then move they would.

"Say again, Colt."

"Stand by one, Boss."

Caraway let go of J. J.'s sleeve and the two ducked around the backside of the building.

"Repeating, helo has spotted one of the LVRS." A slight change in pitch told J. J. the helo was moving. Light from above spilled over the edge of the roof, but since the spotlight was directly overhead J. J. and Caraway remained in darkness.

"Can you make it off the compound?"

"Not without being seen," Caraway answered. "My bad, Boss. I lingered too long."

"Yeah, I saw that. You just get back here alive so I can kill you." J. J. and Caraway exchanged glances. Moyer continued. "I can see the helo on the monitor. It's moving to the building directly south. It sees the LVRS. You got seconds. Move out!"

Caraway was moving before Moyer finished the sentence, J. J. a half step behind. Halfway across the empty portion of the lot and still several meters from the fence, J. J. slowed. The next maneuver required it.

The moment Caraway reached the fence he turned and linked his fingers to form a flesh-and-blood stirrup. J. J. took several more steps, planted his foot in Caraway's hands, and boosted himself up the fence. He threw a leg over the top, feeling the bent ends of the chain-link top digging into his thigh. He extended an arm to Caraway, who had already begun to climb, seized the back of the man's vest and pulled. The chain link dug deeper into J. J.'s thigh, but he pushed the pain from his mind. If he lived, he would have time to complain later. Otherwise, it didn't much matter.

Caraway got both hands on top of the fence, and as he did, J. J. heard a new sound added to the *thumpa-thumpa* of the helo—the noise of a metal roll-up door opening. Facing three men armed with automatic weapons held no appeal for J. J. He swung his other leg over the fence and dropped to the ground. Caraway followed. They turned to run down the alley.

Then everything around them lit up.

"They spotted us, Boss," J. J. said into his mike, still running. To his own ears he sounded calm and his words conversational. His jackhammer heart said otherwise.

J. J. pulled his 9mm from its holster. "Light," he said.

"Roger that," Caraway answered. "Now."

The two stopped, swiveled on their heels, and raised their weapons. Each fired three shots and the spotlight went out. The helo banked and pulled away. It banked again and J. J. lost sight of it.

"If they didn't know where we were before, they do now." Caraway started back down the alley. "Anyone awake within a mile of this place heard that."

"Boss, we took the light out. Proceeding on foot."

"Roger. I count two men on foot to the south. They just made it over the fence. Third man still back at the ranch."

That was good. Two against two were better odds, even if the other two could fire six hundred rounds a minute. Fortunately the AK-47 clips held only thirty rounds, maybe forty if they favored the larger clip. Of course, it only took one properly placed round to do the job. They may not be outmanned, but they were outgunned at the moment.

"I miss my M4," Caraway said.

"I miss your M4 too."

A sharp pop came from behind them.

Caraway grunted, stumbled forward, and fell.

JULIA CENOBIO HEARD A cell phone ring. She heard shouting. She heard the rumble of the metal overhead door clatter as it climbed its tracks. The combined sounds pushed through the locked bathroom door.

"Mamá?" Lina said.

"Hush, sweetheart."

"What's going on?"

"I said, hush." Julia stood, fingering the shiv. "Get behind me, children."

"Why Mamá?" Even in the dim light, Julia could see the fear on her daughter's face. Nestor stood with his spine straight and his fists clenched, but the young boy's face couldn't conceal his terror.

Julia stepped to the door and placed her ear close to the dirty surface. She heard the footfalls of running men and a *thumpa-thumpa* that made her think of a helicopter. A few seconds later she heard gunfire.

"Blessed Jesus, protect us."

Julia backed away from the door. She had a decision to make. If she interpreted the sounds correctly, two men had left. That meant only one remained. If he opened the door . . . Julia looked at the sharpened metal rod in her hand. Would she have the courage to do it if she had to? She looked at the tear-dampened face of Lina and the determined stance of her boy and decided she did.

☢ ☢ ☢

MOYER LOST VISUAL ON J. J. and Caraway once they were over the fence. He watched as the monitor showed two armed men chasing his soldiers. He was about to key his radio when the cell phone chimed.

"Something has happened," Rich said. "The motorcade came to a quick stop, then the first car and the van turned down a side street away from our building. The third vehicle, also a van, resumed course."

"The helicopter spotted our video setup. It also found Colt and Billy. They're on the move, with two hostiles behind them."

Rich's tone didn't change, but Moyer knew the man well enough to sense his anxiety. "On our way."

"No. Stay with the two vehicles. Cenobio must be in one of those cars. If we lose them, we may never find them again. We'll join you. We'll take turns tracking them."

"What about Colt and Billy?"

"Cenobio is our mission. Do it, Shaq. Do it now."

"Understood."

A van sped past Moyer's location, headed toward the target building. Moyer was five miles away, near the range limit of the video equipment.

Jose bolted to his feet and removed a 9mm pistol from one of the thin shelves in the panel truck, strapped it on, then reached for an M4 and its clip.

"What are you doing?" Moyer asked.

"You don't need me to chase the caravan. Billy and Colt need me for backup. They're packing only pistols."

"Cenobio is our mission. We have to go after him."

"Boss, we don't know Cenobio is in the caravan; we *do* know that two of our team need some help."

"We're over five miles away."

"Get me as close as you can, Boss. I'll make the rest of the way on foot."

Moyer looked back at the monitors. Everything looked quiet, but he knew better. J. J. and Caraway were hidden from the cameras. So were their pursuers. He moved from the chair by the monitors to the driver's seat of the panel van and started the engine. "Hold on."

CHAPTER 45

HECTOR CENOBIO'S HEAD HIT the side window of the van as it turned abruptly. He raised his tied hands to the part of his skull that smacked the glass and rubbed. "What's happening?"

"Sit still and be quiet." Miguel Costa held a cell phone to his ear and spoke in rapid Spanish. "How many?" He looked over his shoulder again. "No, I don't think we're being followed. Stay over the area. . . . I know your light is out; just do what you can."

Costa rang off then dialed a number. A second later he spoke in a tone Hector had heard before—the tone Costa used when speaking to Foreign Minister Santi. Santi had overseen Hector's delivery to the caravan but refused to go further. He had returned to the helicopter and flew away. "Trouble. You were right to send a helicopter with us. The pilot saw two men in black on the roof of the building. He also spotted what looks like two surveillance video systems." There was a pause. "Yes, sir, we've changed course. I've ordered the extra men to the building's location to help with the search." Costa rubbed his forehead.

"Stress headache?" Hector asked.

"One moment, sir." Costa moved the phone to his other hand then backhanded Hector across the mouth.

Pain like hot needles shot through his head. He tasted blood and noticed a gash on the back of Costa's hand caused by Hector's teeth. If the wound hurt, he didn't show it.

Costa raised the phone to his ear again. "No, sir, no problem. Just clearing up some static."

Hector bent forward and spit a stream of red liquid between his feet. The blow had been hard enough to loosen a tooth and set his ears ringing. Straightening, he moved his head in a slow circle trying to drive the wooziness from his head.

"Understood, sir. We're moving to the second location. No, sir, I don't have a status report on the woman. That will be my next call." He closed the phone.

"Will I get the back of your hand if I ask what is happening?" Hector looked into the man's eyes and didn't like what he saw. There was a blackness there, as if his eyes floated in a tar pit.

"We've had a slight change in plans."

Hector nodded. "I'm only guessing, of course, but are there new players in this game?"

"You'd be wise to sit in silence."

"You said you were taking me to see my wife and children."

"That has been delayed." Again Costa looked over his shoulder. He spoke to the driver, a young man with an old scar on his right cheek and a tattoo of a knife dripping blood on the back of his neck. "What have you seen?"

"Nothing. There are headlights about a half kilometer behind us, but the car doesn't approach."

"You tell me if it gets any closer."

"I will. Where do you want us to go?"

"I will tell you in a minute." Costa entered another number into the phone. "Status report." It was an order, not a request. Costa listened then nodded. "Send three other men in pursuit. I want the other three on the perimeter. Send one of them to the roof. I want to know what they were doing up there." Again he listened. "And the woman?" More nodding. "Good. Keep a guard by the door."

Hector did the simple math. Three additional men in pursuit. That meant one or more guards were already pursuing whoever was responsible for the upset. Three on the perimeter would bring the number to over six plus one. Costa had mentioned "the guard by the door." Singular. Three plus three plus one plus whatever number might have already been in pursuit. Eight? Nine? Maybe ten guards. Ten was such a small number, but it seemed so large now.

Please, Lord, keep my family safe.

☢ ☢ ☢

SANTI PACED HIS OFFICE, looking for something to throw. Unfortunately anything other than crumpled paper would cost him a fair amount of money. Anything worth throwing was a collectable.

He forced himself to calm then ran the situation over in his mind. Two men had been seen on the roof of the building where he and his team held the wife and children of a renowned nuclear physicist. Caracas had more than its fair share of crime and violence—every city of its size did. But the odds of a couple of street thugs trying to break into the building through the roof were too small to be realistic. Nor did the behavior fit the pattern of a burglary. A common criminal would have gone in through a window or broken down the door. No, this had to be something far worse than two hoodlums looking for electronics to sell on the street.

He stepped to the window and gazed into the dark jungle, yet seeing none of it. His mind was elsewhere, on the streets of industrial

Caracas. Two men on the roof, an injured American with a military tattoo—this could only mean one thing: the Americans knew of their activities. He took a few mental steps backward. What he was doing with Cenobio was not official Venezuelan business. President Chavez knew of the plan but kept his distance. "I need deniability," he had said, with a smile that nevertheless showed his approval.

Santi was familiar with American military operations. He had studied their tactics in Afghanistan, Iraq, Somalia, and Central America. They were here, and they were a problem.

How did they find out about the scheme? Did he have a traitor in his midst? For the moment there was no way to know.

Santi stepped to his phone, dialed a number, and identified himself. "I want a military helicopter sent to my home right away. I want another in the air and moving to a location I will give you. How long will that take?"

The voice on the other end said the aircraft would be airborne in ten minutes.

"You have half that time."

☢ ☢ ☢

FOR A MOMENT J. J. thought Caraway was praying; then he made out several of the whispered words. No one prayed with that kind of language.

"Hang in there, man," J. J. whispered.

"Lucky . . . shot. Just . . . a flesh . . . wound." Caraway grunted between words.

The hole in Caraway's right leg was anything but a flesh wound. Every step made things worse and left a bloody trail. Caraway couldn't put weight on the leg, making J. J. think the round had shattered the thigh bone. He prayed this wasn't the case.

The last five minutes had passed like days. The moment Caraway hit the ground, J. J. spun and unloaded four rounds in the direction of the two men chasing them. They were still a block or two behind them, too far for J. J. to know if he had done any damage. With adrenaline fueling his muscles, J. J. pulled Caraway to his feet. "Can you stand?"

"On one leg. Man this hurts."

J. J. let go to retrieve his partner's weapon and slipped it into Caraway's shoulder holster. Moving to Caraway's side, J. J. put an arm around the man's waist, grabbed his belt, and pulled up, taking some of the strain off the injured leg. Caraway threw an arm over J. J.'s shoulder. "You want me to lead, Colt? I'm a better dancer."

J. J. had to admire Caraway's composure. They were being chased by two men with automatic weapons, he was bleeding and in great pain, but still he joked. "You better let me lead. I've seen you dance. It ain't pretty."

"Yeah, but have you seen me . . ." His head tipped forward and he groaned. "But have you seen me dance while drunk? Now that's . . . entertainment."

"Let's go, Fred Astaire." J. J. led them between buildings and down another alley. Overhead he heard the helicopter moving in slow circles. Without its powerful spotlight, it would have trouble spotting them. Nonetheless, every time the sound of pounding rotors grew sufficiently loud, they ducked under an overhang or next to a dumpster.

"It's only a matter of time, Colt," Caraway whispered. "We took out their light, but I'll bet your left arm . . . they have . . . FLIR."

Forward-looking infrared. The thought had already occurred to J. J.

"Jesus."

"Ha! I knew it. When the going gets tough, even you can't resist swearing."

"I wasn't swearing. I was praying."

J. J. leaned Caraway against the wall of a dark industrial building next to a doorway. He ran a hand along the door's surface.

"It didn't sound like praying."

"How would you know?" J. J. placed his gloved hand on the doorknob and turned. Locked. Still, it was what he was looking for.

"What are you doing?"

"The door is wood. So is the frame. All of the other doors have been metal with metal frames."

"You thinking of . . . buying the place?"

"Not on my salary." J. J. pulled his knife from the sheath around his hip and placed the tip between the wood doorstop and frame. He worked into the soft material until the point touched the metal tongue of the doorknob. He moved the blade back and forth until the doorstop parted from the jamb enough for J. J. to move the knife up and over the tongue. He tipped the blade and worked it until he could feel the backside of the mechanism, the angled portion that allowed the tongue to hit the strike plate and depress, freeing the door to close and lock. A few seconds later the door opened. Without a word, J. J. took hold of Caraway and helped him through.

Just as he stepped across the threshold, he heard the helo pass overhead.

CHAPTER 46

J. J. PROPPED CARAWAY AGAINST a wall and silently closed the door. The lock was still good but wouldn't hold up against a solid kick. He holstered his weapon and pulled Caraway's arm over his shoulders again. He handed his flashlight to Caraway. "Take this. Make yourself useful."

"Hey, I may be bleeding to death, but I can still take you out."

"Yeah, sure. Whatever." If Caraway could still shoot off his mouth, it meant there was still enough blood in his body to feed the brain.

The flashlight beam cut the darkness, illuminating a dirty floor and a set of steel shelves holding boxes of various sizes. They stood in a room about the size of a two-car garage. A door in a wall a few steps ahead stood open. "Let's go." J. J. did his best to bear Caraway's weight. Sweat poured from his brow, his back aching from the odd angle it had been in for the last few minutes. They slipped through the door and faced an abyss of darkness.

"I don't suppose it would help to turn on the lights," Caraway said.

J. J. knew he was joking. "Yeah, it would help the bad guys find us. Move the light around some."

Caraway did, and the beam fell on work tables, machines, and rows of stacked metal chairs in an expansive room. He moved the light to the right, and it fell upon white-topped tables with folding legs piled one atop another. On one of the tables rested a stack of long, wide cardboard.

"Looks like the place makes folding tables and chairs." J. J. moved to the largest work surface, the one with sheets of cardboard. The table had been made from two-by-fours. As gently as he could, J. J. lowered Caraway to the floor, removed his knife again, and cut the man's pants leg from ankle to pocket. "Give me the light." Caraway surrendered it then laid back on the concrete floor.

J. J. directed the beam over the wound. He saw a small entry hole in the back of Caraway's thigh and an ugly exit hole with flapping skin just off center on the front of the leg. Three things bothered him: the amount of blood oozing from the wound (at least it wasn't spurting), the fact the exit wound was at an angle from the entrance wound, and the bits of white specs embedded in the flesh. The last two items confirmed his suspicions—the bullet had hit the bone and shattered it.

"How . . . bad?"

"You won't be dancing anytime soon, but you'll have a great scar to show the grandkids." J. J. cut off the split pant legs and formed a tourniquet. He could hear Caraway grit his teeth as he applied it four inches above the wound.

"You know you're going to have to leave me."

"Yeah, right. You know we don't leave our people behind. You're stuck with me."

"Sweet as that is, Colt, I'm an anchor around your neck. Stop trying to be a hero."

"I'm not trying to be a hero; I'm trying to annoy you."

"You were always good at that."

"I do what I can."

"Seriously, J. J. You gotta bolt. I left a blood trail a blind dog could follow. It's only a matter of time before they find us."

"Forget it. The rest of the team will be here in a few minutes."

Caraway shook his head. "You know better than that. Boss said there were incoming vehicles. There's a helo circling overhead. I'll bet you dollars to donuts that caravan is carrying Cenobio."

"Makes no difference."

"Of course it does, stupid. Cenobio is the mission. We're expendable."

J. J. did know, but admitting it would gain nothing. "If I leave you, I'll have to tell Moyer why. I don't think I want to do that." J. J. studied the wound again. The blood flow had slowed.

"If you don't leave me, you'll be dead."

"Let's see—death or Moyer, Moyer or death. I think I'll take death."

That made Caraway chuckle. "I see your . . . point." Caraway stiffened and moaned. "Man, this hurts."

J. J. rose and began moving folding tables and stacking them on edge against the side of the table facing the door. He worked as fast as he could. Five minutes later he had constructed a wrap-around barricade enclosing their position. The concept was simple but unproven. The folding tables had tops made with a laminate sheet over particle board. Particle board was dense and heavy but not enough to stop an AK-47 bullet. Several tables, however, might provide enough protection for J. J. to pop whoever came through the door. He doubted he could hold them off for long, but it was worth the try.

"Help me up." Caraway struggled to one elbow.

"Forget it. It's past your bedtime."

"I'm serious, J. J. I'm not gonna die on my back. If I'm going out, I'm going out like a soldier. Now help me."

J. J. started to object again but couldn't. He would make the same demand of Caraway had the situation been reversed. He stood and bent over Caraway. "This is gonna hurt."

"It already hurts. Just do it."

J. J. pulled Caraway close to the table and positioned him in front of a slot formed by the vertical edges of the stacked tables, a slot that faced the door. The slot was wide enough to shoot through. When J. J. turned Caraway onto his stomach, Caraway didn't moan, didn't groan—he whimpered. The sound of it broke J. J.'s heart.

"Be sure to keep your head to the side."

"Are you telling me how to soldier?"

"Wouldn't think of it."

"I have one more favor to ask, Colt, and I want your word on it."

"You can do your own work when we get out of here."

"Just listen, smart guy." Caraway turned his face away from J. J. "If I don't make it, promise me you won't let them put that stupid billy-goat nickname on my tombstone."

"You're kidding, right?"

"So help me, Colt. If you let them do it, I'll dig myself out of the grave and stalk you for the rest of your life. Imagine my corpse sitting beside you in church."

"I'd be happy to have you in church any way I can get you."

"You know what I mean. Now promise."

"I promise, pal, but I'm not giving you permission to die."

Caraway turned to J. J. and said softly, "Thanks."

Only one word, but it carried a lifetime of meaning.

MOYER KEPT ONE EYE on the streets and one on the sky, watching for the helo. "I can't get much closer without being seen."

Jose sat in the passenger seat, automatic weapon in hand, pistol and extra clips for both weapons attached to his vest. There would be no blending in tonight. Anyone who caught sight of him would know that he was dangerous. "Just say when."

"I'm having trouble with this," Moyer admitted.

"You have a job to do. This is mine. Let's not talk about it, Boss. Let's just do it."

Moyer looked at the GPS display. "You'll have to run at least two clicks through the alleys. I won't know when or how to extract you."

Jose studied the display, committing it to memory. "Nothing like an impromptu mission to get the blood going."

Moyer checked his mirrors and, seeing no other vehicles or people on the street, pulled to the curb. Jose exited without a word. Moyer pulled away. Thirty seconds later he heard something new: the sound of another helicopter.

He felt sick in a whole new way.

ROB LAY IN HIS bed staring at a Rolling Stones poster on his wall without really seeing it. The only light in the room came from a nightlight that been in the wall socket since he was three. He should have removed it long ago but never had. If it were left up to him, it would be there another thirteen years and that fact bothered him.

Earlier that day he had gobbled two hamburgers with an Army chaplain. He pretended not to care, not to listen. He had gone along with the unexpected meeting for only two reasons: it might save him a lecture from his mother about being gone all night, and he wanted to drive the Camaro. What a sweet ride. But it wasn't the talk or the car that kept him awake; it was a nagging sense of guilt.

Lately guilt had held no sway with him. He had enough apathy to drown any sense of responsibility, and he had lived that way for the last year and a half. The older he got, the more he despised his life and his father. Having Dad someplace else in the world was like having shackles removed from his legs and wrist. Or so he told himself. Truth was he didn't feel free at all. Sure, he could stay out late or, as last night, not come home at all, but he found no satisfaction in it. The guilt stole the sense of pleasure his adolescent mind told him he deserved.

A sound came from the kitchen. He listened for a moment and heard the refrigerator door open and close. He looked at his clock: 3 a.m. Someone else couldn't sleep. Rob assumed it was his mother. His sister never got up in the middle of the night. His mother hadn't been home when he returned from school; she'd probably been with the pregnant woman in the hospital.

Rob swung his legs over the side of the bed and, without knowing why, rose and opened the door to his bedroom. Since he slept in an old pair of shorts and a T-shirt, he didn't bother dressing.

The fluorescent lights in the kitchen glowed too brightly for the hour. He stepped to the breakfast bar and saw his mother dressed in a pink robe and matching slippers. Her disheveled hair looked as if a bird had nested there. Rob couldn't remember the last time he had seen his mother with anything other than perfect hair. What surprised him most, however, were her eyes. They seemed empty and dark, as if someone had spooned out her soul.

"You okay?" Rob asked.

Stacy jumped. "Oh, you scared me. Don't sneak up on me like that, especially at this hour."

"Sorry."

She lowered her head and sighed. "No, I'm sorry, Rob. I shouldn't have snapped. You just startled me."

"Next time I'll whistle or something."

"I haven't heard you whistle since you were a boy. I'm fixing some hot chocolate. Want some?"

"Yeah, okay."

Stacy pulled another packet of instant cocoa from the pantry, then poured more milk into the saucepan she was using to heat the cocoa.

"Wouldn't the microwave be faster?"

"I guess so. Sometimes doing things the old way is relaxing. My mother always made cocoa this way."

Rob slipped onto one of the bar stools. "Whatever works, I guess. I take it you can't sleep."

"I was going to say the same thing to you." She stirred in the mix. "I haven't been sleeping well since your dad left."

"How come? He's left plenty of times before." He regretted the tone. "That sounded worse than I meant it. Force of habit, I guess."

"I know it's hard on you too, just in a different way." As she spoke, Stacy removed two mugs from the cabinet and set them by the sink then returned to stirring the hot chocolate.

"You gonna ask?"

She set the spoon down. "Ask about what? You being out all night or about Chaplain Bartley?"

"Both, I guess."

She shook her head. "Not tonight. Truth is, my brain is fried. I'm just going to trust you."

The words punched him in the chest. "I fell asleep at a friend's, and yes, I met with Bartley. He let me drive his car."

Stacy turned. "He let you drive an Army-issue car?"

"I wouldn't be seen dead in one of those. He let me drive his '68 Camaro."

"Wow. Should I be afraid?"

Rob smiled. "No. I behaved myself. I've only had my license a couple of months; I'm not ready to lose it."

"Those are beautiful cars." She poured the hot liquid into the mugs then carried them to the breakfast bar.

"So why are you up?"

"I told you. I can't sleep."

"Why can't you sleep?"

"Just getting old, I guess." She sipped from the cup. "Drink your hot chocolate."

"Mom, you've been nagging me about telling you what I'm doing and where I'm going. It's time you be open with me. You never get up in the middle of the night. What's eating you? Is it that woman in the hospital?"

"Lucy? She's part of the problem. I'm worried about her."

"The chaplain said he thinks you're carrying some kinda burden and that I should be sensitive to it. Well, he's right. I can see something is chewing you up."

"It's nice of you to ask—"

"You don't get to ask what's going on in my life and expect an honest answer if you won't be honest with me." He stood.

"No, wait." Stacy set her cup down.

Rob returned to the stool.

"It's your father. The day he left I got a call from a doctor. A *civilian* doctor."

"That doesn't make sense. Why would a civilian doctor call you about Dad unless . . . he's sick and hiding something."

Stacy nodded, and Rob watched as a tear began to run down her cheek. She didn't bother wiping it away. Rob's stomach went into freefall. He looked into the cup of hot chocolate as if it held some answers.

"Apparently your father went to see the doctor the morning he got called up. At first the doctor didn't want to talk about it, but I tricked him into telling me the truth. I guess I shouldn't be telling you that."

"You got a right to know." Rob was surprised by how soft his words came out. "What did he say?"

"He wants to run some more tests." The tears began to flow. "Not certain . . . blood . . . intestines . . . cancer . . ." Her shoulders heaved with each sob.

A moment later Rob held his weeping mother in his arms.

His eyes burned.

CHAPTER 47

JOSE'S FIRST THOUGHT AFTER exiting the panel truck was of his wife. The image of her face, the smell of her hair, the music of her laugh struck his mind with such force he almost doubled over from the pain of it. By the time he had taken his third step down the dark alley the likeness of his children played on his mind. He could hear each voice, see them sleeping soundly in their beds, arguing over which cartoon to watch, and driving him insane with inane questions. He would pay any amount of money, endure any kind of pain, to be annoyed like that again. Their mother lay in a hospital fighting for her life. They might lose her and he wouldn't be there. Instead, he might end up lying on the street, afloat in a sea of his own blood. For all he knew, his children would be orphans before the sun set on the coming day.

By the time he took his fifteenth step, those images and thoughts had been packed away in the vault every soldier kept in his mind. In a single fluid motion, Jose dropped the night-vision goggles over his eyes. The dark alley came alive in yellow-green hues. He started jogging. Moyer had dropped him off a little over a mile away from the target building. Without equipment Jose could jog a mile in less than eight minutes. With gear it took closer to eleven. Not track star speeds but respectable for a man his age. But even eight minutes was an eternity in a battle situation. He picked up the pace.

Keeping close to the westernmost buildings, Jose plodded forward, the barrel of his automatic weapon pointed at a spot on the ground three feet in front of him. His eyes scanned the alley ahead and each door and window he passed. At this hour every business was closed, but that didn't mean a janitor couldn't suddenly emerge from an alley door with a mop and bucket in hand.

The darkness combined with the tall concrete tilt-up buildings to form a stygian valley. He whispered, "Yea, though I walk through the valley of the shadow of death . . . check that . . . though I jog through the valley of the shadow of death . . ."

He stopped at every intersection of alley and street, peeking around corners to assess threat or locate observers. So far the only movement he had seen was a bit of paper blown by a breeze and the scurrying of a rat startled by Jose's footsteps. In training they called this urban warfare. More and more battles were fought not on open fields but in city streets. His tours in Iraq had all involved working through dangerous streets that harbored snipers or men with rocket-propelled grenades. Pavement was the hallmark of twenty-first-century warfare.

He had no idea where J. J. and Caraway may have gone or what condition they might be in. He planned to make radio contact once he got closer to the scene. For now, he followed the sound of the helicopter thunder. The overhead sounds had changed, doubled in intensity. Another helicopter had arrived and, like the first, was using a spotlight to search the streets. As much as it concerned Jose that there were now extra eyes in the sky, he felt thankful for one thing: The enemy just might lead him straight to his friends.

☢ ☢ ☢

MOYER STUDIED THE GPS display. He was one street over from Rich and Pete.

"Shaq, report."

"Target vehicles remain on previous tack. We're following about a half mile back."

"Have the helos spotted you?"

"Negative, Boss. Best guess is they're searching for Billy and Colt."

"Agreed. Jose is on foot and heading to the scene."

Rich's momentary silence said more than words. "Understood, Boss. I still think we need to go back."

"No can do, Shaq. God knows I want to, but we stick with the mission." Moyer heard the first syllable of a curse before Shaq caught himself. "Stay on the vehicles, Shaq. In a few moments I'll cut up to your street and we'll switch places so they don't get suspicious. In the meantime I've got to make a call."

What Moyer wanted to do was radio his members on the ground, but his radio was behind him in the van. To reach it he'd have to pull over, and he didn't want to lose the seconds. He had to trust his men, trust their training.

Moyer slammed his fist on the steering wheel. He forced his mind to calm, picked up his encrypted phone, and punched in a two-digit number. He formulated his words while he waited for the call to connect.

☢ ☢ ☢

"WHAT ARE YOU DOING?" Caraway's words were two levels below a whisper.

"I'm going to do a quick recon of the building." J. J. pulled his night-vision goggles on. Both he and Caraway had used them to change the video-surveillance batteries but removed them for the close-up work with the gooseneck spy cam. Night-vision technology had many advantages but was more a problem than a help when dealing with small objects up close. When the chopper had arrived on scene and Moyer ordered the bugout, they hadn't had time to don them again. Now with a few seconds free, J. J. decided to take a better look around the inside of the building's work area. Night vision worked on a complex electronic principle of light amplification, meaning there had to be at least a small amount of light available. Dim moonlight worked well outside, but there was no moon inside. J. J. reached for his flashlight and turned it on.

"What do you expect to find?"

J. J. knelt by Caraway. "Roll on your side."

Caraway did, and J. J. pulled two 9mm clips from the man's vest and set them within Caraway's reach. He then took Caraway's weapon, ejected the partially used clip, and replaced it with a full one.

"You didn't answer my question."

"This is an industrial building. I'm betting there's an industrial first-aid kit. Kick back while I go look. Feel free to shoot anyone who comes through the door—just don't shoot me. I'm the only guy in the world who likes you."

"Yeah, right. We've been buddies for years."

J. J. stopped and stared at Caraway through the goggles. "We have the future to fix that." He rose and started his search, pointing the flashlight ahead of him. The goggles multiplied the dim light, providing greater visibility than the flashlight could on its own.

The wide room was filled with stacks of cardboard, spools of binding wire, several large compressors, and a woodworking area with sheets of particle board. About half of the work area contained parts of metal folding chairs. J. J. assumed the metal parts were made elsewhere and assembled here for shipping.

Two minutes after he started his search, he found what he was looking for: a two-foot-by-three-foot blue metal box with a red cross and the words EMERGENCIA MEDICO painted on the front. J. J. removed the case from the wall and returned to Caraway.

"Miss me?" J. J. removed the night-vision goggles and pointed the flashlight beam at the first-aid kit.

"More than life itself, sweetheart."

"Okay, now you're scaring me. It must be the blood loss." J. J. removed two large steripads and a roll of Corban wrap. He placed the sterile pads on each wound and held them in place with the self-adhering wrap.

Caraway made no complaints, but his body language betrayed the pain he was experiencing. J. J. touched the man's face. His skin was cold and clammy. Shock was setting in.

In the kit J. J. found a bottle of 800mg ibuprofen tablets. "Just what the doctor ordered: Ranger candy. Can you swallow this without water?"

Caraway put the large white pill in his mouth and bit. It took four tries but he managed to force the pill down. "You know, too much of this stuff is bad for your liver." Caraway laughed at his joke. J. J. feared delirium was just around the corner.

A voice poured from J. J.'s earpiece. "Colt, Billy, this is Doc. Do you read?"

J. J. keyed his mike. "Doc, this is Colt. We hear you."

"I am close to the scene. Status report."

At first J. J. couldn't believe what he was hearing. "Are you . . ." He didn't want to use the word *alone* in case others were listening. "Are you coming to the party stag?"

"Yep. Couldn't get a date. Status report."

J. J. decided cryptic talk was useless. Their cover had been blown, men were searching for them, a helicopter circled overhead— better to go with direct communication. "Billy took one in the leg. I'm okay. We're about half a click from the scene. West-facing building. Wood door."

"Roger that. On my way."

The exterior door exploded open and two beams of light pierced the darkness. Caraway was the first to fire. A half second later, the room was filled with the explosive reports of gunfire. The acrid smell of spent gunpowder clogged the air.

THE SOUND OF A firefight poured through Jose's earpiece. He stopped for a moment, crossed himself, and sprinted down the alley, no longer caring if he were seen or not.

THE RADIO COMMUNICATION POURED over Moyer's radio just as he hit the END button on his phone and was preparing to dial Shaq again.

"Billy took one in the leg. I'm okay. We're about half a click from the scene. West-facing building. Wood door."

"Roger that. On my way."

"Roger—" *BANG. Pop-pop-pop* . . .

Moyer recognized the sound of 9mm pistol fire and that of automatic weapons.

Something inside of him died.

CHAPTER 48

IT TOOK EVERY FIBER of Rich Harbison's highly developed sense of discipline to keep from cranking the steering wheel and heading north on the next street available. Despite his reactive instinct, he kept the accelerator pressed just far enough to match the speed of the van and car in front of him. Following at this distance took concentration. At any moment the suspect cars could make a sudden turn and speed down a side street, and Rich would be impaled on the horns of a dilemma. He could accelerate and give chase, which would alert his targets that they were being followed, or he could let them slip away. A thought occurred to him. If he lost them, Moyer might feel forced to let him and Pete go after J. J. and Caraway.

That's when the greater principle of what he was doing came to the forefront. They were not police chasing car thieves; they were not tracking down a drug lord; they were risking their lives to keep safe a man who could further Iran's nuclear weapons program. Rich didn't have the look of an intellectual, but appearances—especially his appearance—could be misleading. He might be basketball tall and have the look of a dumb jock, but he was more knowledgeable about world affairs than most men. That knowledge kept him focused on the vehicles ahead. In the summer of 2008, the Israeli military conducted exercises meant to show their ability to attack key locations in Iran. For weeks the world wondered if the Middle East would become, as one Iranian leader said, a fireball.

"They're slowing." Pete sat in the passenger seat rubbing his legs and shoulders. Rich didn't have to ask. Pete was still stiff and sore from his run-in with the car. Every two hours he took pain meds— Tylenol first, ibuprofen two hours later. The in-car calisthenics were Pete's way of getting ready for action.

"They're testing us to see if we're following them." Shaq kept his speed the same. To slow might give them away. "They're going to figure out they're being followed."

The cell phone on the seat between them delivered Moyer's voice. "I'm behind you, Shaq. Peel off and I'll follow for a while. Take the next street over and parallel our course."

Shaq looked in his rearview mirror. It took a moment for him to spot the panel truck. Moyer drove with his lights off.

"Roger that." Shaq turned north and immediately increased his speed.

J. J. FELT A MOMENT of joy when he heard Jose's voice. Another gun and a medic were just what they needed, but the joy faltered when he realized Jose was the only reinforcement on the way. That meant Moyer and the others must have followed the caravan. Caraway had been right. J. J. knew it all along, but an unspoken hope had taken up residence in his brain. The hope died when the wood door caved in.

Caraway fired a half second before J. J. The sound of their weapons bounced off the concrete walls of the building. Two bursts of AK-47 fire joined the chorus then everything fell silent. The moment the door slammed open, two beams from flashlights sliced the darkness. One light dropped and rolled to the side, casting its beam along the concrete floor. The second light moved to the side. J. J. realized he and Caraway had shot the same man. How many did that leave? He knew two men had been pursuing them—Moyer had seen them exit the building. Had others joined the chase? What worried him was the van Moyer said was headed to the building. It could be filled with half a dozen armed men.

A soft glow pushed some of the darkness from the storage room. J. J. donned the night-vision gear and peered over the bolstered work table. A man lay unmoving on the floor. He could see the beam from the other light sweeping over the body then the door frame that separated the back entry room from the cavernous work area. That was their advantage. The attackers had to come through that door to get them unless they found another door. J. J. knew there had to be other doors. Behind him was a metal roll-up, but it was locked down tight. A standard-size door was positioned next to it. Unlike the back door, it was metal in a metal frame.

"Come on, come on," Caraway mumbled. "I can't stay conscious forever."

J. J. whispered. "I see one down. One is behind the wall." A movement just beyond the exterior door caught his attention. "There's movement just outside."

"Swell, they brought friends."

Someone outside yelled and J. J. saw several men charge through the door firing their AK-47s. The night vision amplified the muzzle flashes, stabbing J. J.'s eyes. Bits of wood and particle board flew through the air. J. J. ducked behind the makeshift barricade. Caraway returned fire.

J. J.'s ears roared. Wood shrapnel stung his hands and face. He raised his 9mm to fire, but his hand went empty and pain shot down his arm. He turned his head in time to see the butt of an AK-47 coming at his head.

A new blackness filled the room.

"WE THINK THEY'RE HEADED for the airport." Moyer heard Pete over the cell phone. "I've been looking at the map. The airport makes the most sense."

The thought had occurred to Moyer. The caravan changed directions immediately after the helicopter spotted J. J. and Caraway. Perhaps they had planned to go to the airport after picking up the woman and children. It made sense, but Moyer had no way of proving it. He kept this eye on the distant tail lights, hoping to stay far enough back so as not to alert the others to his presence but still maintain contact.

"Understood," Moyer said. "My guess is they'll head to the private plane area. Maybe they have a corporate jet standing by, or a small plane to take them to another airfield."

"Sounds right," Pete said.

"Yeah, it sounds right, but I can think of thirty other permutations."

"Just thirty, Boss?"

Moyer didn't answer. Something caught his attention—something that made his hopeless situation seem impossible: the sound of a helicopter overhead. These rotor sounds were different than the earlier ones; these had the distinct sound of a military chopper. Moyer rolled down his window to hear better. Not huge. Not a Russian-built MI-17. Its size and five-blade rotor would have a deeper pitch.

"I'm hearing the new helo. Sounds close." Moyer did his best to spot the craft but couldn't lay eyes on it. A second later a bright light shone down on the vehicles he was trailing.

"Boss, Pete saw it go overhead. It's an A109M."

The Italian-made light helicopter was light, agile, and could be armed with anti-tank missiles, rockets, and machine guns. He cursed under his breath. The craft probably left Fort Tiuna, the military headquarters in Caracas, shortly after J. J. and Caraway had been discovered.

"What now, Boss?"

"Give me a sec." Moyer ran every scenario he could think of, and every one ended with him and his crew dead on a Caracas street. The light that bathed the van and car a half mile ahead moved. It was headed straight for him. The pilot must have seen him when he flew over. The fact that Moyer had been driving with his headlights off could only be seen as suspicious.

"We got trouble, guys. I've been spotted."

Rich's voice came over the phone. "You gotta bail, Boss."

"Negative. Listen. We've only got seconds. Here's what we do."

SANTI RODE QUIETLY IN the back seat of the Bell 412 helicopter, listening to the radio transmission from the other military craft that flew closer to street level. He was just an observer at the moment and his helicopter an airborne command center. He hated being in this position. Bringing in two military craft would raise questions. He had planned to keep the whole operation secret from everyone, especially the military. If things went wrong, President Chavez and his administration would be publicly humiliated, and Chavez didn't tolerate attacks on his prestige.

This Bell 412 was a simple observation-and-transport craft. It carried no arms. That didn't matter, he reminded himself. The A109M had enough weaponry to handle any shooting that needed to be done—if he could convince the pilot that firing a machine gun at people in the streets was the right thing to do. As foreign minister he could give many orders and people would rush to obey them, but the military was different. If he demanded the pilots to shoot men on the ground, they would first radio in for permission from their commanding officer. There was no telling how that delay might affect the outcome of these events.

The pilot leveled off five hundred feet higher than the 109 and a kilometer away, moving in a slow circle around the van holding Costa and Cenobio and its escort car. He could see them clearly beneath the 109's spotlight. He also noticed a truck a kilometer behind the van driving with no lights. Santi ordered the military craft to illuminate the truck.

JOSE ARRIVED AT THE alley leading to the structure where J. J. and Caraway were hiding. He slipped down the lane and ducked behind a dumpster—a battered van was parked in the alley next to an open door. He forced his breath to slow and his heart to calm. He snapped down his night-vision goggles, which made the taillights of the van seem to glow like miniature suns. He squinted through the lenses. He counted four men entering the van, and the vehicle pulled away. He had arrived too late.

Jose waited a moment then moved to the still-open door. This was the site J. J. had described. The shred of hope he held that the van was just making a delivery or picking up product evaporated. With the barrel of his M4 raised, Jose stepped into the building. A dark puddle rested near the threshold of another door that led into a work room. Once confident the building was clear of hostiles, Jose raised his night-vision goggles and turned on the flashlight mounted to the rail of his weapon.

He saw a large work table with a makeshift barricade made of folding tables stacked on edge. The tables bore several bullet holes. Jose moved to the other side and counted a dozen spent 9mm shells. He also saw another pool of blood. What he didn't see were bodies. That gave him another thread of hope.

Jose jogged from the building and started down the alley.

CHAPTER 49

NOTHING ABOUT THE PLAN was right. It occurred to Moyer that it was less a plan and more of a reaction. He had no choices, no alternatives. If the military chopper fired on him, or just forced him to stop following the caravan, he would lose Cenobio for good. In very little time, the enemy would deliver the physicist to the airport and he would be out of reach.

The light from the helicopter bathed Moyer and his truck. There was no more hiding. Most likely their cover had been blown when Pete landed in the hospital and then escaped. Still, they had remained out of reach to this point. No longer—it was now or never.

"Go!" Moyer shouted into the cell phone. He slammed the accelerator to the floor.

HECTOR CENOBIO HAD BEEN looking out his window and up at the sky when everything went white. He snapped his head back and blinked his eyes. "What's going on?"

"Reinforcements," Costa said. "It seems you have friends. Who would send trained military men to rescue you and your family?"

"I don't know what you're talking about."

Costa looked at his cell phone. "I am told that two men tried to break into the building where we are keeping your wife. You have friends in the military?"

"My wife, my children—they are all right?"

"Yes. The two men failed. They've been captured. One is injured badly. He may not live." Costa smiled. "The uninjured one may not live either."

"I want to see my family."

"Perhaps later. Your friends have changed everything."

Hector struggled for words. "I don't know who they are."

"Perhaps they are not friends. If they know how valuable you are to certain countries, they may not be here to rescue you at all."

"What do you mean?"

Costa turned in his seat to face Hector. "Killing you would be easier than rescuing you."

Hector looked outside and tried to deny the truth of the words.

He failed.

THERE WERE NEW VOICES—SEVERAL of them. Julia Cenobio stood next to the door, her ear just an inch away. She heard excited chatter in a Middle Eastern tongue. She heard a man scream in pain. Another man moaned. Was one of them Hector?

☢ ☢ ☢

J. J. REGAINED CONSCIOUSNESS SLOWLY. A moment ago he was on the beach, sitting on a blanket, as a lazy ocean of deep blue rolled and tossed small waves on the shore, creating a backbeat to the song of gulls overhead. Next to him sat Ronnie—tall, trim, blonde hair to her shoulders, and skin painted brown by gentle tanning. They were holding hands.

J. J. had never held Ronnie's hand. He had only seen her in church and during Sunday-morning Bible study for single adults. More than her good looks attracted him to her. She never hesitated to participate in the discussion, always offered educated opinions, and glanced at him frequently.

Last Sunday was going to be the day when he asked her out—the day when he would gather the courage to approach, chat, then spring the question: "May I introduce you to the best tacos in town?" A lousy line, but she had once told the Bible study group of her love for Mexican food. He had committed that to memory.

A breeze pushed through J. J.'s hair. The briny smell of the ocean seemed like perfume. He turned to Ronnie and she to him. She leaned closer. He could smell the lotion on her body, the sweetness of her breath.

Their first kiss hovered a moment away.

Scorching pain crossed his left cheek and ignited every neuron in his brain. He felt himself falling. Concrete replaced the soft white sand of the beach. J. J.'s head bounced off the floor. A coppery-tasting fluid filled his mouth. He opened his eyes. Someone spoke in a language J. J. didn't understand, but he had heard enough of it over the years and during missions to recognize Farsi.

J. J. tried to rise, but he couldn't move. Instinctively he reached for his sidearm. His arms didn't respond. A second passed before he realized he had been bound to a wooden chair. He and the chair lay on their sides. Several blinks later the fire in J. J.'s head subsided enough for him to take in his situation. Memories inundated his mind like a tsunami coming ashore. With the recollections came the pain from his injuries. He recalled the gunfire and the butt end of an AK-47 landing on his nose. He tried to inhale then realized he couldn't draw air. He could feel the swollen tissue of his face. The impact had broken his nose.

Again someone said something in Farsi. Despite the language difference, J. J. knew an order when he heard it. Two men righted him. Duct tape secured his wrists and legs to the chair.

"I see you're awake. Did you enjoy your nap?" A thick accent weighted the English words.

J. J. looked around and recognized his location, although he had never been inside the room. He had, however, been on the roof above and seen it with the gooseneck spy cam.

"I asked a question." The man—short and wiry with a scowl J. J. assumed he had been born with—raised his fist.

"Ease up, mate. No need to hit me again."

"What . . . what was that?" The man laughed. "Was that supposed to be an Australian accent? Pitiful. Laughable."

"New Zealand," J. J. said. Before they had left on the mission, they had been reminded that if captured, the U.S. would deny any involvement.

The tormentor looked at the others in the room. J. J. scanned the faces he could see: five men, all under thirty years of age, all with angry looks on their faces. He also saw the door leading to the small bathroom and wondered if the Cenobio woman and her children were still held captive there. A motion behind him drew his attention. He turned his head and could barely make out Caraway in his peripheral vision. The best J. J. could tell, his partner was alive, unconscious, and bound to a similar chair.

His captor leaned close to J. J.'s face. "I have been to Australia and to New Zealand. You sound nothing like what I heard there."

"I'm still working on my act."

The man lifted a booted foot and placed it on J. J.'s thigh, leaned in, and put his weight on it so that it pulled the tissue of J. J.'s leg toward the seat. The pain was worse than J. J. thought it could be. "Let me tell you who I think you are. You are American soldiers, Special Operations most likely. If not that, then you're with an American mercenary group."

"And who are you?"

"What? You want to ask questions of me? The way I see it, I'm your captor and you're my prisoner. I will ask the questions."

"I guess you got me there. Wanna trade places?"

The man removed his foot and delivered a fist to the tender side of J. J.'s head. The chair toppled over again, and two men righted it.

"You are military trained. Your appearance does not fit the typical soldier, but all that means is that you are not typical. Why are you here?"

"Jungle cruise. I went on one at Disneyland and wanted to try the real thing. I heard Venezuela had a great ride." J. J. steeled himself for another blow that didn't come.

"My time is short, soldier. I have no patience with infidels, especially military infidels. If the situation were different, I'd take my time with you—maybe several days or weeks. Bit by bit I would get the information I want, but time is a luxury I don't have."

"You want me to come back later?"

"How many are in your unit?"

"What unit?"

The man looked at his cohorts. "Always they begin this way. Brave, strong, as if pain means nothing to them. The American military train their men to resist interrogation. They call it SERE training—Survival Evasion Resistance Escape." He spoke like a concerned teacher. "Their soldiers go into the field thinking they can resist any torture. It is not true, and do you know why?" He bent over J. J. again. His breath smelled sour. "Pain changes the brain chemistry. An injured dog will bite its owner who is trying to help the creature. Soldiers like you resist for a while, but the pain begins to alter the brain. Over time you begin to rationalize your behavior. Memories become blurred. Orders get confused in your mind. Soon you begin to think you're doing the right thing. Do you know how I know this, infidel? I learned about the brain in medical school."

"Is that where you learned to throw a punch? Release me and I'll show you a better way."

"The problem today is time, so I'm going to have to dispense with the more sophisticated approach."

"Sorry to cramp your style."

"I ask again: How many in your unit?"

J. J. looked away but said nothing.

"What do you call your friend?"

"What friend?"

"The man behind you. The man whose leg you bandaged. The man you were willing to die for."

"Oh, him. He was just trying to sell me a timeshare." J. J.'s heart picked up speed.

The man J. J. started thinking of as the evil doctor sighed and stepped from sight. "Turn him around."

The two who had righted the chair spun J. J. around to face Caraway, whose face had become ashen, the color of the concrete walls that surrounded them. Doctor pulled a knife from his pocket and cut the wrapping loose and removed the bloody steripads. He seemed unconcerned that Caraway's blood covered his hands. He studied the wound.

"A nasty business, gunshot wounds. Of course, you probably know that. How many of my Shi'ite brothers in Afghanistan and Iraq have you killed? Take your friend here—as you know the point of entry was the back of the thigh. The entry wound is fairly small, but the exit wound . . ." He took hold of a loose flap of skin and pulled up. Caraway, although deep in shock, moaned and twitched his leg. The wound began to bleed again.

J. J. closed his eyes. A second later something hit him on his broken nose. He did his best not to cry out in pain. Pain forced tears from his eyes.

"I insist you watch this. I'm doing you a favor."

"You're sadistic."

"Why, yes, I am. I didn't start off that way. I wanted to help humankind, and so I studied medicine. But that was before infidel soldiers like yourself killed my father, my mother, and my sister." His face turned hard. "Tonight, you killed one of my men."

"Was he one of the guys shooting at us?"

"He was my brother. My only brother. Tell me, soldier, which of you shot him in the face?"

"It was kinda dark."

The doctor nodded, bent over Caraway again, then began to pound his fist on the wound. Caraway came to and screamed.

"Leave him alone! He's almost dead already."

"Then it won't matter if I speed things along." He turned to one of his men. "Bring me a pencil." The man disappeared into the office area of the industrial building and reappeared a moment later. The blood drained from his face as he handed the writing instrument to his leader.

J. J.'s heart beat so fast that he felt certain it would either blow through his sternum or simply explode. Either would be fine with him.

"I ask again: How many in your unit?"

J. J. shook his head.

The doctor plunged the pencil into Caraway's wound and left it. The screams made J. J. tremble. For the first time in his life, he wanted to kill a man with his bare hands.

WHEN JULIA TURNED, SHE saw her children covering their ears. They had never heard a man cry in such pain. Neither had she. The sound of it rattled around in her soul and scaled her spine with icy fingers. Tears poured from her face. Scream after scream pushed through the locked door; only slightly muted, it rebounded off the tile walls. She couldn't silence the sounds, couldn't force them from her ears. They stabbed at her consciousness, branded her eardrums. She knew if she survived, she'd carry the hideous cries with her forever.

Julia prayed the prayer of the desperate, of those so stunned, so shocked, that whole sentences were beyond their capabilities.

"Oh, God, oh, God, oh, God." She hated herself for her next thought, but the hope didn't come from the rational part of her brain: She prayed the screams came from someone other than her husband.

CHAPTER 50

ALONE. JOSE HAD BEEN taught to work with a team, but his team was in two different locations and he was between them. More than anything he wanted to use his radio to report what he had found, but he couldn't. J. J. and Caraway were in the hands of hostiles, and if Jose used his radio, they were certain to hear. He had taken a few moments to call Moyer on the cell phone, but the call refused to go through.

He had never felt so alone. His wife and child hovered near death's door. Two of his team were in the hands of the enemy. The three other members of the team were miles away with problems of their own.

The logical part of Jose's mind—the part that stored his instincts for self-protection and survival—screamed for attention. He refused to listen. He had learned long ago that courage was defined by what a man did when nearly overcome with terror. This night he would live or he would die. This night would be whatever this night was intended to be. If that meant bleeding out in the street, then so be it.

He forced one foot in front of the other, slowing only at inter-
sections of alley and streets, and continued forward in the darkness
of the night and the ebony dawn of his soul. With every stride his
apprehension gave way to the steel of determination. With every
step he forced back fear. Nothing mattered but getting to J. J. and
Caraway. Nothing. Let hell release its minions. They would find
one man determined to do what had to be done.

☢☢ ☢☢ ☢

THE PANEL TRUCK SPED along the road. Moyer had only a few seconds
to make his move. If he had outlined this plan on paper, every one
of his superiors would have nixed the idea and wondered about his
sanity. It made no sense, had little chance of working, and would
probably end in his death.

As he closed the distance between him and the two vans, he
thought of his wife, his daughter, and his son. He didn't know what
happened after death. Maybe J. J. did. He felt a moment of sadness
that he had never availed himself of the opportunity to discuss it
with him. Well, he would know soon enough.

The light from the A109 fell behind him but would only take a
few seconds to catch up. Moyer kept his gaze fixed on the vehicles
ahead. They had maintained course, but in a moment they would
certainly bolt, hopefully not before he or Rich could do what
needed to be done.

The speedometer read ninety miles per hour and rising. Moyer's
grip on the steering wheel turned his knuckles white. He waited.
With every second that passed he expected machine-gun fire to cut
him and his vehicle in half.

"STOP THAT VEHICLE! SHOOT it!"

"I'm sorry, Minister, but we have orders not to fire our weapons within the city. I must await clearance."

Santi had heard the pilot ask for permission to fire, but that had been close to thirty seconds ago. No doubt their commander was seeking permission from a higher-ranking coward. "I am ordering you to open fire on that truck. There are terrorists aboard, and they are endangering an important diplomat from our country."

"I have yet to receive permission, Minister."

Santi pounded the seat like a child. "I will hold you personally responsible if you do not shoot that truck right NOW!"

Nothing happened.

Santi snapped up his cell phone. "Behind you. Behind you!"

THE MOMENT COSTA PUT the phone to his ear, Hector saw him crank his head around to look behind him.

"Go, go, go!" Costa ordered the driver.

"What? Why—"

"GO!"

The driver hesitated long enough to pull the van from behind the lead car then drove the accelerator to the floor. He had hesitated too long.

Something struck the lumbering van. The back of the vehicle slid forward. Hector watched the driver's head snap back then forward as he tried to straighten the van, but it refused to cooperate.

Hector turned and saw another vehicle pressed against the back bumper.

POLICE CALLED IT A "pit maneuver." Moyer had seen it done a dozen times on television but had never attempted it himself—just one more thing wrong with the plan. The engine's roar lessened for a moment as Moyer allowed his truck to slow enough to keep control when he made contact. The van steered abruptly into the oncoming lane but a second too late. Moyer determined not to miss his only chance.

He matched the van's maneuver then floored the gas pedal. His front bumper touched the right rear bumper of the van. Moyer steered slightly to the right forcing the back of the van to move sideways, its rear tires breaking traction with the asphalt. He turned the steering wheel a few inches to the right. The driver of the van lost control.

So did Moyer.

The van and Moyer's truck, both with high centers of gravity, slid sideways then tipped over. Moyer had time to see the van tilt onto two wheels then begin to roll. The next thing Moyer saw was pavement rising to meet his side window. He threw himself to the right and grabbed the passenger seat.

Metal screamed as it skidded along the macadam. Glass exploded and filled the cab with tiny fragments. Moyer waited for the vehicle to roll, but its tall sides kept it from doing so. Eternal seconds passed as the vehicle continued to slide, the sound of grating metal stabbing his ears.

The truck came to a halt. Moyer wanted to wait a moment, to take a few seconds to get his bearings, but moments might cost him his life and bury his mission. He popped his seat belt, fumbled for and flipped the switch that turned on the overhead lights, and scrambled into the cargo area. The floor stood vertical and to his left. Equipment lay strewn across the area where Moyer walked. The monitors that Moyer and his team had watched diligently were damaged beyond repair, not that it mattered. They'd never be used again.

Snatching an M4 from the weapons rack, Moyer stepped over the detritus of equipment, batteries, radios, and weapons. He twisted at the handle to open the back doors, but it wouldn't budge. Moyer had no time for this. He kicked the handle twice and the left-hand door—now the "bottom" door—swung open and crashed to the pavement. Moyer raised his weapon and stepped into the night.

He had less than two seconds to do what had to be done next.

The darkness disappeared in a glare from above. The helicopter's beam covered him.

RICH POWERED HIS SEDAN down the side street. He had no idea how fast he was traveling, but he knew it wasn't fast enough. Pete had already drawn his sidearm. Neither man spoke. Neither needed to.

The car bottomed out crossing an intersection. Rich hit his head on the roof and pain pierced his skull and neck. He would worry about that later—if later ever came.

"It's the next street," Pete said.

"Got it."

Based on Moyer's last communication, Rich and Pete should be slightly ahead of the two-vehicle caravan. They assumed Cenobio was in the rear van. Rich hoped they could snatch him safely, but he understood the unspoken order: The hostiles would not be allowed to take the man. Not alive.

Rich hit the intersection and turned the wheel hard to the left. The sedan began a short four-wheel drift, its tires screaming the arrival of two more players. Rich noticed the overturned van and truck first. Then he saw Moyer step from the truck and the light from the chopper shining down on him.

"Shaq, behind us!"

Rich snapped his eyes to the rearview mirror. The other vehicle in the caravan was pulling a U-turn, its tires spinning on the pavement and sending smoke into the air.

"Hang on."

Cranking the wheel as far to the left as it would go, Rich again floored the accelerator. Like the car behind him, the sedan made a tight U-turn. Rich's turn, however, didn't clear the curb. The car lurched as the right front tire jumped from street to sidewalk back to street again. The force of the impact threw Rich into the door, his shoulder hitting the window so hard he was surprised the glass didn't break.

Rich steered directly for the oncoming car as if planning to ram it. The performance was convincing—the other driver flinched and steered away. Rich wouldn't let him off the hook. He rammed the driver's side door, pushing the car sideways several feet.

White air bags exploded into the faces of Rich and Pete. A half second later they deflated. With ears ringing from the crash and the explosive air bag deployment, Rich threw his door open. He saw Pete do the same.

The impact must have been harder than he realized because Rich staggered to the side two steps. By the time he gained his footing, two men had exited the passenger side of the car and raised Uzi-style submachine guns. Rich didn't take time to identify the weapons properly. Instead he raised his sidearm and squeezed the trigger. Before he felt the recoil of his weapon, he heard a percussive bang from his right. Pete had already squeezed off a round, followed by another. Man number two, who had crawled from the backseat, dropped backward, his face blank and his forehead bearing a large hole that hadn't been there a moment before. Man number one had been in the front passenger seat. Rich's shot hit him in the neck. A second shot entered the skull just above the man's right eye.

A movement in the driver's seat drew Rich's attention. The driver had raised a similar weapon. Rich stepped to the side just as the driver's already fractured window erupted into shards. Rich aimed, pulled his trigger twice, and the driver ceased firing.

Another shot to his right. Pete had shot another man who had crawled across the backseat. He never had time to raise a weapon.

A new sound—automatic fire. Rich spun on his heels. The military helicopter had opened up with a blast of machine-gun fire aimed right at Moyer.

CHAPTER 51

THE PAIN HAD BROUGHT Caraway back to consciousness, and J. J. wished with all his might it hadn't.

"I repeat: How many in your unit?"

Perspiration poured from Caraway's face, a face that had turned as white as a lily. "Six thousand," Caraway muttered. "Or maybe seventy thousand. I'm not good with numbers."

The doctor-interrogator lost his temper and landed a hard fist to Caraway's gut. J. J. could hear the air leave the man's lungs. Caraway coughed, and J. J. saw blood come from his mouth. J. J. strained against the duct tape, but it refused to budge. Although it was Caraway being tortured, J. J. could feel every blow as if it had been delivered to him.

"I can do this all night," the doctor said. "You can save yourself a great deal of pain by cooper—" A cell phone chimed. One of the other men handed the device to the doctor.

"Yes." His face blanched. "Where? We're on our way." He said something in Farsi. J. J. didn't understand the words, but he knew the look. Something had gone wrong.

"What is happening?" one of the men asked in English. This one had a Spanish accent.

"We are needed. Everyone into the van."

"What about them?" the Hispanic asked.

"Where are they going to go? I need every man."

They exited through the office door. J. J. heard someone lock the door and rattle the handle.

"Go get 'em, Boss." Caraway's voice was barely above a whisper.

"Caraway, you still with me?"

"Where would . . . I go?" He gritted his teeth. "I don't know how much longer I can hold out."

"Just hang in there."

He shook his head. "Fading fast. You pray . . . pray that God kills me."

"I won't do that, man. We're not finished yet."

"My fault. I shouldn't have hesitated when . . ."

"It's not your fault. Save your strength."

Caraway moved his lips, but no words came out.

J. J. struggled against his restraints. It was hopeless.

Caraway lifted his head but was too weak to hold it up. His head lolled back. "Pray . . . the pain . . . pray for me, Colt. Pray for my soul."

"Hang in there, pal. Just hang in there."

"I'm serious. Pray for my soul."

"I will. I will."

Caraway's head dipped forward.

☢️   ☢️   ☢️

THE MOMENT MOYER'S FOOT touched pavement he raised his M4 and sent a burst of rounds toward the light. Just before he pulled the trigger he heard the loud rumble of machine-gun fire. The chopper was shooting at him.

Moyer's bullets found their mark first, the spotlight. He dove to the side as a stream of .30-caliber rounds punctured holes in the asphalt, sending bits of debris flying. Moyer landed on his side, rolled to his back, and instinctively switched the weapon to full-auto mode. He pulled the trigger hard and bullets flew into the air at nine hundred rounds a minute. He heard his ammo hit the metal skin of the craft. The problem with firing on the A109 was, like many military helicopters, the A109 had armored seats, protective shielding over key areas, and redundant systems. Nonetheless, Moyer emptied his clip, aiming at the rotor system in hopes of doing enough damage that the pilot would have trouble controlling the craft.

He would need to get lucky. Real lucky.

The helicopter pulled away, circled, and began a new approach, nose pointed at Moyer. Moyer scrambled to his feet and bolted for the panel truck. The metal sides of the truck would provide no protection. The helo's machine gun could cut through the siding as if the truck were an aluminum can.

The *pop-pop-pop* of handheld weapons worked their way through the truck's siding. Moyer bolted from the truck, two clips in his hand. In a move practiced more times than he could remember, Moyer released the spent cartridge holder and slammed a new magazine in its place.

The helo realigned but further away this time. More gunfire. Moyer glanced to his side and saw Shaq and Junior moving his way, each firing round after round of 9mm bullets at the craft. Each ejected a clip and replaced it with fresh ammo. They carried only two magazines, one in the weapon and one back-up. They would soon be out of ammo.

Moyer raised his M4 to his shoulder, sighted, and squeezed the trigger, again aiming at the rotor assembly in the slim hope he could cripple the craft. He saw the muzzle flash of airborne weaponry, but Moyer stood his ground. Just as the weapon began to dry fire, starved of ammunition, a strong hand grabbed his arm and jerked. A hot stream of machine-gun rounds skipped past him just inches from his body.

"Thanks, Shaq."

"Look." The big man pointed to the helo. The craft was spinning on its axis. "Looks like we took out its tail rotor." The helo began to spin faster.

The helicopter pilot fought to keep control, but it was clear he was going down. Moyer didn't wait to watch the crash or try to determine which industrial building was going to have an A109 sticking out of its roof.

Moyer jogged around the panel truck and made for the van. The side door had been opened and two men had managed to crawl out. One held a gun to the head of the other. Moyer recognized Cenobio from the photo sent to him from stateside. Blood had dried below his nose from a split lip—his hosts had been unkind. The other man wore a determined look. Moyer raised his sidearm, as did Rich and Pete.

"One move and I kill Cenobio," the man said.

"You do and you will die before he hits the ground," Moyer said. "Let him go. There's no way out."

The man motioned upward to another helicopter. "There is always a way." Moyer didn't turn to look. He could hear the aircraft in the distance.

Pete did turn. "Bell 400 series. Doesn't look militarized."

"Keep an eye on it, Junior."

The Hispanic man with a gun pressed against Cenobio's temple raised an eyebrow. "Americans. Figures."

"Let the man go," Moyer ordered.

"Stay where you are. I *will* kill him. What will you tell your masters when you tell them you let Dr. Cenobio die?"

"We don't have masters, just higher-ranking officers."

"Still, you go home empty-handed." He pushed the muzzle the deeper into Cenobio's flesh. The scientist's face twisted in pain.

"What makes you think we've come to save him?" He paused a second. "Shaq?"

"Got it."

Moyer nodded. "Take the shot."

The sound of Shaq's 9mm discharging echoed down the dark street.

☢ ☢ ☢

THE PAIN FROM COSTA'S twisting the business end of his handgun into Hector's head hurt more than the backhand he had received earlier, but the pain disappeared when he heard the oldest of the three men say, "What makes you think we've come to save him?"

How much worse could things get? Held at gunpoint by one of his abductors, he now faced three assassins. As if to punctuate the observation, the large black man fired his weapon. The noise engulfed him and he flinched, waiting for the bullet to pierce his chest. Instead, he felt something wet against the side of his head. The gun that had been pressed against his temple was no longer there.

There was a pain in his chest. His heart had stopped beating for a moment then restarted, sending a sharp thrust through his sternum. Hector took a stuttering breath and touched the center of his chest. He forced himself to look: His hands were clean. Slowly, Hector turned to see Costa on the ground with an angry red hole above the bridge of his nose.

The older man stepped forward and took Hector by the arm. "Are you all right?"

"Considering everything, I guess so."

"Good. We don't have much time."

"Who are you?"

"Let's just say we're friends and leave it at that."

Hector nodded. "My family. They have—"

"We know and we're working on that. Right now, you have to trust us." He turned. "Shaq, Junior."

"The helo's approaching, Boss."

"I've had my fill of helicopters," the man called Boss said. He turned, raised his automatic weapon, and unleashed a torrent of bullets. The helo banked away.

"I see smoke," Junior said. "Nice shooting."

"It's easier when they don't have strategic armor. Check the van."

The younger two approached the overturned vehicle slowly, peering in through the windshield. "Driver looks dead. I don't see anyone else," the larger man reported.

The Boss nodded. "Okay, listen up . . ."

J. J. LEANED FORWARD THEN sat back hard in hopes of breaking the chair. Maybe he could free a hand and start working on the tape that bound him, but he couldn't create enough force to fracture the oak. Despair began to set in. Then something occurred to him.

"Mrs. Cenobio . . . Julia . . . can you hear me?" Nothing.

Pushing with his feet J. J. scooted the chair closer to the bathroom door. "Mrs. Cenobio, my name is J. J. I'm here to help you . . . actually, I need *your* help. Can you hear me?"

A muted sound pressed through the door. "Yes . . . yes, I can hear you. Who are you?"

"I'm part of a team here to free you and your husband, but I need your help."

"The guards."

"They're gone for now, but they might come back. We have to act quickly. Can you come out here?"

"I'm locked in."

J. J. examined the doorknob. It was a cheap, simple affair with a twist latch. If he had one hand free he could easily twist the lock into the open position, but even that was beyond him. He contemplated turning the lock with his mouth but doubted he could do it.

"Are they really gone?" she asked.

"Yes, for now. I think they went after my friends."

"Okay . . . okay. Wait." She said something else J. J. couldn't hear. He assumed she was speaking to the children.

J. J. started to speak when he heard an explosive bang and the bathroom door shook in its frame. A second later it happened again, then again. A little above and to the right of the lock a splinter-laced hole appeared. Several more times the door shook, and with each impact the hole grew larger. J. J. had no idea what she was using as a battering ram but it was working. A moment later a white, flat, hard object punched through the hollow-core door. J. J. recognized it immediately. The woman was knocking a hole in the door with the lid to a toilet tank.

He heard grunting and more of the hard porcelain lid appeared. The tank top disappeared back into the bathroom, and a delicate hand replaced it and fumbled with the outer lock. Two seconds later the door opened slowly, and the tear-smudged face of Julia Cenobio appeared. Before opening the door all the way, she glanced around the room.

"Stay with me, children." She stepped out and her children followed her. They looked frail and frightened beyond words. Julia stepped to J. J. She held something in her hand.

"Is that what I think it is? Is that a flush arm from a toilet?"

"Yes."

J. J. shook his head. "Lady, no matter how many times I tell this story, no one is going to believe me."

"You sound American."

"I am. Can you free me?"

Julia studied the duct tape. Then she looked around the room.

"I'm afraid they took everything from us."

Julia nodded, lifted the metal bar she had sharpened on the concrete floor, and cut one of J. J.'s hands free. She started on the other arm.

"Is he dead, Mamá?" the boy pointed at Caraway.

"I don't know, sweetheart. Try not to look."

J. J. understood. Caraway looked as if he had been run over by a tractor. Blood pooled beneath his injured leg. Once his hands were free, he took the makeshift knife from Julia and cut away the rest of his bonds. It took five minutes for him to free Caraway, who continued to draw breath, although J. J. didn't know how.

CHAPTER 52

JOSE DUCKED BEHIND A stack of cardboard boxes when the battered van came speeding down the street. It rode heavy, as if weighed down with equipment or a full load of passengers. Even in the dark, Jose could tell it was the same van they had spotted after setting up the video recon systems. Once he was certain he was out of sight of the van, Jose pulled the encrypted cell phone from his vest and dialed Moyer. No answer. He then tried Rich, who answered on the fourth ring.

"Doc, that you?"

"Shaq, I can't reach Boss."

"He's here. We have the package but have to beat feet."

"I'm near the building we had under surveillance. A van just tore down the street. I'm sure it's the same one that brought the woman and her kids."

"Did you see who was in it?"

"No. Too far away. But I'd assume hostiles are inbound to your location."

"Roger that. Boss is headed your way. He's in a 1958 Chevy pickup."

"Say again."

"Boss is coming in. Look for an old pickup."

"Understood . . . I think."

"Any word on Colt and Billy?"

"Negative. Will report soon."

Jose ended the call and wondered what he had missed.

☢ ☢ ☢

SANTI SCREAMED AT HIS pilot, "What are you doing? Turn back. We can't lose them."

"I can't do that, Minister. We're losing oil pressure."

"You said we were too far away for them to do any real damage."

The pilot shook his head and struggled with the controls. "Maybe it was a lucky shot. I don't know. I do know that we're losing oil, and if I don't get us on the ground soon the engine will seize and we will drop like a stone."

"Can't you hold our position just a little while longer?"

"We must maintain forward motion. If the engine stops, I can use autorotation for a controlled crash. If we are hovering when the engine stalls, we will fall with no hope of survival. I'm going to find a place to set down."

It took all of Santi's willpower not to scream at the top of his lungs. Three men had killed six of his people and snatched Cenobio. He had watched his most faithful mercenary collapse to the ground after being shot in the head. It was all falling apart.

He snapped up his cell phone again and placed a call to the man he had ordered to the scene a few minutes before. "My helicopter is damaged. You must get Cenobio back. Do you hear? Get him back!" He slammed the phone on the seat next to him. The helicopter descended. "Let me talk to your commander."

"With all due respect, sir, I'm a little busy now."

"I want to talk to your commander."

The pilot did something Santi couldn't see. "Go ahead."

Santi began talking before the commander could speak. "I want another helicopter in the air. Now."

☢ ☢ ☢

"YOU AMAZE ME, JUNIOR." Moyer buttoned his vest and began stocking the cab of the classic truck with loaded weaponry.

"I wasn't always the fine, upstanding soldier I am today, Boss. I learned a few things back in high school."

"They taught you how to hot-wire an old truck in high school?"

"It was one of the lesser-known classes. You can drive a stick, can't you?"

"Ain't nothin' I can't drive, Junior." He slipped into the cab.

Shaq approached. "There has to be a better way."

"Just follow the plan and get Cenobio out of here."

"I think you're taking an unnecessary risk."

"You can file a complaint with Colonel MacGregor when we get back. Besides, you were the one that wanted to go back for Colt and Billy."

"I know what I said—"

Moyer snapped his head around. "Shaq . . . Rich, you have your orders. Carry them out." Shaq's ebony face darkened all the more. "Understood?"

"Oorah, Boss." His expression softened. "Don't get dead."

Moyer held out his hand and Rich shook it. Then Moyer dropped the old truck in first gear and slipped the clutch. As he pulled away, he saw Rich put Cenobio in the back of the sedan. The car had sustained damage but was still operational. Pete had checked for leaking fluids and cut away the deployed air bags. The car started up and headed in the opposite direction, and Moyer shifted into second.

JOSE'S PROBLEM WAS A lack of knowledge. He had no idea if J. J. and Caraway were in the building he approached; if they had been carted off in the van; if their bodies were lying in some alley; or if heavily armed gunmen waited for him. He just didn't know, and there was only one way to find out.

According to the book he should wait for Moyer to arrive, but the amount of blood Jose had seen behind the work table barricade likely meant that one of his team was well on his way to dead.

Staying in the shadows, Jose reconnoitered the perimeter of the building and saw no guards. That didn't mean a half dozen men didn't wait for him inside. He did notice that the front gate lay wide open, which fit with the speed of the van. Perhaps the bad guys had all hightailed it out.

The sound of a vehicle on the street sent Jose sprinting to the other side of the street, where he hid in the narrow space between two buildings and raised his M4. The vehicle, an older-looking truck, stopped a block down. A man exited and moved stealthily across the street then started toward Jose. Through the night-vision goggles, Jose recognized Moyer's gait. A moment later, his cell phone vibrated.

"Whatcha got?" Moyer asked.

"No sign of hostiles. Front gate is open. Doors are all closed. I was just getting ready to check the windows."

"Meet me at the southwest corner of the fence. We'll go in together."

"You come alone?"

"Shaq and Junior are busy."

Jose didn't bother to ask. If he lived he could hear the whole report later. All he had to do now was rescue J. J. and Caraway, escape Caracas, find a way home, and a dozen other small matters.

"DO YOU THINK THIS will work?" Pete asked.

Rich glanced at him then tilted his rearview mirror to better see Hector Cenobio stretched out on the backseat as he had ordered him to. "Not a chance."

"Yet we're going to try."

"Boss said to do it, we do it. Besides, the last part of the plan couldn't work either, but it did. Maybe it's our lucky day."

"Do you feel lucky?"

"Luck or no, we're committed." Shaq fought with the steering wheel. "Man, this thing is a bear to drive. The alignment is all out of whack."

"Ramming other cars can do that." Pete leaned over and looked at the gauges. "At least it's not overheating. You know, the rental agency is going to charge you more for scratching the paint."

"I figured as much. I'll gladly pay it if—" Shaq tilted the rearview mirror up. "We got company."

Pete turned. "I don't know about you, Shaq, but I'm getting real sick of these guys."

"On the floor, Cenobio."

"I'm already lying down on the seat—"

"ON THE FLOOR!"

The rear window exploded. Shaq pressed himself down in the seat. Pete popped his seat belt, turned, and lifted his M4.

The front window shattered, sending a million spider-web cracks through the whole glass surface, the safety laminate holding the shards of glass together.

"I can't see," Rich barked.

Pete lifted his weapon and smashed the butt of the stock into the window repeatedly until he created a hole. Rich stuck his head out the window. Pete lowered his weapon and started pulling the windshield out of its track.

"That'll do it," Rich said. "I can see enough. How about returning the favor?"

Pete turned in the seat again, aimed the automatic weapon out the back window, and pulled the trigger. Spent cartridges flew from the chamber and hit Rich in the head. He didn't complain.

"Talk to me."

"Looks like a single vehicle—a van I think. Hard to see because of the headlights. Shooter is—" Pete fired a burst, "*was* hanging out the window."

"You know how to fix the lights."

The sound of several bullets hitting the trunk of the car made Shaq crank the steering wheel left then right.

"I need two seconds without the evasive maneuvers," Pete said. He spoke calmly as if all this were a video game.

"Ready?" Shaq asked.

"Ready."

Rich straightened the car and Pete released three quick bursts. Rich looked in his mirror. One headlight disappeared. The van veered right, then left.

"I saw steam," Shaq said.

"I hope so. I was hoping to take out the radiator while I was at it."

Shaq zigged then zagged as the sound of gunfire erupted from behind. "Hang on, we're coming up on our turn."

"Hanging—"

The car turned sideways as Rich pressed the accelerator even harder and jerked the wheel to the left. Pete grunted as he hit the passenger side door. As the car straightened, Pete released three more bursts out the back window. In the mirror Rich saw the van overshoot the intersection. Steam passed in front of the remaining headlight. Rich had shot up the radiator and maybe hit an oil line.

"Caught the tail end of the van. He's moving fast."

"Hang on," Rich said again as he made a sharp turn on a side road, backtracking their previous direction. At the next street he turned right. "Anything?"

"No. I heard brakes. If they want us, they're going to have to search for us."

"Stay sharp. They can't be more than a block or two away."

☢ ☢ ☢

HECTOR LAY OVER THE driveshaft hump in the backseat, covering his head to protect himself from the hot cartridges regurgitated by the automatic weapon. The noise was deafening, the smell of burnt gunpowder gagging, and the fear almost overwhelming. "I should have been a meteorologist," he said to himself, then returned to praying for his family.

CHAPTER 53

J. J. CUT AWAY THE tape that held the unconscious Caraway in the chair and eased him to the floor. He then reapplied the tourniquet. He looked around the large room, hoping for another industrial-class first-aid kit, but found nothing.

His mind raced. What to do next? Their captors could return any minute, but he couldn't move Caraway without further endangering his life. He also had a frightened woman and two terrorized children to rescue.

The sound came from the front of the building, near the entrance door, by the window. They were back, and this time he was certain they would kill Caraway, him, and maybe the woman and children. "Get back in the bathroom," he said. He picked up the sharpened metal bar Julia had crafted and started for the front of the building.

"No. I've had enough of that space."

J. J. didn't have time to argue. He moved to the office area and placed his back against the wall, the shiv clutched in his right hand. He heard the doorknob jiggle then stop. He tried to peer around the wall to see if the door had opened. It hadn't.

This was madness. He was a single weary soldier with a weapon made from a toilet, going up against a half dozen heavily armed enemy combatants.

The window exploded and J. J. took a step back. Two men charged through the opening. J. J. swung his arm in a wide horizontal arc then stopped. The blade was an inch from the throat of Jose. Just behind him, with the barrel of his M4 pointed at J. J.'s head, stood Moyer.

J. J. lowered his arm, bent over, and took several deep breaths.

"Gee, Colt," Jose said. "I thought we were friends."

J. J. straightened and embraced the medic. "Sorry. I thought you were a bill collector."

But Jose had spotted Caraway and already moved to help him.

"You okay, Colt?" Moyer asked.

"Yeah. A little worse for wear."

Moyer frowned. "Report."

"Six men. Some Iranian, some Hispanic. They got an emergency call and bolted out of here. Caraway is bad. The things they did to him . . ."

"Save that for later, soldier. We're clear for now?"

"Clear."

"Good. We're leaving. Kill the lights and open the big door."

☢ ☢ ☢

SANTI STOOD OUTSIDE THE Bell helicopter, pacing in the grass of the infield of a community baseball diamond where the pilot had set the craft down. Any other night Santi might have admired the pilot's skill and daring in landing the crippled craft, but all he could think of at the moment was the interminable time it was taking for another helicopter to find them and land.

Two minutes later a massive Russian-made MI-17 thundered overhead, hovered, then landed in center field. Santi was moving to the craft before it had fully settled on the grass surface. The moment he had his safety belt fastened, he said, "Go!"

The craft lifted from the ground, leaving the crippled helicopter and pilot behind. The MI-17 was heavily armored, heavily armed, and designed for military operations. There was room in the compartment aft of the two-pilot cabin for a dozen more people. A soldier manned the massive machine gun.

"See if you can shoot us down now," he mumbled to himself.

☢ ☢ ☢

RICH TURNED THE HEADLIGHTS off and cruised the back streets, taking a circuitous route to their destination. Cenobio sat in the middle of the backseat, swiveling his head from side to side. He and Pete studied each street, looking for the van that had been chasing them. So far there had been no sign of it.

"Only a couple of hours left before daylight," Rich said. "I'm seeing more vehicles on the road."

"What, you think a smashed-up car with no front or rear window might attract attention?" Pete sat with his M4 pointed between his feet.

"If I was a cop, I'd stop me."

"Yeah, me too."

"I'm not leaving without my family," Cenobio said.

"I'm sorry, Dr. Cenobio, but you are. It's the only way."

"I'm not leaving Caracas without my wife and children."

Rich sighed. "I have a wife and kids too, Doctor, and if I were in your situation, I'd be saying the same thing. We have men trying to rescue your family now. Once we have you safely out of country, the bad guys won't need your family."

"And they will be free to kill them."

He was right. "We're doing our best to make sure that doesn't happen."

"If things had gone a little differently, you would have killed me, wouldn't you? To keep me out of the hands of the Iranians, you would have killed me."

Pete looked at Rich.

"Yes," Rich said.

"What a world we live in. How are you going to get me out of the country? The foreign minister is behind all of this. He is a powerful man."

"We thought he might be involved."

"You haven't answered my question."

Rich nodded. "I know."

He maneuvered the car away from the streets of the industrial area and toward the ocean. Several large structures lined the coast, and small private piers stretched like fingers into the black ocean. Each pier glowed under dim mercury-vapor lights, giving the impression they had driven into a ghost world.

Several trucks plied the coastal road. Rich did his best to avoid them, but he couldn't remain out of sight forever. He looked at his watch. "I hope we're not late. It's so unfashionable to be tardy."

"Just imagine the damage to your social status," Pete said.

Rich noticed Pete's fingers drumming the stock of his M4. Rich couldn't blame him. His heart was drumming the inside of his rib cage.

"That's it." Pete pointed to a small pier a dozen yards beyond the road.

Rich steered off the coastal road and proceeded down a thin strip of rutted and warped asphalt, the kind of damage caused by eighteen wheelers. The sedan, already battered and shot up, bounded down the uneven surface. He began to feel hopeful.

They parked near the shore end of the pier and exited the car, eyes searching every shadow. They saw nothing.

Waiting was the hardest work of all.

The three men stood by the car, gazing back at the street.

The soft sound of water lapping the pier's pillars and caressing the stone breakwater hung in the air. Any other time Rich would have found it soothing. At the moment he found it annoying, and it seemed to increase in intensity.

"You guys looking for a ride?" The voice came from behind him.

Rich and Pete spun, bringing up their weapons. They found themselves face to face with a giant bug.

"LOST THEM? WHERE?" SANTI held the cell phone so tight his fingers ached. "Hold on." He spoke to the pilot. The craft banked and headed for the commercial district southeast of Caracas. "We will be over the area in a few minutes. Keep searching."

J. J. AND JOSE LOADED Caraway in the back of the pickup. Moyer directed Julia Cenobio and her children into the front seat. The boy sat in the middle, the young girl on her mother's lap.

"How is he, Doc?" Moyer asked as he rounded the back of the truck.

"Not good, Boss. Shock and blood loss. I wish I could give you better news."

"Keep him alive. This is going to be a rough ride back here. There's nothing I can do about it. Stay low. Keep your weapons at the ready. Clear?"

"Oorah," they said in unison.

Moyer slipped into the driver's seat.

"Where are we going?" Julia asked.

"Hopefully to meet your husband." He dropped the old truck into gear and pulled onto the street.

THE BUG WAS HOLDING an automatic weapon in Rich's face. Two other bugs did the same with Pete and Cenobio. It took a long second for Rich to realize the bug was a man wearing a diving mask. "I take it you're our way out of here."

"Name?" the bug demanded. "And it had better be right."

"Master Sergeant Rich Harbison."

The man looked at Pete.

"Staff Sergeant Pete Rasor."

"Lieutenant Coffer." The men lowered their weapons. "Nice car."

Rich glanced at what had once been a fine-looking vehicle. "I'm just borrowing it."

"Remind me never to loan you anything. Can you swim?"

"Um, yeah, why?"

The man turned to Pete. "What about you?"

"Love swimming."

"And you?" He nodded to Cenobio who shook his head. "Not at all?"

"I hate the water."

"That's too bad. Follow me." He turned and headed to the stone breakwater next to the small pier. Rich took Cenobio by the arm and followed the man.

"What's going on?" Cenobio asked. "Who are they?"

"Navy SEALs," Rich said.

"You know," Pete said, "if word gets out that SEALs saved our bacon, we'll never hear the end of it."

"They're not saving our bacon, Junior. We're allowing them the privilege of participating in our mission. They need the experience."

"Works for me."

"Watch your step," Coffer said. "Some of the stones are loose."

Moving as fast as footing would allow, Rich, Pete, and Cenobio followed Coffer under the pier. The two other SEALs crouched on rocks just below the brim of the breakwater, watching the streets. Rich noticed several dark packages just above the waterline. Coffer grabbed one and held it up. For the first time, Shaq noticed the man wore a similar device.

"This is a closed-circuit rebreather. Several hours of training are necessary to use one properly."

"Just give us the basics, Lieutenant. People are looking for us." A two-lens dive mask had been attached to the breathing unit, the same kind of mask that gave the SEALs the human-bug look.

"So I hear. A rebreather will let you breathe underwater without scuba tanks. In a nutshell, it turns your exhalation into breathable air."

"Under . . . underwater?" Cenobio said.

"Yes, sir."

"I told you I can't swim."

"No problem, sir. All you need to do is breathe and go limp. My men will take care of everything else."

"I don't know if I can—"

"You can," Shaq said. "Continue, Lieutenant."

Coffer slipped one of the bag-like devices over Pete's head. "It slips on like this. Straps go around the side. Make it snug but not so tight it restricts your movements." He held up a hose and mouthpiece. "This goes in your mouth. You hold it in place by biting on these rubber protrusions. Breathe normally."

"How far do we have to swim?" Rich asked.

"Not far, Master Sergeant, about three miles."

"Three miles? You're kidding, right?"

"No, sir."

"Cenobio can't swim. How do you expect him to last three yards, let alone three miles?"

"No worries. You're in the hands of the United States Navy."

Rich looked at Pete. "Suddenly I'm terrified."

"Keep your weapons as long as you like, but once we're underway, I suggest ditching them. That or sling them over your shoulder. You'll need both hands free.

Five minutes later Rich stepped into the inky black of the ocean. Next to him the other two SEALs led the terrified physicist into the water.

CHAPTER 54

J. J. LAY IN THE truck bed to the right of Caraway. Doc lay on the other side. They tried to give the injured man as much room as possible while keeping themselves from view of anyone driving by. Dawn was still a couple of hours off and the streets in this district remained empty except for the occasional delivery truck.

The night's events had taken their toll on J. J.'s mind and body. Weary and aching, he wondered if the impact from the butt of the AK-47 had split his skull. Jose wanted time to examine him, and J. J. couldn't blame him. He knew he looked a mess: bloody and swollen face, split lip, and broken nose. Still, he felt thankful to be alive for however much longer that would last.

Overhead stars gleamed and flickered, distorted by the thick marine air. They seemed so close, almost touchable. Since elementary school when he first began to hear and take seriously the things taught in church, he had imagined that God lived somewhere behind the stars, as if the night sky were a dark blanket just waiting for someone to pull it aside to reveal the glory of heaven. J. J. longed to reach up to the stars with his hand, to seize that blanket of nighttime sky, to see for just a moment the glories of God's neighborhood, but he kept his arm down, his fingers on the 9mm pistol Moyer had given him.

Next to him Caraway groaned, stirred, then fell comatose again. J. J. took this as a reminder. As requested, he began to pray for Caraway's soul.

☢ ☢ ☢

THE PICKUP HAD THE suspension of a rusted truck, and it transmitted every bump, every pothole to its passengers. Moyer felt guilty about every bounce. The ride had to be hurting the men in back, especially Caraway.

"Thank you for coming for us," Julia said.

"I was in the neighborhood." Moyer studied each intersection. Somewhere out there was a battered van filled with armed and extremely angry men. The last thing he wanted to do was cross their path. Not with a woman, two children, and an injured man dying in the back.

"How is my husband?"

"Last I saw him, he was well. It looked like someone may have popped him in the mouth, but beyond that he was okay. I'm sure he'll be a little bruised from the accident."

"Accident?"

"The van the abductors used to transport him met with a little trouble."

"What kind of trouble?"

Moyer kept his eyes moving from side to side looking for anything that might prove a danger. "Someone ran them off the road. The van turned over."

"Someone?"

"I'm sure the guy meant well."

A loud knocking broke into the conversation. J. J. rapped the back window again. Moyer looked in the rearview mirror. J. J. pointed at his ear then at the sky.

Moyer began to swear under his breath.

"WE HAVE ANOTHER TEAM," Rich said.

"I know," Coffer said.

"At least one is wounded."

"I know."

Coffer stepped deeper in the water. Rich laid a big hand on his shoulder. "A wounded man can't swim three miles."

"I know that as well, Master Sergeant. My orders are to get you and the men with you safely away from the coast without getting killed. That's what I'm doing."

Rich turned the man around. "Look, I want to know there will be someone here waiting for them."

"There will be, and with all due respect, Master Sergeant, I have no intention of chatting with you until you're satisfied. You have your orders, don't you?"

"Yes."

"And who gave them to you?"

"My team leader."

Coffer nodded. "Then I suggest you follow your orders so I can follow mine. Now are you going to let go of me, or do I have to break that arm?"

Rich considered telling him to give it a try but gave in to the logic and his training. He removed his hand. Coffer turned and took two more steps and slipped into the water, turning on his back like an otter. Clearly the man was comfortable in the ocean. He pulled his mask over his face and slipped beneath the surface.

Pulling his mask over his face, Rich slipped into the ocean. He could see Coffer a few feet below the surface pointing an underwater light at him. Rich moved toward the light. Coffer grabbed his arm and pulled him close then redirected the light to a thin, white nylon line. He pushed Rich's hand to the line and motioned with the light for Rich to follow it, and so he did.

The bottom dropped off slowly but was steep enough that Rich was soon fifteen feet below the surface. The blackness of the predawn hours was nothing compared to the ink now surrounding him. His heart rate ratcheted up and beat like the piston of an Indy car. He reached forward and felt something hard, metallic, and cold. Rich could go no further.

He could see nothing in front of him or to his right or left. He turned and was surprised to see Coffer's light so close. Coffer swam to his side and pointed the light up the line. Further up, descending in the gloom, swam the other two SEALs, with Cenobio between them shaking like a leaf in a hurricane.

Coffer pointed his light downward and Rich saw what he had touched moments before: a torpedo-shaped machine. It took a moment for Rich to realize they were underwater scooters—devices that could pull a man through the water. No wonder the SEALs weren't concerned about a three-mile swim.

The scooters—Rich knew the Navy had to have some special name for the things, but he wasn't in a position to ask—hovered a few feet above the ocean floor. Coffer raised one of devices and lifted a nylon strap with a loop in the end. He motioned for Rich to put his hand in the loop. He did. One of the other SEALs did the same with the second scooter, while the third helped Cenobio with his strap.

Rich took several deep breaths. The air tasted metallic. A moment later Coffer pushed away from the bottom, fingered a control, and the scooter began to move. A high-energy light mounted to the scooter cut through the murky water, illuminating bits of plant material and sparkling silicate. Rich let himself go limp, and with his free hand took hold of Coffer's ankle. There was nothing more he could do.

The ocean bottom dropped away, and Rich let Coffer drag him into blackness.

THE EBONY WATERS RUSHED along Hector's body, chilling him. His body already shook from shock and fear. Over the last few days he had been abducted, shown photos of his family in peril, backhanded, shot at, abducted again by men apparently sent to rescue him, and now towed beneath the surface of the ocean. He doubted anything else could surprise him.

A passage from the psalms came to mind: "Where can I go from your Spirit? Where can I flee from your presence? If I go up to the heavens, you are there; if I make my bed in the depths, you are there." Hector had never doubted the Bible, but he found himself hoping those words were especially true. In the darkness, submerged in the depths, Hector began to pray again, his lips dancing on the rubber mouthpiece.

He estimated they were less than twenty feet below the surface. He didn't know much about diving, but he did know the deeper they went the more dangerous the environment. He also knew some of the physics of water. For example, that water conducts sound very well. That fact made him wonder about the deep pounding sounds he was hearing.

SANTI GAZED OUT HIS window as the pilot of the MI-17 continued to increase his spiral search pattern. Santi had directed him to the spot where the firefight had ended the lives of several of his men. Costa's body, as well as those in the escort car, still lay in the street. He did, however, see one difference. The vehicle that had rammed the escort car was missing.

His jaw tightened as he thought. He had to get into the mind of the abductors. Where would they go? Certainly not the airport. They must know that security would be on alert. If they stayed in the city, they would need a place to hide. Every hotel in the city now had the pictures from the hospital security camera and would be watching for those men.

Several good roads led away from the city. They could be fleeing, intent on making it across the border, but they wouldn't get far. He had alerted local police and border guards. The car, with its smashed front end, would be easy to spot. No, they'd have to ditch the vehicle and take another. Of course . . .

Santi let his thoughts trail off then spoke to the pilot.

"Head toward the water."

MOYER ROLLED DOWN HIS window to hear the heavy chopper better. He kept the pickup well within the speed limit, hoping to appear like an unconcerned driver on the way home from a late-night job. Of course, that would end the moment the chopper flew overhead. Three men lying in the bed of the truck, two with weapons, would be a giveaway. He wished they had been able to cover them with a tarp.

The sound of the motor was beefier than that of the helicopters they encountered earlier. Someone had called out the big guns, and that wasn't good. After a moment he decided he was hearing something like an MI-17 Russian-made chopper. He couldn't be sure, but the powerful rotor pulse indicated a large five-blade craft, and Moyer knew that Venezuela had twenty of the beasts. Whatever it was, it probably carried a heavy machine gun and maybe rockets.

"Mrs. Cenobio, I need to ask a favor."

She snapped her head around to face him. He had tried to sound confident. Apparently she heard more than he intended.

"What?"

"I want the children to get on the floorboards and stay there. I know there's not much room, but it needs to be done."

"Why? What's wrong?"

"Please, Mrs. Cenobio."

"Mamá, is something wrong?" the little girl asked.

"Children, you're going to ride down here now." She pointed to the space at her feet.

"There's not enough room," the boy said.

"I'll make room."

She guided the girl to the floor and raised her legs to the seat so the boy could squeeze beside his sister. As they passed beneath a streetlight, Moyer saw tears on her face but she said nothing. She was, he decided, a very brave woman.

At last, through the windshield, Moyer saw a dark object in the sky. The profile matched his guess that the helicopter was an MI-17. He took no pride in that. The only sensation he felt was raging concern. Their M4s would be no match for whatever the Venezuelan military had put onboard the flying gun station.

Then he realized the chopper was moving away from them and toward the shoreline—the last place Moyer wanted to see it go.

CHAPTER 55

MOYER STOPPED THE TRUCK beneath the canopy of a closed gas station. A large, lit sign out front listed the price of fuel. Moyer did a quick conversion. Less than eighty cents a gallon. Had his life and those in the truck not been in imminent danger, he would have found it worth commenting on.

"We can't win a firefight with .50-caliber machine gun," Jose said. "And if he cuts loose with a rocket launcher, we'll be barbecue."

"What we need is a shoulder-fired Stinger missile," J. J. said. "I don't suppose you have one in your pocket, Boss?"

"Fresh out." Moyer looked at Caraway. "How's he doing, Doc?"

Jose shook his head. "Not good, Boss. He needs serious help. He's barely hanging on now."

"How long can he last?"

"I don't know. He's tough, but he's lost a lot of blood. To be honest, Boss, I'm a little surprised he's still with us."

Moyer looked toward the horizon. "Time is of the essence, huh?"

"Yeah."

Running a hand across his chin, Moyer studied his fallen team member. The longer he waited, the greater the chance Caraway would die, but the odds were against his making it anyway. In the cab Julia Cenobio sat with her arm around the children. He then turned his eyes in the direction of the helicopter and wondered what its next move would be.

"Help is out there," Moyer said, nodding toward a shore he couldn't see, a shore still several miles distant. "But getting there may be impossible."

"I don't suppose the bad guys in the van have decided to call it a night," Doc said.

"I doubt it," J. J. answered. "They don't seem the type."

Moyer had to make a decision. "Okay, here's what we're going to do. I can't promise this is going to work. Truth is, I'm clean out of great plans."

"We're with you," J. J. said. "Just say what, then say when."

Two minutes later Moyer started the truck and pulled away from the filling station and back into the open.

SANTI TAPPED THE SHOULDER of the flight engineer, the third member of the flight crew, and pointed. "That is the car."

"It looks empty. And I don't see anyone in the area."

Santi dialed his cell phone and gave the location to the man on the end of the line. He then keyed his mike and spoke to the pilot. "Circle the area. Look for three or four men."

The pilot acknowledged the order and began a spiral search pattern centered on the car.

WHEN THE HIGH-INTENSITY LIGHT first illuminated the massive black bulk, Rich thought they were about to collide with a whale. A second later he realized they were about to collide with a nuclear submarine. He didn't know whether to be relieved or not.

Coffer slowed and hovered just above a hatch behind the submarine's narrow sail. He took Rich's hand and thrust one of the scooter's handles into it. Rich made certain he touched none of the waterproof switches. Less than a minute later the other SEALs arrived with their human luggage, staying back just a few feet and directing their lights at the hatch. The hatch opened and a handful of tiny bubbles escaped.

Taking the scooter from Rich, Coffer pushed the device through the hatch then motioned for Rich to follow it. The compartment on the other side of the hatch was dimly lit by lights recessed into a metal bulkhead. Rich found the ladder and used it to pull himself downward. The scooter floated by and Rich seized it so it wouldn't interfere with the others coming through the hatch. One of the SEALs entered, then Cenobio and Pete. Within a minute everyone was inside and Coffer closed the hatch.

Coffer descended the ladder and nodded to one of his men, who turned to a panel mounted to the side. Within seconds the pressure on Rich's body increased. There was a gentle rush and the water drained. Soon they were standing on solid steel in a narrow room with a curved ceiling. Rich felt as weary as he had ever been, though he had done no actual work to get to the sub but allowed himself to be towed for three miles.

Coffer opened a hatch in the bulkhead and stepped through, followed by the others. Coffer spit out his mouthpiece, and Rich and the others did the same. Once the last inch of water had been expelled, the door from the lockout trunk opened. "This way, gentlemen."

On the other side of the hatch stood a stately man who looked more like an English teacher than a naval officer. He wore the khaki uniform of a commissioned officer, a silver eagle pin affixed to his collar.

"Welcome to the *Jimmy Carter*, gentlemen. Sorry you had to use the back door." He shook the hand of each man and looked each in the eye. "I'm Captain Jay Stern, skipper. I think I know the answer, but which of you is Dr. Hector Cenobio?"

Cenobio raised a trembling hand.

"I am glad you're safe." He turned to a short man with weathered skin. "COB, let's get some dry clothes for these men. Make sure they get a warm meal, and find a place in officer's country for them."

"Aye, sir."

"This is James Reid, Chief of the Boat. He'll make sure you're taken care of." Stern started to leave.

"Captain," Rich said. "We still have men in Caracas."

"I've been made aware of that. Your team leader has been in contact with Ops Command."

"We need to go back for them. We have wounded."

"My orders are to provide safe passage for Dr. Cenobio. We're pressing our luck hanging out so close to Venezuelan-protected waters."

Cenobio pushed forward. "Sir, my family . . . my children."

Stern's face softened. "I'm sorry, sir, but—"

"Begging the captain's pardon," Coffer said. "Sir, if it were one of my men, I'd want to go back. Some of my men will volunteer. With your permission, sir, I'd like to try."

A sailor in a blue coverall uniform handed Stern a piece of paper then disappeared back to where he came from. "The saber rattling between the U.S. and Venezuela has been going on for some time," Stern said. "SECNAV is dialing us back. Apparently the administration is trying a more diplomatic approach." He opened the paper, read it, then read it again. He raised his head and looked at Rich. "Your team leader is making a run for the beach."

"Captain, please . . ." Rich ran out of words.

"Lt. Coffer, your men rested enough to go again?"

"Aye, sir, just give the word."

Stern took a step closer. "Let's be clear on this, gentlemen. Venezuela has a navy. It might be Little League but they could do us some damage, and I have a lot of men on this boat who have families too. So long as we remain a slow mover this close to their waters, we are in danger. We are at our best on the move, not idling. So do this, do it right, and do it fast. Clear?"

"Clear as rain, Skipper."

Stern swiveled on his heel and left.

Rich took Coffer's arm. "I'm going with you."

"Me too," Pete said.

"Negative. My men are trained for this kind of thing."

"You're not hearing me, Lieutenant. We're going with you. If it were your men, would you leave the heavy lifting to someone else?"

Coffer didn't respond. Instead he looked deep into Rich's eyes.

"Go ahead," Rich said. "Offer to break my arm again."

Coffer smiled. "Maybe later. Right now, we've got work to do. We'll get you some fresh weapons."

Ten minutes later, still wet, Rich and Pete hung onto the rope handhold on the side of a large Zodiac rigid-hull inflatable boat as Coffer attempted to eek out a little more power from the motor.

CHAPTER 56

MOYER COULDN'T SHAKE THE feeling that he was driving toward disaster. It was difficult enough to lead healthy, highly trained soldiers into battle, but taking a mother, her two children, and a man more dead than alive into harm's way was nothing short of crazy. If there were another option, he'd take it, but none existed. Their window of escape was fast closing, and any further delay would ensure Caraway's death. No matter what Moyer decided, it would be a bad decision.

Given how long the helicopter had circled the departure point, Moyer figured that Shaq and Pete's car had been located. Moyer pulled onto the coastal road and drove at a leisurely pace, his eyes following the flight pattern of the helo. They were circling—no, spiraling—in a search pattern, giving him a brief moment of hope. If he could time it right, Moyer could speed to the departure point when the helo was on a northbound course, its tail turned to Moyer. And just maybe there would be some friendlies waiting for them.

Moyer turned to Julia. "I need you to listen to me, okay?"

"Yes. Okay."

"I don't know everything that's going to happen, but I need you to be focused and brave for the children. Can you do that?"

"Yes, of course." She looked at her son and daughter tucked into the tight floorboard space.

"That helicopter is searching for us. It's not looking for this truck, but any vehicle in the area at this time of night will draw attention. That means we have to get in and out of the car as fast as possible. In a moment the chopper will turn north and be unable to see us, but the pilot will turn back this way again in a few moments."

"What do you want me to do?" Her voice was calm and firm.

Moyer smiled. Dr. Cenobio had married well. "There's a small pier extending from the jetty into the water. I've seen it on satellite photos. That's where my men took your husband."

"Is he safe?"

"I haven't heard. Communication has been by encrypted cell phone to my country and from there to others. When we get there and I tell you to go, I want you and the children to run to the water's edge and hide under the pier. Can you do that?"

"I think I can . . . Yes, I will do that. What happens after that?"

"I'm not really sure." Moyer's intestines cramped and churned, but for the first time in weeks, it didn't seem important.

The refurbished truck moved easily down the coastal road. Moyer saw several cars headed in the other direction, as the city was coming alive with early risers. Moyer wondered if he'd see the sunrise. He glanced at the Cenobio children and thought of his own. He ached for them and wished with all his heart he could hold them one more time.

The helicopter banked and started north.

Moyer slammed the accelerator to the floor.

The vehicle responded immediately. Whoever had rebuilt this beauty knew his engines. Were the situation not so dire, he would have felt bad for stealing the truck.

Ahead, and several hundred feet in the air, the MI-17 began its turn south sooner than he had expected. For a moment Moyer considered calling off the run and trying again on the next pass, but there would be no "good" time. There was just *this* time.

Moyer killed the lights as he came close to a wide, warped asphalt road. The dips, potholes, and grooves, combined with the truck's speed, made for a rough ride. Moyer thought of Caraway in the back and started to ease off.

A hard rap on the back window drew Moyer's attention. He looked in the rearview mirror and saw the headlight of a large vehicle. Steam, lit by the one working headlight, poured from the front. Moyer couldn't see the vehicle clearly, but he would bet a month's pay it was the battered blue van they had seen before and that Jose had spotted leaving the industrial building.

The back window of the truck fragmented, and Julia screamed, as did the children.

"Down. Get down now!" Moyer grabbed Julia's head and pushed her forward over her crossed legs. This would keep her head low and—the thought sickened him—provide one more barrier between the gunmen and the children.

Moyer glanced back through the shattered window. J. J. and Jose sat up like dead men rising from a coffin, and M4 and 9mm fire filled the air. The driver of the van hadn't expected gunfire from the bed of the fleeing truck. He swerved and lost traction, and the van spun but stayed upright.

Moyer kept pressing forward, his eyes bouncing from the road ahead to the killers behind them. The van's tires spun in loose dirt then regained traction. J. J. and Jose held their fire for the moment, as ammunition was limited.

Another shot clipped the top of the cab, and J. J. and Jose returned fire in several bursts. The pursuing van's remaining headlight died.

Moyer stole another glance behind him in time to see Jose's head snap to the left as something hit the back of the cab.

"No. Oh, no."

Then Jose turned back to the van and let fly another burst. He was still alive and able to raise his weapon, alleviating Moyer's fear that his medic had just taken one in the head. The truck shot past the sedan Rich and Pete had used to bring Cenobio to this place. He slowed and turned the truck sideways, the passenger side facing the ocean. He killed the engine and shouted, "Go. Go now!"

He threw open his door and exited holding the M4 he had kept between the door and the seat. He began firing, not in bursts, but shot after shot, aiming for the driver's seat of the oncoming van. The van slowed, swerved, then plowed into the parked sedan. A man's arm and head appeared in the open driver's side window, as if he were taking a nap.

J. J. was the first out of the truck bed, and he too fired at the van. Several men poured from the vehicle and took up position behind the crumpled sedan. Moyer switched to auto-fire and sprayed a hail of bullets just above the hood and trunk of the car as he scrambled behind the truck. Jose had already pulled the unconscious Caraway from the bed and set him on the ground—Jose was bleeding from a nasty gash in his cheek.

Snapping his head around, Moyer saw Julia and the children scramble down the breakwater. Once they were at the water's edge they would be shielded from any stray bullets.

Thunder came from overhead. Moyer didn't need to look, didn't want to look, but he did. The MI-17 gunship was headed their way.

The helicopter's searchlight flashed to life, washing Moyer and his men in a cascade of light. Moyer and J. J. fired into the light then directed their weapons at the two air intakes above and behind the cockpit. The craft pulled away but didn't leave the area.

"Bought us some time," J. J. said.

"Why hasn't the chopper opened up on us?" Jose asked. "He's got to have at least a .30-caliber onboard—maybe a .50."

"Not to mention rockets."

"Beats me." Moyer rose and fired several shots. "Watch the building to the left. If one or two reach that position, they will have a straight shot at us."

Several more rounds pounded the truck.

The helo approached once more, and Moyer opened up on the craft. He could see small flashes as his copper-jacketed rounds rebounded off the chopper's skin. Then he heard something that chilled him: the click-click-click of dry firing. J. J. had expended the clip of his 9mm. A moment later Jose's weapon made the same sound.

Moyer handed his 9mm to J. J. and his only extra M4 magazine to Jose. He had no idea how many rounds remained in his own weapon, but he knew there couldn't be many.

Jose peeked over the back of the truck and sent a stream of bullets into the back of the vehicle then returned to his position. "Why can't cars blow up like they do in the movies?"

The helo approached again and the three men fired on it.

Moyer's gun quit. "That's it for me." Better to die with an empty gun than a full one.

Again the MI-17 backed away. They should all be dead now. One rocket, a few bursts from the craft's machine gun, and they'd be toast. Yet the pilot seemed uncertain. Why? Moyer glanced to the side and saw an armed man at the edge of the large commercial building to the left. "Left!"

Jose turned and fired in one instinctive motion. The man disappeared behind the corner for a moment then fell to the ground in full sight.

"Great shot," J. J. said.

"Odd. I thought I had missed." Jose returned his attention

"We have to keep them pinned behind the car."

"You mean like they have us pinned behind the truck?" J. J. asked.

"Exactly. They can't have much ammo either."

Moyer glanced back to the pier. He saw no sign of the Cenobio woman and her children. He took that as a good omen. If he couldn't see her, the hostiles couldn't either. Fortunately the helo was preoccupied with them and not what might be going on at the waterfront.

Another movement near the building caught Moyer's eye, but this time he didn't shout. Three men quickstepped from the break-water's edge to the back of the building. One figure was taller and bulkier than the rest. Shaq! "Reinforcements have arrived."

Before J. J. or Jose could respond, the large man moved to the corner closest to Moyer and the others. He waited three seconds then unleashed a torrent of bullets. Two of the men went behind the building, flanking the hostiles. Moyer heard more weapons fire. While guns blazed, a man in a wet suit ran to the truck from the breakwater. He carried an M4 with a M203 grenade launcher on the rail beneath the weapons barrel. While the other three men showered the sedan and van with bullets, the man Moyer realized was a SEAL popped up and launched the grenade. He dropped down again.

The explosion was like music to Moyer.

"I'M AWAITING APPROVAL, MINISTER. I cannot open fire without orders from my commander."

Santi was beside himself. He screamed into the microphone, "You can see foreign nationals attacking our shore!"

"I see a gunfight between two groups of men. From here I can't tell who is who."

Pounding his hand on the wall of the craft, Santi continued his rant. "Don't be an idiot! I'm telling you which ones to shoot. The other pilot followed my orders."

"I don't know anything about that. I'm sorry, Minister, but I was given strict instructions from my commander to clear all action with him. He said you might ask me to do something like this."

Santi looked out the window and saw several new combatants—then he saw the explosion. He turned to the young soldier manning the 12.7mm gun. "I order you to shoot the men by the truck."

"Hold your fire," the pilot ordered.

The young man looked at Santi then the pilot.

"I said fire."

"No, sir."

Santi released his safety belt and pushed the young soldier aside. Suddenly the craft twisted up and to the left, making it impossible for Santi to aim the machine gun.

"Turn us back around!"

Loud popping noises filled the cabin. The pilot pulled away.

"They are shooting at us again," Santi shouted. "Engage them!"

He heard the pilot report that they were taking fire again. He then heard the base commander order them to pull back.

Santi couldn't believe his ears.

CHAPTER 57

"THEY'RE RETREATING," MOYER SAID, his eyes fixed to the flying hulk as it pulled slowly away.

J. J. looked over the back of the truck. "Maybe our new friends scared it off with the grenade launcher."

"Maybe, but why didn't he fire when he had the chance?"

The man in the wet suit slapped Moyer on the shoulder. "We can figure that out later. Right now I think we should take advantage of the break in action."

"Who are you?" Moyer asked.

A familiar voice from behind him said, "That's Lieutenant Coffer, Navy SEALs. I said he could come and play."

Moyer saw Rich standing over his shoulder. He then turned and shook Coffer's hand. "For Navy, you're pretty punctual."

"We aim to please. Now let's get out of here. We have a Zodiac at the pier."

"There's a woman and two children—"

"Safe and with us." He looked at the other two SEALs. "Let's get the wounded man to the Zodiac."

Before they could move, Moyer said. "We got him. You provide cover."

Coffer nodded. "Make it quick. The helo is making me nervous." Sirens in the distance pierced the thick marine air. "And sounds like company is on the way."

Jose took charge. "Boss, you take the right shoulder, Colt the left. Shaq take his right leg. I'll take the wounded limb. Junior, we're going to need you when we reach the rocks." He leaned over the unconscious Caraway. "Sorry buddy, but this is really going to hurt." He looked at the others. "On three . . ." He counted and the team lifted Caraway from the ground. His body went stiff, and he released a pitiful groan.

Three minutes later the Zodiac was skimming across the dark water with all on board.

"FOLLOW THEM! DON'T LOSE them."

"I have them on infrared," the pilot said.

"Good. Once they're away from the shore you can shoot them."

"Not without permission."

"I give you permission. I am the foreign minister. I order you to fire on them." Santi's frustration with military protocol had reached the boiling point.

"I'm sorry, sir, but you are not in the chain of command. However, I will convey your wishes to the commander."

THE ZODIAC BOUNCED, AND with every vertical change Caraway moaned. Coffer piloted the craft, zigzagging across the surface as fast as the burdened boat would go. Moyer took a second to check on everyone. Julia sat at the bow, her arms wrapped around her frightened children. J. J. and Jose hovered over Caraway. Rich and Pete kept their weapons trained on the MI-17, which followed three hundred feet up and fifty yards behind. The two remaining SEALs did the same. Coffer kept his eyes forward, moving them only to glance at a handheld GPS unit. Behind him, the lights of Caracas grew more distant, and Moyer felt glad to see them go.

The Zodiac slowed. "Why are you stopping?"

"Wait," Coffer said with a smile. He looked at his GPS unit. "Any minute now."

Moyer glanced up at the helo. "Make it a short minute. That beast—"

A rumble from beneath the water cut Moyer off. He turned in time to see a smooth obelisk, darker than the black ocean, puncture the surface. Seconds later, a round, black bulk like a four-hundred-foot-long whale appeared. Waves from displaced water rolled beneath the Zodiac.

"Wow," Pete said.

"Kinda makes you wish you enlisted in the Navy, doesn't it," Coffer quipped.

"I wouldn't go that far," J. J. said.

Coffer raised his voice. "Gentleman, you have ninety seconds from my mark. Trust me—you do not want to be outside when that thing begins to move. Clear?"

"Clear." The men spoke in unison.

Two hatches aft of the sail opened, and a stream of armed sailors poured from them like ants—one of them carrying a Stinger missile launcher. Moyer snapped his head around to check the helo's position. A U.S. nuclear sub sitting on the surface made a tempting target. The captain was risking his boat and crew to save them. An ambitious Venezuelan pilot armed with two rocket launchers might find the target impossible to resist, whatever his orders.

Coffer powered the Zodiac and directed it at the submarine. The nose of the rubberized craft climbed the hull of the sub. The submarine sat low in the water, the deck less than three feet above the rolling surface.

"Go, go, go!" Coffer ordered.

Before Moyer could move, a pair of sailors grabbed the children and pulled them from their mother's arms. A third sailor lifted the woman from the boat and led her to the hatch. Moyer reached for Caraway, but Coffer waved him off.

"Let us do that. We train for this."

Moyer and his team yielded, but not one took his eyes off their comrade. The pain of the move brought Caraway to, and he screamed in pain. The scream, Moyer reminded himself, meant the man was still alive. He followed the others to one of the open hatches.

☢ ☢ ☢

"YOU CANNOT LET IT go!" Santi yelled into his microphone. "That's an American submarine. It's in our territorial waters. Use your rockets."

"Sir—"

"If you do not fire now, I will make sure your career is over."

"Sir—"

"I may not be in your chain of command, but I have authority you know nothing about. Now, fire on that submarine!"

"Sir, there's a radio message coming in for you."

"Your commander? Maybe now he will listen to reason."

A voice came over the speakers in Santi's helmet. A familiar voice.

Santi sputtered then said, "Yes, Presidenté. I understand. Yes, sir."

As he removed his helmet in resignation, Santi thought he heard the pilot say to the copilot, "I wonder whose career is over now."

☢ ☢ ☢

COFFER LED MOYER TO the command area of the submarine and showed him where to stand. A distinguished-looking man studied a video display of the surface. From where he stood, Moyer could see the image coming from the periscope.

"Sonar, conn, any new contacts?"

"Negative. We still have audio of the chopper. No other contacts."

"Very well," said the man whom Moyer took to be the captain. "Take us deep, XO. Make turns for fifteen knots."

"Aye, sir," a middle-aged man with dark skin replied and turned to two men who sat at a set of complicated-looking controls. A man in his fifties stood between them. "Make our depth four-zero-zero feet, four-degree down bubble. Make turns for fifteen knots."

Almost immediately the sub lurched to life and a vibration ran beneath Moyer's feet. Minutes later, satisfied that his orders had been carried out, the captain said, "XO, you have the conn."

"Aye, sir, I have the conn."

Moyer felt he should come to attention, but he was too tired to straighten his spine.

Coffer stood erect. "Captain, may I present, Sergeant Major Moyer. Sergeant, this is Captain Stern, skipper of the *Jimmy Carter.*"

Stern extended his hand. "Happy to have you aboard. I understand you've had a rough day."

"I've had better."

"The Chief of the Boat will see to it that you have a change of clothing, a hot meal, and a bunk."

"I have a wounded man—"

Coffer interrupted. "Already being taken care of."

The captain nodded. "We have the best corpsmen in the navy, as well as a ship's physician. We'll do everything we can."

"Thank you, sir. I also have a man whose wife and baby are back home in the hospital. He may lose both of them."

"I understand, but I can't do much about that right now. In about three hours we will rendezvous with a surface ship. You and your team will be transferred to it, and from there you will be flown to the States. Frankly, sir, you were lucky we were in the area. If Venezuela and Columbia weren't at each other's throats again, we might have been on the other side of the world."

"Understood, sir, although I have a team member that might call it a miracle."

"A Christian man?"

"Yes, sir, he is."

"Good. If I were you, I'd do everything I could to keep him on my team."

"He's a good soldier."

The captain nodded then addressed Coffer. "Fine job, Lieutenant. Please congratulate your team for me. I'll talk to them individually later."

"Aye, sir. Thank you, sir."

To Moyer, he said. "I'll show you where we can wait for a medical report on your man. In the meantime I would like to meet your team."

☢ ☢ ☢

MOYER, J. J., RICH, AND Pete sat in the crew mess drinking hot coffee and eating scrambled eggs, steak, rye toast, and hash browns. Moyer had heard that submariners ate better than any branch of the military. Now he believed it.

Captain Stern and Coffer sat with them, listening to Moyer and the others tell their stories. From time to time Moyer noticed sailors in the mess looking their way.

Coffer explained, "Ship's captains don't usually sit in the crew's mess."

"I thought we'd have more room here," Stern said. "Open space on a submarine is rare. Besides, the officer's mess is being used."

"I don't suppose this would be a good place to have claustrophobia." Moyer looked around the room.

"Psych testing weeds those folks out right from the start," Stern said. "Not many men qualify for this duty. It's not easy spending six months underwater."

Moyer began to speak, then Jose and a sailor entered the room. Jose had insisted on assisting, or at least observing, Caraway's medical treatment. Moyer stood, as did the rest of his team. He didn't like the look on Jose's face.

Jose shook his head. "He lost too much blood. We tried to compensate, but it was too little too late."

Stern stood and laid a hand on Moyer's shoulder. "I'm sorry, Sergeant. Do you want me to call the chaplain?"

Moyer sank to his seat and stared at the table in front of him.

"Boss . . ." Jose began.

"Get that wound on your face taken care of. Colt, go with Jose and get checked out."

"I'm fine—"

"Do it, J. J. Maybe they can fix that nose."

"Yes, Boss."

HECTOR COULD NOT SIT still. Every time he sat down at the table in the officer's mess he popped up and began pacing again. He gripped a cup of coffee in his hands as if it were a life preserver. He ran a hand through his salt-crusted hair. He had been offered a shower but refused. He did exchange his wet clothing for a blue work suit of the kind worn by many of the enlisted men.

He sipped his coffee but couldn't taste it. His mind had no room for anything other than rampant worry and the images of his wife and children. A few moments earlier he had felt a motion that made him think the submarine might be rising. Several gauges were mounted to the wall, and he watched as the depth indicator flashed lower and lower numbers, as if it were a countdown. Then the gauge hit zero feet.

The pacing resumed. Fear chewed at his insides as if a ravenous animal was feasting on his organs.

Motor sounds, sailor sounds, ventilation sounds grew in intensity with each moment. He forced himself to breathe deeply. There was nothing for him to do but wait and pray. He begged God for the safety of his family. He bargained with God, offering his life for theirs.

"Papa?"

Hector spun. His daughter, his son, his wife stood at the room's threshold.

Hector dropped to his knees and held out his arms. He didn't need to call them. They rushed to his embrace. They cried. He wept. Hector pulled them as close as possible, then tried to pull them closer still.

"My Lina. My Nestor."

Then he rose. Julia stood by the metal table. Her hands trembled. Tears dripped from her face.

"Julia . . ."

She fell into his arms and dissolved into sobs. Hector felt no shame in adding his tears to hers.

Nestor hugged one of Hector's legs, Lina the other. Hector turned his eyes upward. "Thank you . . . thank you . . . thank you . . ."

EPILOGUE

CHAPLAIN BARTLEY STOOD AT the head of the casket, which hovered over a grass-green tarp that concealed the cold hole in the ground of the military cemetery. Moyer had tried to listen to the sermon but failed at every turn. His mind refused to focus on anything but his sense of failure. Stacy stood to his right, holding his elbow. Rob stood to his left, wearing a suit that looked a size too large. His son had offered to attend the funeral. Moyer didn't ask why. He was just glad to have his boy near. Gina, always a sensitive child, didn't want to come. Moyer couldn't blame her. He hated funerals.

He scanned the crowd that stood around the open grave. A memorial service had been held a short time before. The graveside service would be short, which Moyer appreciated. Standing with him were the other members of his team. J. J. stood as if his spine had morphed into a steel rod, his face still puffy and his eyes black from the broken nose. Moyer could see the emotion boiling beneath the surface.

Jose, the wound on his face caused by a bullet that very nearly killed him, stared at the coffin. Moyer had only seen him at the debriefing session and the funeral. He spent every hour by his wife's side. Yesterday they received the encouraging word that Lucy might be able to carry the baby almost full term—at least long enough for the baby to live once free of the womb. The danger remained, but now there was hope.

Rich stood with his head down, his wife by his side. Next to him Pete moved his fingers into a fist then released them over and over again.

Moyer wondered about the Cenobios. When the transport plane from the aircraft carrier they had been transferred to landed, the State Department had taken charge of the physicist and his family. He assumed they were returned to Canada.

As the chaplain read from the psalms, Moyer's thoughts ran to the news in the morning's paper. An article told of how a group of drug smugglers had engaged military personnel and were killed. A second story told how Venezuela's foreign minister, Andriano Santi, had suddenly retired from public service.

It had been seven days since the mission, and Moyer had spent a portion of each of those days wondering why the helicopter had not fired on them or the submarine. Several ideas had been floated, but Captain Stern's idea, shared in the crew mess while they awaited word of Caraway's condition, seemed most plausible.

"Venezuela has a fairly robust military, but nothing like the U.S. We have more aircraft and ships in mothballs than they do in active service. They also have a difficult country to defend. They're not that far from the U.S.; we can have jets and cruise missiles pounding them in less than an hour. Would you want to fire on a vessel knowing it would bring a response like that? Chavez and his goons may talk big, but when it comes down to it, their Boy Scouts don't want to go toe to toe with us."

". . . in Jesus' name. Amen."

Moyer looked up and saw Chaplain Bartley nod. Now came the hardest thing Moyer had to do. He and his team stepped to the flag-draped coffin, circling it. Silence bathed the area. Moyer called his men to attention. "Present arms!"

The men delivered a military salute done only at funerals. Rather than a snap gesture, each man slowly raised his hand to his cap. The salute seemed to last forever. Moyer could hear people shuffling in discomfort. From the corner of his eye he caught a glimpse of people wiping their eyes.

Seconds passed as the salute continued. A short distance away, a bugler blew "Taps." Everything in Moyer melted. A tear ran from his eye. Across the casket he saw J. J.'s hand shake.

The salute ended and the team stepped away. An honor guard approached and, in a well-practiced tradition, removed the flag and folded it into a tight triangle. The lead member of the guard turned, walked to Moyer, and presented him with the flag. Moyer took it in his upturned palms. The guard member took one step back, came to attention, and saluted. Then he stepped away.

Moyer's hands began to tremble. He took several deep breaths. He felt his wife touch his arm, willing strength into him. Rob laid a hand on his shoulder.

Moyer stepped forward then crossed to a woman he had met only a short time ago: Orla Caraway seemed like a chocolate Easter bunny left in the hot sun. To her left stood a man with his arm around her shoulders; to her right was a young boy clinging to her hand. The child let go when Moyer approached.

"On behalf . . ." His words evaporated. He took a deep breath, held out the flag. "This flag is presented on behalf of a grateful nation as a token of our appreciation for the honorable and faithful service rendered by your father." He extended his arms and the boy took the flag.

Taking a step back, Moyer offered a salute, then turned and stepped to his wife's side. He couldn't look at her for fear of losing control of his emotions.

Chaplain Bartley said, "This concludes our service." Slowly the crowd dissipated.

"I need a few minutes," Moyer said.

"Of course," Stacy replied.

Rob started to leave, stopped, and embraced Moyer. Moyer took his son in his arms and began to weep. A minute later Rob pulled away and joined his mother as they walked to the parking lot.

Only five men remained around the coffin.

"ANGIODYSPLASIA," THE ARMY DOCTOR said.

"Not cancer?" Moyer asked. He glanced at Stacy.

"Nope. It usually affects older people, but it's not unheard of in men your age."

"Treatable?"

"Yes. Ninety percent of patients stop bleeding without treatment. We'll have you well and tormenting low-ranking enlisted men in no time. Oh, and the next time you have a medical problem, come to us. It makes us look bad when Army personnel go to civilians for diagnosis."

"Will do, Major."

"Good, now get out of here. I have sick people to care for."

ACKNOWLEDGMENTS

I WANT TO THANK my king, Jesus Christ. I hope this book will help every reader find hope in Him when facing Certain Jeopardy and in every other situation in life.

Al Gansky, you deserve more credit for this book than I do.

Jonathan, thanks for prodding me in a direction I would never have considered going without your advice.

To all the folks at NSB, thanks for helping me keep my out-of-control life under control.

Keith and Kelly, I am glad that I know you.

Jeff, Tom, and Steve, you are my inspiration for Pauley.

Finally to Dawn, you mean more to me than words can say. Thanks for partnering with me on this book and in life.